"The Council of Protectors seems to believe that they can teach the three of us to behave as natives of Belsar Four, and to speak at least one of the languages, and I see no reason to doubt them. They do not know, you see, whether the persons or events responsible for the attack on the Unity's base was also responsible for the attack on the scouting party that checked it out. Belsar is a dangerous planet. Banditry is commonplace; there are also savage wild animals. What they need most is simply someone who can survive long enough to gather the information the Council needs. And they do not even know what that is. We are not even sure that the natives of Belsar were responsible. It is possible that there is someone on Belsar who should not be there. That is the function of the Council of Protectors—to prevent the exploitation of unevolved worlds. . . ."

And when it came to survival qualities, there seemed to be none in the civilized worlds as qualified as the three who had survived the terrible Hunt of the Red Moon: Dane, Rianna, and the monstrous Aratak.

THE SURVIVORS

by

Marion Zimmer Bradley
and
Paul Edwin Zimmer

DAW BOOKS, INC.
DONALD A. WOLLHEIM, FOUNDER
375 Hudson Street, New York, NY 10014
ELIZABETH R. WOLLHEIM
SHEILA E. GILBERT
PUBLISHERS

Cover art by Richard Hescox.

DEDICATION
To our mother:
Evelyn C. Zimmer
without whom, obviously,
this collaboration would have
been quite impossible.

First Printing, January 1979

8 9 10 11 12

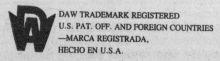

DAW TRADEMARK REGISTERED
U.S. PAT. OFF. AND FOREIGN COUNTRIES
—MARCA REGISTRADA,
HECHO EN U.S.A.

PRINTED IN THE U.S.A.

CHAPTER ONE

A whole Universe to wander around in, Dane Marsh grumbled to himself. *A Galaxy at my feet. And where do I wind up? In the city of Dullsville, on the planet Tamel*

Around him the living unit was quiet; too quiet, with a controlled purr of conditioned air, smoothly adjusted to the proper flow, cleansed, recycled and scented with a faint tang of salt sea air which could have been instantly adjusted to mountain pine, the delicate fragrance of a scented flower garden in the sun, or the pungency of a beach at low tide. The only sound, blotting out the background hum of machinery, was a faint, almost subliminal crash of distant surf . . . as artificial as the sea air, but soothing. The light could vary, at the faintest touch of a button, from a moon-lighted beach to the brilliance of a blue-white sun, or anything in between. And none of it was real. It was all a mockery. Comfortable, even luxurious. But a mockery just the same.

Dane looked up to the wall display which dominated the main room where he sat; the Samurai sword which hung on the wall. Vaguely, the sight of it made him ashamed of the luxury around him.

That was real. Terrible, but real. Basic, gut-level, life-and-death reality. And now look at me. . . .

It wasn't the Samurai sword with which he had fought through those eleven days on the Hunter's World, under the Red Moon, winning through, in the end, to riches and freedom. *That* sword still hung on the walls of the Weapons Museum on the Hunter's World. But the first thing Dane had done with the wealth he'd won on that world—well, almost the first thing—was to commission a replica of the Samurai blade with which he had fought there. A telepath, a curious little creature from one of the protosaurian races, who looked like a man-sized Gila monster back on Earth, had combed

Dane's mind and memory for every detail, not only of appearance, but the feel of it in his hand, its weight, the hiss it made in the air, the tension of its length in the muscles of his arms, all the details which had registered on Dane only below the level of his consciousness. Then a skilled craftsman had forged it, and finished it, until nothing but logic could remind Dane that the original Mataguchi blade still hung in the Armory on the Hunter's World. This was his sword. . . .

A silly gesture, really. Sentimental—as sentimental as the long pale braid of Dallith's hair that he kept hidden away in his most secret hiding place in his room. Romantic, and fake, as much a fake as the tang of sea air in his room and the distant crash of mechanical surf in the sound system. That part of his life was over, and rationally, Dane knew he did not regret it. At first the peacefulness of this civilized, mechanized, Utopian world had been welcome, after the long nightmare of the Hunt, and the Red Moon. For a long time he had wakened, sweating, from dreams in which every multiformed creature thronging this centralized, civilized world near the center of the Unity, became a disguised Hunter, one of the shape-changers of the Red Moon, on his trail once more. Many times he had wakened struggling, shouting, clutching for a sword no longer needed, waking Rianna with his cries. Not that she had minded. She had her own nightmares, and sometimes Dane thought they were worse than his. Or was that just a remnant of consciousness from his life on Earth, before the Mekhar ship had whisked him from his lonely yacht in mid-Pacific, a remnant which told him, against all the logic of the Unity, that Rianna was a woman and therefore weaker than himself and to be protected. The truth he knew to be otherwise; Rianna was no weak woman, but had fought at his side on the Hunter's World, his companion, his sword-mate, his love. And he had come here willingly to be with her while she filed the reports of their long ordeal on the Hunter's World for the central intelligence agency of the Unity. Willingly. At first.

Rianna . . . she would be home soon. In the Unity, here at Central, there was no such thing as marriage, but he supposed in every way that mattered they were mutually committed in a relationship which, on Earth, would probably have been called so. At least it had never occurred to either of them that they could or would separate. They had been through too much, together, to part now.

Dane walked to where the window would have been if a

central living unit had allowed any such anachronistic devices; touched a panel and the wall became transparent. From a perspective which would, on Earth, have been that of a second-story window (actually he was about half a kilometer up, but the view was an illusion which every Living Unit in this structure shared) he looked out on Festival in the streets of a City that covered half a planet, a city that was not, except by Dane, called Dullsville, on a world that was not called Tame. But was.

There had been a time when Dane thought he would never tire of watching the crowds that thronged these streets, lizard-men, cat-men, bird-men—or, to use the terminology of the Unity, the enormous Galactic civilization, protosaurians, protofelines, protoavians; and others, people of every conceivable species of sapient. The phenomenon known as Universal Sapience took many forms. There were several hundred planets in the Unity—and nearly as many more outside it—bearing sapient life; and over a hundred of them must have been represented in the crowds below.

And a sizable number of these crowds were protosimians—so-called; Dane would have called them *human*. Some looked as human as he did himself and could have walked in any city on Earth without exciting a second look. Others would have created a riot or a panic, with sleek fur, with long prehensile tails (he still remembered the time he had seen a bizarrely beautiful protosimian woman combing her hair with a prehensile tail which held a jewelled comb) or by the ability to count to fourteen on their fingers, or toes, or both. Scattered here and there in the crowd were a few—a very few—tourists from worlds so different that they must trundle along in protective atmosphere suits or even environmental tanks. He had never thought he could tire of this infinite variety. He had watched it obsessively, even though he knew that the watching triggered nightmares in which the aliens became protean Hunters, shifting shapes and flowing like liquid to take him off guard, assuming protosaurian, protosimian, protoursine shapes, now and then muting into his own face, or the face of lost lovely Dallith, and he would wake shrieking. . .

But now he dreamed he was in a padded cell.

On Earth an atavistic drive for adventure had driven him to climb mountains, to earn black belts in karate, judo and various other martial arts, to visit every hidden hole and corner of a world with diminishing numbers of blank unmapped spaces, and finally brought him out in the ocean, alone in a small boat, easy pickings for the Mekhar slave ship which had snatched him away. At first he had hunted for adventure here, too, thinking that in the vast reaches of the Unity, there must be new and strange adventures.

But if you climbed a mountain here, there was a little robot following you around, with a forcefield that followed you up the slope, to catch you if you fell, or even if you looked as if you were going to fall. He had learned to fly one of the little airboats which people used here, and had zipped around the planet three times, revelling in the speed—until he had realized that the damned thing had so many safety devices that he might as well have been in one of the environmental tanks used by methane breathers; he couldn't have crashed it if he wanted to, and if, unimaginably, all three of the fail-safe backup systems had gone wrong, an automatic monitoring machine would have brought a rescue team literally within seconds, no matter where he was on the surface of the planet.

He had even taken up their equivalent of hang-gliding, though protosimians were not supposed to have the reflexes for it (it was a protofeline sport), enjoying the knowledge that he was riding the treacherous upper-air currents buffeted by air-cars and jets, riding the jet stream, with an oxygen mask, had given him a brief sense of excitement—until he realized that every glider unit had an electronic safety net which made it as safe as a kiddie car; and then he had given up. It took the fun out of it.

Rianna couldn't understand.

"Do you *want* to break your neck?" she had asked him, and he had told her, emphatically, not.

"Then what difference does it make? You still have the excitement of traveling on the jet stream, riding the currents, the view is the same. If your reflexes are really good enough to be doing it at all, you will never need to know that the electronic safety nets are there at all. And if you *do* need them, at least you won't get killed for a minute's inattention."

Dane had despaired of making her understand. She was right, of course. Faced with instant and immediate death, he had fought like a fiend, to survive; and he had been as terrified, as desperate, as she was herself. He didn't want to die.

"But it spoils it, to know there's no penalty if I fail. There's no—no premium for skill or courage; I could do it just as well if I were a fat clumsy bumbler or a sickly child of ten!"

"Dane," she said gently, understandingly, "you've already proved your courage. You don't have to keep on doing it. I know you're brave. You don't have to keep on proving it, even to yourself."

Dane had almost hit her. It had been their nearest approach to a serious quarrel; and afterward he had realized that from *her* point of view she was probably right. How could he explain that it wasn't his courage he needed to test, but his skill, his resources, that he was built in such a way that he needed real, not pretended, challenges. Now they simply didn't talk about it.

At Rianna's suggestion he had hunted up the fashionable studios where off-world arts were taught, including half a dozen or so exotic combat forms. He sampled the sword skills of half a dozen barbarian planets, learning new tricks and refining his own skills. His only rewarding occupation, at the moment, was fencing against a huge bird-like creature who used a sword long enough to be called a spear, and was skilled enough to make the combat equal—but Dane was winning with more and more regularity.

He had thought, now and then, of opening a martial-arts studio of his own; but then he would be committed to stay here; and he wanted to be free to leave, when Rianna finished her work of recording and reporting. With the wealth he had won on the Hunter's World, it would be possible to hire a small spaceship and an experienced pilot; and there were worlds in the Galaxy still to be explored.

If they were lucky, finder's fees, or the records Rianna could make for the Unity's archaeological and anthropological research services, would recoup what they spent on it; and fortunately, Rianna was almost as eager for the project as he was. But her work seemed to stretch out endlessly; every time she thought it was nearing completion some new agency or bureau or administrative unit wanted a new report or more information. He would have thought she would have been wrung out a dozen times over, but it seemed there was no end to the information they wanted and she could give.

And while they waited, Dane was bored, bored, bored. The Samurai sword on the wall seemed to mock him, in the black-lacquered rack he had had made for it.

A silly, useless gesture, a shrine for something I am not sure I believe in. The way it was set up, it looked like a

Shinto shrine, and it gave him a point of reference. In a sense, a very real sense, it was a center of his life.

But for the rest of my life, am I going to be looking back to that time, instead of looking ahead to new challenges? He told himself this was silly and morbid. Once they could get Rianna's work wound up!

She was the equivalent of what would be, on his world, an advanced professor of a science which translated out, through the translator disk which all civilized sapients wore embedded in their throats or other vocal mechanisms, as "Study of sapient civilizations past and present." It represented a cross between anthropology and archaeology, in Dane's eyes. But when she finished her reports, she would have the opportunity to do original, *individual* research.

Most scientists on her level had to settle for joining some kind of Foundation, and most such Foundations were protosaurian or protocanine; protosimians, humans, were not believed to have sufficient tenacity or reflective skill for sciences of this kind. So that the wealth won on the Hunter's World fulfilled a dream and a challenge for Rianna too; sufficient funding for the kind of research she really wanted, without the endless jockeying for funds, internal politics, trying to retain integrity while getting into the good graces of the Important People who could let you in, or keep you out, of your desired research.

Some things must be the same in all cultures and civilizations. It sounds just like University and Government programs on Earth. Dane said so and shattered another of Rianna's illusions—she had somehow cherished the idea of Dane's world, of Earth, outside the Unity, as a kind of romantic primitive paradise.

He turned away from the endless panorama below, reaching toward the opaquing button on the wall—then, something he had seen registering after he had actually seen it, stayed his hand, searching in the crowd for what he had seen. A slightly built woman with brilliant red hair, and beside her—

He had seen the two together countless times . . . but not for a long time now, not since they had come to this world. Next to Rianna, moving through the festival crowd toward the entrance of the enormous living unit structure, was a huge proto-saurian, grayish-green, and although many protosaurs looked alike to Dane, this one he could never mistake.

Aratak! Aratak, the giant lizard-man who had fought at

their side through the Hunt, and with them had survived it to freedom and wealth ... Aratak, *here*!

But Aratak, philosopher, fighter, was at the other end of the Unity! After they had gone together to Dallith's world, to inform the empaths of Spica Four how she had died, Aratak had left them, had returned to his own people, and the peaceful, quasi-monastic disciplines of a devotee of the Cosmic Egg.

When he thought of Aratak, he had pictured him light-years away, in one of the swamps he thought delightful, buried to his nostrils in the mud which his integument required, and meditating quietly upon the philosophical precepts of the Egg.

What was Aratak doing *here*, in the sybaritic surroundings of Festival, on this central world of the Unity? What had prompted Aratak to leave his peaceful meditations?

Some requirement of the Galaxy-wide bureaucracy, probably. He had never known quite what position Aratak held in his own society—though Dane assumed he was a high official of some sort—but he had assumed that with his Hunter-won wealth Aratak would buy the freedom to spend his life in pleasant, peaceful meditation. He had not expected to see Aratak again for years or decades, if ever! For whatever reason, the thought of greeting the huge protosaur, his friend and companion on the long Hunt, filled him with delight.

They were out of sight now, evidently inside the structure (it was too enormous to be called simply a building) and coming up the long shafts of elevators and lifts. Then the warning chime rang from the entrance, a door slid noiselessly back; Rianna stepped inside, and behind her, wriggling his huge scaly bulk through a door designed only for ordinary-sized humans, came first the claws, and then the enormous fanged muzzle, and then the leathery bulk of Aratak.

CHAPTER TWO

When Aratak had completed the lengthy, and difficult task of squeezing his ten feet of grayish, rugose hide through the small doorway—Dane was reminded of a man crawling into a doghouse—the spacious room was suddenly small. Dane, embarrassed, thought of a place he could have taken, near the spaceport, which would have had room for almost any conceivable entity. But this had seemed more comfortable, because it *was* scaled for humans, or human-sized creatures.

The programming of the entrance kept wanting to shut itself on Aratak and finally Dane and Rianna had to hold it back with their hands; even so, Aratak had a few scrapes on his leathery integument. He finally drew the last segment of his tail inside, and Dane tried to frame some convenient apology, but all he could find to say was "Does the Divine Egg have nothing to say about the difficulties of visiting friends who live in mouseholes?"

Aratak rolled up his eyes, saw that he could not rise without banging his head on the ceiling, and shifted himself to a comfortable kneeling position on the floor. His deep, gentle voice vibrated through the translator disk in Dane's throat.

"The Divine Egg, may his wisdom live till the last sun burns into darkness, has said that wherever one meets with old friends is a Great House and rich with joy." Dane was used to the translator disk by now and would have had to listen very carefully to hear the actual hissing syllables of Aratak's native tongue. "It gladdens my liver to see you both. I trust your life here has been happy and filled with rich fulfillment?"

"Well enough," Dane said, without enthusiasm.

"Overworked," Rianna laughed.

"You are then well content with your pattern of life upon this world?" Aratak asked. His face held a strange expression which Dane had not yet learned to interpret.

"Well," Dane said slowly, wanting to be honest with his friend, but not wanting to complain—and after all, wouldn't complaints sound silly and ungrateful?—"I think perhaps I've been in one place too long. We've been thinking about hiring a small ship, and seeing a bit more of the galaxy; there are unexplored worlds, and unrecorded worlds . . . oh, this one is pleasant enough, but—"

"To tell the absolute truth," Rianna said, breaking in vehemently, "he's been bored out of his mind!"

"Oh, come, Rianna—"

"Out of his mind," Rianna repeated, not budging an inch, "He thinks I don't know it, but I do. I've been swamped with reports and information-authorities myself! I've been doing reports on the Hunters, and reports on the project I hadn't finished yet when the Mekhar slave ship caught me. I think that if I see another record box or voice scriber again I'll explode! I can't wait to get back to field work again."

"Is it so, truly?"

"It is," confirmed Rianna, "Aratak, may I offer you some refreshment?"

"A drink would be welcome," he admitted. "This planet is unpleasantly dry, and my metabolism suffers."

She went to the panel where foodstuffs were delivered by pneumatic tubes to each apartment, began to punch out instructions to the computor to deliver refreshing drinks for protosimian tastes. "Dane? Wine or tea?"

He came and helped her carry the drinks; Aratak's size made it impossible for him to move into any of the smaller rooms in the apartment without overturning too much furniture, so they each dragged in a cushion and sat down in the lee of the enormous protosaur.

"So you are longing to return to field work, Rianna? Tell me, where had you intended to begin? Or had Dane some particular desire?"

Rianna said, "I was hoping to get up an expedition to the companion planet of the Hunter's World—the one we called the Red Moon—and investigate the ruins we found there, and the—the beings there, whatever they were."

During the Hunt, Rianna had been missing for a night and a day, and they had believed her dead; but she had reappeared with a story of being concealed underground, and assisted, by a race of beings who dwelt in the dark and whom she had never seen, remnants of some ancient and unknown, unrecorded civilization. "I'm dying of curiosity—but I think this time I will leave it to someone else to make the reports afterward!"

Dane chuckled. Aratak asked "Have you made so many arrangements already for this project that it cannot be altered or postponed?"

"We haven't really even started yet," Dane confessed, "I found out where to hire the spaceship and where I should apply to engage an experienced pilot, but everything else has had to wait till Rianna has finshed her work! Don't tell me you want to come along!"

"If I were to tell you this, would you be enraged?" Aratak asked, and Dane laughed—he had forgotten how literal the translator disk could be. Irony, sarcasm or exaggeration did not register.

He said "If you told me that, Aratak, believe me, we'd both be overjoyed—wouldn't we, love?" he added, glancing affectionately at Rianna.

"We would indeed," she confirmed, "and it would be simple to arrange for a ship with room enough for you, and for appropriate protosaurian provisioning. Aratak, are you actually considering coming with us?"

Even through the flatness of the translator disk, Aratak sounded regretful. "I fear it is not possible," he said, "but if you have not yet made so many plans that they cannot be altered, perhaps you would postpone that project for a time, to interest yourselves in a different proposition I have been asked to convey to you?"

Dane felt an almost physical prickling of interest, of curiosity. Intuition? He should have guessed that Aratak would not have come here merely for a social call!

Aratak sipped slowly at the "wine" which the computer had delivered; actually it smelled to Dane rather like a fermented root beer which had begun to spoil, but Aratak savored it with apparent pleasure.

"I was recently contacted by a member of the Council of Protectors," he told them, "It seems that they have a problem, and they believe that we can help them."

Dane had never heard of the Council of Protectors. That didn't surprise him; the Unity maintained a truly vast bureaucracy of organizations, Federations and splinter-group associations, enormously overlapping in the huge star-Federation. It was entirely too much for one human mind to take in.

At first this had troubled him, until he found out that Rianna, too, knew only the names and functions of those agencies with which she had business. The Unity, of course, was not a government at all, but a kind of philosophical construct, dedicated to maintaining peace and trade among the scattered star systems.

Aratak said, "The Council of Protectors have been studying the culture on a Closed World, a recently discovered planet—" Dane understood, of course, that he meant recently discovered in Unity terms, which was probably longer than all their combined lifespans—"A planet still in a barbaric state of development. As usual, the Council is trying to gain a thorough understanding of its society and cultural structure before we reveal ourselves or attempt to bring this world into the Unity. It's rather a curious place—presents some features which ought to interest you, Rianna. For instance: there are two distinct sentient species at a similar level of sapience, one a race of protosaurians not physically dissimilar to my own, the other composed of protosimian sapients—"

"What?" Rianna said, her voice lifting in excitement, "Is this Belsar Four, Aratak?"

"It is indeed. Do you know of it, Rianna? This simplifies my task considerably."

"I've been following the controversy over Delm Velok's Lost Starship Theory. Anadrigo's comments seem not much to the point; parallel evolution could not—"

"Wait, wait," Dane said, "Hold on! —I mean, stop for a bit, and fill in some information before I get completely lost!"

Rianna laughed. "I'll tell you what I know, and Aratak can go on from there, for us both. Belsar Four is a puzzle to scientists in my field. Normally, a sentient race fits into the local ecology. Most protosaurian races have evolved on planets where mammals never developed at all, or remained very small and unimportant. If the protosaurians were sapient, they exterminated any possible mammalian competitors at an early stage in their development; while in other conditions—I remember that you told me, Dane, that your protosaurian giants were not sapient, they had small brains and being unadaptable to changes in climate and planetary ecology, they became extinct. Is that true?"

"Quite true. A dinosaur—er—a saurian of Aratak's size would have had a brain roughly the size of my thumbnail, and without any cerebral cortex to speak of, thus preventing the development of anything like sapience. One of our scien-

tists—John Lilly—theorized that sapience was an inescapable
accompaniment of a certain critical size of the cortex."

"Elementary," Rianna said, "We call it Methwyk's Axiom,
and it's the first thing a biologist in the field of sapientology
learns. Anyway," she went on, "Belsar Four has a highly developed protosaurian race, and also a fully developed mammalian ecology, with no other competing saurian or reptilian
forms at all—in fact, no other reptiles of any sort, as nearly
as I remember, certainly none of any size, or complexity.
Delm Velok's hypothesis is that the protosaurians of Belsar
Four are descended from the crew of a lost, wrecked starship, probably from the Sh'fejj Confederacy—that's one of
the oldest space-going races in the Unity, probably in the
entire galaxy. The protosaurians on Belsar Four are very
similar to the basic Sh'fejj type."

"There are few differences among sapient protosaurians,"
Aratak rumbled, "far fewer than among varying species or
ethnic types of protosimians. The gravity of a given planet
determines our size—some of us are not much larger than
protosimians, and there are one or two small protosaurians,
dwarfish races who compensate by some powers such as telepathy for their lack of strength, but in general, my protosaurian brothers are mostly of races indistinguishable from
myself. With certain cosmetic manipulations, I would cause
little comment on any planet inhabited by descendants of the
Sh'fejj, and their females would find me quite acceptable as a
mate."

"But there is another scholar, Anadrigo," Rianna said,
"who drew up a long list of physical differences—though he
admits those might be caused by mutation or acclimatiza-
tion—and did a linguistic analysis to demonstrate that there
is no trace of any Sh'fejj language, either in grammar or vo-
cabulary, in any of the Belsarian languages studied so far. He
also cites native annals and native epic poetry which indicates
that the protosaurian race has been there from a time before
Sh'fejj starships could possibly have reached so far; *his* theory
is that this race developed intelligence in order to avoid whatever catastrophe killed off their original environment. But
there isn't enough evidence on either side. Not yet. The
planet was discovered only—well, not within my lifetime, but
certainly within my grandparents'. And only the most basic
research has been done. So we have only theories, no solid
evidence."

"It seems likely, daughter, that we may never have such

evidence," Aratak said somberly. "About ten Standard Units ago—" (the Standard Unit was a period in use all over the Unity, it appeared to be taken from an average mean time division of all the major planets; Dane didn't understand completely how it was derived, but he used it anyway; it seemed about five weeks in his own reckoning)—"the Unity base on Belsar ceased to report, and the last message was peculiar and incomplete, as if—" he pondered for a moment, "as if the sender had been interrupted—suddenly, perhaps even by violence. There was something in that message about aborigines inside the perimeter."

Rianna asked, "Doesn't anyone know what happened to them?"

"An expedition was dispatched to Belsar Four at once, of course, to investigate. Messages received from their personal communicators indicated that they found the base completely deserted—with the forcefield and some of the emergency defenses turned on full. But there were no bodies, and no obvious signs of violence. Almost their last message told that they were attempting a journey to the nearest city-state, to see if they could learn anything there." He paused, and went on sadly, "The final message stated that they had been ambushed by natives in the hills; there was only one survivor, and nothing has been heard from him since."

He looked around at them, with a long, deep sigh.

"As you both have reason to know, very few of the Unity Agents have any skill in personal combat, or the use of primitive weapons. One or two of those on the Belsarian base, we thought, did have some such training; but they were all on the Base when whatever happened to them happened. Or else they were somewhere outside the Base—and are still wandering around out there, with no way to communicate with the Unity at all."

Dane looked at the huge protosaurian in wild surmise. He was beginning to see the drift of Aratak's remarks. Was it weapons experts they wanted, men trained in personal combat? Aratak's next remarks confirmed his guess.

"So the Council of Protectors is trying to find some weapons experts. Apparently they believe that anyone who could survive the Hunt—" his scaly face was unreadable, but small fidgeting motions told Dane that he was uncomfortable—"must be such an expert. They believe that I, for instance, can be disguised, without much difficulty, to pass as one of the protosaurian race on Belsar, a native; and the pro-

tosimian race is not unlike your own. But if your life satisfies
you so richly—" he paused.

"They want *us* to go?" It was almost a cry of delight, the
first trace of excitement since he had given up hang-gliding
beginning to build up inside him. Then he frowned. "But wait
a minute—this sounds more like a job for the Space Marines,
if you have any, or for a psychic investigator. We don't know
the languages, or the customs, and if the planet is a barbarian
one outside the Unity, the natives don't wear translator disks,
do they? And barbarian tribes—we had some of them even
on *my* planet—are very choosy about people observing local
customs and manners. It's not like the Unity, where anything
goes, as long as you don't do it in the street and frighten
the—" he gulped, understanding that the proverb would
mean nothing, and amended quickly, "block the traffic."

"The Council seems to believe that they can teach us to behave as natives, and to speak at least one of the languages,"
Aratak said, "and I see no reason to doubt them. They do
not know, you see, whether the persons, or events, responsible
for the attack on the Base was also responsible for the attack
on the scouting party. It is a dangerous planet, you see. Banditry is commonplace; there are also savage wild animals;
what they need most is simply someone who can survive long
enough to gather the information they need. And they do not
even know what that is. We are not even sure that the natives
of Belsar were responsible."

Rianna picked up on that immediately. She said, "I suppose
it's possible that the people on the Base could have been
raided by a Mekhar slave ship?"

"Entirely possible," Aratak confirmed, "there have been
Mekhar ships, and also Kirgon, sighted in that sector, though
of course we have had no actual reports of unauthorized
landings."

Dane said, "If the forcefield on your Base was full on, how
could natives get inside? Wouldn't it take something like a
Mekhar ship to get through a forcefield of that kind?"

"It's possible." Aratak said, "but of course, we don't know.
Natives might have gotten into the station when the forcefield
was turned off, or have taken keys from Base personnel who
were waylaid outside. But it is also possible that there is
someone on Belsar who should not be there. That is the function of the Council of Protectors—to prevent the exploitation
of unevolved worlds by the Mekhar, or the Kirgon."

Part of Dane's mind was still clamoring, *What an adven-*

ture! I want to go! But a saner part temporized, examined the story carefully. "I'd have thought, with a whole Galaxy to recruit them in, there'd be any number of swordsmen—er—weapons experts for the Council to choose from."

"Not many in *this* sector," Rianna said, adding bluntly, "and most of those who do take it up are dilettantes, and would curl up their toes and die if they were expected to use them seriously, in a life-and-death fight! Maybe some of them might not, but the Unity wouldn't like the idea of testing them to find out! They *know* we're capable of fighting for our lives if we have to."

"Another thing," Aratak added, "the species must be right. Protofelines are sometimes fierce enough—but the Mekhar do not belong to the Unity, and in any case, a protofeline on Belsar would be such a curiosity that the natives would either kill him out of hand—or treat him as a god. Certainly he would not be suitable for a quiet investigation. It is very important that they find a protosaurian and two protosimians who are accustomed to working together."

Two? Dane jerked his head up sharply, in protest, but Rianna was already speaking.

"It hardly sounds like a pleasure trip. But, damn it, it's tempting! Though I suppose I'd get stuck with making the report after this trip too! Though I've been wanting to have a look at Belsar Four, and I knew I wouldn't get permission, not in my lifetime!"

"Sounds too dangerous," Dane said, feeling secretly relieved that she was not going to rush off blindly, all enthralled by the prospect of digging up more ruins of the ancient whatchacallums. For himself—to his own surprise—he discovered that he wanted to think it over a little more.

Rianna was staring at him in disbelief. "Too dangerous? That from *you*, Dane? And all I have heard from you, for days, is that you are stifling here on this supercivilized world!"

"I am," Dane said with dignity, "and I'm thinking seriously about going. Trying to take all the factors into consideration, which is more than you seem to have done. And it's a dangerous planet—according to Aratak, it was a dangerous world even before people started disappearing out of forcefields and so on." *Too dangerous for a woman*, was what he had started to say. But he didn't; he knew better. Instead he said, "It doesn't sound the right place for a—a peaceful archaeologist and scientist."

"My *dear* Dane, virtually every world visited by any Unity scientist is a dangerous world!" Rianna's eyes were flashing danger signals; Rianna had a real red-headed temper—that's what they would have called it where Dane came from—but to give her credit, he hadn't seen any signs of it in a long, long time. "Even before the Hunt, I was used to dangerous worlds—I didn't have to play with swords and cruise around on little boats to get a taste of danger! Almost any worthwhile world visited by an anthropologist has dangers *you* can't even imagine! Are you implying that you intended to charge off with Aratak, and leave me here, at the tender mercies of the recording machines?" She scrambled to her feet, regarding him with fury. "That settles it, Aratak! I'm going with you whether this overgrown tree-badger does or not!"

Tree-badger? Dane opened his mouth to demand an explanation, then realized that his translator disk was playing games again. What would Rianna gather from it if he called her a bunny rabbit? Evidently it was some creature from Rianna's own world, to which she felt Dane was at the moment comparable. He wished he knew how. . . .

"Rianna," he said gently, making up his mind to try one more time, "this may be one thing for a barbarian from a backwoods world, like me. But you are civilized—"

"How civilized was I on the Hunter's World?"

At the back of his mind the picture formed; blackness, the Red Moon hanging like a neon mountain in the sky, the dark slumbering forms of their companions—*Dallith, the lost, the beloved, Dallith, dead because he, Dane, had gone berserk and forgotten his duty to his companions of the Hunt, Dallith living, sleeping while he and Rianna kept watch, Dallith, sleeping the last peaceful sleep she was to know in life; and Rianna's voice in the darkness, saying, "I'm less civilized than I ever believed. . . ."*

"You've only seen three, maybe four planets in your entire life!" Rianna flared at him, "I'd been on that many dangerous worlds before I hit puberty!" Her voice, the present, seemed very far away; less real somehow than the bush-clad slopes of the Red Moon, the brick-red disk of the Hunter's World hanging above them; the spider-man moved through a corner of Dane's mind, twirling his deadly spear, Cliff-climber moved catlike at his back, and Dallith . . . *Dallith.* . . .

Dane shook his head as if to clear it of cobwebs. Hell, this planet—what was it, Belsar?—however dangerous it was, was probably a Sunday-school picnic compared to the Red Moon and the long Hunt! In a single flowing motion he was across the room and down by his knees before the sword-rack. His hand closed on the long curved scabbard; he bowed his head for an infinitesimal space, then rose smoothly to his feet and turned to face them, the scabbarded sword held like a briefcase in his hand, his thumb crooked over the guard as though to keep the blade from escaping.

We're going, together, he thought, but even in his mind it was not to his companions he spoke, but to the sword. Aloud, to them, he only said, "Okay, when do we leave?"

CHAPTER THREE

"Good God," Dane exclaimed, "the planet's got chicken pox!"

Even through the translator disk the words could not have conveyed much to Aratak, but he chuckled at Dane's tone and joined him at the viewport.

"Its integument does indeed suffer as if from the attack of insects," he commented. "Indeed, it presents more the appearance of a dead satellite under bombardment by meteorites than a living world with an atmosphere which would burn up such missiles. It is a riddle, my friend, which I cannot read, but the Divine Egg has truly remarked that if we knew all things, no challenge would be left for sapient beings and we should all die quickly of boredom, or sink into swamps with only our nostrils above water, with nothing to contemplate but the known and the dull."

"The Divine Egg seems to have had something to say about almost everything," Dane murmured, but Aratak's invisible but sharp ears had picked up the murmur.

He said, with the extreme politeness he used when he was ruffled, "It is the business of a philosopher to make comment upon those matters in life which those of us who are entangled in worldly affairs have no leisure to contemplate."

"I spoke carelessly," Dane agreed, "I should have said that

the wisdom of the Divine Egg is rather fitted to an ancient
and venerable sage than to one in embryonic form."

"The Divine Egg," Aratak remarked, "was eternally favored in that all during the millennial span of his wisdom he
preserved everlastingly the wonder of the newly hatched, as
indeed all sapient beings must do if they are to rejoice fully
in the endless diversity of Creation. It is said," he added, with
a knife-thrust of his rare sarcasm, "that his wisdom was so
great and all-embracing that he could even imagine wisdom
residing in the protosimian creatures, since the Creator of All
could not, he said, have created anything which was not—for
some reason and for some purpose—worthy of Its own
Divinity."

"I'm sure he did us too much honor," Dane said wryly, but
then backed off—there was no point in exchanging sarcasm
with the saurian philosopher, and at that game Dane knew he
was beaten before he started. "Seriously, Aratak, how could a
planet with oceans and an atmosphere develop craters like a
dead moon?"

"Seriously, I have not the faintest notion," Aratak said, "it
is not within the realm of my competence. If it were not a
planet in its earliest stages of life, with a newly evolved and
barbaric culture . . . but there is no point in discussing non-
existent contingencies. It is barely possible, I suppose, that
life may have come late in this planet's created existence, after a span of time spent as a dead satellite to some other
sun—suns in formation do sometimes capture satellites of
other suns, especially here, so deep in the Cluster—and life
does then evolve upon them, with the new bombardment of
cosmic rays. This is rare, but it does happen," he concluded,
looking at the oddly cratered planet that was Belsar Four, beyond the viewport.

From where they hung, in an orbit only a few thousand
kilometers above the greenish-dark world, Dane could see
blue oceans striped with bands of cloud, a single massy continent located in what he thought of, automatically, as the
"Northern" hemisphere because it was at the top of his visual
field, and another smaller one which looked, just a little, like
South America tilted improbably on its side.

Rianna came up to them, carrying a computerized printout
of the surface below them. She pointed to a spot on it.

"The shuttle will drop us here. Aratak, your friend Dravash wants a final conference on the bridge; that nameless

friend of his insisted." She shuddered. "Ugh, that chap gives me the creeps!"

"Dravash?" Aratak stared in dismay. "Are you repelled by the aspect of the Sh'fejj? I dislike the thought that I too might repel you in this guise, my dear one."

"Oh, no, not Dravash himself," Rianna said, "and now I've gotten used to it, you look almost normal to me. In fact," she added tartly, "I'm tempted to say it's an improvement!"

Dane had to conceal a grin. He had never suspected the big lizard-man of vanity; but since the transformation into Sh'fejj disguise for this planet, Aratak had indulged in what most humans would have called *sulking*.

Aratak's greenish-gray integument had been dyed with chemicals to a silky blue-black; the color of the dominant Sh'fejj, the protosaurian race who had first taken to star travel. They were still the most widespread of the Unity's protosaurians. Aratak was larger than most of the Sh'fejj—few of them were more than two meters high, and Aratak at full height was nearly three—but he would pass. The transformation had been necessary in order that he might pass, on Belsar Four, for one of that planet's dominant race, although they were not true Sh'fejj. He had also been informed, by the ship's Medics, that this transformation would help to soften and moisten his integument somewhat, helping to retard the damage it would otherwise sustain in the climate of Belsar.

Aratak had accepted the need for the change—but he distrusted all protofelines, and the ship's Medics (like most of the Medics in the Unity) were protofelines. And he had not ceased to grumble about the transformation. Far worse was the need to conceal his gill-slits; they were only vestigial in the Sh'fejj, and the Medics had suggested cosmetic surgery on them, which Aratak had curtly refused. When Rianna tried to persuade him, he had asked her sharply if she would consent to having her external ears amputated.

He wore a loose decorative scarf with a high "collar" effect, concealing them. Dane hoped it would be enough. If the climate of Belsar was really as hot as he had been told, it might stand out like a down parka in the Amazon rain forest!

Now Aratak said, turning the talk away from his own appearance, "If the aspect of the Sh'fejj does not repel you, or that of Dravash, what has excited your revulsion, Rianna?"

"That nameless chap Dravash's involved with," Rianna

said with a grimace. "The Farspeaker, or whatever he calls himself."

Aratak shrugged. "Once we have left this ship, Rianna, the Farspeaker will be our only means of communication with civilization. The Divine Egg has wisely remarked that it is ill to aim insult at a bridge to safety, even though it may be splintery to the feet. I too find the Farspeaker uninviting, in character and personality. But his faults, and candor compels me to confess that they are many, appear to be an inevitable accompaniment of his many talents. Would you rather feel we were wholly out of contact, as on the Hunter's World, my dear?"

"I understand it's really not much better than that," Rianna said sullenly. "It's not as if they could step in and pull us out again if we got into trouble."

"No," Aratak said, "but should catastrophe overwhelm us, at least they will know through the Farspeaker what has befallen our expedition, and perhaps others sent after us can avoid our worst mistakes and succeed where we failed."

Rianna shuddered. "You're a real comfort to me, Aratak! Come on, let's not keep the Captain waiting, or they'll think Dane and I have gone off for some standard protosimian hanky-panky!"

She turned irritably toward the door of the cabin, and Dane, following her, grinned at the wryness in her voice. In the worlds of the Unity, protosimians—what Dane himself would have called *humans*—far from being a dominant species, were regarded as one of the most unstable and untrustworthy, being at the mercy of what most of the Unity's people regarded as a dangerously prevalent sex drive. Most races have a strictly seasonal cycle of fertility, and at all other times could keep their attention strictly on the work at hand. Aboard Unity ships, for instance, crews were protofeline, and the females given season-retardant drugs to keep them from disrupting ship's crews. They became fertile females only on their home worlds, and there was some annoyingly intense curiosity about the fact that Dane and Rianna shared a cabin.

Dane had, to some degree, gotten used to this; it was the one off-color joke which was appreciated by all the species of sapient beings in the Galaxy, the constant sexuality of protosimians, who had no decent sense of time and place. But it still inhibited him, from time to time. He had to regard it as a joke or it would have driven him crazy.

Now he followed Rianna along the long, curving corridor of the Unity ship. It was staffed mostly by Prrzetz, the proto-feline cat-people. Although a highly ethical race of scientists, they physically resembled the Mekhar who had kidnapped Dane from Earth some time ago. Dane had learned not to flinch from them, but something inside him—the primeval monkey, he thought wryly—still cowered a little when a Prrzetz good-naturedly bared its teeth.

In the ship's central cabin—although in fact there were no charts, only computerized printouts behind translucent panels along the walls, moving and flowing with the ship's progress in space—the Prrzetz captain was waiting for them with Dra-vash.

Dravash was a Sh'fejj, silky-black, small only by contrast with Aratak; he reminded Dane of nothing so much as a small iguana which had somehow grown seven feet tall and learned to talk.

"I see you have managed to induce your protosimian com-panions to come here, Aratak," he said. Even through the translator disk his voice sounded rasping and harsh. "I still feel this was unwise. A contingent of Sh'fejj, with you to guide them, would have been more trustworthy."

Aratak rumbled, "I can vouch for Dane and Rianna. They proved their worth on the Hunter's World."

"Perhaps." But Dravash regarded Dane in no friendly fash-ion. "I still feel that a true fighter would have been willing to come without his mate. And protosimian females, as is well known—"

Rianna snarled something under her breath that came through Dane's translator as "Stuff that down your wind-pipe!" Aloud she said, with silky persuasiveness, "Would the worthy Sh'fejj Agent of the Protectors care to attempt two falls out of three with my humble self? If he still believes I should be at home hatching my eggs, this might help to per-suade him that I have other functions on this journey."

Dane kept his mouth shut. One of the first things he had had to learn in the Unity was that Rianna was more than ca-pable of fighting her own battles, and that the one thing he ought not to do was to open his mouth in her defense.

Protosaurian faces were not easy for humans to read; but Dane had been around Aratak long enough to know that Ar-atak was amused and Dravash was not. Nevertheless Dravash backed down. He said, "Save your fierceness for our enemies, good-female-colleague." Through the translator Dane could still hear the rumble of a special mode of speech used only with respect toward members of another sapient species. Rianna heard it too and was mollified.

"And now that we have exchanged adequate courtesies and compliments," the Prrzetz captain said sharply, "will my worthy passengers be pleased to get down to the business at hand? Dravash, you have given us the co-ordinates of the Unity base down there; do you wish to be landed in full daylight? If not, we must land you as soon as possible."

"Very well," Dravash said, "but I beg you, wait a few moments until the Farspeaker joins us."

Dane tensed; only once during this voyage had he set eyes on Dravash's companion, the "Farspeaker" of whom Rianna had spoken. Now, hearing a thick swishing shuffle in the corridor outside the chartroom, he knew that the Farspeaker, unsummoned, had come to join them.

Why should the creature excite such revulsion? An albino crocodile would not have distressed him unduly. The Farspeaker was of Sh'fejj origin, in general, but his leathery hide was a dull off-white, and the gill-slits, not vestigial in this individual, were pinkish, and fringed at the edge with crimson. Dull crimson eyes were deep-set in his reptilian skull. He dragged himself painfully along in a walker, the mechanical support holding him only partially upright, his upper body hunched over it and his scaly dirty-white dorsal appendage trailing along uselessly behind. As he came into the chartroom he looked neither to one side nor the other, and even through the translator disk his voice seemed flatter and more mechanical than most.

"My courteous compliments to all here." But from his tone he might as well have been sneering obscenities at them all. "Dravash, have your party assembled?"

"I believe so, Consecrated One."

The albino Farspeaker hitched the mechanical walker a little closer so that he could brace himself in it; nevertheless he seemed to sway from side to side a little, so that Dane watched him in horrified fascination, sure that the repellent creature would tilt too far to one side or another and come crashing down.

"What it can profit to ally yourself with protosimians I cannot imagine," the Farspeaker's voice clicked on with distressing precision.

Dravash said defensively, "The natives of Belsar Four—"

"Are quite properly subject to our kind and need not be consulted. . . ."

"Respect, Consecrated One, but no sufficient number of Sh'fejj adequately trained in primitive survival and combat techniques could be located in the limited time—"

Farspeaker waved that aside. His droning voice moved on, toneless and mechanical. "I have informed my surrogates that you will be dropped in a shuttle ship precisely one Standard Unit before the sunrise of this completely repellent planet. This will give you adequate time to take such shelter as is necessary to preserve your useless lives. Have your revolting companions undergone such transformations as will make them as disgusting as the natives of that foul and loathsome planet beneath us?"

"As the Consecrated One can clearly see—"

"I do not waste sight on such matters," the Farspeaker interrupted him sharply, "Since you take perverted pleasure in contact with these disgusting beings, fulfill your worthless office without further delay, if you are capable of so infinitesimal a right action for once in your useless existence."

Dane felt his anger swelling within him.

That washed-out lizard thing acts like he had all Creation in his hand and comes on as if he's lord of all he surveys. Where does anything that repulsive get off with calling us names?

Dravash, however, spoke with humble deference—a departure for the proud Sh'fejj who was to lead their expedition. "Aratak, Consecrated One, has been transformed to a suitable color for a Sh'fejj. There is no concealment for his extraordinary height and bulk, but if need be he can be passed off as a giant—a freak or a monstrosity, exhibiting his enormous size and strength."

Aratak blinked angrily several times, then gave a philosophical shrug and subsided.

"As for the protosimians, they too have had the colors of their hide and fur transformed to conform to the appearance of the natives of Belsar Four."

"It renders them even more revolting," the Farspeaker droned, "but may serve to prolong their meaningless lives for a time, while the Unity gathers the knowledge for which you were sent here."

That's big of you, buddy, Dane thought, but he did not speak aloud. He and Rianna had both had their hair dyed to a rusty brown, and their skins darkened several shades; he already knew that only the cooler of the G-type stars would permit fair-skinned types like himself and Rianna to survive infancy. Redheads like Rianna were a rarity; fair-skinned blond types like Dane himself limited to a scant half-dozen planets among hundreds, so that even on the crossroads Administration city where he had lived with Rianna, Dane attracted stares—polite, concealed stares, but still, stares, and on a less civilized world he would have collected a crowd.

"I myself prefer them this way," the Prrzetz captain said, looking at Rianna's dark skin and dusky hair, "They no longer bear the superficial resemblence to the Kirgon which made me fear them. My apologies, worthy beings," he added politely to Dane and Rianna, "but although I know you and your male companion are *not* Kirgon, the paleness of your fur created a reflex of internal fear I could hardly control; it is a relief to look at you now without a purely visceral urge to regurgitate my food from fear."

This came as a shock to Dane—that the protofeline Prrzetz captain had feared *them*? He murmured to Rianna, "What the hell are the Kirgon?" and she whispered, "Race of slave-takers outside the Unity; *hell* is right. They make the Mekhar look like housepets."

That gave Dane a new view of the transformation. He hadn't really resented it; he knew that the medication which added protective melanin to darken his skin and hair would protect him, that without it, he'd be fried alive under the sun of Belsar Four down there; and Rianna wouldn't be much better off. But he felt odd when he looked down at the unfamiliar color of his skin, and it was even odder to look at the normally red-headed, pale-skinned Rianna, now dusky as himself; her green eyes looked strange indeed, looking out from the darkness of her dyed skin.

Dravash said, "Even if it were not physically necessary for their comfort on Belsar Four, and for their concealment among the natives, the color white would be regarded with superstitious taboo down there, according to the few reports we have had; it is not even allowable in clothing. But our protosimian colleagues have most graciously submitted to this alteration, and now they are ready to accompany us."

The Farspeaker said, ignoring that, "Our bond is made, Dravash. But in the event that you are killed or made prisoner, we must not rely upon this one bond alone. I must touch each of these in turn so that I can reach them if the need is great."

Dane stiffened. *That* hadn't been in the bargain. He had known of the telepathic bond between Dravash and the Farspeaker, but the thought of incurring some such bond himself—and with a creature as repulsive as the Farspeaker—turned his stomach. A glance at Rianna showed him she was equally unwilling.

"Why is that necessary?" she appealed to the Prrzetz captain. "We have the Communicators, for necessity—" she touched the tiny, super-miniaturized transceiver around her neck, disguised as a piece of elaborate jewelry; it had been constructed to patterns smuggled out of Belsar Four by earlier teams of scientific observers.

The Farspeaker clacked, "Mechanical communication devices are unreliable; they can be stolen, you might have been deprived of your hands, your speech organs or your wits. The team which disappeared was equipped with such communicators, and nothing has been heard of them. This way I can monitor what happens to you, and relay the results to your betters. Do *you* protest, when *I* have agreed to endure a contact so disgusting?" The loathing in his voice was the first real emotion he had displayed.

"Consecrated One, our worthy female colleague intended no disrespect—Rianna, assure him that you intended no disrespect—"

"I intended no disrespect," Rianna said tonelessly, for the translator disk. Under her breath, in the common language she and Dane were beginning to share, she whispered, "Not disrespect. Detestation."

Dane whispered back, knowing that the protosaurians would take no notice of them, "It's probably mutual, at that, honey."

Dravash's yellow eyes glinted at Rianna; but he said nothing, and stood quietly before his albino partner, waiting.

"Aratak." The Farspeaker focused his dull crimson eyes on the enormous lizard-man; after a moment he said in disgust, "Your thoughts are as dull as those of an insect browsing in a swamp, awaiting the toad that swallows him."

Aratak's voice was calm. "The Divine Egg has wisely told us that peace of mind is a jewel worthy of the crown of all life."

"If your Divine Egg was as great a fool as you, he would still be the wisest of his race," the Farspeaker said with something between a snort and a snarl, and Dane stared—would Aratak let this slur upon the great philosopher of his kind

pass unremarked? But Aratak, though his eyes glinted, merely
remarked, "The Divine Egg is as he is, now and forevermore,
Farspeaker," and moved away from his interrogator. "I thank
you, Farspeaker, for an entirely new experience. No philosopher would willingly forego such a happening."

Farspeaker looked at Dane and Rianna. After a moment
Dane felt something strange. For a moment he could not
identify it; then a conviction began to steal over him that the
Universe was a sickening, hostile place, that each of its varying creatures was uglier than the last, that every one of them
inspired varying degrees of loathing and revulsion and that
they in turn regarded him with similar disgust. Caught in the
waves of this sickening self-hatred, Dane found himself looking upon a ludicrous apelike creature, upright, of a repellent
golden-brown color, its hair crudely dyed dark, and at its side
a female of the same foul sort, its body distorted with the re-
pugnant secondary sexual characteristics of proto-simian females, sensed the hateful look of horror on its face and its
own waves of emotion, revulsion, loathing. . . .

The contact broke. Sweating, Dane was aware that for a
moment he had been in total mental contact with the little albino telepath, had seen himself through the protosaurian's
eyes. A line from a Terran poet flashed through his mind, *O
would some power the giftie gi'e us, to see ourselves as others
see us.* . . . How many of us, he wondered, could stand it
more than once? If the world looks like that to the poor creature, no wonder he hates everything and everybody!

"Your pity is as repulsive as your appearance," the Farspeaker said harshly, "but now I can discover what has happened to you in the event your wretchedly inadequate
communicators cease entirely to function or your stupidity
fails to include adequate information in your reports." He
swayed in his walker as if exhausted. "I must seek solitude to
cleanse myself of the contamination of your presence."

None of them spoke while the shaking creature dragged
himself slowly and painfully from the cabin. But Rianna
moved closer to Dane, stretched her hand to him, and he
closed his fingers around hers. The touch, her quick sympathetic smile, somehow eased the self-loathing wakened in him
by the shock of contact with the Farspeaker.

Dravash's voice was more gentle than was usual with him.
"The poor fellow isn't as bad as he sounds, you know. He's
really a rather good creature at heart; he wouldn't harm an
insect that stung him, really."

Aratak said enigmatically, "I rejoice that sapience has many forms. It is good, no doubt, both for you and the Farspeaker, that a bond between you is possible; I equally rejoice that the Unity requires no such bond of me." He shook himself—rather, Dane thought, like a large dog emerging from a muddy swamp—and said to the Prrzetz captain, who had sat during all this with his eyes rigidly fixed on his viewscreens and computer printouts, "Show us, I beg of you, where we are to land."

The catlike Prrzetz touched buttons and the blurry pictures of the land below them enlarged tenfold, a hundredfold, a thousandfold, seeming to leap toward them from the viewscreen as if they were falling rapidly toward the surface of the planet; an illusion, Dane knew, but so compelling that he, and even Rianna, gasped.

"Here," he said, "near to the northeastern shore of the large main continent there. If you are fortunate, the small shuttle will land you within a few meters of the small station built for the Observer crew that was lost, and you will be safe there, unseen, before the day breaks."

"And you believe we can pass there unnoticed—"

"I believe so," Dravash said, "We will attempt to pass ourselves off, if we must travel in that area, as travelers from Raife—which, as you will recall, is far distant, on the western shore of the continent."

That was true, Dane thought, as a tidal wave of "memories" from the intensive course of educator tapes and hypnolearners flooding through him, to the natives of Kahram down there, travelers come from Raife will be as exotic and strange as—his mind sought still for Earth's equivalents—as a Chinese would have seemed in Marco Polo's Venice. Raife is so far away from them—and, as I remember, divided by the Grand Gorge which cuts the continent nearly in half—that the distance will cover any small lapses any of us make in speech and local custom.

Rianna was thinking along the same lines, but they brought her to different conclusions. "Won't this make us even more conspicuous than we'd be anyway, with Aratak with us?"

Dravash said sharply, "We could not possibly disguise ourselves well enough, or speak the language sufficiently well, to be anything *but* strange. There is no way we could possibly appear as natives of the Kahram rain forest. Since we cannot be inconspicuous and blend into the scenery like a camouflage-cat . . ." Dane shuddered at what the translator disk

made of the native name of the fiercest of the predators of
the Kahram rain forest—"we might as well be so enormously
conspicuous that no one will believe we could possibly have
anything to hide."

Dane supposed that was a valid point of psychology, but it
still gave him the shivers. Abruptly he recognized the sensation; it was much the same he had felt on the eve of their
landing on the Hunter's World; excitement, and a strange,
tonic fear, bracing him, making him very much aware of
small things going on. It was not unpleasant at all; rather the
reverse.

He wondered, *am I just an adrenalin junkie, then? Do I
get some kind of emotional high from danger?*

Rianna had accused me of that . . . impatiently, he put
the thought aside, as Dravash gestured them into a small com-
partment adjacent to the hangar-well of the shuttle which
would drop them, and said, "Our weapons and rucksacks are
there, ready for landing."

Silently, Dane strapped his on, watching Rianna do the
same. A short, heavy knife was belted into the sheath at her
waist. She wore a short, wrapped leather kilt and boots high
to the knee, the upper part of her body covered with a close-
fitting knit garment—not unlike a ski sweater—and a
wrapped over-garment which went around her twice but
could be rearranged to cover her head for warmth or leave it
exposed to the air, or to fall from her shoulders like a cape if
it was too hot. Her curly hair, dyed black—Dane missed the
cheerful fire of its normal bright red—had been cut to a
curly cap around her head, and a brilliant blue kerchief tied
around it. Around her neck a variety of amulets and necklaces jingled gypsy-fashion, concealing among them the single
small microcommunicator.

Dane's costume was similar, his leather kilt somewhat longer, his boots not quite knee-high. The clutter of pendants,
amulets and other trinkets were a jingling nuisance at his
neck—he supposed he would, sooner or later, get used to
them. Drawing a deep breath, he strapped the Samurai sword
at his hip, adjusting the belt to the precise height he liked,
where the hilt was at his hand. He touched it surreptitiously,
not looking at any of his comrades.

Aratak wore a long thin knife, slid into the same narrow
case he used to hold eating instruments and brushes for cleaning his long teeth. Dravash had a short, ugly-looking knife
not unlike a machete.

"This does not seem the best of planning," said Aratak thoughtfully, "to send in only one team. It would seem that since one team has vanished without trace already, it might have been wiser to have two or three teams to investigate, to find out what is going on—"

Dravash said irritably, "Of course that would have been wiser! But we could not find sufficient members for such teams—at least, not teams adequately trained in the basics of survival under primitive conditions! Considering that we were restricted to protosimians and protosaurs, and could not recruit among the adventure-loving races—" he added, with a glance at the Prrzetz captain. "Do you really think—"

He broke off, but Dane was sure he had been about to make some tactless remark, such as, Do you really think we would have entrusted a mission of this importance to protosimians?

Dane wondered; how could a Galactic civilization, like this one, have lost all sense of adventure?

Civilization, he thought. Maybe that was the answer. People grow up accustomed to comfort and convenience. Now that everyone has what he needs to make life good for him, there is just too much to risk. When life is all danger and hardship anyhow, the risk of death is just one more of the many ways to die, since death is always just around the corner. But in a society like this, there is just too much good life to risk. . . .

The thought struck Dane as infinitely depressing. As life grew better, happier, safer, did it also lose some indefinable edge which made it worth living at all?

Or don't most people even know about that edge? Is it something limited to primitive throwbacks like me? Sure, even on Earth, I had to go farther and farther away from civilization, to find anything exciting enough to make me feel I was living. . . .

Well, anyhow, he was on the edge of an adventure now. Again he touched the sheath of the Samurai sword with surreptitious fingers, wanting to draw Rianna close to him, shoulder to shoulder, sharing this moment with her. But he knew that it would annoy and embarrass the protosaurians if he did, they would see it as just one more manifestation of protosimian rut and inappropriate sexuality, so he only grinned at her and waited.

One by one he ran over in his mind the various dangers ahead. The enormous tigerlike beast Dravash called *camouflage-cat*, who might conceal himself anywhere in the rain forest, plunging upon them without warning; the existence of this dangerous, but not very intelligent predator was probably the reason for the lack of sapient protofelines on Belsar Four. It lived on monkeys and apes—of which for some reason there were a considerable number—and was not averse at all to dining, now and then, on an accessible member of the protosimian dominant race of humanlike creatures.

A sword, Dane thought, *should take care of the camouflage-cats quite nicely*. But he wished Rianna's knife was longer.

Dravash said they have a nasty habit of jumping down on you from the trees....

Then there was the other predator they had been warned about in the educator tapes; a slinking silent creature not unlike the terrible wolverines of the arctic circle on Earth; this one fought with desperation, and its least bite could be poisonous as well. Fortunately they were rare....

Dravash asked the Prrzetz captain, "Have your experts finished analyzing the metal flotsam which was found drifting here two rotations ago? If it was any part of a Kirgon or Mekhar ship...."

The Prrzetz shook his head, cat-whiskers flicking from side to side. "No fear, Dravash. Radiation data have shown us it is old, old . . . probably older than the civilization down there on Belsar Four. It must have been jettisoned from some Unity ship a thousand generations ago and been floating through interplanetary space ever since. Possibly some historians will find it interesting; I have recommended it be sent to the Unity museum." He made a curious purring sound. "I suggest, friends, that you prepare to board your shuttlecraft, if you wish to be landed before sunrise at the Observer station, since dawn approaches the eastern coast of the continent." He indicated, on the flowing viewscreen, shifting behind its translucent panel, the creeping line of light across the planet's face.

Dane took Rianna's hand as they moved toward the small shuttle ship. She said, "What if we are seen landing?"

"What if we are?" Aratak said. "On a planet as primitive as this one, if anyone should see us land, even in full daylight, he is likely to believe he has seen a delusion or a dream, or has undergone a mystical visitation from gods of some sort. Remember what Dane told us of landings on *his* world?"

The landing craft was small, not over ten meters in diameter, and almost precisely disk-shaped; this, Rianna had told Dane once, being the most efficient shape for riding the gravity currents of the planetary field. Rianna and Dane climbed through the hatch; Dravash followed, and finally Aratak forced his huge bulk through the doors which had never been designed for anyone his size. He too was draped with knitted shawls and scarves, a collection of amulets and jewels around his enormous neck; concealed among them, as well as the twin of the communicators he and Rianna carried, was a resonator keyed to the forcefield which surrounded the Unity's Observer base, making it invisible to outsiders. There was no seat inside the shuttle which would hold Aratak without crumpling—Dane had seen him try to sit on ordinary furniture aboard the Prrzetz ship, his first day in his cabin had broken down the bunk—so he curled up on the floor.

Rianna said, "I wish I could carry a recorder or a scriber. There must be fascinating things here . . ." but she sighed, knowing she could not carry any visible item of obvious offworld manufacture. "And there *are* limits to micro-miniaturization! The day they perfect a recorder I could hide inside a bracelet, I'll be in heaven!"

Dane said, "You'll just have to keep a diary." But she looked at him without comprehension, and it suddenly struck Dane that he had never seen Rianna write. Her notes and memoranda were kept on tiny spools of thin fine wire, an enormously sophisticated recorder of "memory wire" which kept its own coil and refused to be tangled despite its superfine size; it was capable of recording not only her voice, but, by some process Dane didn't understand at all, reproducing pictures as well, when fed into the appropriate playback machine. It was small—pocketsize—but that was, at present, some kind of ultimate limitation on the size of the thing, and it was definitely too bulky for this kind of trip!

It would be strange, he thought, if she really *couldn't* write. He'd have to ask her about it . . . then he forgot it again, as on the viewscreen below them, the clouds and striped bands of continents slowly separated into patches of land and water, rolling hills and thick vegetation, a canyon which seemed at a swift glimpse about twice the size of the Grand Canyon on Earth—but he didn't get more than a quick look at it—and the view from space gradually resolved itself into a landscape. They were hovering a few thousand meters over a thickly forested area, through which they could faintly see the course, outlined in a thicker green, of a great and winding river.

The operator of the landing craft, a young Prrzetz with striped hair growing low like fur on its forehead, manipulated dials and controls with delicate long claws. "I can drop you as near as you wish to the Unity base," it said—Dane had no idea whether the Prrzetz was male or female, there was no way for a protosimian to tell at a glance—"The homing device is still working. What *can* have happened to the beings within it?"

"That," Dravash said grimly, "is what we're here to find out."

The ship touched down, quietly, gently. Dravash said with a quick look that took in all four of them, "When we land, we begin at once to speak the local language of Kahram; all of you have learned it proficiently from language tapes, and at any moment it is possible that you will be overheard. I do not wish to hear a single word in any Unity language even when we are alone, lest we grow careless. Is that understood, my colleagues?"

Aratak said, "A wise precaution."

"Okay by me," Dane said. Only Rianna demurred.

"I see no reason for that. If we speak an unfamiliar language, will the natives of Kahram not simply assume it is some tongue from distant Raife?"

"We cannot assume that some bystander will not understand the languages of Raife better than we do," Dravash said somberly. "Furthermore, good female colleague, one of my duties is to discover whether there are invaders on this world, Mekhar or Kirgon or unknowns, who should not be here. I need not say to you that if we speak a word of any Unity language and there are such illegal aliens here, our lives are not worth *that*." He snapped his teeth as if snapping up a fly.

Rianna flinched at the clash of the enormous teeth.

"I understand. Very well, Dravash, you're in charge."

Dane touched the hilt of the Samurai sword again. It felt firm, *alive* under his fingertips.

It would be easy to get superstitious, to think, as long as this sword is by my side, I'm okay. . . .

He hoisted his rucksack, strapped it on. The others were doing likewise, Rianna's across her shoulders like his own, the two protosaurs with packs slung across their hips—or where their hips would be if they were human.

*Not a lot, to face a strange and dangerous planet
with. . . .*

"Let me go first," Aratak said wryly as the hatch opened,
with a soft whining sound. "Then if I get stuck you can all
push from behind."

His bulk completely blocked the hatch; Dane, standing behind as the protosaur struggled to force his scaly body
through, felt impatient. A new world, waiting . . . he supposed he would never be quite free of the sense of wonder
and strangeness. Rianna would never quite share it. From
girlhood she had grown up with a galactic civilization as her
birthright, new worlds everywhere. But Dane had grown up
in a world which did not believe that any others held intelligent life, and he could never take it for granted, never.

With a grunt of savage effort, Aratak forced himself free
of the hatch and dropped to the ground. Through the opening
came the thick sweetish smell of heavy, damp, half-rotted
vegetation. Dane scrambled through the hatch, let himself
drop four or five feet into the darkness, landing on soft wet
tangled turf.

It was dark, the thick darkness before dawn. Around him
was a small clearing, not more than a hundred meters or so;
at the edge of the clearing thick trees rose, and in them Dane
heard soft rustles and inexplicable sounds, sleepy birdcalls,
felt the moist air on his face. It was raining very lightly, a
soft warm drizzle. He could just manage to see the blackish
loom of the trees, a deeper darkness where anything might be
lurking . . . as Rianna landed beside him, his hand found the
hilt of his sword, and he sensed without seeing that her hand
was on the haft of her knife. Dravash was a darker patch in
the murk beside them and he could smell, very faint, the
strange dry lizard-musk of the Sh'fejj.

Dravash said in the language of Kahram, "We must move
clear, give the landing craft room to take off." With quiet
precision he reached out, linking the four of them, his dry
claw touching Rianna's fingers, Dane's shoulder; past them
Dane sensed that his free hand found Aratak in the dark.

"This way."

"This way," came a ghostly echo.

"You're in charge," Rianna said in the language of
Kahram but Dane heard the ghost-echo again, *It is you who
have the right to give orders* . . . and knew what was happening; Rianna's translator disk, embedded in her throat
muscles like Dane's own, was picking up everything she said

and providing a running translation which Dane's own translator picked up, too. What he *heard,* with his ears, was Dravash, or Rianna, speaking the terse language of Kahram, which he knew through the educator tapes; but what he sensed, through the translator—which was so much a part of his senses now that he had almost forgotten what it was to be without it—was Rianna subvocalizing in her own language, or perhaps the way the translator disk rendered it.

Eerie. He supposed he'd get used to it, sooner or later; but it was the first time since the early days after he'd been implanted with the translator that he had been really *conscious* of the gadget in his throat. The translator disk didn't work by telepathy—the technology behind it was completely beyond Dane's comprehension, though Rianna had tried to explain it several times and been exasperated when he couldn't follow her explanation—"It's *perfectly* simple," she told him—but it wasn't telepathy, and Dane was just as glad. His one taste of telepathy, with the Farspeaker, had made him aware that telepathy was probably unendurable for ordinary species. The few races that had it were so alien that few other races could interact with them.

No, that's not true, Dallith was a telepath, an empath from Spica Four—we interacted with her, we loved her. . . . Dane cut off the thought, angry at himself for giving way to it. He must not think of Dallith, lovely lost Dallith, whom he had loved and who had died in the last battle under the Red Moon. . . .

The four members of the landing party moved slowly toward the edge of the clearing, under the lee of the dripping trees. It was so dark that they only heard the hum, did not see the landing craft take off, but they felt the blast of searing heat it left behind, and the vibration made Dane's teeth and eardrums ache.

Rianna said in an undertone, "If there *are* Kirgon on this planet, or Mekhar, they'll have infrared scanners—" She had to say the words in the Unity language, and Dravash frowned, but held his peace, knowing there was no Belsarian equivalent—"We have left a mark they can read from here to the poles."

And again the ghostly echo of her voice through Dane's translator disk.

His skin prickled as they moved under the trees; the educator tapes had informed him, not only of the camouflage-cats and their tendency to leap down at unsuspecting prey, but snakes, venomous or given to strangling their prey, could be hanging from those trees. . . .

"The Unity base is in this direction," Dravash said, in Kahram, and again the running commentary from his translator disk, *over this way*. . . . Dane tried to tune it out; it was a distraction. Slowly, hands linked, they moved through the trees. Dane's hand clenched on his sword-hilt; the strange smells of the alien jungle bombarded nostrils and brain, and he felt as if every separate nerve were quivering.

Aratak fumbled among the chains and pendents at his neck with a small metallic clashing. He held up one of them and Dane recognized, beneath the ornamental carving which made it look like an amulet of some kind, the forcefield key.

"Dravash, observe. The forcefield is still on, full strength and undisturbed. Nothing could have broken through; there is no artifact on this planet which could penetrate a Level One forcefield, let alone the Level Three which confronts us. Therefore they must have left this place of their own free will and been overtaken outside by disaster, rather than being attacked from beyond the field by some native intruders."

"*Supposedly* there is no such artifact on this planet," Dravash reminded them.

It was growing light away to the east. Flashes and streaks of whitish brilliance were lightening the sky, and a bird called stridently from a high branch. Something flapped off heavily in the distance. The rain continued to fall, the heat steaming up from the ground to meet it. Dane felt damp and soggy, but Aratak stretched luxuriously, evidently enjoying the moisture, the warmth.

"There is the Observer Base," Dravash said, holding up the forcefield key; Dane could see nothing but mirrored jungle, then, abruptly, as Aratak twisted a dial which looked like a crude carving in disguise, it rippled, wavered, and the reflected curtain of jungle listed a little, gave off a flicker which showed them a line of carefully planted native vegetation, green and purple with chlorophyll and cyanophyll, and behind it, a glimpse of low hutlike buildings which wavered and were gone again.

"Use your key," Dravash reminded them. Dane twisted the forcefield key in his hand and the wavering jungle was gone. He walked toward the building. Rianna disappeared behind the wavering curtain of jungle, then as suddenly reappeared as her own key lowered the field of vibration. Anyone without a key, sight and sense of direction subtly distorted by the broadcast vibration of the field, would simply wander *around* the concealed base behind the forcefield, never seeing it or knowing it was there, believing they had moved in a completely straight line.

Now they were all inside; past the forcefield lay blankness, even the view of the jungle blanked out, and Dane heard Rianna draw a long breath, saw her release the hilt of her own knife. Her knuckles were clenched, white with tension. He laid a hand on her shoulder, knowing how she felt; in here they were safe. No vicious animal or predator could get through the forcefield.

They were safe.

For a time. Until whatever had gotten in to take away the original crew of this Base broke through to take them too. . . .

"There is the main building," Aratak said. "Let's go inside and see if there are any clues to what happened—whether they left of their own free will, just walked out one day and never came back, or were taken away. If they did, there must be some sign of it. Or whether they're still lying dead in there."

"They aren't," Dravash said, "the first crew found that out."

Dane heard Rianna's breath catch in the growing light; but she said nothing. He reached for her hand, remembering. The first crew, like the original staff of the Base, had vanished without leaving a trace. . . .

Well, that's what we're here to find out.

"Before we go into the buildings," Aratak said, "let us inform the Prrzetz captain that we have safely achieved the inside of the Base."

"A good thought." Dravash pulled out his communicator, spoke into it; his thick dark forehead ridged and his eyes flashed with annoyance.

"What is this?" He shook it, spoke again, finally said, "What is this? Aratak, give me your communicator." He took it from the giant, repeated the process; then, frowning, he took Rianna's and finally Dane's. At last he sighed.

"Perhaps it is the dampness, or some electrical condition in the atmosphere. But the communicators appear to have been stricken with a simultaneous malfunction. I must await the Farspeaker's waking, and make my report through his mind."

"The Divine Egg, may his wisdom endure, has rightly said that anything built by the claws of mankind may fail, but the sapient mind alone is worthy of trust." Aratak added, grimacing, "I would as soon not have proved the wisdom of this particular maxim quite so swiftly."

So much, Dane thought, for their elaborate backup communicators. They were alone on Belsar, and out of contact with the Unity—except for a telepath who hated their guts!

"Come on," he said roughly, "let's get inside and see what further pleasant surprises they've rigged up for us inside the Base there!"

CHAPTER FOUR

The front of the main building was open, a kind of long porch filled with enigmatic shapes. An open door, large enough for Dravash, but small for Aratak, led into a darkened interior. Rianna was already on the porch and Dravash fumbling for some kind of light switch, but Dane said, "Wait," and went back toward the rim of the enclosed space, where the forcefield again raised its invisible shimmer.

He had listened again and again, on the ship that had brought them here, to that enigmatic final message from this station. Most of the tape had been the equivalent of a ship's log, monotonous notes about weather, a kind of "eight bells and all's well," routine reports of sunspots and small variants of solar radiation, without the slightest interest for anyone except professional planetary observers, and, Dane suspected, not much even to them. And then there had been the sudden interruption of a second voice, asking a question. Not even a frightened voice, just curious.

Look. Are those natives? How did they get inside? Is something wrong with the forcefield?

No. They can't be natives. They're—

Then silence. No static. No screams. Not even the click of a switch. Just the silent hissing of the mechanical recording machine as it played itself out to the end. Nothing.

Not a clue. Dane shivered, knowing he stood on the spot

where the mysterious "They" who were *not* natives, must have attracted the curiosity of the Unity observers inside the station. For an idiotic second he bent down to look for tracks, then common sense washed that away, just as the rain—and weather for the last three months or so—would have washed away any traces of whatever intruders they had seen. He went back up toward the outside porch—it was really a kind of covered walkway at ground level, beaten soil with a few heat-wilted blades of grass, thinning as they came nearer to the covered machines which lined the outer wall of the building. Dane wondered why they hadn't put them inside where they could have had the benefit of air-conditioning.

But then, neither Dravash nor Aratak appeared to be bothered by the heat, and the Unity observers had been, most of them anyway, Sh'fejj and similar protosaurian types.

If it's this hot here right after dawn, he wondered, *how are we going to stand it at midday?*

Dravash was moving along the row of machines now, warily looking round, his big body tensed as if to spring. He made Dane think of a hungry Tyrannosaurus Rex.

Aratak investigated just inside the darkened door and lights sprang out above each machine panel. "Whatever happened to them," he said, "they had time to turn out their lights."

Dravash said impatiently, "No, no, our first investigating team did that." His voice echoed oddly in Dane's throat disk. "You remember their report said that lights and cooling system—although I fail to see why cooling equipment should be desired for the delightful climate of this planet—were still operating in one or two of the living units."

"Shouldn't we try their communicator?" Rianna asked, pointing. "The first investigating team called from it."

Dravash made a small startled movement, seeming as surprised as Dane would have been if a housecat had suddenly spoken up and reminded him of something he had forgotten. "Quite right," he grunted, and stepped over to what looked like a closed upright player-piano against the outside wall of the building. "I thank you, *Felishtara.*"

My thanks to my good-female-colleague, Dane's throat disk echoed his words, and he shook his head, puzzled; *Felishtara* was a Kahram honorific he had believed equivalent to *Lady.*

Dravash thrust up a panel at the front of the machine, revealing a recessed, concave screen, then lifted the cover from where the "keyboard" would have been, if it had really been a piano. Below it was a bank of bewildering controls, but even Dane could recognize the small hand-held item he pulled out as some kind of microphone pickup.

"You will recall," he began ponderously, "that in the final message from the first investigating team, sent out after—ha! What have we here?"

Here was a small cube of black crystal perched on the keyboard between two rows of colored buttons. Atop it was a card on which a mechanical scriber had imprinted a few of the hieroglyphs which served as a universal written sign language among all the multi-cultural complexity of the Unity. Each symbol stood for an *idea,* and was completely independent of any lingual sound system. It was, to Dane's way of thinking, enormously unwieldy, much more so than any possible universal phonetic language could have been. He started to puzzle it out, knowing only half a dozen of the more elementary symbols—enough to help him find elevators, staircases, rest rooms or protosimian food-serving areas in the city of the Unity—but Dravash saved him the trouble.

"Urgent—scout report—study carefully," he read aloud. "Now I wonder. Is this just a transcript, or is it their original?" He pressed a button on the side of the cube. No audible sound came from it, but Dane's throat disk vibrated suddenly, almost sub-vocal, a crackling whisper.

Sh'fejj calendar eight-four-oh-nine-seven-three, egg-hatching of the . . . and an incomprehensible string of numerals. He assumed this was the date and time of their arrival at the Belsar Four base; an assumption verified when the numerals ceased.

"Upon arrival at Belsar Unity Base found compound deserted, forcefield activated, lights burning inside buildings, but no response to any kind of signals. Investigation found no bodies, nor any signs of violence. One or two personal items in living quarters were in disarray but this appeared to indicate rapid abandonment rather than struggle; this and other indications caused us to make a preliminary evaluation that all personnel upon the Base had evacuated rapidly. . . ."

"We heard this before," Rianna whispered. It was the transcript of the bafflingly brief report of the investigating team, but this must have been the original from which the sound-transcript had been made. It made Dane's skin crawl, that mechanical disembodied voice whispering, without sound, directly into the disk embedded in his throat. *Eerie!*

"Communicator unit panel open, sound unit on, microphone hanging by its cord. Several of the defense systems were on." The tone of the report suddenly altered: "In short, it looks as if everybody suddenly put up what they were doing and went out for a walk. Food was being prepared in one living unit; it had grown cold and spoilt. Items of clothing were abandoned on the floor. In the laboratory, every experimental animal has been removed and the cage doors are open, indicating that the laboratory animals were set free before the Base personnel abandoned the Base, or were taken with them."

There was a long pause, and the four clustered around the cube thought that the message was over, then the voice began to vibrate silently in Dane's throat-disk again.

"We are taking native disguise and will proceed to the city of Rahnalor, in Kahram. We will attempt to make a report from there. Expedition-leader Vilkish F'Thansa reporting."

The voice stopped. Dane's skin prickled as the silence drew on; a second crew had vanished without trace, into a mechanical silence, there was nothing more, there would never be anything more of either crew. . . . Dravash had reached out to turn off the cube when the whispering voice began again and Dravash physically drew back, startled, his protruding eyes blinking rapidly in surprise; for this was where the report they had heard on the ship had ended, vanished into silence.

"Vilkish F'Thansa reporting, probably for the last time. I make this record and leave it here for any investigators who may be sent to follow us. I will leave the voice-cube concealed within this communication unit, which was in perfect working order less than a single digestive period ago and now will not function even for a moment. My chief technical officer, M'Kash Valsaa, has examined the unit thoroughly and gives it as his opinion that it is functional, yet we can receive no response. It is possible that it is still transmitting to the ship; if so, I beg that Captain Javgash shall send someone down to take us off this planet. But I have no such hope; my personal communicator, which I have set to monitor this signal, is not functioning, it is receiving nothing, and M'Kash and I cannot even receive one another with our communicators. A more thorough inspection of the living quarters and laboratories has revealed some puzzling things. There was an open carton of food on a table with eating utensils nearby; the molds upon it indicate that the eater had been interrupted in the midst of his meal and never returned. I have checked my inventory of native disguise which indicates that no more than three men could have left the Base in native disguise prior to our coming; yet there are over twenty of the first crew missing. I have sent my men out to scout the immediate area thoroughly before departing for Rahnalor; yet I have received no report. I can only assume that their communicators have been overtaken by the same mysterious malfunction which has seized mine and that of M'Kash! I have attempted to re-summon the men without success. Evidently no communicator on this planet is functioning anywhere; or if they are, I cannot receive their signals."

A brief, hissing silence; then once again the voice of the ill-fated Vilkish F'Thansa—why, Dane wondered, did he immediately assume that the leader of the investigating party had been ill-fated? The message this time began in the middle of a sentence and Dane wondered what had been omitted—or erased?

"—without sign of a struggle, and most important, no record of a spacecraft landing on any of the monitoring or skywatch equipment. The obvious explanation which first occurred to me was that a Mekhar ship had landed and captured all Base personnel. I have, however, made a thorough examination of the automatic recording instruments and they show no sign of a spacecraft landing close enough to endanger the personnel of this Base, and no sign of tampering. Furthermore, any Mekhar crew seizing the personnel of this station would hardly have freed or taken the laboratory animals; they would have left them to starve, having no use for them. I have determined to go on to Rahnalor as planned, alone; perhaps I shall overtake my crew, perhaps not; perhaps I shall discover what has befallen them, or share their fate. I take no credit for this decision; I would be equally afraid to remain here. I shall leave M'Kash, whose wound is not yet healed, to report if the communicator should begin to function again, and to add to this report if anything should happen while I am gone. May the Mothers of my clan have pity on me! If I should not return, I respectfully report that the news of my death be recorded within the walls of F'Thansa. . . ."

Like an interruption, another speaker . . . although how Dane knew it was another speaker, and not the soundless subvocal mechanical whisper of F'Thansa, he could not tell; was there, perhaps, some subtly different rhythm to the second speaker?

"Captain! Is that a man?"

"I do not know, M'Kash. It is a large white creature, but larger than any man could be unless he lived to a truly venerable age!"

Dane glanced at Dravash, remembering that F'Thansa would have meant, by a *man*, a protosaurian Sh'Fejj like himself; and that protosaurs did not cease to grow at maturity but continued to grow throughout their lifespans, so that size was, within limits, a reliable indicator of extreme age.

"But *white*? Captain, the inhabitants of this planet are manlike, but of our color! Can it be an illusion, an apparition, a deformed creature like one of the Farspeakers?"

"Remain here, M'Kash. I shall investigate."

And silence. Silence, for so long that Dane felt the hair shudder on his scalp. At last:

"M'Kash Valsaa reporting. One standard digestive period has passed. Nothing to report."

A faint buzzing sound signified the end of the transmission.

"M'Kash Valsaa reporting. Two standard digestive periods have passed. Nothing to report."

Buzz.

That was all. That was really all, this time. The silence stretched on and on, and finally there was not even the faint mechanical hiss of the cube, and Dravash touched the button. Forgetting his own rule, he rumbled a phrase in Sh'fejjhi which Dane's translator disk rendered as "Poor lost eggs!" Then he straightened and shook himself, looking more than ever like an alert Tyrannosaurus Rex.

"I want to check those spacewatch instruments myself! And then I want to get as far away from this place as I can!"

Dane agreed strongly, but felt that if he were in charge of this party he wouldn't even have wanted to wait to check the instruments!

"The Divine Egg—" Aratak began, but Dravash checked him with an impatient snort.

"No proverbs now, colleague, I beg you! I'm busy!"

He strode over to one of the mysterious massive shapes against the wall and began examining it.

Dane forced himself to relax, looking round him. The rain had diminished to the merest drizzle, making the faintest of sounds on the covering. Dane turned his back toward the wall of the building—well away from the door—hoping that this would lessen the feeling that *something* was going to land between his shoulder blades at any moment. He had the creepy feeling of being watched. After hearing that record cube, he hoped they wouldn't have to go inside the deserted base at all. He kept close to Rianna, which wasn't difficult. Closeness to another human being gave him a faint feeling of security which he wished his common sense would stop telling him was illusion. Some instincts were best followed. . . .

Grass grew part way under the sheltering roof, paler and sparser as it edged closer to the inset blocks of something like concrete which supported the heavy machinery. Closer in, the ground was mostly bare tramped soil. He straightened suddenly. Tracks! There was no rain in here to wash them away, and nothing could have gotten in to disturb the ground since that first investigating team had followed the Base personnel into limbo.

"Stay here," he said to Rianna and, moving to the edges of the roofed space, knelt to examine the ground. Aratak raised his head, alert and curious, but when he moved as if to join him, Dane waved him back. Dane moved all along the edge of the covered area, examining the trampled soil carefully, giving careful attention to their own fresh tracks, particularly to those of the two protosaurians.

The dirt was dry and crumbled, and of course wind had gotten in, though rain had not, to blur the edges of the marks. Finally Dane straightened, kneeling upright by the edge.

"Captain," he asked Dravash, "the people who staffed this Base—they were all saurians, Sh'fejj, were they not?"

"What else?" asked Dravash absently, not looking up from the machine he was studying.

"And the members of the investigating team, too?"

"Yes, to be sure." This time the black iguana head lifted from the blank bluish screen of an unknown instrument, where obscure green lines traced themselves in meaningless curves—to Dane—over the surface every few seconds. "Have you found some clue?"

"I'm not sure." Dane frowned at the dim marks in the ground before him, remembering, long ago in Australia, when he had spoken to a very old aborigine who could still read tracks in the ancient way and had taught Dane who had passed in the desert outback more than half a year before. Dane had never had anything like *that* kind of tracking skill. But still. . . .

"Do you know anything about them personally? For instance; do you know if any of them were as big as you, or as Aratak?"

The Captain made a puzzled, interrogatory sound.

"Mostly, I should imagine, they were a great deal smaller; this sort of thing is usually a young man's work. Why do you want to know?"

"It's been too long to be sure, but these tracks—here, at the edge, in the mud, where it must have rained in once and then dried out—indicate there was at least one saurian here who must have been around Aratak's size. Maybe even bigger."

"I don't understand what you are talking about." Dravash left the machine and came over. Dane pointed to the outsize track he had discovered. Dravash stared at the ground in puzzlement, then suddenly jerked his head. "Wait a minute," he said. "Are you referring to the impression made by feet in the ground?"

"Of course," Dane said.

"Ah!" exclaimed Dravash, "Now I understand; I was on a joint expedition with a group of Prrzetz once, and one of them was always able to tell you what kind of animals had been around, he was always sniffing at the ground and smelling it. It was always a mystery to me, how he knew, but he was usually right. He tried to teach me, but I couldn't seem to pick it up. So protosimians can do that too?" There was real wonder in his voice.

Rianna said, "Most hunting species develop the ability in their primitive stages, Dravash. According to old records, the people of my world used to do it too, though it's a lost art with us."

Dane understood at the edges of his mind that she was saying he was closer to the primitive than she; but it didn't matter now. Dravash looked down at Dane with a sudden respect.

"Very wonderful, that. What can you tell us about the creature?"

"Very little, Captain. Only that it must have been about Aratak's size and weight. That footprint's pretty old, but see, you can tell how deep it went when it was fresh."

Dravash actually bent down and put his long lizard snout against the ground, trying to see; finally he straightened, with the little twitch that seemed the equivalent of a rueful headshake.

"Sorry; to me, I fear, dirt is dirt. As I finally had to tell my

Prrzetz friend years ago. Tell me, could you recognize the creature if you smelled it again? RR'sais could."

Dane shook his head. "Our people only use our eyes, not our noses."

"And you can actually see. . . ." The ridges over Dravash's eyes wrinkled up.

"Look," said Dane, beckoning Aratak toward them, "See the imprint there, and how long the foot must have been? Now look at Aratak's foot—the length. Does anyone *your* size, or smaller, have a foot that length?"

"If he did, he would belong in a museum of monstrosities," Dravash said.

Rianna asked, "Are you quite sure Aratak didn't make that print?" She was kneeling, studying it.

"I am sure of that," Aratak said, loosening the scarf which covered his massive gill-slits, "I moved from the walk there, directly to the machines."

"Anyway, it's an old track," Dane said. "Look how the edges have crumbled."

"You're right," she said. "And now I see there are some differences in the toes—claws—whatever," she finished impatiently.

"Which means," Dane said, "that a saurian of Aratak's size, or bigger—or else that monstrosity Dravash was talking about—stood over here at least once since this Base was established."

Dravash muttered, "Now I wonder . . ." and went back to his machines. Aratak moved out from under the covering roof and stood in the warm drizzling rain, obviously feeling refreshed by it. Rianna was still kneeling by the big footprint.

"I can see now what you are talking about," she said, and Dane nodded. "What I can't understand is why Dravash couldn't!"

"His species have never been hunters," Rianna said. "He may not have the right kind of eye coordination to focus on them properly. The Sh'fejj never needed—"

She was interrupted by Dravash himself, who had returned to the machine with the puzzling green traceries. He had opened it up and was fumbling around inside it; now he jerked his head up, looking somehow more cheerful, as if he had found something that pleased him.

"I may not be able to make any sense of marks in the dirt," his deep voice boomed, "but I can read a record-tape! Poor F'Thansa was wrong. He may not have had time for the exhaustive tests he should have made, or didn't go back far enough. It *is* possible for an offworld ship to have landed here. About ten standard units before the last report from this Base, there are fluctuations in the radiation readings which could have been made by cosmic rays, yes—but they *could* also indicate the energy flows of a starship landing a few thousand measurements from here. There are two similar fluctuations earlier. And the sky searcher has picked up what could have been ion deposits."

Rianna asked, "Then there was a spacecraft—"

Dravash twitched his eye-ridges again. "No, he was right about that; there was no spacecraft, aircraft or any similar powered vehicle within measurable distance of this Base, at the time the staff here went—wherever they went. But that only means they came overland."

Aratak said, "It's hard to imagine Mekhar doing that—or even Kirgon."

Again the eye-ridges twitched. "What I believe now is that this planet has been discovered by some new spacegoing race—one we haven't seen before, about whose habits we know nothing. This solar system is right on the fringes of explored territory, and there are a lot of stars out there. There could easily be something worse than the Mekhar around here."

Dane caught Rianna's eye, and he wondered if the same crawl was up her spine that was prickling with his. If there was a spacegoing race worse than the Mekhar, the interstellar slavers who had captured him and Rianna and deposited them to fight for their lives on the Red Moon, he never wanted to encounter it.

The Mekhar had been protofelines. They would stand out on this world like . . . like a giant anteater wearing clothes, on the streets of Dane's own Terran cities!

But they might not be Mekhar. Again he stared at the huge saurian footprint, crumbled by months of exposure to wind and weather; and quite suddenly he shuddered, his hand going uncommanded to the hilt of the Samurai sword at his hip.

"All this means," said Dravash, striding purposefully toward the front of the building, "that the sooner we're all away from this Base, the happier I'll be about it. It's obviously being monitored in some way. But it took them two or three hours to come after the man Vilkish F'Thansa left here, and once we're out in the jungle, we'll be harder to find. Are you all ready to leave? Is there anything here you wish to examine? Aratak?"

He did not ask Dane or Rianna, and Dane tensed, frowning slightly. That could begin to get on his nerves. He was ready to concede that Dravash was at the head of this party. But if Dravash was going to act as if Dane and Rianna weren't there at all. . . .

Aratak stepped inside the building for a moment, and moved around inside. Dane heard him strike a piece of furniture and growl faintly. Then he called.

"Rianna? Dane?"

They followed him inside. He had his head and part of his enormous forequarters inside a kind of closet; he withdrew a long, leaf-bladed spear.

"Since there may be camouflage-cats—" he used the native word, rashas, but Dane felt his throat disk eerily echoing, *camouflage-cats,* "I would feel safer if you were carrying this, Rianna. It is not quite as long as the one you had on the Hunter's World, but no doubt you can manage it equally well."

Rianna took the spear, hefting it, testing its weight and balance. "Feels all right," she said, and Dane could see the tension in her jawline. "Thanks, Aratak."

Aratak rummaged again in the locker. He said with the door muffling his voice, "This contains—I recalled from one of the earlier reports which I studied—items of native manufacture. Unfortunately there is only a single spear, but as I recall, that was Rianna's preferred weapon. And some of the other items may be useful." He drew out one or two of the short, machete-like native swords. "Perhaps we should each take one of these." He strapped one at his waist. It looked strange there. "Dravash?"

The Sh'fejj shrugged. "It might be useful for hacking our way through the underbrush, if we must. And since it is of native manufacture, it might be safer if Dane carried one. You could leave that alien weapon of yours here—"

"Not a chance," Dane said, his hand closing around the hilt of the Samurai sword. "This one goes where I do." He didn't elaborate. He'd already been over that once with the Sh'fejj.

Aratak said, "There also seems to be an optical instrument of native manufacture—" He handed Rianna a small collapsing telescope.

"That must be from Dalass or Sharna," Dravash said,

naming two of the Belsar cities not far from Rahnalor. "The protosaurians there grind lenses. I'll admit that and the weapons might come in useful, but I hope you aren't going to load yourself down with too much junk!"

Aratak withdrew his massive forequarters from the closet, unruffled. "I do not believe there is anything else here which might be useful. Clothing, mostly, and jewelry. However, the Divine Egg says that only a fool will undertake any action without providing himself with the proper tools."

"If the stars," Dravash said, "were as close together as your proverbs, we wouldn't need spaceships. And if your proverbs were as far apart as the stars, I could concentrate in tranquility upon the necessities of this journey! Come on. Let's get away from this place!"

CHAPTER FIVE

The heavy vegetation around the Base was mostly a screening hedge, surrounding the forcefield, planted by the original expedition to conceal the visual anomalies which might have drawn attention to the forcefield in the open. Dane supposed that on a jungly planet like this, planting a thick screening hedge was a matter of sticking a few roots in the ground and stepping back in a hurry before the resultant jungle growth hit you on the chin.

Dravash brushed a branch aside and stepped into bright daylight, his black scales glittering. Dane could see beyond him a low wall of natural stone with a glassy surface; there was a cleft in the wall, and Dravash went through. The others followed. Dane, glancing back, saw apparently only a patch of undisturbed jungle. The forcefield was again concealing the Base, and he wondered if an observer—if there had been any sapient observers within several miles, them apparently stepping out of nowhere.

which he fervently hoped there weren't—would have seen

A blast of hot spicy air struck Dane in the face, and he

found himself staring down a long slope covered with sun-dried grass. Dark twisted trees that reminded him a little of apple trees shook their deep green leaves with each burst of the hot wind from below. From the branches of one, small owl-like brown birds blinked at the travelers, and with strangely mournful clicking sounds, burst from the tree in a whirr of short wings, sailing off down the slope. On the branches they had looked like owls; in flight they resembled partridges. He stared after them, sudden homesickness like a fist around his heart.

Owls and partridges. But they weren't. Apple trees and pines, sunset beyond the Golden Gate bridge, the crimson of turning maple leaves in autumn, Adirondack fishing streams, Fujiyama, Tahiti. The Rio Grande, the Hudson . . . all gone! Lost to him forever, somewhere in interstellar space! His fingers tightened around the lip of the scabbard, his thumb pressing down the guard. It didn't hit him like this, very often. . . . He watched his feet pick their way across the alien soil.

A small animal that was not quite a rabbit exploded from grass and bounded down the slope.

Sweat burned Dane's eyes. Every step down the long slope, the temperature rose. The grass was golden, seared by the sun; the heat hellish, with a sticky humidity.

The slope was longer than it looked. Far below, a faint wrinkle showed the course of a tiny stream at the bottom of the valley—but, he remembered from the map, that tiny stream was a substantial river. They began the long trudge down the slope. Beyond it, the swelling mass of green, look-ing almost like a bed of moss at this distance, grew up the farther slope.

By the time Belsar stood at the zenith, Dane's head ached in the fierce molten glow, and the glare of the sun seemed to fill the whole sky. His eyes burned and he wished that the items of native manufacture had included sunglasses. Dried sweat caked his body; he was glad the others were downwind.

Now, if only it snowed here now and then, it would make short work of this. There was, he remembered, a little snow around the poles themselves, and the original survey had found evidence of glaciation which, a few million years ago, had covered most of the planet. Well, there had been hot periods during the Terran interglacials too, he remembered, with hippopotami in England and elephants in North America. Planets had hot periods and cold ones, and it was just his luck to have hit this one in a hot period.

And they were still high in the mountains. As he remembered the maps he had studied on the ship, they would have to descend several thousand feet before they reached the city. How hot would it be there?

"When do we rest?" Rianna asked. Dravash turned, surprised. His race has evolved on a world hotter than this. But Aratak stopped and hunkered down beside them.

"They come from cold worlds, Captain," he explained. "Are you well, Rianna? I had truly not realized how severe this climate might be for you."

"It's not all that bad, yet," she said, "but I can't go on forever in this heat, and neither can Dane."

A black scaled claw gestured down the slope. "There's water down there," Dravash said, "Can't you make it that far? If not, I suppose we can rest here—for a while, anyway. But if anyone is looking for us—"

We're a burden to him, Dane thought, scowling down the slope. It wasn't that bad, in Earth temperatures—and if he had been in condition. Which, he decided ruefully, he wasn't. Too much soft living in Dullsville.

"I can make it," Rianna said. "But just a minute." She fumbled in her pack, held out her hand to Dane, small white tablets cupped in her palm.

"Salt. You'll need it in this heat."

"Right." He should have thought of it himself; he'd wandered around in the tropics enough to know the danger. Sunstroke had not been one of the risks which had drawn him to this planet (come to think of it, why *had* he come, he wondered), but if today was any sample, or worse, if this was a *cool* day, it might prove one of the worst.

Although, so far, things looked completely peaceful. . . .

They went on. One of the owl-things sailed over them, clicking sadly. A creature with the general outlines of a small deer was grazing near the stream. It looked up as they approached, saw them, and took flight in a series of long, graceful bounds.

Across the river tangled greenery swelled into a forest, so thick that Dane had to think of it as a jungle. As they crossed the last level space this side of the river, occasional disquieting sounds reached them; hoots, an odd, faraway, long moaning scream. The apple-like trees grew thicker as they approached the river, and a new kind of tree appeared, with feathery leaves and soft-looking brownish trunks, like a giant variety of sumac. Waving from the forest he saw palm-like fronds which brought him a sudden homesick longing for a coconut. Or a banana.

The grass was thicker here, too, and made him pick his step uncomfortably, afraid of snakes; after a time he picked up a fallen branch to probe with before each step, and Rianna, after watching him curiously for a while, asked, "What are you looking for?"

"Snakes."

"*Snakes?* What ever for? Do they interest you?"

"No, of course not, but on this world we don't know which are the poisonous ones."

"Poisonous? Snakes?" The idea startled her. "You mean that snakes are poisonous on your world? What do they do, grow stings on their tails like a fishkiller? How very strange!" The very idea seemed to amuse her, and after a moment Dane chuckled too.

"Although you wouldn't laugh if you'd seen anyone die of rattlesnake bite," he said, suddenly sobered.

"Bite? A *snake?* You mean snakes have *teeth* on your world, and poison?"

"Fangs," he said, "hollow teeth with poison glands."

"Oh. Like a deathbird," she said. "I see."

The idea of a poisonous bird shocked him, and kept him watching the sky suspiciously for a long time afterward. Yet why not? On his own world, snakes and birds had a common ancestor, reptilian at that.

But that little interchange had made him think. The Earth-like appearance of this planet might conceal deadly traps. Snakes might not be poisonous—but then, anything else might be. The birds. The deer. *Anything. . . .*

An insect the size of a hummingbird flew by. Another, even larger, hung on gauzy wings above the stream. A flock of what Dane had begun, in his mind, to call click-owls lifted from the trees as they approached the water.

Dravash drank sparingly, while Dane and Rianna gulped sweet wetness from the swift-flowing current and splashed water over one another. But Aratak hunted down the stream until he found a wide deep pool and submerged himself up to the eyeballs. Several small rodent-like creatures exploded from the pool, horrified, and scampered to hide themselves in the jungle.

Dravash snorted and sat down on the bank, watching them

all disdainfully. Dane would not have been startled if Dravash had pulled out a pipe and lit it (although the idea of a seven-foot black dragon puffing a pipe made him laugh to himself). The Captain reminded him of an old Norwegian skipper he had met once; the same business-like manner, gruff speech, and the same patient impatience with other people's quirks. The same brisk competence, too. It made him feel better.

"Poor Dravash," he said to Rianna, "He doesn't like being saddled with protosimians."

He had used the Kahram language they had learned from the tapes, and Rianna looked mildly puzzled; she repeated it, and he heard the translation from his own translator disk, and amended it. "Burdened."

"Well, you must admit, we've been mostly a nuisance so far. From what I've heard about the Sh'fejj Homeworld, this would be a delightfully cool, pleasant day. And, of course, he probably expects us to go into a mating dance any moment." Her eyes met his with a flicker of glee. "If it weren't so hot, I'd be tempted, just to be annoying!"

"How about a swim instead," Dane said, who had been eyeing the water. "Aratak looks pretty comfortable out there."

She nodded, and looked at him with a small giggle as Dravash watched them shedding their clothes, his thick eye-ridges twitching.

I know what Rianna means. It's a temptation to put on a show for him. But Rianna's right, it's just too hot. He headed toward the pool where Aratak floated. Shortly, while Dravash stared at them in bewilderment and mild dismay, the three of them were frolicking in the cool water, Aratak gleefully hurling great waves of water over his smaller friends, darting about them in the pool with amazing speed. Dane found this a little unnerving, though he didn't say so; although long accustomed to Aratak's appearance on land, somehow the slither of his swimming motions touched off some subconscious, perhaps even instinctive fear. He looked just too much like a crocodile; Dane had to stop and remind himself that this was Aratak, whom he trusted completely, and—yes— loved.

Dravash was actually stamping with impatience when they left the water, and although it was beneath his dignity to remonstrate with either Dane or Rianna, he wriggled his eye-ridges reprovingly at Aratak.

"Have you disported yourself long enough with your protosimian companions?" he demanded, as if reproving a colleague for wasting time playing with a couple of dogs.

As always, Aratak was unruffled.

"The Divine Egg has rightly remarked that bathing, like
eating and sleeping, is among the few wholly innocent
pleasures of mankind, doing no harm to any and giving
pleasure to all."

Dravash rolled up his eyes and wrinkled his brow as if im-
ploring, "God give me patience!"

But all he actually said was, "In the next valley, if ?
remember rightly, there is a camping place which should be
safe. In traveling through the forest with protosimians, we
should watch the trees for rashas."

Camouflage-cats, the translator gave an eerie echo.

Dane wondered if the rasha was really as dangerous as the
reports gave out. The Earthly leopard—and as nearly as he
could make out, the rasha, or camouflage-cat, was about like
a leopard, though larger and considerably bolder—normally
fed on monkeys and apes, including man's closest cousin the
chimpanzee; and would go after a human child quickly
enough if it had the opportunity. But more often than not
they left adult able-bodied humans strictly alone, being smart
enough to realize how dangerous this particular monkey
could be. Hadn't the rashas of Belsar learned that lesson yet?

The Sh'fejj, without any comparable predator on their
world, might have exaggerated the danger.

"I'll lead the way," Dravash was saying, "You bring up the
rear, Aratak. If we keep the protosimians between us, they
won't be too exposed."

*I thought we were supposed to be taking care of them, on
this trip, not the other way around!* Dane silently seethed at
this, until a tardy sense of humor made him grin. Suppose he
and Rianna had been asked to escort a pair of, say, three-
foot-high creatures descended from chickens, through a wood
filled with savage and oversized foxes? The creatures might
be very brave and completely sapient—but he'd still have a
few mental reservations!

They were out of the direct sunlight in the forest, so it was,
in a way, cooler; but the still, dead air was suffocating. They
walked single file, following what Dane thought of as a deer
trail—except that someone from the Base had unobtrusively
lopped off enough of the low branches to allow Dravash and
the two humans to walk erect. Aratak still had to duck much

of the time, but Dravash strode along unhampered; the trail
had been built to Sh'fejj height.

Over their head the roof of leaves grew thicker, and away
from the clearly marked trail the tree trunks were hidden by
vines and thick brush. Dead leaves whispered under scurrying
feet; unseen creatures voiced mysterious cries, though on re-
flection Dane supposed the mystery was mostly a version of
Where, oh where is my dinner? A large bird flapped heavily
off a branch, multishaded feathers drab in the gloom, vanishing among the leaves with an eerie howl—a sound which had
startled Dane when he heard it earlier.

Later, a troop of small monkeys burst chattering through
the branches overhead, screeched defiance at the travelers,
and swarmed away into the deeper shadows of the forest.
Dane looked after them in surprise. They had looked, and
even more strangely, *behaved,* just like monkeys in game
preserves on Earth. He was no expert on monkeys, and
couldn't tell whether they were actually identical with any
terrestrial species, but the overwhelming impression was that
this band of monkeys could have been transported to a Bor-
neo jungle and nobody could have told the difference—except, perhaps, an expert.

Still, if humans basically identical to his own species had
evolved on different worlds, it probably wasn't surprising that
lower simians had done so, too. And he and Rianna were
enough alike, though they had evolved light-years apart, to be
lovers, mates. He looked at Rianna, just ahead of him on the
path, thinking that with her new coloring she seemed almost
a stranger, a dusky princess, exotic and alluring. Mysterious.
He grinned to himself, thinking how it would irritate Dravash
to know that his protosimian colleagues were *behaving* like
protosimians, wasting time on such thoughts. About that mating dance, now.

Well, he and Rianna were going to have to risk shocking
the protosaurians sometime, he thought. Maybe tonight when
they made camp. After all, being protosimians they were expected to behave that way, and if they were going to have the
name, they might as well have the game. . . .

A violent rattle of leaves and a sudden savage yowl
brought his head up, to see spread claws and gleaming eyes
in the air above him.

He dropped to one knee, his sword flying from its sheath
and sweeping left to right above his head. He felt the edge
slice flesh, straining muscles in his forearm. Something wet

and sticky poured blinding into his eyes, and a heavy weight drove him to the ground, gravel and twigs digging into his back.

He was drowning in fur. Rianna was screaming his name; then the weight was suddenly lifted, and he saw daylight again, and Rianna's face, pale with horror.

"He's covered in blood! Dane—*Dane!*"

"It's not my blood." Dane sat up, wiping thick goo out of his eyes. Aratak was holding the cat-thing at arm's length, like a grown man holding a kitten by the scruff of its neck. Blood cascaded from its middle; Dane's sword had sliced it nearly in two, and the hindquarters hung limp, but the forequarters were still scrabbling wildly for purchase. Then, with a tiny mewing sound, the life went out of it, and Aratak dropped it, with a fastidious shudder, at one side of the path.

Dane's hands were shaking with reaction as he cleaned and sheathed the blade. It had been close. He had dropped to one knee just in time; the clawed forelegs had missed him cleanly when the camouflage-cat sprang, clawing air over his shoulders just as the rasha's chest had struck him in the face, knocking him down. If his first blow hadn't nicked the spine, the powerful hindclaws would have torn him apart.

A few feet above the spot where his head had struck the ground, leaves and earth were shredded where the great claws had thrashed in agony . . . Dane shivered. It was a good thing he wasn't one of those people who get sick at the sight of blood; his face and shoulders were coated with it. To say nothing of his hair. He grimaced with disgust and hoped there'd be enough water at the camp to wash off the blood-stink.

Dead, the rasha looked small and almost harmless. The fur was a mottling of yellow and brown, with black stripes like a tiger's to further break the outline. No wonder the damn thing had been nearly invisible until it jumped! Camouflage-cat was a good name for the thing!

And man, it seemed, was strictly a favored item on its dinner menu. He wondered what the odds were against being attacked by a leopard on your first day in Africa?

He looked up to find Dravash's eyes on him, and the black dragon head nodded, as though in approval. Dane thought *What do you think of that for a protosimian, friend?* But all he said aloud was, "Let's try to find water so I can wash off this junk. Bathing isn't even a luxury in a case like this—the smell of blood is going to have every scavenger in the jungle on our trail, and I'd rather they'd dine on the remains of our cat friend there."

CHAPTER SIX

Five days they traveled through the mountains, following the trail across ridge after ridge, each lower than the last. As they descended, it grew hotter, and the jungle thicker. New kinds of trees appeared, and an infinite variety of bushes, vines and thorns. Especially thorns. Dane was no longer surprised that the clothing he and Rianna had been provided with was leather; fabric trousers or kilt would have been in tatters by the end of the first day, and at the end of three they'd have been naked. Even the protosaurians, with their thick hide, bore a few scrapes and scratches.

Twice they had been attacked again by rashas. One had impaled itself neatly on Rianna's spear until a swift slash of Dane's sword had taken off its head. The other had been caught in mid-leap by Aratak's huge paw. For a moment the giant lizard-man had regarded the struggling, spitting creature with detachment, then hurled it accurately into the very center of a nearby thornbush. The beast clawed itself frantically out and scrambled off into the jungle, looking very much, Dane thought, like a cat who has been caught on the table with the Thanksgiving turkey!

On the fourth or fifth day Dane observed to Rianna that the Captain seemed happier about being stuck with Aratak's pet monkeys, now that he'd seen them in action.

And certainly Dravash was warming toward the humans. At night, while weird cries resounded from the jungle around them, and dozens of eyes reflected the small light of their fire, Dravash would tell stories of the strange worlds he had visited, or talk with them of the strange people with whom they would soon be dealing. For Dravash, long ago in his youth, had been with the hidden Observer teams on this planet.

But he still winced at each new proverb from Aratak.

And their communicators were silent. They were well and truly out of contact with the Unity, except for the rapport which, Dane supposed, Dravash still entered from time to time with Farspeaker.

As they left the Base farther and farther behind, more and more new growth encroached upon the trail, and in places, they had to struggle and cut their way through with the machete-like knives.

Dane thought it was the sixth day when the overgrown trail led them into a deep valley, suddenly opening into a broad natural clearing. Deerlike creatures bounded away at their approach, and Dravash pointed to the far end of the clearing, where a gray-white strip of stone ran along beside a deep river.

"Our first objective," he said, "I have remembered correctly. It is the old Caravan road."

The river was broad and muddy, well below the level of its banks. A sheer wall of jungle grew from the farther shore. Insects the size of birds flew by on filmy wings. Something large was swimming along in the center of the stream, a huge rodentlike head followed by a Vee of ripples, but it dived as they neared the bank, before Dane could get a good look at it; Dane decided it must be an Aporra, a creature not unlike a hippopotamus in size, weight, and ecological function—it fed on grass and fresh-water weeds at the bottom of rivers and was highly prized by the natives for meat. Dane wouldn't have minded some fresh meat—but he and Rianna could never have eaten anything that size, and it would have been wasteful to kill it and leave the carcass for the scavengers.

One of the large insects flew too near Aratak. With amazing speed, a huge hand shot out and snapped the creature out of the air. Dane averted his eyes and shuddered slightly as the lizard-man stuffed the bug in his mouth and chewed. He'd nearly thrown up the first time Aratak did that.

"Delicious," Aratak exclaimed, "Truly, this planet abounds in rich foods!"

That settled it, Dane decided. Tonight he'd try to knock one of those click-owls out of the trees and decide if they tasted as much like partridges as they looked.

Dravash, whose dietary habits were not unlike Aratak's, nodded in impatient agreement—though, Dane noticed, his own big eyes were looking around for another of the big insects—but the Sh'fejj flinched as Aratak added, "Truly did

the Divine Egg remark that he who is content with simple
fare has little to fear from misfortune, for all of nature com-
bines to provide him with rich contentment, and a full stomach will soon provide the answer to the other troubles which
besiege the unquiet minds of mankind."

Dane could see Dravash meditating on a sarcastic reply.
But he said nothing; evidently he had already learned that it
would be a waste of breath. While Aratak lived and breathed,
he would continue to muse aloud on the wisdom of the
Divine Egg, and it was just as simple as that. Dravash only
said mildly, "It is a pity one cannot dine on philosophy as on
food and drink, Aratak, and then we should never hunger."

Aratak picked a chitinous fragment of wing from his long
teeth and remarked, "Alas, philosophy alone, without meat
and drink, is but thin fodder; but meat and drink alone, un-
seasoned with philosophy, will not long nourish any sentient
being."

Dane supposed it was a good thing that the reptiles had already begun the changeover to native foods which they must
all make, and which would become total when they assumed
their roles among the native population. So far, though, Dane
and Rianna had only sampled—cautiously—a very few of the
native fruits and roots; they had had no time for hunting, and
had relied on the emergency rations at the bottom of their
rucksacks. But once they made contact with a caravan, they
would have to switch entirely to native cooking.

Dane looked at the swirling water where the Aporra had
dived, and thought about a bow and arrow. The natives, for
some reason, had never developed or used such weapons,
hunting only with spears. One night, back in the forest, he
had actually begun work on a bow, but the saurian had
reacted with horror; as if, Dane thought, Dane had recommended entering the native city wearing spacesuits and carrying laser pistols.

*Haven't you learned anything from the tapes and educa-
tors? The protosimians here don't use bows—or any missile
weapons! Nobody but an outlaw will even throw a spear!*

Dane had protested—he thought they simply hadn't developed the bow—and Dravash looked at him in angry disgust, as if Dane were simply verifying his preconceived ideas
about all protosimians and their stupidity.

*They know what bows are. Didn't you see the replica of
the wall paintings of Kishlor?* Dane had, but evidently hadn't
paid enough attention, and Dravash had repeated it, growling

with angry emphasis. *They don't use any kind of missile weapon! It's their strongest taboo . . . even children are taught it's dishonorable and wicked to throw a stone!*

It was the first time Dane had ever heard of a successful taboo enforced against an effective weapon. It puzzled him. But he still had a lot to learn, and he knew it.

They turned on to the road. Great blocks of whitish stone had been fitted together, without any kind of mortar, but so closely that Dane judged it would be hard to slide the blade of a knife between them. He remembered being told that at some time in their history, it had been built by building a wall in a ditch; the earthen outwalls had long since worn away, and the countless feet of generations had hollowed the stone into a gentle curve. The recent rain had left a little water at the bottom of the channel thus formed—not enough to be carried off by the outlets which had been cut, very old but not nearly so old as the road, to carry off flooding. The two protosaurs splashed along in the water, evidently enjoying the mud on their huge leathery feet in the same way a city-dweller might enjoy walking on grass after paved sidewalks; but Dane and Rianna moved out to the edge of the stone, where they had to pick their way along widening cracks where jungle growth and creepers had forced their way into the once-tightly-fitted rifts between stones. However, the jungle growth had been trimmed away quite recently— Dane supposed it was a cooperative venture among the tribes and cities whose caravans used the road, each caravan doing its part in driving back the encroaching jungle.

Along the bank of the river the verge had been kept clear, and Dane, stepping off the road, studied the muddy ground for tracks. Since learning that no one else in the party had any awareness of tracking, he had set himself to learn the prints left by the native beasts and discriminate between the different feet and the tracks they left. Similarities to Earthly analogues helped; but even more, his concern with local ecology was stimulating his memories of the vast supply of records which had been hypnotically driven into his head. That made sense; if you *use* a skill, he knew, it sharpens.

There were, he knew, men even on Earth who would have laughed at his small skill in tracking; men who could have read a clear trail where he saw only shapeless scratchings in the dirt. But some tracks in the mud of the bank were clear. Here was a set of three-toed, webbed prints he believed to be that of an Aporra, and he had no trouble at all recognizing

the pug-marks of a rasha and deciphering the story they told.
The beast had come out of the jungle, stopped to drink at the
water's edge, and climbed briefly up on the road; Dane could
see the wet spots at the edge of the stone, where he—or she;
the female rashas were equally large and even deadlier—had
smeared water on the stone. The faint traces led across the
road and into the jungle ahead of them. He wondered uneasily if the camouflage-cat was waiting for them up ahead, and
made sure his sword was loose. He opened his mouth to warn
the others—now they were actually on a road constructed by
civilized beings, they might think they were out of the jungle,
and they weren't—when Rianna stopped, turning to him.

"Listen," she said, "What's that noise?"

Dane listened; heard a distant musical chiming, like the
sound of sleigh-bells. *Here comes Santa Claus, here comes
. . .* the sound was ridiculous, under the brazen sun wringing
sweat from his forehead; the reflected sun on rock was rising
up under his kilt, and he felt as if he stood inside a blast furnace.

The shelless holes which served the protosaurians for ears
were less acute at gathering distant sounds; it was some
minutes before Dravash raised his head, hearing the
strengthening bell-sounds.

"Ganjir bells," Dravash said. "There must be a caravan
coming. You people had better let me do the talking." He
had switched languages on them, changing from the local ar-
got of Kahram, which they'd all been talking, to the "High
Speech"—an ancient protosaurian language, somewhat modi-
fied by dropping or altering some sounds protosimians found
too difficult, which—again Dane remembered from the learn-
ing-tapes—had been, like Latin in the Middle Ages, a trade
tongue between widely separated cultures.

The chiming grew louder, and where the road curved before them, Dane could see tall, indistinct forms through the
trees. Aratak laid his huge paw on Rianna's shoulder and said
something Dane didn't catch. She laughed.

The four of them stood together in the center of the road.
Dane strained to see through the fringing trees, unconsciously
stepped back, closer to the jungle, then remembered and shot
a quick glance back over his shoulder. Nothing; the foliage
was still and unstirred.

*Hell, that cat's probably miles away by now. Cats are ner-
vous animals. It's not likely to jump out with a caravan coming up, making that much noise.* He wondered if that was

why they wore bells. Make enough noise, and they'd frighten away most of the beasts in the jungle. . . .

Burning heat, sleighbells, sweat-drenched clothes and Christmas carols running in his head over the sound of bells . . . *winter wonderland! Bah, humbug!*

Another step, and he could see tall shapes, black and gray and brown. The bells grew louder. Suddenly they came around the curve and he could see them clearly, great black-and-white mottled beasts, long-legged like camels but humpless, swaying beneath bales bound with heavy coarse cloth. Tiny chiming bells swayed on their leather harnesses. Beside them men—protosimians, anyway—in grayish coats, feather headdresses and lots of jingling neck-chains and amulets not unlike those Dane and Rianna wore, led the beasts by ropes linked to the halters on the mournfully gentle, vaguely bovine faces of the ganjir; swaying long necks, thickly muscled, covered with a magnificent ruff. Dane vaguely remembered that the wild ganjir was antlered like a moose, but only small stubby knobs remained to these domesticated beasts; probably they were dehorned as calves.

The man at the head of the caravan saw them, and spoke to his ganjir, tugging the beast around to stand sideways, blocking the road. He shouted. Dravash, who was walking ahead of the others, turned to speak to Dane, annoyance on his face.

What now? Dane wondered. *Does he want me to interpret?* Dravash, raising a hand to gesture, suddenly froze, and Dane saw his eyes fasten on something in the forest behind him. Something rustled, half-drowned by the sound of bells and leaves.

Dane jumped, pulling out his sword with what seemed agonizing slowness. Before he heard Dravash's warning shout, he heard the familiar rustle of leaves; his sword seemed clumsy as an iron bar in his hand as he pivoted, bringing the blade up over his head, seeing the rasha come to earth in a crouch and spring. The blade snapped down, crunching through bone, as the great talons opened and closed less than a handspan from his face. The sword was almost torn from his hand as the great cat crumpled, the blade trapped in its skull.

Shouting drowned the bells.

He wrenched at the blade, his foot on the head of the still twitching rasha. He had to use both hands to wrestle it free. Mounted men came riding up on beasts quite different from the ganjir, these with vaguely horselike lines, but horned and

bob-tailed; their leader, on a wine-red beast, pulled up where
Aratak and Dravash stood in the middle of the roadway. He
stood up in his stirrups and whistled, a shrill complex signal;
two of his fellow outriders put spurs into the flanks of their
riding beasts and wheeled their mounts over the edge of the
road and into the jungle. Dane, giving his sword a cleaning
swipe on the fur of the dead rasha, blinked in amazement at
the way the mounts and their riders wove their way into what
he would have considered impassible tangles of brush and
vine. Half a dozen men followed on foot, running with spears
levelled and ready.

The leader settled down in his saddle, looking down at the
party of four with a face not at all unfriendly. His skin was a
deep mahogany red, under black hair streaked with gray. He
had a sparse gray stubble of beard. A tall green plume rose
from his headdress.

Dravash, who had waited in silence while the leader
dispatched his party to see if bandits, or more rashas, were
lurking out of sight, finally spoke, in the High Speech:

"A safe road and a good trade to you, trail-master; may
the Saints and the Blessed Ones watch over your road. We
are travelers from Raife, traders who have come to trade our
poor jewels for the rich goods of these strange lands. We became separated from our caravan during the confusion of an
attack by bandits and have been wandering in the forest for
days, until we came to the road. I am Thrava'ash Effiyim of
Borchan, and this is my beloved Elder Kinsman, A'aratakha,
of the same city and clan."

Dane listened carefully, trying to memorize the precise
sound of Dravash's name and Aratak's in the High Speech.
This, he knew, would be the real test of their disguises. These
men were traders and travelers who had been farther to the
west than anyone else they were likely to meet on this world;
it was not unlikely that some of them had been to Raife. Or,
at least, mingled with men and protosaurians of Raife in the
markets of western provinces. They would know more of that
half-legendary land than any of the sedentary folk of
Rahnalor itself.

Dane felt tension twisting the muscles between his shoulders as the leader looked down at them.

"From Raife," the leader said at last, "You are far astray,
Noble One, but we shall find a place for you among us, and
for your servants. Indeed," he added, his eyes moving to
Dane, "your bodyguard there we will be glad to have with us;

he slew yonder rasha with a swiftness I have not often seen. But we have heard no word of a caravan attack in this vicinity; where was it attacked?"

"Alas—" Dravash gestured vaguely into the thick jungle through which they had come, "I cannot tell, for all these lands are alike to me, and of one strangeness! Never before have I been east of Tivilish! The last town we passed through, I think, was called Vish—or. I cannot speak the name," he concluded with a quite authentic twitch of his eye-ridges, "but we have been wandering in these forests now for eight or nine sunsets; I have no idea where we are now!"

The Caravan-master frowned. "We are about seven or eight days' march west of Vashilor, and twenty days north of Kishlor," he said. "It is possible—"

He broke off as a man came running from the jungle. He wore a short blue robe and carried a long spear. Three others followed, dressed in the short gray coat, not unlike—Dane thought—a judo *gi*, which wrapped over their leather kilts.

"Bandits ahead, Caravan-master," he said, then added quickly, "No connection with these folk. I don't think any of them saw us; I have Odhai and Jandhra watching their camp."

Behind him Dane heard hoofbeats, and turned quickly, braced to see a villainous horde of cutthroats, but it was only one of the mounted outriders, returning to report.

"There is Jandhra," said the Caravan-master, and addressed himself once again to Dravash. "You and your folk had best get back with the others, Sir. It looks like there's trouble ahead. My son will show you—" he lifted himself in his stirrups, glared around, then bellowed:

"Joda! *Joda!* Where has that star-cursed brat gone to now? If he had—*Joda!*" he roared again, enraged, and the man in the blue tunic spoke up.

"I shall be honored to take charge of the travelers, Caravan-master."

"What? What?" The Caravan-master blinked, his rage settling into a scowling displeasure. "Oh—I thank you, Spearman. You go along with Master Rhomda, then, Noble Ones, and he'll see you safely settled among your own folk. And when I get my hands on that brat . . ." he turned away, with an irritable jerk of his head, to speak to the outrider, and the blue-clad man shifted his spear to rest on his shoulder with an expert move that made Dane blink. He was dark-skinned and muscular, in the short blue tunic that set him off from the ordinary gray-coated men; he wore low boots that looked like rawhide, and leg-wrappings above them that protected his bare legs from jungle growth and venomous scratches. He was not very young—he was too clearly in command of himself and everything around him for that—but his hair was an even black untouched by gray, and he moved like a youth in perfect training.

"If the Noble Ones will come with me," he said, and led the party back toward the line of ganjir. Dane had seen Master Rhomda's eyes take in his sword, rest for an evaluating moment on Rianna's long spear. But outwardly his attention was focused correctly on Dravash and Aratak; *they* were the leaders of the party.

Rianna and I are just servants. Bodyguards.

In the back of Dane's mind, somewhere among the masses of data he had been forced to absorb, so quickly, something was clamoring for attention; something alerted by that blue tunic. But he could not quite remember what it was.

Men who wore that blue tunic . . . there was something very important about them. Well, he was ready to believe that Master Rhomda was important, over and above being in charge of the caravan's bodyguard. He looked like somebody.

He's the one we've got to watch out for! He's the one who will see through our cover story, if anybody does!

CHAPTER SEVEN

Close up the ganjir smelled like sheep, a heavy smell of wool and lanolin. Their long noses were really small prehensile trunks, like those of a tapir or an elephant seal; these writhed out for a full four or five inches from the mouth as they sniffed the air, twitching, nervous as the man who led them. The men crowded around Master Rhomda, hurling questions.

"Spearman, what's happening?"

"What is it? Are we being attacked by bandits?"

"Who are the strangers? Have you caught the bandits?"

"Don't be a fool, if they were bandits Master Rhomda wouldn't leave them their weapons! Hey, one of them's a girl, that one with the long spear!"

"Wasn't that a rasha screaming?"

"Master Spearman, Master Spearman, tell us what's going on!"

"Wait, wait," Master Rhomda said, gesturing the crowding men back, good-naturedly, "All in good time."

A young man—a boy, really, fourteen or fifteen—came pushing through the crowd. His face wore a sullen, rather frightened look. Against the dark of his face a thick white scar reared up from the eyebrow through his scalp, dividing the hair with a thin bald line. The man in the blue tunic motioned to him.

"Your father is looking for you, Joda. I m afraid he's angry."

The boy shrugged defiantly. "That is nothing new. Are we being attacked, Spearman? Who are these strangers?"

"Travelers from Raife," the Master Spearman said, and Dane heard startled exclamations from the crowd thickening around them, "Your father wanted you to look after them. Yes, there are bandits ahead of us," he went on in a kindly voice, "but our outriders know where they are, and they may not attack such a large group; in any case, they won't be able to surprise us."

Under his calm reassurance, most of the men clustered around the Spearman had gone back to the ganjir they tended. But not all.

"Come on, pretty thing, stay and talk to me a while," Dane heard a wheedling voice behind him, where Rianna was. "I've got something nice for you—" the voice broke off in a gasp that was almost a scream. Dane whirled, just in time to hear the man with the wheedling voice hit the ground. Rianna still had hold of his arm. She wrenched the wrist and fingers back with a subtle twist, and as the man began to rise he gave a choked scream; the movement brought pressure against his wrist.

"I will *not* be pawed," said Rianna. She pressed, very lightly, on the fingers, grinding the wristbones against each other, straining the tendons to screaming point. "I want this—very clearly—understood. Now."

"I didn't mean anything!" He gasped with the pain, writhing. "Let me go! I won't do it again!"

Several men had left their ganjir again and moved in to

watch. Some laughed. But one, not far from Dane, muttered, "She needs taming, that one. How about it, should we teach her a lesson?"

"Umm," said his companion, "Might be fun, at that, four or five of us could certainly handle her."

Dane's hand found his sword-hilt, but he heard Master Rhomda's quiet voice.

"Four or five dead fools. Have you seen her friend in action, Dando? The one with the sword?"

One of the drivers, a massively muscled man with a broken nose and cauliflower ears, twisted his ruined face in a discordant grin. "You'll protect us, won't you, Spearman?"

"I?" Rhomda shook his head, smiling. "I have more regard for my health than to protect a fool who meddles with another's woman. There are camp-followers enough with the caravan; why strive with one who wishes to protect herself?"

Rianna had released the unwise ganjir drover; he was sitting flat on the ground, holding his abused wrist. She picked up the spear she had thrown down, and came to join the rest. Dravash was watching in eyeridge-wriggling disgust, and Dane could almost read his thoughts, *these protosimians, at it again!* Aratak was watching them in puzzled concern. The boy Joda had not taken his eyes from Rianna since the whole affair began.

"Follow me," Rhomda said, curtly; the episode was over.

Dane strode along behind the Master Spearman, his mind worrying at the confused mass of facts stored in his brain. *Spearman.* Yet they all carried spears, even as Rianna did; even some of the drovers had spears tucked into the harnesses of their animals. Why should the special title apply only to the man in the blue tunic?

Rianna caught his eye, and he asked in an undertone, "All right, love?"

She nodded, with a grin. "I could have managed that one before I was ten years old." She motioned him to silence. "Quiet. I think this is the real leader of the caravan; the Caravan-master is just the head of the guard."

They were approaching four ganjir who bore no loads, but were yoked to a large, wooden-wheeled cart, brightly painted in colorful abstract designs, shell-shaped and huge. Dane stared at the servants who clustered about the carriage. Humans, certainly—but not of the same race as Rianna and himself, not like any protosimians he had seen. Certainly not the same race as the drovers, as Rhomda and the boy Joda.

Chinless, with small heads and heavy brow ridges, they reminded Dane of reconstructions he had seen of the pithecanthropoids of Java and Peking. Great manes of deep reddish hair covered their heads and grew in a kind of crest down their shoulders and backs.

On Earth, evolving man had killed off all his poor relations; here the dominant protosaurian race had preserved at least two different species of simians.

Perched inside the carriage, a silky-black, richly robed protosaurian—Dane knew by the crest of webbed spines on the head that it was a female, and by Rhomda's deference that she was someone extremely important—the Master Spearman bowed almost to the ground.

"Noble One, I bring you travelers from Raife," he said, and turned to Dravash. "Behold the carriage of the Noble Mother OOa-nisha of the House of Thefrassha, of Rahnilor." With another deep bow, he fell back, allowing Dravash and Aratak to approach the great cart.

"Well met, Honored Mother," Dravash said, introducing himself. The saurian lady bowed, addressing Aratak as "Venerable," a title to which his great size entitled him, and at her invitation, the two great saurians climbed into the cart, indicating their "servants" with the merest flicker of a gesture. The Honored Mother made a faint gesture of recognition, which Dane interpreted as giving them permission to exist in her orbit, and Dane felt a touch on his arm.

"Hungry?" Master Rhomda asked. "Your owners shouldn't need you for a while. Come along, I can find you some—"

At that moment the sharp thudding of hooves broke through the other sounds, and a sharp set of whistles trilled out, summoning.

"There goes dinner," Rhomda said, chuckling, as the horse-like horned beasts appeared, hurrying along the road. "Looks like the Old Man's made up his mind to attack the bandit camp, and a good thing too, there are too many of them this close to civilized country. Come along. You too, Joda," he added to the boy. "If you aren't here this time when your father wants you, you know what he'll say, and there's only so much I can do about it."

Rhomda made another of those chillingly fluid spear-motions as he turned, and Dane's mind suddenly dislodged the fact he had been trying to remember all the time; the blue robe, and what it meant. It was the badge of the Anka'an Order, an ascetic brotherhood of elite spearmen whose philosophy and discipline had reminded Dane, at the time, of the Samurai of his own world.

All around them the dark men were running, spears in hand and their short machete-like swords at their waists; he felt inside himself the tension that made them run. He glanced at Rianna, but she did not see him, her face set in a hard line he had first known on the Hunter's World. It was coming now. He could feel the tingling flutter in every nerve, a strange hollow wobble at the pit of his stomach.

The caravan-master slid down from his maroon steed. Dane's mind irrelevantly provided him with the native name for the beast; *khostli*. He watched the caravan-master's eyes quickly taking stock of the men gathered around him, saw them narrow as they fastened on Joda, an angry flush discoloring the dark face. Evidently the kid had done something to make his father angry—and worried, too; but the caravan-master had no time for an erring son now.

"Listen men," said the caravan-master, "we've located the bandit camp ahead of us. We could attack it and take them by surprise—they don't know yet that we're coming, and the camp itself is too strong to attack. But they'll have scouts out, watching the road. And when they see the caravan coming, they'll leave the camp, and come to attack. And I'll be in the jungle behind them."

He paused, letting the plan sink in. Dane saw various expressions on the faces around him, fear, admiration, excitement. Here and there in the group bulked the enormous figures of protosaurians, their black scales glittering in the sun with bluish lights, their reptilian countenances all but unreadable.

"So all you have to do is walk into the trap, pretending you don't know it's there. They'll be depending on surprise, and expecting a lot of confusion and running around. The one thing they won't expect is a solid defense. And when we hit them from behind, they'll break and scatter." He flashed a quick look around the group. "Master Rhomda, you take charge of the defense of the caravan. Get the ganjir moving, and be ready for them when they come. Send a few of your men back to guard the Honorable Mother's carriage. May the Blessed Ones send us good fortune!" He vaulted back into the saddle of his *khostli*, and walked it over to where Dane and Rianna stood beside Master Rhomda and Joda. He leaned from the saddle and his voice was a low hiss.

"Stay by Master Rhomda, boy—and this time, try to fight

like a man! If you shame me further, you had better be lying dead when I meet you again!"

He straightened, facing Rhomda with a look of grim defiance. "I leave the defense in your hands, Spearman. And I charge you, take care of—" he broke off, swallowed whatever he had started to say, but for an instant Dane saw a terrible pleading soften the grim old face. Then it was washed away by anger. Anger, and stubborn pride. "Take care of the Honorable Mother and her valued guests, and see that the men don't panic!" The eyes spat venom at his son and he wheeled the khostli and called a command to his men. Hooves hammered on the stone road.

Joda's head was bent, staring stubbornly at the road. Master Rhomda touched his arm gently.

"Joda, your father—" he started, then shrugged. "No time for that now. Come along!" The terse command included Dane as well, and Rianna. *At least he takes her for granted, though I don't see any other women fighting with the men in this caravan!* Rhomda spoke to the men along the long line, and sent Joda to speak to the others; in a few moments the ganjir bells were chiming smoothly as the long line of tall beasts plodded along, swaying under their heavy loads and bales.

Walk into the trap and pretend you don't know it's there. Dane tried to whistle, found his mouth too dry. He wet his lips and tried again; a few moments later he laughed, realizing he was whistling "Jingle Bells."

He wriggled his shoulders, trying to ease the tension there. He thought about the short, wickedly curved blades these people carried, and wondered how they used them. Dravash had shown Dane what he remembered, but the protosaurian had never been a fighter, and what he had shown Dane gave him no hint of the subtleties of a whole world of different styles and schools of weaponry he was about to test!

He remembred hearing, from friends who had settled in Central America, that the Mayas had never bothered swatting flies. Just cut them out of the air with their machetes.

Well, there are plenty of flies around, and he didn't notice any of these fellows cutting at them.

Through the jingle of ganjir bells he heard Rianna's voice, quick and low, at his side.

"Do you think the plan will work?"

"Ought to," he said briefly, irritably, not wanting to talk; she sensed it and grinned tightly at him, turned away.

A long shadow stretched across the ground beside his own. He looked up to see Aratak striding beside him. Neither of them spoke, but a comforting strength seemed to flow through the three of them. They were together again. . . .

"Be ready!" Rhomda's warning was passed down the line. The ganjir picked up the prickling unease of their masters, and the bells jangled more furiously as the creatures shook themselves, or struggled against their lead ropes.

Joda's fingers were running nervously up and down the pallid scar that stood out, a white slash, against his dark skin. His teeth were set.

"How did you get that scar?" Rianna asked suddenly.

The boy shot her a look of pure fury.

"How do you think I got it?" he snarled at her, "I was combing my hair and the comb bit me!"

Touchy brat, Dane thought, turning away his eyes. *But he isn't proud of that scar. Some kids his age would be, in a culture like this one. I wonder how he did get it?*

Then a wild chorus of shouts from the jungle tore the thought away, raking along his nerves. Brush crackled as men swarmed out of the thick undergrowth, waving spears and machetes and yelling horribly.

Rhomda yelled something, turning to run toward the bandits. Joda, his face set and furious, ran after him.

Machetes hissed free of their sheaths. Spearpoints glittered in the sun as the ganjir drovers left their beasts and gathered swiftly into an effective fighting line.

Dane was running too, his sword still sheathed. He saw half a dozen men converge on the blue-robed Master Spearman, saw Rhomda's lance flicker out to catch the nearest bandit in the throat, then sweep to the side, knocking away other spears that stabbed at him, then dart out again.

A swordsman was running at Joda, the short blade whirling in his hand. The boy hesitated, thrusting his spear out in front of him, trying to hold the attacker back. The blade shone brightly, a blur of silver. The spear thrust in, but the short blade sheared the shaft below the head, and the boy fell back, trying to block with the pointless spear.

And Rhomda, spinning effortlessly away from his own attackers, knocked the blade away with the butt of his spear and with another dancing step drove his point into flesh, pulled it free again, and was turning, sweeping the air to bat aside the thrust that came at him from behind.

A spear was driving toward Dane's throat. He jumped

aside, and as the spearpoint passed him, the Samurai blade whistled free from its sheath, its point tearing a red line under the bandit's ear. A fountain of blood leaped from the artery as the corpse fell past, burying the spear in the ground.

Dane's left hand joined the right on his sword-hilt, as he saw, past him, Rianna's spear drive into the belly of a man who screamed and crumpled over it; saw, over her head as she bent to retrieve the spear, Aratak lashing out with a great scything stroke that laid three headless bodies at his feet. All around them men yelled and died.

He caught a fragmentary glimpse of Rhomda's blue robe, of Joda stumbling back, blocking a lance thrust awkwardly, but effectively enough, with his machete blade. Then he was fighting for his own life as a keen edge whined toward his face. His blade came up, scraping it aside, and fell again to crunch through bone and brain. Then he wrenched it free, slammed it with all his force against a spear-shaft punching toward his chest. He stepped in, past the spear-point, with a short flicking chop that sheared through the wrist and a second step buried his point in the bandit's windpipe, changing the scream into a choked gargle.

As he stepped back, jerking his blade down and out of the attacker's throat, he saw Joda stumbling back toward him, heard the boy cry out and saw blood burst through a sudden hole in the back of the white coat as something red and sharp poked through. The boy fell, screaming, his sword spinning away end-over-end. The bandit raised his spear for the death-stroke, and Rianna, the bright blue scarf fallen from her hair, leaped in, her lance driving into the man's chest. His eyes goggled at her across the spear; blood dribbled out of his mouth and he fell across Joda's body.

Dane was at Rianna's side by then, and his sword swatted aside a lance that drove toward her. Then she had her own spear free, and killed the attacker. A small group of bandits dropped back before Aratak's vast charging form—then hesitated as hoofbeats cut through the sound of battle.

Khostli riders leaped their mounts through the bushes, shouting. The bandits wavered, panicked, ran.

Khostlis brown, black, blue pursued them; with whoops of triumph the ganjir drivers ran to join the pursuit. Rianna, dropping her spear, turned and began to tug the bandit off Joda's body. Aratak bent, heaved, and tossed the corpse bodily into the bushes.

A wine-red khostli pounded up; the grizzled caravan-master leaped down and ran toward them. Joda groaned and sat up, clutching at his bleeding shoulder. Rianna pulled the scarf—which had only fallen around her neck—from its place, and wadded it up, thrusting the thick pad hard against Joda's back where the blood still dribbled through.

The old man's face, taut with concern and horror, changed, twisted with fury and scorn.

"We've healers enough, *Felishtara*," he mocked. "No need to trouble yourself with that cat's meat!" He glared angrily at his son. "Wounded again, I see! In the back this time, no doubt?"

"He stood his ground and fought, caravan-master," It was Rhomda's deep voice. The Anka'an spearman looked and sounded as calm as if he had been at a picnic instead of a battle, though the blue shirt was crusted with blood. "He was not the only one to suffer a wound in this fight. And you have the spearwoman from Raife to thank that you have a living son to rebuke instead of a corpse to bury."

The old man's eyes narrowed. "So! Even a woman fights better than you, my son!" The mockery in his voice dug deep; he half-turned, bowing to Rianna, speaking in the formal sing-song of ritual speech.

"Noble Warrior-lady, will you honor my house and take my worthless son into fosterage for his training in the arts of weapons and war, that he may come to honorable manhood under your guidance?"

Dane could see that it was meant as a jest; a final touch of salt for the boy's wound. The expected refusal—for surely a woman would be even more contemptuous of such a weakling than any man could be—would be another lash to beat the boy with, for the rest of his life.

"Very good," said Rianna calmly. "I accept."

That rocked him. Dane saw the scorn melt from the old face, the sneer go slack with shock as Rianna's words sank in. Dane suddenly felt sorry for the old fellow, though the caravan-master didn't deserve it. Surely this offer, and its acceptance or refusal, was a serious matter in this culture, perhaps the most serious thing that ever happened between a boy and his father; and an ill-timed jest could gravely affect the fortunes of his house.

"*Felishtara*—?" the old man's voice was suddenly shaky, pleading; but Rianna spoke firmly.

"I accept your son into my keeping in fosterage, to be trained in the arts of a warrior. I am a stranger from Raife; I am ill-taught in your language; is there some formal phrase of acceptance I have not been taught, that I should say before you know my acceptance?"

The old man swallowed hard, seemed to shrink visibly where he stood. Long minutes passed while Rianna, ignoring him, knelt to tend the boy's wound.

"Very well," the caravan-master said at last, forcing himself to stand erect, "I wish you better luck with him than I have had, *Felishtara*." He looked down at Joda, who lay with his eyes shut, teeth clenched as Rianna worked on the ragged wound in his shoulder. All the old man's stifled anger burned in his words.

"You heard that, boy? *She* is your master now! You will learn from *her* what I could not teach you about manhood!" He strode angrily away; but as he drew farther from them his figure sagged once more, and he walked as though a great weight hung round his neck.

"Well done," Master Rhomda said with a brief nod of acknowledgment, and walked away.

"Very strange," said Aratak, who had been listening in silence, "Am I correct in my belief that the caravan-master is this child's—" he hesitated over the sound of the Kahram word, mispronouncing it slightly—"Father?"

In Dane's throat, the translator disk echoed, soft and eerie; *Male mother?*

Rianna nodded. A huge protosaurian, obviously some kind of medic, came up and took over from her the task of cleansing and treating Joda's wound.

"Very, very strange," Aratak repeated, "I must meditate on this. Are you sure that your action was wise, dear one?"

"Yes," Dane demanded, "Why *did* you take him on?" He looked at Joda, who seemed to have lost consciousness. "I admit I was sorry for the kid too, but this seems to be a little extreme."

Rianna smiled faintly. "That had nothing to do with it," she said, dropping her voice to a pitch that could not be heard an arm's length away. "Now we have a native guide who is honor bound to assist me in all matters, and keep secret all my doings, however strange they may seem to him. Don't you remember from the—" she stopped and glanced around; no one was near them, but she still did not use the Unity word, rephrasing. "Don't you remember, this is considered a more sacred and binding relationship than the usual clan and family ties. Even if he should find out the truth about us—which I am not planning to tell him—he will be honor bound to remain loyal to us. And I'm sure he will be useful."

Dane shrugged. The kid might, after all, have access to useful information, if they could manage to ask him the right questions. But he certainly would be nothing more than a burden if they had to do any more fighting. And he wasn't a particularly likable kid.

The old caravan-master stayed away from them for quite a while. Of course he was busy—there were bodies to be buried, and after they had moved on, there was doubtless much to demand his attention.

It was not, in fact, until after the caravan had camped for the night that he spoke to them again.

Belsar was setting behind the wall of vines. They had just finished helping the servants of the Noble Mother OOa-nisha set up her pavilion—which was the size of a small circus tent. The four travelers and Joda had been invited to share it with her household. Dane wondered what Dravash had found to say to her; all through the battle, her servants had later reported, she and the Sh'fejj stranger "from Raife" had been closeted in her carriage, talking endlessly.

Dane was meditating over his own attempts to strike up a conversation with the ape-men; the creatures were a little smarter than a chimpanzee, Dane decided, but not much. And at that he might be wronging the monkey tribe.

Dane himself would have preferred to sleep in the open—but that, he knew, would have been strange behavior indeed. The natives of this planet, according to one of the tapes Dane had studied, held a firm belief that the night sky was the abode of millions of demons, all hungry and malevolent. Dane supposed it was inevitable on a planet as thickly forested as this one, where the night sky was rarely visible through the trees, that the natives should regard the stars in the same way they regarded the eyes that clustered inside the forest at night, regarding their fire.

Besides, the tent kept out rashas.

The evening meal was cooking, separate meals for humans and protosaurians. Dane stood at the door of the tent, beside Rianna, sniffing hungrily at the delicious odor of a roast haunch of ganjir turning over a fire, and trying hard *not* to smell whatever incredible mess was being cooked for the Honorable Mother and the two travelers she had invited to be her guests. Dane was sure they hadn't *really* preserved the camp's garbage for a few weeks to let it ripen, and were cooking it all up now as a choice insectivore tidbit; it only smelled that way. When the smell had reached Aratak, his eyes had actually glistened in anticipation; so he wished Aratak and Dravash a good appetite—it could hardly be worse than raw bug—but he wanted nothing more than to move out of range of the smell.

He heard a cough, and turned to see the caravan-master approaching. Dane was surprised; he had expected the old man to go on avoiding them.

"Your pardon," the old man muttered, his eyes dropping away from Rianna, "but—you are travelers; has either of you, perchance, ever seen a blade such as this? It is a wholly new weapon to me; I thought, perhaps, in your travels. . . ."

He held out a long-bladed knife. The weapon was different from any Dane had ever seen; as he took it in his hands, trying to envision the kind of wound it would make, Dane felt a sudden dislike and revulsion for anyone who would use such a blade even in hunting, let alone in combat, against any living being.

It seemed more like a shovel than a knife, like a V in cross-section, an open equilateral triangle that gave it *three* sharp edges. They all drew together, at the point, in jagged, almost microscopic saw-teeth. Worse still, the surfaces were pebbled, like a rasp.

It was not the clean efficiency of a killing weapon. It was a torturer's blade, designed for tearing living flesh asunder in little bits. Oh, it would kill—but the barbs, the pebbling, the dished center of the V—these were redundant in a killing weapon. They were meant only for causing pain.

"Let me see that," Rianna said sharply, and Dane handed it to her, his face twisting in loathing. His eyes fell on the handle. It was neither wood nor bone, and certainly not any metal Dane knew. It could have been some kind of plastic, or ceramic metal . . . nothing you'd expect to see on a barbarian world!

"Kirgon!" Rianna whispered, half aloud. "Dane, Dravash has to see this, right away." She called into the tent, and the Captain and Aratak came out, as she turned to the caravanmaster again.

"Where did you get this?" she demanded. Her voice was sharp, angry, and he reacted to it, almost defensive.

"Off a bandit's corpse, where else? Do they make such blades in Raife, then? If so, I do not admire them!"

Rianna shook her head, no. "Not in Raife. Farther away than that—oh, much farther. But once I saw such a blade as this, only once."

Firelight gleamed on Dravash's needle fangs as he looked up.

"Kirgon work, without a doubt."

Rianna demanded, "But what is it doing here? How did it come into the hands of a common bandit?"

The caravan-master demanded, "Do you know the land from which this blade comes?"

Dravash weighed his answer for a long time, before he spoke.

"No one can tell you that, venerable sir. Yet I have known of raiders who come from very far away, bearing such blades. I cannot tell you the name of the land from which they come, nor point it out to you upon any map. I can only tell you that they are said to be evil beyond all imagining."

"Looking upon their blades, I can well believe it," said the caravan-master, "And when I look upon it, I wonder that the Blessed Ones would allow such creatures to exist."

"The ways of the Blessed Ones are beyond my fathoming," Aratak said, and the Caravan-master nodded.

"That is certain, whatever else is in doubt, but their ways are not for us to question." He shook his head as Dravash would have given back the strange weapon. "The Saints forbid I should stain my honor by having such a thing in my possession! Keep it safe, Noble Sir, and bring it to the attention of those whose business it is to be aware what evils are abroad in the land. Worthy Sir, *Felishtara*—" he bowed to Dane and Rianna—"I bid you a safe and pleasant night." He paused and looked up at the sky, still light, but rapidly darkening. "I shall be glad to be inside my tent tonight. They do say the power of the Star Demons has grown in these lands lately."

"What do you mean?" Dravash asked sharply, and the old man blinked.

"It's probably nonsense, fools jumping at shadows; but I've heard garbled stories of monsters prowling about, like no animal that could be killed with an honest spear. Probably some hysterical fool saw a tree trunk in the moonlight and believed it was after him, or was afraid to admit he ran away from a rasha he was not brave enough to kill, and invented a monster to justify his own cowardice. But you can never tell what may happen when Star Demons are about."

They watched the Caravan-master plodding away in the dusk, the plume above his head nodding as if with discouraged agreement.

"Well," said Dane at last, "there's *one* question we can ask Joda."

The boy's pallet was set up near Dane's and Rianna's; and what a nuisance *that* was going to be, Dane thought. But then, cultures of this sort could probably not afford to put a high value on privacy. It wasn't too likely that Joda would pay the slightest attention to whatever they did—all Dane had to do was stop minding. And talk Rianna out of minding. . . .

The shoulder wound was healing nicely. Barbaric this planet might be, but there was nothing backward about their medical technology. It might have a few things to teach the Unity. Dane was no expert, but he remembered that this had been cited as one of the prime bits of evidence for a lost Sh'fejj starship, though Anadrigo had pointed out that medical technology was not necessarily dependent on other advances. Lens-grinding had been an early art on this world, and that had led naturally to the discovery of germs, and that in turn to asepsis and bactericides.

Joda was asleep and there was no question of asking him anything for a while. Dane crawled into his pallet and realized that right now it didn't matter whether they had privacy or not, he wasn't going to behave like a protosimian tonight. He was too damned tired, he could feel sleep creeping down his forehead as soon as his head touched the rolled blanket he had folded for a pillow. He would sleep, and sleep, and sleep, and he wondered if anything would wake him up.

And yet he did wake up, hearing the sounds of naked feet moving on the grass just outside the tent. He gripped the handle of his sword in the darkness, and lay listening.

Someone moved in the darkness of the tent. Rianna still lay curled against his body, breathing deeply, heavily asleep. Then someone was silhouetted against the tent flap, between them and the dying fire.

Joda appeared briefly as the curtain drew back, silhouetted for an instant against the firelight, and vanished again into the night.

Dane rolled softly away from Rianna; she made a soft sound but did not wake. Sword gripped in his hand, he followed.

Outside the stars blazed suddenly down, an army of

torches against the velvet sky. There was no moon here and no need of one. Belsar was deep in the Galaxy and the stars were so thick and close they made the sky blaze with multi-colored light. Dane stared at the sky in awe for a few moments, then remembered Joda and his mysterious errand. He set his teeth, braced for some kind of treachery—he couldn't imagine what or why—and looked around the clearing.

Joda stood a little way from him, in the clearing. He wasn't doing anything. He was just standing there, one hand resting on his wounded shoulder as if it hurt him, and staring up into the sky. Just standing, and looking up.

Dane shook his head, smothering a yawn. He suddenly felt very stupid. What the hell was he doing out here spying on the kid anyhow? Why wasn't he in bed, sleeping off the exertions of the day, and the new exertions tomorrow? So Joda got his kicks counting stars, why the hell *shouldn't* he? In the old phrase from a vanished Earth, it was neither illegal, immoral nor fattening. He turned and his bare foot scraped on a stone; Joda turned and saw him.

"Aren't you afraid, traveler from Raife?" he asked, and his voice, his face, his whole body were one big sneer. "The Star Demons up there will steal away your courage and destroy your common sense! If they're feeling nasty they just might swoop down from the sky some night and carry you off into the sky to eat! Why, don't you know the Star Demons will chill your bones and make your hair fall out and your teeth ache and turn the milk sour from your favorite khostli? If it weren't for the vigilance of the Blessed Saints, they'd probably burn the world up! Better get back safe inside your tent before they chew you up into little tiny pieces!"

Dane stared at him. Finally he said, "Do you believe all that, Joda?"

In the starlight, he could see that the sneer had faded from the boy's face, leaving only puzzlement.

"No," Joda said, "but don't you? Everybody else does."

Dane shrugged and smiled at him. "I never worried too much about what other people believed."

"And you really aren't afraid of the stars?" Joda demanded. He sounded almost angry.

Dane shook his head. "No. I never met any Star Demons, and if I were going to be afraid of something, I'd pick something I'd met, something I knew could hurt me."

"It's very strange," Joda said in a quiet voice, "I'm a very great coward, traveler from Raife. My father says I am only fit to end my days in the belly of a rasha, and he is probably right. I'm stupid and clumsy, and your spearwoman is so much better at fighting, that I am afraid of her, too. When I face a battle I always think I will die of fear before any foe has a chance to come at me. I am even afraid of the ganjir, quiet as they are, and that is folly, I grew up working close to them, my little sister can lead them out to the fields without half as much fear as I. And yet I have never been afraid of the stars. I am such a coward I know I am not fit to live to manhood, and yet for some reason I do not fear the stars. And you are the only person I have ever met who is like me, not afraid of them."

He paused; in the brilliant starlight Dane saw anger knotting his face.

"They tell us, in the village, that demons live in the stars, and that gods and saints and the Blessed Ones live under the ground to protect us. But I don't believe any of that! It's nonsense, it's like the tales the old grandmothers tell, about a gnome who steals the children's shed milk teeth and plants them under the ground to grow new rocks! Fairy tales! I don't believe that there are any gods, or Saints, or Blessed Ones, or demons from the stars either! And if I did—" he looked up at the blazing sky again, and said, his voice very serious, "If I did, I think I would believe that it was the other way round, and that the sky there was the abode of the Saints and Blessed Ones. Look, traveler from Raife! How can anything so beautiful as that possibly be evil?"

Dane said "You're right, you know. There's nothing to be afraid of." And then he began to wonder if he had done right, putting this kid at odds with the taboos of his own culture.

"Is this because you come from Raife? Do they not believe in the Star Demons, in Raife, traveler?"

"My name's Dane," he said, "and I never heard of Star Demons till I came here." Well, that was true enough. "But lately I heard that there are stories going around about Star Demons actually appearing here—frightening people, carrying them off—I'm a long way from my own country, and I'm always interested in strange things. Strange occurrences."

"Superstitious rubbish," Joda snapped, "Tales to frighten children! People carried off by Star Demons and forced to work for them, mysterious weapons no human hand could forge, Demons prowling the woods as monstrous animals, the

Saints appearing to drive the Star Demons away—all rubbish, all contradicting each other!"

Maybe, Dane thought, remembering the Kirgon blade, *the kind of creatures who used that kind of weapon would make any ordinary demon look tame. Meet up with one of those, kid, and you won't need a demon!*

And what, he wondered, would these people ever do to us—even the boy Joda—if they had a hint of where we really came from? If the stars are evil, and we came from the stars—what would we be in for, if they found us out?

"There's no reason to be afraid of the stars," he said, "but the damp of night isn't good for an unhealed wound, either. Go inside the tent and get some sleep, why don't you?"

"You're not my master," the boy spat at him, *"she is!"*

Dane's softening toward Joda abruptly vanished again. *Rotten, spoiled brat! No wonder even his own father can't stand the sight of him! If he was my kid, I'd drown him!*

"Oh, hell," he said. "Stay here, then, catch your death, see if I care!" He went off inside the tent, fuming. *Star Demons, indeed!*

CHAPTER EIGHT

"But it was white, I tell you! I swear it!"

Dane set down the wooden bowl of sweetish native beer he had been drinking, a chill running down his spine. The voice had come from somewhere near the back of the great shadowy room that served the purpose of a tavern.

"White? You've been out in the midday sun too long," another voice derided, "How could a demon from the stars be white? Maybe you saw a vision of the Blessed Ones, or one of the Saints—"

"It wasn't no saint, and nothing from the Blessed Realm," the voice insisted, "I saw the thing, I tell you, and it was *white.*"

A chorus of derision greeted the voice. "You *saw* it? Hah, you see a Star Demon, you won't be around to tell tales about how white it was!" One voice rose above the others, and Dane rose silently and made his way back along the wall, holding the wooden bowl carefully, and threading his way between tables. He was hearing in his mind the voice on the scout report-cube that Vilkish F'Thansa had made just before his mysterious death—or disappearance. *A strange white form.* For once it seemed that his recent practice of haunting the tavern at the midday hour, when almost all of Rahnilor sought shade and repose, was beginning to pay off. For weeks now he and his party had lived in Rahnilor, carefully following down the slightest leads about what could have happened to the vanished party of Sh'fejj from the Unity base. But so far, there had not even been a rumor. The earth might have opened and swallowed them up whole.

And any lead was worth following up, now. Even one so nebulous as a drunk at midday, talking about some unexplained white form. He paused, listening for the voice which had spoken, or the ones which had interrupted him; then he saw the speaker, a querulous old man, white hair above a crinkled brown nut of a face.

"How did you come to see this marvel—and were you sober when you heard it?"

"Sober and thirsty and hard at work," said the first speaker. He was a tall burly man with work-hardened muscles and a stubborn face, dressed like a khostli drover. "I was hacking away the brush to clear my field for the late planting, and this—this *thing* comes over the fence, grabs a calf and was gone before I could shout. It was terrible. *Nothing* moves that fast. Not a rasha. Not a granth. Not a bird! And it was *white*! White as your hair, whiter than an eyeball!" He tilted his head back, took a long drink from his bowl, wiped the foam from his lip, and stared at them belligerently.

The old man said, "How do you know it was a Star Demon?"

"What else could it have been? You tell me that!"

"White is the color of purity, the color of the Blessed Realms," said the third man at the table. He was small and dapper, with an embroidered jacket and a feathered headband of green and scarlet plumes. "It could not have been a Star Demon. Animals are born white, sometimes. What made you think it was a demon?"

"The way it moved," the first man insisted stubbornly. "No animal, not even a freak, moves that fast. I spent enough years keeping rashas away from my cattle, I know all about how they move. And if it wasn't a Star Demon, what was it? It had six legs!"

They stared at him, half dismayed, half derisive.

"Ah, that's too much," said the old man. "Now you're making it up. You saw *something*, and because you can't admit you couldn't kill it, you call it a Star Demon. Animals born white are extra fierce, they have to be or they couldn't live; since everybody can see 'em in the jungle. You saw a freak rasha."

"You show me a rasha with six legs! Or a granth! I tell you, it wasn't a rasha; moved more like a granth. . . ." Dane remembered this was the fierce, highly intelligent weasel-like predator, "—only faster, even, than a granth. And *it had six legs!*" He stared, defiant.

"If it was moving all that fast, how'd you count the legs?" demanded the old man, but the third man said quietly, "No, listen. That's what the Spearman told me. He said he followed its trail for miles, and there were more feet than four could make; and they were all wrong somehow. Maybe he saw the thing the Spearman was tracking. But that was away down near the Great Gorge. You say this thing had six legs? And big enough to carry off a calf? Only thing I ever saw had six legs was a bug this size—" he measured with his hand on the table. "Some kind of big freak bug out of the Great Gorge, maybe? Could be *anything*, down that way!"

"It wasn't anything like a bug," the farmer said. "More like a granth, only it had a long, low body, about so high—" he measured off the floor, "and a long tail. And it moved in fast and straight. You know how a granth comes in, in a rush sidewise, nipping with its head down? Well, this one came in charging straight, grabbed the calf up whole and made off with it faster than ever. *You* know how a granth kills first, head down, nipping and biting, knocking you over with a big paw and then biting at the throat? Well, this one didn't move like that, just came in head on like ganjir charging, reared up, grabbed the calf and hauled it off still bawling. Big calf, too, and it didn't even slow it down!" He shook his head, marveling, and signaled for more beer. "If that doesn't sound like a demon, I don't know what *you'd* call it!"

"Sounds like you'd been out in the sun too long," the old

man said, scoffing; but the slender man in the feathered headdress shook his head, the plumes bobbing.

"Maybe not, Gran'fer. Out beyond the Great Gorge, I heard they had an outbreak of Star Demons, carrying off folk in broad daylight, and such like; though that never made much sense to me, I thought Star Demons only came out at night, or what's the world coming to?"

"Your pardon, good folk," said Dane, edging closer to the table and signaling the waiter, moving through the scattered tables, to bring fresh bowls of beer, "I could not help but overhear your talk. I am a traveler from very far away—" Deliberately, he spoke Kahram a little less well than he could have done, "—but on the road here I heard of some—some people who vanished completely after seeing a strange white form they thought a demon. Is it true that—that others of this kind have been seen?"

Three pairs of eyes swivelled toward him as the slender man in the feathers said, "You. You're one of the bodyguards came with those jewel sellers from Raife—the giant and his partner. No, you'd not have heard of such things in Raife, I expect. But down below the Great Gorge, near Peshilor, they had an outbreak of Star Demons, carrying off men in broad daylight, and cattle. They sent for the Anka'an Order, and by the help of the Blessed Saints, managed to kill some of them, and the others went away. But there must have been one left to frighten our farmer friend here, and carry off his calf. They were hunting them for two moons, down there; terrible stories there were, of men being burned up by fire the demons threw on them, whole villages being carried away in the bellies of great metal carts."

"That's what the Spearman told me," the farmer said. "Said I was lucky the thing took only a calf and not one of my children." He shuddered. "I hope they track it down and kill it! Master Prithvai can say all he likes, but we folk in the villages have enough to fight, with rashas and granths, and the fodder burning up in the fields in a dry year, without being plagued by Star Demons too! Where are the priests, if they can't keep demons away?"

"Demons, demons, I don't want to hear any talk about demons," said the old man, his shrill voice trembling, "I tell you, the thing was a white rasha, a freak born that way, and Master Prithvai talks about demons to justify what the Anka'an Order takes from us for guarding! Why don't they put that much time and energy into hunting down rashas like the one who took my son ten years ago? They didn't call out the whole Anka'an Order then, they wouldn't even send a single spearman! Kill one rasha, they said, and there'll only be more!"

"He's right, though," the slender man said. "Rashas are too many to kill them all. You cannot blame the Anka'an Order because there are rashas in the world."

"Ha!" said the old man angrily. "Maybe they couldn't kill them all, but if you put the whole Order to work, together with every man who's ever lost a child to a rasha, you could kill them off to where it would be safe to live in sight of the city, at least! If we really worked at it, we could kill every rasha in the valley, drive them all back into the hills or into the Great Gorge! The Anka'an Order, with all their fancy talk about how the Saints have given the rashas the right to live—kill them all, I say, to the last claw! We could do it, if we tried!"

"And then who would keep the wild ganjir and the deer out of our fields?" asked the slender man, with maddening logic. "The rashas kill them, and we kill the rashas, and it all comes out even in the end, as Master Prithvai says."

"You city folk," the old man snarled. "You live inside walls, and if a rasha takes a farmer's child, you shrug and jabber about bearing the ills of the world, but you don't lose *your* children to the rashas! And the First People are just as bad, preaching about the Great Chain of Life—when everybody knows the rashas won't eat *them*, or even their eggs!"

Dane left them to their argument; he knew he'd get nowhere by interrupting. He knew from the map that the city of Peshilor was downriver from Rahnilor, beyond the Great Gorge, where Thundersmith Falls flowed into what he had heard called the Eye of the World . . . the large landlocked sea ringed by mountains, one of the enormous craters which had so startled Dane when he first saw the planet from space.

He went into the street, feeling the sun sear at his eyeballs and the heat strike like an opened furnace door. Gauzy white awning stretched between the buildings to keep out the worst of the sunlight by day, and shelter men from the baleful influence of the stars at night. Some of the narrower streets were roofed over completely, for the same reason; Dane had ceased to wonder that men here feared the sky. As he crossed a brief open space between two of the awnings, he knew he was cringing from the open sky just as the natives did.

It wasn't just the sudden terrible blaze of heat burning at

his scalp and shoulders, though that was bad enough. The heat surged up even through the soles of his sandals. The packed earth under his feet felt as if he were walking across the surface of a very hot griddle.

Rahnilor was two cities, really. The inn was in the human sector; above him, on the heights, the city of the First People rose, flat-roofed structures intended to concentrate the very heat that the human inhabitants found so difficult to endure, and had built *their* city to minimize. Dane ducked his head between his shoulders and hurried under the next awning.

The protosaurian city of the First People had been there first, he remembered, surrounded by the rude villages of those who labored for them, and by broad fields of plants inedible to them. Later the lower city of Rahnilor had grown up in the valley, the home of a peaceful agricultural tribe who had traded fur and produce for the iron and finely worked steel that was still a saurian monopoly. Then had come the Barbarian Invasion—and Saint A'assioo.

At the end of the shaded street, Dane came out into the open market square. Heat reflected from the stone scorched his legs, and he pulled up the hood of the jacket he wore to shield his head from the sun, though he hated the way it cut off his side vision. A constant noise of ganjir bells jangled as the great beasts stirred in the heat. Hawkers sang out their wares, and the voices of a thousand merchants whined, droned, argued over prices.

Dane slitted his eyes against the light that blasted up from the pavement, wishing the protosimians here had thought of inventing sunglasses. He began to make his way through the brightly colored booths and carpets where the merchants spread their wares. Farmers hawked their produce, jewelers their crafts—passing a jeweler's stall, Dane saw some pieces displayed, made from the exotic "jewels from Raife" which had been their ostensible reason for coming here to trade. They'd come here first several days ago, he and Aratak; Dane standing behind him in the stance of a paid bodyguard, ostentatiously glaring at the passing crowd, while Aratak haggled with the local jewelers; then Aratak had packed up the remaining supply of the jewels—and a considerable supply of the local money—and dismissed Dane, open-handedly tossing him a few extra coins, so that Dane could go about their *real* business—looking for rumors in the human ghetto.

Dane moved past swordsmiths, weavers, sandalmakers, hunters with furs of all colors—even a rare white granth skin,

which made Dane think of the belligerent farmer whose calf
had been taken—carvers in stone and wood, musicians and
storytellers gathering small crowds to listen under the cool
flaps of their tents, travelers with spices, herbs and perfumes,
fortune tellers selling amulets and trinkets, luck-charms and
love-charms, and dozens of other merchants whose wares
Dane could not even begin to recognize.

And above all the noise and activity of the market, the
gleaming white statue of Saint A'assioo brooded, with outstretched forelimbs and blind marble eyes; a squat protosaurian muzzle protruded from the hood of the long garment
that shielded the rest of his form, concealing everything but
the outstretched, blessing forelimbs and hands.

The stone was old. Old as the foundations of the city. A
thousand years ago or more, a nomadic horde had swept
downriver and hurled themselves upon the peaceful human
village. It had been then that Saint A'assioo had appeared,
preaching peace to the warlike tribesmen and averting slaughter. The tribesmen had settled in the valley and raised the
vast human city which had grown as the caravan roads that
crossed the ford of the river, here, had brought civilization
and trade. The First People of the City on the hill also re-
vered Saint A'assioo; the mythology of Belsar Four was full
of such protosaurian "Saints," teachers and peacemakers
who had come from some unknown realm to live among men
and bring them wisdom and civilization. Rahnilor was not the
only city founded by such a Saint.

Dane recalled one of the tapes he had studied:

> The protosaurian influence upon the protosimian cul-
> ture of Belsar has been profound and benign. The legend
> of Saint A'assioo disarming the barbarian hordes during
> the invasion of Rahnilor, and Saint Ioayaho's disarming
> of the archers of the conqueror Ashrakhu, were funda-
> mental to the development of civilizations in their respec-
> tive regions. Sermons attributed to these and other
> "Saints," their lives of patient example and their pitiful
> deaths are the keystones of moral and philosophical cul-
> ture throughout Belsar; although much of their early lives
> have been obviously mythologized in order to connect
> them with the underground "Blessed Realm" of all Bel-
> sarian peoples, both are clearly historical figures. It is
> noteworthy that even among the protosimian cultures of
> Belsar, there has never been a single protosimian Saint.

Aratak, of course, had been especially intrigued by the Belsarian philosopher-Saints, and had memorized many of the sayings of A'assioo and other Saints, particularly Saint Ziyamoay of distant Raife; these sayings—at least in public—had now replaced his constant quotations of the Divine Egg. "All wisdom is One," Aratak had remarked, when Dravash twitted him about this, "and this is proven by the fact that not the Divine Egg alone, but also Saint Ziyamoay and Saint Ioayaho said so."

As always, Dane paused for a moment, despite the burning heat, to look up at the imposing, marble-cowled figure.

In the heat and glare and noise, there was something comforting, strong and reassuring in that calm and benevolent figure. He thought, surprised at himself, that even if he did not know it was a statue of Saint A'assioo he would have known it for a Saint of some sort; it reminded him, if he didn't look too hard at the saurian muzzle, of a hyper-modernistic statue of Saint Francis he had seen once in San Francisco, arms stretched out, beneath his monk's robe, to bless the harbor. A line of Belsarian poetry Aratak had quoted ran briefly through his mind; *For us the Saints come to suffer in the sun, though the Blessed Realm is dark and cool.*

Well, the Saints had their mission, and he had his. Shaking off his mood of the moment, Dane moved through the noisy, head-swimming glare of the market, thinking of the tavern and the rumors he had heard.

White. Faster than a granth. Six legs—and that was rare, even in the worlds of Unity. Certainly no native beast. Demons from the stars, who threw fire and carried people away in the bellies of their metal carts. Dravash had better hear about this, right away.

He saw the flash of a familiar blue tunic, threw up an arm in greeting, then saw it was not Master Rhomda, but another of the Anka'an Order, a leaner man, angular, a scarecrow moving with a dancer's grace. His face was thin and hook-nosed. He returned Dane's greeting with an indifferent, courteous gesture, shifted the deadly spear from one carrying position to another with the same elegant precision which was becoming familiar to Dane, and strode away across the square. Dane hesitated, half inclined to hurry after him and ask about the "Star Demons" against whom, it seemed, the Anka'an Order had been summoned. But the strange Spearman was already out of sight, and it would be easier to hunt

up Master Rhomda—who had a friendly interest in the boy
Joda and had dropped in, once or twice, at the house where
Aratak and Dravash were staying.

He reached the opposite side of the market and plunged
into the grateful duskiness of the Street of Strangers—an area
where houses were always available on an arrangement Dane
would have called short-term leases, for travelers and traders.
Dravash and Aratak had taken such a house for themselves
and their "servants"—Dane, Rianna, and young Joda—and
no one had thought to question that they were, indeed, jewel
traders from distant Raife. If they had, indeed, been merchants, this would have been a highly successful trip; the
Council of Protectors, back at Unity Central, had assembled
for their use an enormous collection of jewels, large and
small, which were common and cheap over much of the
Unity, but on Belsar, rare and expensive, though not unknown. They could have lived in modest luxury for the rest
of their lives on the proceeds of the sale. Dane hoped they
wouldn't have to.

The house Dravash had found for them was a large, flat-
roofed, sprawling affair of wood and brick, built around a
central courtyard; there was a section set aside for humans,
and for the subhumans Dravash had hired to do menial work
for them. Dane, Rianna and Joda shared one section of this,
a flat reed roof set on poles, which was kept continuously wet
with a sprinkler arrangement, for coolness inside, curtained
by flaps of thin coarse cloth which kept out insects at night.
Dane found the place damp, and the subhumans who had inhabited it before him had not been of the cleanest habits, but
it was pleasantly cool and quiet.

The sun had lowered enough that a part of the courtyard
was in shadow, and Rianna and Joda were working out there,
in the shadow of the long wall. Rianna was taking her position seriously; she had spent long hours teaching the boy the
rudiments of the curious almost-judo of her own world,
which she called by a name meaning, "the art of making an
attacker defeat himself." In addition, she had made Dane
teach him the rudiments of karate, and, finally, exercise with
him in swordplay.

He's improving, Dane thought as he watched Joda and Rianna, rehearsing the moves of the defensive art. Perhaps it
was only that he was not—quite—as afraid of Rianna as he
had been of his father, and that she had never beaten or ridiculed him; his stance no longer had the mixture of cringing

sullenness and insolence which had turned Dane against him
from the first. Intensive training was beginning to wash the
awkwardness out of his limbs.

"No, no," Rianna said, watching him sharply, "You still
back away at the very minute you should charge! Like this—"
she made a swift movement toward him and, unavoidably,
he flinched.

*He must have been beaten within an inch of his life. It
would make some kids defiant. It only made him more timid
than ever. Beatings are no cure for cowardice, but that must
have been exactly how the kid's father went about it.*

Rianna stopped in mid-stride. She said, with a gentleness
that Dane found surprising, "Joda, don't you know yet that
I'm not really going to hurt you? My defenses were wide
open—look. All you had to do was catch me like this—" and
she reached out to take his arm in the hold she intended, but
again, he cringed and drew out of reach.

"You did hurt me, the other day," he defended himself.
"Look, I've still got the bruise!"

Rianna's temper flared; she opened her mouth for a sharp
retort.

"Someday you will meet someone who really *intends* to
hurt you, and if you aren't ready—" she began, then, visibly
mastering her irritation, said quietly, "Then you had better go
over there on the sand, and practice falling some more, until
you know that falling won't hurt you as much as you think.
Your worst enemy isn't the bruises you get, it's your fear of
them."

Cringing, sullen, the boy went off to the opposite side of
the court, and Rianna, mopping her forehead with one of her
gypsy scarfs, came toward Dane.

Dane, looking after Joda, said, "He's pretty hopeless, isn't
he?"

"Not really," Rianna demurred, "but of course he doesn't
fit into this culture at all."

"I think," Dane said, lowering his voice so that the youngster wouldn't hear—he was dutifully practicing the elementary exercises of relaxing and trying to fall completely limp
in the pit of soft sand—"that he'd be a misfit on *any* world."

"Why don't you like him, Dane?"

"I don't know. He's—" Dane searched for the right word
"—he's nasty. Mean. Sarcastic. Cowardly. I just can't stand
the sight of him, and that's a fact."

Rianna shrugged. "This world is pretty hostile to anybody

who doesn't have the courage or fighting skills to face it. How would you feel if you'd had to face nothing but hostility all your life? You'd probably be aggressive in mean, nasty little ways, too."

Dane doubted if anything could have made him *that* obnoxious, and said so.

"The trouble with you is," Rianna said, sharply, "you have no imagination. Basically you're a lot like the poor child's father; you despise him because he isn't as brave as you are! If he'd grown up on a civilized world, he'd be in a University somewhere, learning to be a scientist or an astronomer or something suited to his talents and interests! And he'd be a different youngster! I'm just trying to help him *survive!* Why can't you *help* me, instead of being so hostile? He was doing fine, until you came in, and then he froze up again because he knows that you despise him and you're hostile!"

Dane said, scowling, "Maybe I'd just better keep out of his way!" Why in the world had Rianna become so indecently protective of the boy? He had never suspected her of a maternal instinct, and it didn't suit her! He said, "We seem to spend all our time these days quarreling about that damn kid!"

Her face softened. "We do, don't we? I'm sorry, Dane." She slipped her arm through his. "You're not jealous, are you? Goodness, he's only a child!"

Jealous? Dane wondered No, not in that way, exactly, though it was true that he resented the amount of time and energy Rianna spent on the youngster; and of course she had less time for *him.* He said, squeezing her arm close to his side, turning to press his cheek against hers, "Well, you've got to admit that having him around all the time does inhibit us a little—doesn't it, love?"

She smiled up into his face, in the old intimate way, and murmured, "We'll have to figure out something we can do about that."

But Joda had evidently been watching them out of the corner of his eye, and seeing that Rianna's attention had turned to Dane, he came toward them again.

"Will you show me that attack again? I'll try to do it, this time, without backing away."

Rianna touched Dane's lips lightly with her fingertips and her mouth formed the whisper, "Later," which he heard as an eerie whisper from the translator in his throat. He tended to forget about it for days at a time. Then she smiled resignedly at Joda and took the carven board, resembling one of the short native blades, which they used for practice, moving into the shaded, smoothly trampled area they used.

As he fell into a defensive stance, she moved to correct him.

"No," she said, "You've got to have your feet farther apart. Remember what I said about finding your own center of balance; imitating my stance won't work because I'm a woman and my weight falls differently. Find where your own body is centered. Now as I come at you—" she advanced on him, moving the blade down in slow motion, "just bend, and let my own movement carry me on, and over—" She allowed herself to trip over him, catching herself in midair. "Now let's try it at something like normal speed, shall we?"

Her wooden sword blurred toward his head. He wriggled aside as she had shown him, reaching up for the wrist, but seemed to freeze in mid-movement; the wooden sword whacked his arm painfully, and the boy yelped and clutched at the bruised spot.

"I can't do it," he whined, "I'm too clumsy! I'll never learn!"

"Nonsense," Rianna snapped, then added, with a smile of patient encouragement, "It hit your arm this time instead of your head, didn't it? That's an improvement."

The boy fingered the scar on his head, nervously, looking sidewise at Dane with that furtive look Dane loathed—*Why in hell can't he look me straight in the eye? He acts just as if he expects me to kick him, and that makes me feel just like doing it!*

"It's getting late," Rianna said, "and I'm getting hungry. Go and wash up, why don't you?"

Dane asked, "Where are Dravash and Aratak?" The boy's lesson had diverted him again from giving Dravash the important news he had heard in the market—once again, he thought resentfully, the kid was getting in the way of the job he'd been brought here to do, and he glowered at Rianna.

"Dravash is sunning himself on top of the oven," Rianna said, referring to the central part of the house which the humans found impossibly hot, "and Aratak is bathing again."

Joda snickered. Bathing had become Aratak's secret vice; despite the rain on the first day of their landing, which had given Dane a completely false impression of the climate, this planet was far more arid than Aratak's own, and despite the transformation of his skin, Aratak found it uncomfortable.

There were none of the moist pools of rich, sulphurous mud
which abounded on Aratak's native world, so he had taken to
bathing in the ornamental pool with which the house was
equipped; it quickly became apparent that this was a notable
eccentricity, almost a scandal, so they tried to keep the extent
of his bathing secret. Dane supposed the subhumans gossiped
about it among themselves, but he didn't imagine anyone listened except other subhumans, so it probably didn't matter.
Still, he wished Aratak would do his swimming at night.

"Better come along and find them," Dane said, "I've
learned—something." She nodded to show she'd understood
and turned to Joda.

"Take your blade, and practice cutting on those logs, as I
showed you, until time for nightmeal."

The boy went off, and Dane and Rianna went back toward
the main part of the house. Rianna, for these lessons, had
adapted the local men's dress—wrapped kilt and short hooded
jacket discarded indoors; but she had added a tight band
around her breasts when she was doing anything active.
When she went out into the city—which was seldom—she
had to wear the local woman's dress, bare to the waist over a
long tight wrapped skirt, which inhibited her movements, and
nothing above it except a head-veil and many jingling amulets. She was sweating freely with the heat and exercise, and
her hair curled in tight frizzy little ringlets all over her head.
Dane watched her striding along the courtyard with her free
walk; dear and familiar, the darkness of her skin and hair
adding an almost exciting note of alienness and mystery. In
spite of their year together, she was still strange to him and
she might always be. He thought abruptly that this was the
first time they had been alone, even for a little while, since
Rianna had adopted the boy. He laid a hand on her arm, to
hold her back a moment, then sighed. This was important;
they'd better get to Aratak and Dravash with it. Protosaurians
already thought that protosimians, with their apelike instincts,
were all too ready to delay the important work of the world
to pay attention to their overriding and uncontrollable sexual
drives, and he wasn't going to add further fuel to that flame.

She smiled, evidently following his thoughts, but nodded,
gesturing him toward the door of the "oven"; they never went
inside. It was like a blast furnace, and it was Dravash's favorite spot.

The enormous black Sh'fejj was lying inside, very quietly,
the transparent inner membranes of his protruding eyes low-

ered to protect them; he was asleep, or communing with Far-speaker.

"I've heard something in the market," Dane began, and Dravash rose, immediately alert. "Tell me. But of course, you are not comfortable in this room, perhaps we should join Aratak. I believe," he added with an air of scornful detachment, "that he is indulging in his incomprehensible habit of submerging his body in cold water. Some day, I am sure, I shall find him quite melted away."

They went toward the ornamental garden of succulents and cactus-like plants at the center of the large courtyard complex; at the very center was a large ornamental pool, marble-mosaicked, with huge floating water-flowers starring the surface with pale violet and blue, and among the flowers Dane made out the huge bulging eyeballs of Aratak, lying mostly submerged. Dravash impatiently motioned him out, and Aratak reluctantly hauled his huge bulk up on the marble verge.

"If you have quite finished this sybaritic attention to the condition of your integument—" Dravash began. Aratak said mildly, "You wrong me, colleague. I was meditating upon the wisdom—"

"Of your holy unhatched one, I suppose," Dravash said, and Aratak's eyes moved upward in resignation. "No, actually, upon the wisdom of the Blessed Saints in choosing the cool underground realms for their permanent abode. Well does the divine wisdom say that it is well to seek ease of body for the most perfect of meditation, and that it is the greatest of wisdom to keep one's mind turned forever upon the holy perfection of the divine regions. And therefore, in seeking perfect comfort, I was actually creating within my mind a metaphysical response to the state of holy bliss—"

"Saints preserve us!" Dravash's brow-ridges were twitching so violently that Dane wondered in brief alarm if protosaurians ever had epileptic fits. "I should have known you would find some religious precedent for your abominable indulgences! But while you have been lying here in—" he choked at Aratak's brief threatening gaze, amended, "in holy and blissful meditations, our protosimian colleague has gone, like a Saint, to suffer in the sun of the marketplace, and has not returned with empty claws. Shall we hear him?"

Dane repeated the conversation he had heard in the tavern, while the two protosaurians listened without comment.

"It sounds," Rianna said, "like a Kirgon slave-hound."

Dravash rumbled agreement. "They come from another of the planets in the Kirgon system. I have never understood their alliance with the Kirgon—"

"I can," Rianna said, "they are equally vicious, amoral and cruel!"

Dravash shrugged that aside as too obvious to need comment. "However, your story makes little sense, Dane. I cannot believe that a few natives, even assisted by the Anka'an spearmasters, could have driven off the Kirgon and killed enough of them that nothing was left but a single slavehound. The Kirgon might indeed be the answer to what had happened to the personnel of the Unity Base—but what happened, then, to the Kirgon?"

"Maybe," Rianna suggested, "they fell to the same mysterious fate that snatched up your Sh'fejj at the Base."

"The albino protosaurs?"

Aratak nodded. He said "I know of no such race. But in the universe there are many things, both inside the Unity and out, which I have not yet encountered. As the Divine—er—A'assioo remarked, the diversity of Creation is truly limitless."

Dravash said, "I find it difficult to imagine a protosaurian race both albino and warlike—warlike enough to vanquish an invading force of Kirgon!"

"I find it possible to imagine such a race," Aratak said, "but I find that I would much, much rather not."

"Oh, come," Dane protested, "It stretches the imagination enough to think of *two* outside civilizations trying to invade Belsar at once—the Unity and the, what-do-you-callems, Kirgons! Now you're postulating a third? Why would anyone bother? Belsar just isn't that important!"

"I do not find it so," Dravash said, "Personally I find it even too uninteresting for much study, and in spite of the delightful climate, intellectually unstimulating. And I beg to remind you, colleague," he added pointedly to Dane, "that it is both inaccurate and offensive to speak of the Unity Base as an *invasion*; it was a scientific expedition, intended to study without disturbing the native civilization in the slightest, and to go away again afterward without affecting them in any manner."

"Sorry," Dane said, "No offense intended. But I just can't stretch my imagination far enough to imagine three alien races converging on one small planet at the edge of nowhere; it sounds like—" he stopped himself, knowing that if he said,

it sounds like a science fiction space opera, they wouldn't
have the faintest idea what he meant. "It sounds too fantastic
for belief. And if there has been a kind of war here between—among—three alien races, why haven't the natives
noticed anything? I would think, in that case, that every city
on the planet would be crawling with rumors and strange
tales—and it took me three weeks to hear this one!"

"Barbarians at this level have no concept of their planet as
a whole," Dravash said, "and news travels slowly. Theoreti-
cally, there could be Kirgon here, Mekhari on the other continent, and your unknown albino protosaurians somewhere
else, and we would have heard nothing of it. After all, you
must remember that a society at this level. . . ."

The mellow booming of the gong by the gate broke in and
a moment later Joda appeared, escorting a messenger, a self-
important human whose short jacket, elaborately embroidered
with symbols, showed him to be a servant in the employ of
one of the great Houses on the hill, from the original protosaurian city.

"I come," said the man, "bearing a message for the honorable strangers Thrava'ash Effiyim and his Most Venerable
Elder Kinsman A'aratakha; is it those honorables to whom I
address my insignificant self?"

"It is," said Dravash, gesturing impatiently, and the messenger proffered a sealed envelope. Dravash tore it open, impatiently, and a strange, thick, musky odor, not altogether
unpleasant, wafted heavily through the room; Dane felt a
curious prickling of his spine, half disgust, half an instinctive,
nearly racial fear. But Dravash straightened with a low,
moaning sound, his mouth opening in what was virtually a
bellow. Aratak heaved himself upright, his nostrils quivering,
sniffing the air as if a foe was upon them; and yet Dane
could have sworn that his expression was one of rapturous
delight.

"Out of the way, quick," Rianna hissed, yanking at his
arm, and Dravash, with a howl of frenzy, charged toward the
gate, followed swiftly by Aratak lumbering after him with
enormous speed. The messenger had stepped aside, too, from
the rush of the reptiles, but he followed them hurriedly out of
the gate and Dane heard them charge down the street, roaring and bellowing in voices that made the ground shake.

He stared after them, in stupefied amazement.

"What—" he muttered, realizing that they were bounding
away like schoolboys on holiday. He heard Rianna giggling,

and turned to her, demanding, "What is this all about? Have they both gone out of their minds?"

"You could say that." Rianna chuckled, doubling over with giggles. "And after all Dravash had to say about protosimians!" She clutched at her middle, collapsing into near-hysterical laughter. Finally she sobered enough to say, "I forgot you don't know all that much about protosaurian sexual customs, do you? Evidently these people here have customs like those of the Sh'fejj, which, when you come to think of it, could be an argument for Anadrigo—"

"What in the *hell* are you talking about?" Dane demanded, and Rianna explained.

"They're cyclic. When a female comes into heat—with the Sh'fejj it's about every three Standard years—she sends out invitations to all the notable males in the neighborhood. I suppose Lady Ooa'hassa, I recognized the symbols on her messenger's livery, must have a liking for strangers and notable travelers. And over the next several days, she holds a small, select and continuous orgy in her private rooms. It's very sensible, really—since every egg must be fertilized separately, it provides maximal genetic variation, and you can see that it would act as a powerful stimulus to the males, to become notable or successful enough to be invited by the females of highest status. This custom has been credited with causing much of the progress made by the protosaurian races."

"But why—but what—"

"Oh, their behavior? Well, now you know why they worry about protosimians. They know that we have no special sexual seasons—so they think we're really like *that*, all the time—charged up, rampaging, and completely unable to think about anything else! With them, it's all or nothing. Once a male has caught the scent—"

"Yes," said Dane, "I wondered about that."

Rianna caught up the discarded envelope and drew out an elaborately embroidered silken kerchief or veil. "It's a—ah—a glandular secretion. When a female comes into heat, she—well—to be blunt about it, she wipes herself with her veils and sends them out for invitations."

Dane chuckled heartily. "And they have the nerve to make remarks about protosimians!"

Rianna nodded. "As I say, once a male has caught the scent, you won't interest him in anything else until the season's over. They won't eat, won't sleep, and so forth, for a considerable time." She thrust her arm through his. "It's a good thing the story you brought us wasn't a major emergency; Dravash and Aratak certainly won't be good for anything else for at least ten days!"

She stared at the pool Aratak had vacated. Suddenly Dane laughed. Now they were really alone—for Joda had vanished, probably in search of the nightmeal he could smell cooking—without even the disapproving protosaurians around. He put his arms around Rianna and kissed her, long and thoroughly.

"Let's have a swim," he said, "and then let's try an orgy of our own. I can't promise to keep it up for ten days—after all I'm only a protosimian—but I'll do my best."

Her mouth met his. "Why not?"

CHAPTER NINE

It was actually eleven days, and there was nothing for Dane and Rianna to do in the interval but guard the house, in the traditional fashion for protosimian bodyguards left in charge of the homes of First People at such times. Dane spent time in the marketplace every day, looking for Master Rhomda; his idea was to try and persuade the Master Spearman to have a drink with him and get him talking about the Anka'an Order's mission to track down the strange "Star Demon." He was sure the Spearman was still in the city; before this, he had encountered him by accident a dozen times. But now that he was actively looking for him, Rhomda was only one of many hundreds of people in the city, and of course he was the one Dane never came across.

There was nothing to do but help Rianna with Joda's training, an abrasive business for each of them. He taught the boy basic karate movements, slowly working him into the simpler *katas*. Again and again he drilled the youngster in the graceful dancing motions, patiently going over the moves again and again, trying to restrain his own annoyance at the persistent complaints and spiteful comments. He was sure he could have done a better job if he'd actually been able to *like* the kid.

But he did the best he could, and already he was beginning to see improvement, see the repeated movements slowly changing from awkwardness to grace. It was a miracle he had seen many times on Earth, in the *dojo*; the discipline slowly seeping through the muscles into the mind, creating harmony out of disorder, shaping mind and body into a unified whole.

He practiced swordplay with the boy too, but that was another problem. The technique used with the short native blade was drastically different from the two-handed Samurai style Dane had studied, and learned to use. He regretted that he had never studied the form the Samurai had evolved for the use of the shorter *wakazashi*, but he remembered, from the few times in his old life that he had seen it demonstrated, that it was not too unlike the European saber style.

He had once—before he took up Japanese martial arts—been reasonably expert with both foil and saber, and now he tried to adapt that to Joda's instruction.

Of course the modern "Hungarian" style of saber fencing, which depended on being able to flick a piece of curved wire around with your fingers, was useless with a blade that had any weight to it; that had become a style for exhibition matches or, perhaps, duelling, but for serious, life-and-death swordwork, Dane wouldn't have trusted it.

But Dane had once been fortunate enough to spend the better part of a year working with a Master of the old Italian school—an amazing little gnome of a man whose reflexes were still lightning-fast after teaching fencing for fifty years. Old Alessandro had taught him the older style, with great looping cuts he had called *moulinets,* left over from the days when the cavalry saber was still an important weapon of war.

And so each afternoon he and Joda took the carved wooden blades out in the courtyard and whacked away at each other with them. Once or twice, to his mild chagrin, while the old reflexes were just beginning to come back, Joda had surprised him, too. For Joda's father had given him intensive teaching with the sword, and taught him a considerable amount. It had never been that the boy didn't know what to do with a sword. But his father's impatient and violent attempts to bully a boy naturally timid into faster learning had only increased Joda's fear and hesitancy, giving him the equivalent of a manual stutter.

Even now, each time Joda made the slightest false move he froze, cringing, as if he expected Dane to strike him—and when Dane, instead, rebuked him in a soft voice and patience, he would answer with a sneer and a sarcastic comment. Sometimes, in desperation, Dane wondered if the boy was *inviting* a kick or a blow; he even wondered if it might not be a good idea to give the kid a good drubbing, just once, to make the boy acknowledge Dane's formal authority over him. If that was part of the kid's cultural expectations—that he could only respect the strongest dog in the pack—Dane felt that he just might have to prove to Joda that he *was* top dog. If Joda felt it was weakness that kept Dane from breaking his neck. . . .

In the end it was only the awareness that if he once resorted to violence, he would only confirm Joda's lifelong expectations of cruelty, that kept him, doggedly, patient and soft-spoken. That—and the shamed knowledge of the pleasure he would personally take in beating the kid black and blue; if he gave the kid the good licking Joda was trying to provoke, he'd be doing it, not to teach the boy a lesson, but to restore his own wounded ego. And so he kept his hands off and his voice disciplined, quiet, refusing to match sarcasm with sarcasm. It was one of the hardest things he'd ever had to do in his life.

But he kept his temper, and realized that it was having at least one good side effect; he was actually learning something, from the kid, of the native Belsarian style, and it would probably come in handy.

If, that was, they ever had anything to do except hang around here guarding a house that didn't need guarding, while Aratak and Dravash attended to their love lives! If, he thought, either one of them ever again made any kind of wisecrack about protosimians, he'd break a reptile neck or two! Talk about being too wound up in sex to pay attention to business!

And, now and then, an occasional word or look from Joda showed the beginnings of a healthy respect. Small wonder; for Dane discovered, through brief overheard comments in the human sector and the marketplace, that he'd acquired what they'd have called, on Earth, quite a reputation. The number of bandits he was supposed to have killed in that attack now outnumbered the original band, and the story of his

sudden appearance in front of the Caravan had been the only
known instance of rashas hunting in packs.

Dane was amused by all this, knowing that Joda, who
defied him at home, and whose main attitude was one of sullen dislike, thoroughly enjoyed the status he had gained from
living in the house of the fighting traveler from Raife and his
spearwoman companion—Rianna had a small but solid reputation of her own, which Joda had been at some pains to re-
peat and encourage among his peers. The brutal joke of
Joda's father had backfired; far from being ridiculed for
being the fosterling of a woman, he was regarded with faint
awe for having the good fortune to be apprenticed to the
"Lady Spearwoman of Raife." And the boy made the most of
it.

At night, Joda would go out into the courtyard to look at
the stars—openly now, without the concealment he had had
to use among his own people—and sometimes now Rianna
went with him. She had the small folding telescope Aratak
had taken from the Unity base, and was teaching the boy to
look through it. On the ninth night of Aratak's and Dravash's
absence, she was outside with Joda, showing him how to set it
up and focus it. This was the first time in his life Joda had
moved among people who did not regard star-watching as an
evil, dangerous and probably immoral perversion; he had
dozens of stories he had invented about the crowding stars in
the cluster.

"That one," he told Rianna, pointing at an enormous blue-
white star, brighter than Venus at the full, "I call it Fireholder, because it is where they store the lightning between
storms. At night after a storm Fireholder hides herself in
clouds so that her skirt full of lightnings can be repaired;
then when a storm comes she shakes out her apron over the
sky and lightnings fall from her necklaces."

Dane met Rianna's eyes. With an imagination like this, it
was a great pity the boy was locked into a culture where the
only possible career for a man was as a fighter.

"Here, *zadav*," said Rianna, holding the telescope for him,
using the word that meant fosterling, apprentice, foster son.
"Twist the ring below your eyes so that it comes completely
clear . . . no, more slowly, just a fraction at a time. See how
it clears. . . ."

He drew a breath of amazement.

"Oh! There are one, two . . . no, three tiny lights like
coals—" he breathed in excitement. "It is true then that Fire-

holder is a woman, for she has her babes about her skirts—"

"If you will look at this one, the color of a coal from the fire," Rianna said, pointing at a low red star on the southern horizon, large and unflickering, which Dane surmised was not a star but a planet, "you will see that he, too, has companions." And when Joda had taken the telescope and was eagerly focusing it, Rianna beckoned Dane over and said, "That will keep him busy for a while; that's the largest planet in this system and has eleven moons. I saw it on the way in, in the shuttle. I wanted you to see something." She pointed to the enormous blue-white star Joda had called Fireholder.

"I believe that must be Berilon," she said, low-voiced, in Dane's ear, "It's only a light-year or so from Belsar, and there's some evidence that one of its major planets exploded, a while ago, into an asteroid belt. Joda may make up harmless clever tales about Fireholder and her lightnings, but the natives call it World-destroyer, and insist that it is the home of the most dangerous of all the star demons. There is a tradition that once demons came from World-destroyer to enslave the souls of men, and that the Blessed Saints had a great deal of work in vanquishing them. Now I wonder. . . ."

"I'm surprised to hear you collecting native superstitions," Dane said. "You're worse than Joda."

"No, but Dane, traditions like that don't just come from nowhere. A name like that—"

"As far as I can tell," Dane said, "those of the stars which have any names at all—and that's not many of them—have names of fear. I don't think it means anything."

"It may not, of course. Just the same—"

Joda rushed up to them, excitedly brandishing the telescope. "I saw it! I saw it, Lady Mistress, I counted eight—no, nine of his companions, though one of them is very small. I think I will call him Spark Dancer, teaching his band of companions to dance in the sky. The smallest of his companions, Youngest Spark, is a very great coward and can only be seen now and then because he is afraid to burn. . . ."

"It's such a waste," Rianna said. "On any other planet he would be in training for an astronomer, not making up tales about stars and demons!"

Joda said, "Where did you get the far-seeing glass, *Felishtara*? Is it made by the First People? Do they have many such things in Raife? Will I go with you there, some day? Perhaps the First People would tell me how such things are made. Do you know how it makes some of the stars so much clearer, *Felishtara*, so that they are clear little circles in the sky, while others are only a little brighter? Why can it make some of them into little horns, and others stay only clear lights?"

"Gently, gently, *zadav*, I have only one pair of ears, and only one tongue to answer a single question at a time," Rianna reproved, smiling. "Let me think for a moment." Under her breath she murmured to Dane, "Do I dare tell him that stars are really suns?"

Dane didn't know. It might bump into the general Unity prohibition about disturbing the cultural level of any indigenous population. He shrugged and said, "Do what you think best, love. He's *your* apprentice." It was a copout, maybe. But Rianna knew the Unity laws better than he did.

Rianna said fiercely, "I hate ignorance!" She took the spyglass from Joda, and said, "In Raife, Joda, some of our best philosophers have a new theory about the structure of the world. They believe that your sun, up there in the day, is a great central ball of fire spreading heat and light to all the smaller balls, and that these balls are small worlds which revolve around the central fire. And that is why it is warm during the day when the sun is looking at us, and cold when we cannot see its face. The red light you call Spark Dancer is such a world too, with his companions smaller worldlets, which turn around him as we turn around the sun."

She went on, putting the "philosophy of Raife" into an elementary lesson in the theory of basic astronomy. Joda curled up at her feet, listening with absorption.

When she had come to a halt, he said, "Is that why you do not fear the stars, Lady Mistress?"

"Yes, Joda. Because the philosophers who have taught me this, have taught me that the stars are suns like our own, and that many of them have worlds like Belsar, and on these worlds are people like you, and me, and the First People, and—and others."

He sat with his chin resting on his grubby hands, thinking that over. He turned up the telescope to the sky again and said in a whisper, "But there are so *many* of them. And if people like you and me could live on worlds up there, demons could live there too. And demons could come from those other worlds."

"The worlds are too far away for that, Joda. Much too far."

"But they can't be *that*, far," he argued, "If our sun is fire, it is close enough that we can feel the heat; my father's campfire will keep away rashas, but only to a little distance, as far as one could walk away from the camp to pass water. And if the sun is close enough to feel the heat of the sun-fire, perhaps the others are close enough for demons to come, and that is why my father and the First People believe in demons from the stars." He looked at the great star he had called Fireholder, and said, frowning in the darkness, "Perhaps demons do live there, and that is why some learned Elders fear it."

Dane thought, *the kid has a mind like a steel trap. It didn't take him long to follow that up!*

"I think perhaps the sunfire is a different fire from your father's campfire, Joda," Rianna said, but she left it at that. It was too much to expect, that the boy could absorb concepts like astronomical distances and solar radiance all in one lesson. "I think we should put away the seeing-glass and go inside to sleep."

Reluctantly, Joda put the glass aside. But Dane had seen him differently; for a moment, as he might have been in a society where he had not been born quite so desperately a misfit.

A few days later, Dane, making his early-morning check of the leased house and grounds, standard for a bodyguard, saw great bulging eyes floating in the lily pool; and after a moment, the huge bulk of Aratak heaved itself out of the pool.

"So you're back?" Dane greeted him, sourly, "It's about time!"

Aratak looked at him with a vaguely puzzled air. "It is the time it is," he commented, "and the Divine Egg has wisely remarked that all things come in their appointed times. Is something disturbing you, dear friend?"

"Oh, no!" Dane said with heavy sarcasm, "It's just fine to be left here wondering what the hell to do about all these rumors of Star Demons, and whatever it was that happened over on the other side of the Great Gorge, while you and Dravash run off to attend to your love lives and leave us protosimians to do the real work!"

"I am glad nothing is troubling you," Aratak remarked serenely, submerging himself to the eyeballs again. "As I said, all things come in the appointed times, love and work and danger, and at this moment it is the hour for my bath. When

Dravash wakes, we shall discuss the appropriate action to investigate the happenings of the Great Gorge."

"That's *fine*," Dane exploded, "You just go right ahead with your bath! That's more important than what's been happening while you were gone!"

"I am glad to hear it," Aratak murmured, even his eyeballs sinking out of sight, and Dane realized abruptly that because of the literalness of the translator-disk, Aratak had taken his words at their exact face value, and all his sarcasm had been wasted. In a rage, he felt like dragging the big protosaur out of the pool and forcing him to confront his own, Dane's sense, that the protosaurians had been goofing off, on holiday—then, tardily, he began to grin. Aratak probably hadn't had much time for bathing in the last ten—no, eleven—days, and nothing *had* happened to speak of while they were gone. Later, retailing his frustrations to Rianna over their breakfast—because, since Aratak was determined to enjoy a leisurely bath, there was no reason to go without food—he found her sympathetic, but still, she shrugged.

"Dane, they simply don't see it the same way we do. With them, when it's there, it's there and there is literally nothing else of importance. When it's over, it's over and that's that, it couldn't matter less, and they literally couldn't understand why you are making a fuss about it now, when it's gone and done with . . . except they'd say that was just like a protosimian, thinking about sex in and out of season, instead of attending to it when the time comes and forgetting about it afterward like a rational being."

"They call that *rational*? At least we can put it aside for something that's *really* important—" Dane grumbled.

"Thank you," Rianna said pointedly, and Dane, meeting her ironic green glance, lowered his eyes, feeling heat in his face.

She relented. "Dane, I know what you mean. I keep forgetting, too—" she lowered her voice, though Joda was not with them, "that you didn't grow up around protosaurians and protofelines and the like. There's a proverb at Unity Central; I've heard Aratak quote it, but you have to remember it, or lose your sanity; *Leave others their otherness*. All we can do is go on from here."

And Dane gradually realized that Rianna was right. The attitude of the protosaurians was simply too alien. They were good-natured, exuberant, like schoolboys just returned from a holiday, but within minutes after Dravash woke, when they summoned Dane and Rianna for a conference, it was instantly apparent that the holiday was *over*; it was time to get back to work. Dane shrugged philosophically, reflected that he and Rianna had enjoyed a kind of holiday too, and left it at that.

"It is obvious," said Dravash in his thoughtful way, "that somehow we must investigate the happenings on the far side of the Great Gorge. But that is not as easy as it sounds. There is no travel on a regular basis between here and Peshilor, which is why traders from Raife are so unusual. Anyone hearing about us assumes, of course, that we must have traversed the Great Gorge already on our journey from Raife, so that we cannot even hire experienced guides without comment. The only way to traverse the Gorge is on foot, of course, and most people simply avoid it; normally we would find a caravan travelling south to the Eye of the World—" Dane recalled the sea-filled meteor crater he had seen from space—"cross the Mahanga near its mouth, then find another caravan running north—which usually would not bother to retrace its steps and enter Peshilor, although there is, of course, some trade. But Peshilor is not a major trade center and we would need some reason to diverge so much from the ordinary trade routes, or for going there at all."

"Would it not be simpler," asked Aratak, "to head out into the wilderness, and find a way across the Great Gorge? I am not wholly unacquainted with mountain country. And we would be unlikely to be followed; the boy Joda tells me that the wilderness is believed to be the home of the most vicious Star Demons. And if the rumors Dane has heard in the market are as current as this, that wilderness is avoided by most travelers. We would not be overseen."

"How long would it take?" Dane asked, looking at Dravash's map, "Ten—twelve days at most. We could afford that much time."

Dravash said, "It would cause too much attention. It is not in keeping with our role as wealthy merchants from Raife. Certainly if we all left the city to go into the wilderness, it would excite attention. But perhaps one or two of us could slip out—"

Dane said, "I've done a lot of traveling in mountain country just as rough as that," and Dravash nodded.

"You and I, then." His eyes went to Aratak's bulk; Aratak, too, came from a swampy world, and despite his disclaimers, was likely to have trouble in mountainous terrain. "Aratak

will show himself in the marketplace between baths, and Rianna can continue to instruct her fosterling. Allow us—" he
frowned, his brow-ridges twitching, "perhaps thirty days; if
we are not back, try to communicate again with the ship; if
your communicators are not working, Farspeaker will make
contact with you. He will, of course, know if anything has
befallen any of us, which is why I insisted upon such a link
being made before I descended to this world. When two expe-
ditions have vanished in defiance of communications, some
extraordinary precaution should be taken."

Rianna grimaced, and Dane knew she was thinking of that
possibility; that Farspeaker would need to establish contact
again. . . .

"If we do not communicate, in one way or another, in
forty days, get back to the Unity Base somehow, and I'll be
sure some kind of craft is there to take you off."

The gong boomed at the gate. Dane said sourly, "Don't answer. They might find a good excuse to take off again, and I
don't think we can wait any longer."

"It seems not likely," Dravash said blandly, but in a moment Joda came in, guiding two visitors; one a black-scaled
saurian, seven feet tall, wearing the distinctive white cloak
which had been pointed out to Dane as identifying the
prestigious Order of Healers in this city; the other was the
scarred, angular Master Spearman, in the blue of the
Anka'an order, whom Dane had seen that day in the
marketplace. He seemed more than ever, with his hairy bare
legs and hook nose, to resemble a gaunt scarecrow.

"The noble lord Haithiyo'asha the Healer," the Sh'fejj announced himself, and the Master Spearman, spinning his
lance point to the floor in token of peaceful entry and respect, said briefly, "Prithvai, Spearman of the Anka'an Breth-
ren." Only his black eyes moved, sweeping the room wall to
wall and floor to ceiling, examining every mote of dust for
hidden dangers. That done, white teeth suddenly flashed a
smile in the thin, swarthy face. The giant saurian, dwarfed by
Aratak, lowered his head in greeting.

"Thrava'ash," he said, "A'aratakha, Venerable Elders. You
will remember me? We met at the home of the Lady
O'ohassa."

"Well met and well remembered," Aratak said pleasantly,
but Dravash only nodded, his eyes watchful and his brow-
ridges twitching.

Master Prithvai, formalities over, relaxed—or seemed to;

Dane would have bet a substantial sum that he knew to a hair's breadth everything that was going on in the room. His hands slid down the haft of his spear as his body dropped into a comfortable squat on the floor. Dane watched, feeling suddenly awkward and alien, like a stage Irishman on his first visit to Dublin, or a blackface minstrel suddenly dropped off in Harlem. Watching the subtle interactions between man and saurian, he realized that Hathiyo'asha and Master Prithvai shared a culture, a common background, in a way that he and Aratak—or even he and Rianna—did not, never could.

"You are both well, I trust?" said Haithiyo'asha in a genial tone, "I could not help noticing, A'aratahakha—even though everything was very confused, as usual—the wound on your neck." He lifted his own clawed hand automatically to the side of his own neck, and Dane thought, with sudden wariness; *Aratak's gill-slits! They're vestigial in the ordinary Sh'fejj!*

"I trust the wound is healing well? Would you care to have me examine it, while I am here?"

Consternation flashed across Aratak's face; very briefly, replaced by bland innocence. Dane and Dravash met each other's eyes, and Dane hoped his face was as unrevealing as that of the Sh'fejj Captain.

"There is no need, Healer," Aratak said calmly, "the wound is healing nicely and has no need of attention."

"Still, it might be well for me to have a look at it," said Haithiyo'asha, stepping forward, "it is a long journey to Raife, and the climate might well aggravate any difficulties. Tell me, will you pass through Borchan?"

The question was directed at Dravash, and it was he who answered, "Yes, I presume so, although our route is not yet established."

The Healer was staring at his hand. He touched the tips of around Aratak's neck—and stopped, frozen. Dane saw the smile vanish from Master Prithvai's face, the dark eyes suddenly alert.

The Healer was staring at his hand. He touched the tip of the long claws delicately against each other, then he raised his eyes.

"I have not been within the confines of Borchan in many egg-hatchings," he mused. "Tell me, is all well within the household of old Eeoffessaway?"

Master Prithvai's eyes swivelled quickly round, though he did not move a muscle, and Dane knew by the tension in those hands that the question was a trap. Dravash's brow-ridges

jerked. Aratak hesitated, just a second too long, then, realizing that it was urgent to say something, anything, quickly,
and careful not to fall into the trap, said coldly, "I have not
the honor of his personal acquaintance, Healer."

Dane, watching Master Prithvai's face, thought, *wrong answer! The man's dead—or never existed!* The spear-point still
rested between Master Prithvai's feet, but Dane, remembering
Master Rhomda in action, knew how that spear could rise to
a striking position at any split second!

The oldest trick in the book—and Aratak walked into it!

Aratak said icily, trying to bluster it through, "As a matter
of fact, Healer, the very existence of the person you mention
is unknown to me. Are you certain you have not confused
the city of Borchan with some other—" he hesitated for a
weighted moment, but concluded blamelessly, "location?"

Dane was acutely aware of the sword at his side, his left
hand cupping the upper mouth of his scabbard, of the tension
in his right hand where fingers strained at the ready, to leap
across his lap and lock around the sword, of the shoulder
muscles ready to whip the blade across. . . . but he knew, too,
that the Master Spearman's eyes saw all these things. He
forced his fingers to relax, but knew his pulse rattled like a
fast train.

The Healer said slowly, his face unreadable, "Since you
have no need of our services, Venerable Elder, we shall take
our leave." He nodded to Prithvai. The spearman's scarecrow
figure straightened slowly, with deadly grace, hands sliding up
the motionless spearshaft with the deliberation of a man determined to make no sudden moves. When he was fully on
his feet Dane's heart lurched and his sword-hand tensed as
the spear reversed itself in a precise maneuver, to thump its
butt on the floor.

Healer and spearman bowed together, a formal bow; then
the Healer strode from the room, and as he reached the door,
Prithvai too turned to follow, turning his back on them all.
But Dane could see the terrible tension in his legs, the set of
his shoulders, and knew that the slightest sound of any of
them following would bring the spear around. . . .

But the door closed behind them, and Dane let out his
breath, and audible sound. Rianna asked, "What was all *that*
about?"

"Either the Healer he named is dead, or someone whom
Aratak couldn't help knowing," Dravash answered her,

"someone, perhaps, whose public death or disgrace created news even from Borchan all the way here."

That would have done it, Dane thought. *Imagine asking an American about the current health of President Kennedy, or Martin Luther King? Or for that matter Charlie Manson or James Earl Ray?*

"In either case," Aratak said, "We had better make our plans very swiftly. They now know we are not what we profess ourselves to be. I am sorry I gave the wrong answer; the question took me by surprise. I had believed that no one from this area would have had enough contact with Raife to know the name of any particular individual, and I thought it sufficient to refuse any claim to his personal acquaintance— *that* was an obvious trap, of course. But in avoiding it, I fear, I fell into a worse. Well does the Divine Egg warn against deceptions and untruth!"

Dravash said wryly, "I'd think more of the wisdom of that Divine Egg of yours if he had warned us all in advance!"

"Wisdom cannot be put to temporary human uses—" Aratak began, but Dravash said impatiently, "In the name of all the Saints, is this the hour for a lecture on philosophy? Don't you realize? We've got to get out of here! There used to be some speculation in Survey, when I was a tadpole, that the Healers and the Anka'an Order maintained some secret information network not available to the general populace. I've also wondered whether the Healers have some degree of psi power they use in their work—did you notice how he reacted when he touched Aratak's scarf?" He sighed. "Too late to worry about it now. We had better start collecting our belongings; we will leave as soon as it gets dark—all of us!"

In his voice was the authority of a man who had commanded starships, and nobody argued. But Dane and Rianna were strapping on their packs when they heard the clamor in the streets, the sudden sound of the gate crashing open and the shouts. Joda came running into their quarters, white-faced, and Dane thought, *Good God, I'd forgotten the kid! We can't take him with us! No, damn it, we're committed to do just that—Rianna is, anyway, which means I am too!* He never questioned that.

He said tersely, "Come along!" The three of them began running toward the main house, Rianna catching up her spear, and Joda, seeing it, awkwardly tugged at his own sword. Dravash and Aratak, inside the house, had retreated from the broken gates; as Dane and Rianna joined them, Dane said, "Quick! Out through the back courts!"

But it was too late; already the mob was swirling all over the grounds, yelling, and now Dane got the gist of what they were yelling.

"Star Demons!"

Men and protosaurians from the market and streets of the city were swarming across the court, swords raised, spearpoints bristling, filling Dane's visual field.

Then Dravash—Dane remembered he had captained explorer ships—leaped to one of the wooden pillars that held up the roof, ripped the beam free, and swung it like a baseball bat. Men fell, and even tall saurians hesitated. Aratak seized a second beam, and Dane ran to join them, both hands holding the blade poised over his head. Out of the corner of his eye he saw Rianna's spear; he could feel her just beside him, at his left. The crowd hesitated; Dane, in that instant of quiet, realized there were not nearly so many of them as he had thought.

Out of the corner of his eye Dane saw Joda crouching next to Rianna, sword drawn, face white, and spared a momentary pity for the youngster as he looked from them to the mob in terrible confusion.

"This way," said Dravash, as the crowd drew back before them. Then Master Prithvai strode through the crowd that parted before him, darting under the great beam Aratak swung down, running straight for Dane. A point of light on the end of a pole was driving toward Dane's throat. He swatted it down with his sword and stepped forward, his own point thrusting out and up. Prithvai's hand swept the air before his throat with the spear butt, knocking Dane's blade away, and the spear point moved in an arc just above the floor, darted out like a snake for Dane's thigh. Dane jumped back, bringing the blade down. The movement spun him halfway round, and he saw Joda, still cowering against the wall, forgotten—*How in hell does anyone find the time to be scared?*—and he whipped his sword up as the spear drew back and extended again, high this time. He knocked the point away, stepping to the side. . . .

And the spear butt came swinging around to catch him in the back of his head.

He had a sudden headache; sparks burned in front of his eyes. The heavy wood had only grazed him; he saw the point flipping up for his belly, and managed to push the sword down toward it. He caught it, not with the blade, but squarely with the length of hilt between his two hands. The scarecrow figure leaped back, a look of respect flashing across his face.

He expected that one to kill me, didn't he. . . .

Dravash had leaped like a raging tyrannosaur among the men, and they were scattering. Aratak had closed with two of the saurians, towering over them like a giant among school children, cracked their heads together and flung them senseless into the crowd.

Rianna had her spear buried in a man's chest. As she struggled to free it, a second closed in and Dane saw her stagger as a spear-butt cracked on her head.

Prithvai's spear was driving at Dane's chest again. He batted it aside, ducked toward Rianna, but the lean spearman bounded into Dane's path. The spear-shaft whipped between Dane's legs. He managed to rock his weight to one side, shifting his balance, but the spear-butt clubbed into the thick muscle of Dane's thigh.

Rianna was down now, a spear poised over her, even as Dane's sword hissed toward Prithvai's face.

And Joda came flying out of his corner, spread-eagled; his weight floored the man who had knocked Rianna down. . . . Prithvai's face disappeared behind a curtain of blood; through it Dane saw Joda's foot come out in one of those almost-judo kicks, and somebody, Dane couldn't see clearly who it was, went down. He was wrenching his own sword free from Prithvai's split skull, leaping over the sprawled scarecrow form. Rianna groaned and sat up, dazed; Joda hauled her to her feet as men scattered before Dane's sword. Aratak at his side, they advanced toward the corridor, where Dravash was still cracking heads with the roof-beam; but the heart had gone out of the attack. Then they were through into the corridor; outside in the hot, muggy air. Dane felt groggy, his head splitting open with pain.

They were back on the Red Moon, Hunters following them. . . . The Spider-man had broken Rianna's spear and Aratak had snatched up one from somewhere for her. . . . He looked up, dazed, into the thick black velvet, jewel-starred, of the night sky, trying to get it clear. A fragment of his mind knew they were on Belsar, but he still moved his head, aching, from side to side, alert for the Hunters in any shape they might assume. . . .

Aratak lifted Rianna in his arms. *Yes, the Spider-man had*

wounded her in the leg . . . then they were off and running. *But it's dark, the Hunt ends at dark,* he thought, confused again, having to force himself to remember that they were not, now, facing Hunters.

Only people. Good people, mostly, but afraid of Star Demons. . . . He ran, trying to bring his mind back to the present, away from the Red Moon. The image of Prithvai's split skull was before his eyes, and he thought with aching regret, *Hell, I didn't want to kill him!* There had been no choice. Anyway, their exit left nothing to be desired. And perhaps the darkness, which native superstition peopled with Star Demons anyway, would keep pursuit away.

Anyhow, they were on their way.

CHAPTER TEN

Somewhere a night-hunting bird coughed in the dark roof of leaves that shut away the stars. Rustles of grass, the faint pattering of paws, told of beasts out in the darkness, going about their nightly business of breeding and feeding, hunting and being hunted, living and dying.

Like us. . . .

Rianna stirred restively in Aratak's arms.

"Put me down, I can walk now."

"We can't go blundering around in the dark anyhow," Dravash said, "We'll have to make camp. Nobody will follow us, not with Star Demons about in the night—so the superstition is useful to us, at least."

Here and there silver pillars of starlight stabbed through the jungle dark. Toward one of these clearings Dravash led them. A burst of wind made the leaves hiss, and Dane realized he was shivering; the heat rushed up into the sky at nightfall, and sweat was clammy cold on his chilled body. His legs ached with running and his head was still sore and confused from Master Prithvai's spear butt.

Well, Prithvai's head is in worse shape than mine. . . .

He could remember little of how they got out of the city; fogged memories of running through an endless maze of cloth-roofed streets, of hiding for what seemed hours, and probably was, in a thick garden of bad-smelling plants, of a nightmarish fight while Aratak unbarred a gate somewhere, of guards frantically slamming a gate behind them rather than pursue them into the night, haunted by rashas and Star Demons beyond the safe city walls. . . .

Flint struck steel in the darkness, and Dravash's face flared in the tiny flame. He fed the fire leaves and small twigs, while Dane wondered if making the fire was such a good idea; it would only draw pursuit, or at worst, show pursuers in the morning where they had camped. Then somewhere a rasha howled, and he decided the fire was a good idea after all.

Hunters. He half expected to see the crimson of the Hunter's Moon rise red above the trees . . . he struggled to get himself under control again. That was then. This was now. All they had in common was *danger.*

The flames leaped up, lighting the clearing. Joda had his hands clasped over his face; Rianna went to his side, laid a hand on his shoulder, but he flinched away in terror.

"What's wrong, *zadav?*"

"I knew it was too good to last!" the boy said wildly. "What is it, what have you done, that the Anka'an Order can order you killed? And you killed Master Prithvai in fight— who are you? What are you? I have never been so—" he stopped, swallowed, and when he spoke again his voice was steady, and he demanded, "One of you tell me what this is all about!"

"Tomorrow," Dravash said firmly. "For now, sleep is what we all need, more than anything else."

Perhaps it was only the habit of obeying the First People; Joda spread out his blankets, but he was still watching Rianna fearfully. *What will we tell him?* Dane wondered, spreading out his own. *How does Dravash expect us to sleep, after all this?* He knew that he, at least, was far too keyed up to sleep at all. He would just close his eyes. . . .

And was wakened from sound sleep by the scream of a rasha. His eyes opened to see the creature struggling in Dravash's grasp; the saurian's heavy knife blade flashed down, and Dravash hurled the headless corpse into the underbrush, picked up the head and heaved it in the other direction. Dane heard weird cooing cries and the sound of pattering feet. The local scavengers, coming in for lunch. He wondered what they were like, then decided he didn't want to know.

Rianna was pressed tight against him. On the other side of her, he heard Joda's teeth chattering. She rolled away from Dane, turned toward the boy, and he heard her murmuring in the dark, soothingly, knew that she had drawn him against her, her shoulder cradling his head. He felt a momentary annoyance. Good God, was he jealous of the kid? That was silly, the boy must be scared out of his wits after all this! Anyway, he was too sleepy to care. He closed his eyes again.

When he opened them again, the sky was dim with the coming dawn, and the stars had gone out. Aratak was hunkered down by the dying coals of the fire, Dravash a long, dark, blanketed form as close to it as he could possibly be without setting the blanket on fire.

"I wanted to let him sleep as long as possible," Aratak said in a whisper to Dane—so low, in fact, that Dane heard him only through the translator disk,—"He fought far harder than I, and he is not accustomed to it."

Around them, the forest was quiet; Dane knew there was little likelihood of a rasha's attack at dawn, but even so, he kept a hand on his sword while he relieved himself. When he got back to the camp Joda and Rianna were awake. Aratak had caught himself a breakfast of raw bug, and was eating it with the same enjoyment, Dane thought, as a city man might enjoy a breakfast of trout fresh from a mountain stream. But Joda stared, wide-eyed, as hot food appeared miraculously from the bottom of the packs Dane and Rianna carried; and Dane saw superstitious fear struggling in the boy's eyes with his love and respect for Rianna. Well, she'd just have to figure out how to explain heat-paks to him, since the alternative was breakfasting like Aratak on live insects.

"You must tell me what this means!" Joda said, staring at the food without touching it. "They called you Star Demons! And now food that grows hot of itself—and looks strange, unlike any food I ever saw—is it demon-food?"

Rianna tugged unconsciously at her hair, and smiled at him. "No, of course not," she said, "Do I look like a demon to you, Joda?"

"I don't know what a demon-woman would look like!" The

hysterical note in his voice was a high, sharp-edged whine now. "You fight like a man—you keep your breasts hidden as if they were deformed, but they're not, they're not—and your eyes, they are strange—"

His voice trailed into silence, frightened. Rianna bit her lip.

"Perhaps," she said gently, "since you are so unsure of us, I should simply say, yes, we are Star Demons, and let you run back to tell the folk of the city where we have gone."

He stared at her; then dropped the food-pak and flung his arms round her, hiding his head against her breast.

"I couldn't do that!" he cried out, "You're no demon! I'll never believe you are a demon! If you are from the stars, then it's as I always believed, and the stars are the home of good, not evil! You are good! I don't care what they say, I know you are good, all of you!"

For a moment Rianna tightened her arms around him; then pushed him gently away. She said, "You're right; I am no demon, *zabav*, and I hope never to be anything but good in your eyes. Pick up your food and eat it; we have not too many supplies, but we should eat while we can. And while you eat I'll explain to you as much as I can."

He retrieved the food-pak and began to eat with his fingers, as she did, watching her and Dane with frightened eyes.

"Obviously," Rianna began, "we're not travelers from Raife. We're from somewhere a lot farther than that." She looked at him, thoughtfully, and Dane followed her concern.

Joda didn't think he believed in Star Demons. But they were, after all, part of his mental makeup, and when it came to the crunch . . . well, anyway the boy had reaffirmed his faith in Rianna. That was something.

"Joda," she said, "do you see that dark bird, sitting on the high tree?" She pointed.

"The diving-crane, on the redflower tree? Yes, I see him."

"How big is he? About the size of your thumbnail, perhaps?"

He looked at her, wondering if she had suddenly gone mad.

"No, *Felishtara*, the diving-crane is a *big* bird—" he spread out his arms to indicate how big.

"And yet," she said, "when I hold up my thumbnail, I can hide him completely from sight."

As if explaining something very simple, Joda said, "That is because he is so far away, that is all."

"Very well. Then I suppose you can understand that the sun—" she pointed to the blaze of Belsar on the horizon, "is a ball of fire larger than the whole world we stand on."

She saw him slowly taking this in. "Then what you said about philosophers from Raife—"

"Is the knowledge of another world, Joda. I know the world here goes around your sun, which we call Belsar, because I have been in a—a kind of metal cart or ship in the sky and seen your world going round it, with your other planets—the one you named Spark Dancer and his companions. And the stars in the sky at night are other suns, like Belsar, only much, much farther, so far you would find it very hard to imagine or dream how far. And some of those stars, or suns, have worlds like this one, and on one of those worlds I was born. And Dane on another, and Dravash and Aratak on others yet. Do you understand?"

"I—I think so." But his tone was doubtful. It was a long and patient explanation, and many times wonder struggled with terror in the boy's eyes while his forgotten food grew cold; Rianna finally stopped and made him eat it, reminding him that supplies were limited. Finally, as Dane had known he must, he put the question.

"But what are you doing here, on *our* world? They say the Star Demons—" quickly he amended, "the star people have come to enslave us, carry us off in their metal carts, torment us—"

"Perhaps that is why," Rianna said, "in our world beyond those stars you can see, we heard rumors that some evil folk had come here to torment and enslave Belsar. We belong— Aratak and Dravash belong, that is—to an—order of Protectors—"

"Like the Blessed Saints?"

She smiled and shook her head. "More, perhaps, like the Anka'an Order, pledged to guard the weaker folk against savages and predators. Dane and I were chosen because we were able to fight and survive on—" she choked back the very words on her lips; Dane heard them already through the translator, though Rianna managed not to speak them aloud. *—on a barbarian or primitive world.* She would not say that to Joda.

"On a world which presents many dangers."

"And," said Dravash, who had wakened during Rianna's explanation and was listening with an impassive interest, "we must move on before the dangers surround us again. Come; this way."

Joda asked "Where are we going?"

Dravash said, "Toward the Great Gorge—eventually. Just now, we are attempting to evade pursuit."

The forest ahead glowed with morning sun; Dane looked at their back trail, plain to his eyes. And there must be trackers on this world better than *he* was! After conferring with Dravash, they took the party up into the hills, seeking rockier ground that would leave fewer traces of their passing.

Once, close to Rianna, Dane said, "I liked the way you handled that explanation. I couldn't have done it."

Her eyes glinted faintly green at him. "I've had to do it before," she said, and Dane felt again the sting of inferiority.

She probably thinks of me as a primitive, not much better than Joda! And again the anger, that had rankled in him since the night before, when Rianna had turned from him to shelter Joda in her arms, surged up.

Does she really care about me at all? Or is it just habit, after what we went through on the Hunter's World? Or even more degrading, he wondered, was it simply that he had seemed exotic, primitive, strange, a change from the over-sophisticated men of her own world? Even on Dane's own world, there were women with what he called a Tarzan complex; seeking educated men of their own level for companionship, but for sexual excitement seeking out men who were nothing more than magnificent physical animals, without offering anything, really, in common but sex. Dane clenched his sword, wishing he could find a rasha to use it on and vent his anger on somebody; wishing for a moment that he was not too civilized to give Rianna a good hard swat across her sneering face. Or had he just imagined the sneer? Or was it Joda he wanted to kick good and hard in the britches?

This was no time to be worrying about that. They were climbing now, and it took all his breath and energy. Glassy stone, hurled up molten by whatever cataclysm had scarred the planet with craters, reared up in great curving ridges out of eroding beds of softer rock, gypsum, sandstone. Here the voracious jungle vegetation could take no root, and Dane led them, quick-foot, over the hard stone for several hours.

Then, as they came over the top of an outcrop, he saw distant movement out of the corner of his eye. He waved the others back, and crawled to the top, flattening himself against glassy green stone. Barely a quarter of a mile away, a small

group of men were moving slowly through the brush, spread
out like a hunting party, spear points blazing in the sunlight
which now came from directly overhead. Among them were
several figures in blue tunics of the Anka'an Order.

Dane reached behind him, whispering to Rianna to pass up
the telescope they had found at the deserted Unity Base. For
a moment he worried—had she taken it out for Joda's
damned star-gazing lessons and forgotten to put it back into
her pack? Then she put it into his hand. He sighted the instrument and peered across the intervening masses of leaves.

Suddenly a face leaped at him in sharp focus.

Master Rhomda!

Dane felt a sudden impulse to crouch down and hide;
through the telescope it seemed that the calm dark eyes must
see him, but the spearman turned calmly away. Dane glanced
at the party. There were at least five of the blue tunics, and
perhaps fifty others, and they were moving through the undergrowth very methodically, searching the bushes with their
spears.

Had they been hastily summoned to pursue the fugitive
Star Demons? Or were they merely hunting the mysterious
white Star Beast, the one Dane had heard about in the tavern? Dane did not want to find out.

Dane scanned the area quickly with the glass, concentrat-
ing on the course of a small stream that ran down from the
hills a little ahead of them, to join with the river below.
There was a fine clear path of bare rock to its edge, but it
would be in plain sight of the men below them.

But a little way downstream, the water veered sharply back
toward them in a wide meander, along a jumble of boulders
and scrub. A stand of tall trees shrouded in vines shielded it
from sight. Dane remembered a spur of exposed rock that
ran in that direction.

This area was becoming definitely unhealthy. Dane
wriggled back down the slope, handed the telescope to Rianna, and explained the situation in whispers to Dravash.
Quickly moving back to the earlier rock spur, he led them
across rock to the stream. In one place he made them leap
from boulder to boulder across soft, betraying turf, glad that
they had all, except Joda, come from somewhat heavier
worlds, and the boy was young and limber. They reached the
stream without leaving a track or a broken twig. Dane
plunged in and they followed him, along the edge where the
water was shallow; although Aratak and Dravash moved out

into the center of the stream where the water was over the heads of the humans. Dravash waded stolidly, ducking the branches that dipped over the water, but Aratak slipped down and swam silently ahead, scouting out the stream.

Dane was thoughtful. If their pursuers were not already following their trail into the hills, they would before long; if Master Rhomda's party had not yet heard of their escape from the city, and were hunting the Star-Beast with six legs, they would certainly soon turn their attention to the more easily identifiable party of "Star Demons." If the searchers were beating the hills for them, the valley was obviously the place to be; but the valley was thickly jungled and they could not hide their trail.

But would the pursuers think to look for them on the far side of the river?

That night they swam the river, Rianna and Joda holding on to Aratak as they drove through the heavy current. Dravash insisted on helping Dane, and after feeling the strength of the river, Dane was grateful for the big Captain's help. Dane was sure they would be safe on the far side; he doubted any human could swim it unaided, and so far their pursuers were all humans.

For several days they moved cautiously through the jungle beyond the river; but sooner or later, they knew, they would have to pass through thickly settled areas, hoping to pass unnoticed through the common people of the villages.

"If," said Joda to Rianna, "you will put on a skirt, give the spear to Dane to carry, and bare your breasts like any decent woman, we will all be a lot safer." That made sense, though Rianna hated the long wrapped skirt and the way it shortened her stride; for they must move between scattered patches of woodland between the fields of various small villages. But there was no disguising the color of Rianna's eyes, though she smeared around them with ashes to simulate the crude cosmetics of the village women; or Aratak's enormous bulk. Sooner or later, no doubt, some rumor of them would reach the city, and they could only hope the rumor would be late, and grossly distorted. And to keep a consistent rumor from rising, of a woman and a man with strangely colored eyes, and an oversize saurian, they sometimes split up; Dane would wander through the rising dust of ploughed fields, between villages, with Rianna and Joda alone, like a commonplace family group, sometimes stalking like a bodyguard behind one of the saurians, to rendezvous at the next village, while the dark-skinned throngs hurried by intent on their own affairs.

A musician played on a small harp with an extra string fastened only at one end, that was used like the bow of a violin, and people danced joyfully in the dusty marketplace. An occasional juggler or wandering mime drew small crowds at a crossroads. But most of the people were farmers and their wives, carrying produce to markets, laboring in fields wrested painfully from the jungle, and perpetually at war with the encroaching tendrils and vines that kept trying to creep out into the ploughed lands.

Once in a marketplace Dravash brought out some coins—the "jewels from Raife" were too dangerous here, they would cause too much comment; that must wait for another big city. He bought a small drum and squatted in the market, starting up a quick musical tattoo that brought crowds running. Joda was shocked—most musicians were human, for it was beneath the dignity of most of the First People—but Dane knew what the Sh'fejj was thinking. Fugitives, people with anything to hide, would be trying not to attract attention. Under Dravash's whispered orders, while Dane and Rianna hid in the crowd, Joda went round the crowd, holding out his turbanlike headgear for the listeners to toss little coins into.

But as they traveled, the patches of jungle between the fields thickened, the villages grew farther apart and poorer. Wooden palisades surrounded the clusters of domed huts, with the cleared fields around them keeping back the jungle, and hopefully discouraging the rashas.

The rashas. It might have been a pleasant trip, without the rashas. The big cats became a more and more constant menace as the travelers finally took altogether to the jungle. Dravash and Aratak, with their greater height and the advantage that the rashas did not find them edible or attractive, took on the task of guarding their protosimian fellow-travelers, and became adept at spotting the great cats roosting in the lower branches. Even so, only Rianna's quickness with the spear kept their talons from Joda on two occasions, and once Dane took a long scratch on one arm that festered and hurt for days. Dane lost track of how many they had killed. He thought sourly, *If the people along here knew, they'd give us a medal as public benefactors.* But when he expressed this thought to Dravash the Sh'fejj frowned and shook his head.

"Not at all. The rashas are the only control against protosimian overbreeding and outstripping their food supply—or destroying the jungle with their villages and disturbing the ecological balance."

Dane didn't care. He still killed as many as he could. As the country grew wilder, a sound began to grow ahead of them. First it was only a background hum, unheard at noon by the buzz of insects; but day by day it grew, drowning out all other forest sounds, a deep mutter that never stopped. Thundersmith Falls.

Click-owls fluttered away as the travelers approached, their mournful cries inaudible in the roar of the falls. Faintly over the growing sounds came a series of shrieks; Rianna pointed up into the trees and looking up, they saw a large baboon-like monkey hurl itself frantically between two trees. It seized the end of a leafy branch, swung into more branches, seemed to bounce upward as its feet touched a lower limb, crashing from one wildly-swaying branch to another.

The foliage shook in the tree it had left. Branches shook beneath the weight of a rasha, leaping behind the ape through the trees. Dane followed the fleeing ape and the pursuing cat with his eyes as they hurtled through the branches, then lowred his eyes and began to walk forward again.

Better him than me.

The earth opened out before him. Ahead, a few hundred feet, the world ended, jungle and ground alike; the sky was barred by a blurred streak of green and purple mottling, below which hung a wall of sunset cloud. He heard—barely, over the thundering roar—Rianna's gasp.

His eyes adjusted, to pick out red-orange cliffs half-hidden in the haze, and miles of flat jungle at their top, all the way back to the horizon; all distant, painted in flat pastels. Like a mirage painted on the sky.

The Divine Egg tells us. . . . Aratak's voice rumbled through Dane's throat-disk; in his excitement he forgot to speak Kahram, and Dane was too awestruck to correct him; anyway, the sound of the falls drowned him out, "that contemplation of the wonders of the Universe will make a mind grow to fit them. Contemplation of a wonder such as this must surely have given some great wisdom to some of the minds upon this world. . . ."

His voice in the disk trailed into a rapt silence.

Thundersmith Falls appeared abruptly through the leaves to their left, a great silver curtain of roaring water.

Niagara pouring into the Grand Canyon, Dane thought.

No. Too big for Niagara. What's that enormous one in Africa?

The jungle thinned. They stood at the edge of vast emptiness. Fierce winds leaped up from the gulf, chill with mist from the falls. Here the mouth of the river had taken a huge bite out of the canyon wall. The wind carried them the terrible hammering of the falls. Sandstone sloped away at their feet; halfway down the glassy rock stood out in jagged spurs, and below that they could see darker rock dropping to the canyon floor.

Halfway down the face of the falls the water fountained wildly, rebounding from jagged splinters of crystal, making multiple rainbows; then plunged into the deep boiling pool at the bottom. Out of the furious spray a stream flowed toward the center of the valley, where mist shrouded the invisible river.

Dane's throat disk vibrated to Dravash's voice.

"That looks like a way down over there." The Sh'fejj pointed. "Perhaps we can all get down." His eyes lingered, concerned, on Aratak. He scanned the slopes below, called to Rianna to bring the telescope, then studied the lower slopes. He turned back to Dane, saying, "I can get him down. There are ledges and outcroppings down there that one could almost drive a crawler down, if the edges were smoothed somewhat."

Aratak looked down into the steep gully, gloomily.

"The Divine Egg has wisely told us that it is easier to sink than to swim," he remarked, "but I do not know if the same applies to climbing up or down hills. His wisdom has not yet applied itself to the matter of speed and control, alas."

Joda was tugging at Rianna's arm and shouting, but Dane could not make out a word he said over the crash of the falls. Probably he was more confused than ever, seeing them apparently conversing without worrying about the noise, but Dane wasn't about to stop and explain the translator disks right now. Joda pointed and Rianna turned to look; she stiffened, beckoned to Dane and pointed.

Dane looked across the arc of the bitten-out edge of the canyon rim, to the rocks at the edge of the falls. After a moment he snatched the telescope, focused it hastily. A small figure in blue stood there—an Anka'an spearman! Others were coming out of the jungle, and the spearman was pointing—

Dane whirled to the others.

"Down, quick! They've seen us!"

Aratak focused his bulging eyes on the followers. Then he pulled Dane's head close to him. "The rest of you should go—make your escape down this slope. Leave me here to delay them." He added, with a twinge of humor, "Better I should delay *them*, than delay you in your descent, as I am sure to do!"

Dravash bared needle fangs. "No. We'll make a stand and chance driving them off."

"There are too many," Aratak said, "Go, sir. What of our mission? Better they take only one of us. And only you can communicate with Farspeaker if we are all killed. I was forced by no one to undertake this mission, and I was fully aware of the risks. Hurry! I will delay as many as I can, but I cannot delay them forever!"

Belsar was sinking behind the trees to the west; the far wall of the canyon was a hazy pink above a streak of silver; below them the rough, tumbled floor of the canyon would give them lots of cover, if they could only reach it.

"No," he said. "Aratak, you and Dravash start down now; you're the slowest, but if you start now, you can make it to the bottom before they're on us, and take cover down there. We monkeys can hold them for a while, at least, and then when they start getting scared of the stars, make it down fast!"

Dravash hesitated, then said, "He's right, Aratak. I hate to leave them, too, but they do have a natural advantage!"

Aratak balked, and Dane knew he was remembering how the three of them, Dane and Rianna and Aratak, last survivors of the Hunt, had stood side by side in the last battle under the Red Moon. But finally Dane gave him a push, said, "Get going," and, reluctantly, the huge saurian started down the gully at Dravash's side.

Dane watched the small figures running along the rim toward them. There were more than he felt like counting, and he thought, grimly; we fought against worse odds under the Red Moon. He pointed to Joda. "Go after them, quick," he said, then realized that the boy could not hear him over the roar of the falls. But the boy saw the gesture and shook his head stubbornly, shouting something Dane couldn't hear. Dane thought, just as well; from the brat's expression, it was something rude.

Rianna had her spear at the ready. She and Joda stood shoulder to shoulder, and Dane, joining them, turned to face the approaching figures. They had seen the saurians descend into the gully, of course, and knew they faced only the humans. But perhaps he could trick them—make them think they were running into an ambush.

"Rianna—" He gestured. "Go, hide behind that rock over there; take Joda with you. Then, when they all get past that clump of trees, hightail it back—er, get back here as fast as you can!" They'd see her moving behind the rock; with luck, they wouldn't see her coming back, and they might think there were others, hiding behind the rock. It might slow them down just enough . . . too bad the noise of the falls drowned out noise, or he'd set Joda to thrashing around in the brush, making a noise like a dozen men back there and yelling to imaginary allies. But that old trick wouldn't work this time.

He stepped ostentatiously behind a tree and from its shelter looked down into the gully. Far below them, the saurians were making their way, too slowly, over the rock, Dravash helping Aratak on the rough terrain. They might have to hold the ambush here, if the saurians couldn't make it.

Time crawled. Pursuers ran. Belsar still hung stubbornly above the far rim of the canyon, fiercely as Dane willed it to sink. Would the superstitious primitives dare to chase them in the dark? Would the Anka'an Order share the superstitious fear? Would Joda break and run away before the fight?

Rianna and Joda came running back. Dravash and Aratak had vanished into the deepening shadows at the bottom of the valley.

"Into the hollow, there, quick," he urged, in a hasty whisper, "Crouch down out of sight, and wait for my signal—and when I give it, be ready to come out fighting, or to run! When Dravash and Aratak are safely on that ledge down there, and out of sight, I want you two to go down as fast as you can, and wait for me on the ledge!"

Rianna opened her mouth to protest; stopped, drew a deep breath, and nodded. A flight of click-owls soared up out of the forest, cries and wingbeats lost beneath the growling of the falls. Dane tensed. The birds had been startled—probably by the men who followed them. But they had been deeper in the woods. Or were their pursuers circling, to come in from the back? Or was there a second party on their trail?

He knelt, peering through the thick leaves. Green leaves, and purple. Dead brown leaves on the forest floor. Tree-trunks shrouded in orange vines. Interweaving bushes.

Was that a flash of white? Sunlight flashed on something; a

spearhead? A belt buckle? A drop of leftover dew? An animal's eye?

"Dane——" It was Rianna's voice in his throat disk, "Dravash and Aratak are down on the ledge."

"Get going," he said, realizing that to shout would do no good; she would hear it through her translator disk or not at all. "Wait for me at the bottom of the long gully." He turned to watch them start down, then turned to the edge of the forest once more. Thank God for the translator disks! Though neither he nor their makers had ever expected them to be used *this* way.

Then, through the leaves, he saw the feet of two men. He watched carefully, parting leaves to see better. Yes, there they were, moving in very cautiously, spears drawn back against their chests, the long knives of the points jutting up beyond their shoulders. Behind them he saw the bushes shaken by the coming of others.

Thundersmith Falls drowned all sound.

His sword was out of his scabbard. He found himself holding his breath, and forced himself to breathe, slow and deep. He was timing the rhythm of their steps in his head. The blade rose, his left hand came across his chest. One more step, another—*now!*

He burst through the screen of leaves.

The arms of the nearest man shot toward him, spearshaft sliding through the leading hand like a pool cue, with Dane's throat as the ball. Dane ran straight in. His blade snapped across his body, batting the spear to his left; then he was raising himself on his toes, the sword flying up over his head—and then all that stretched power was contracting again, ripping the sword down and *through*. . . .

He wrenched his blade free from the bloody mess that had been a man, and spun wildly toward the other spear driving at him, letting the point droop toward the ground, jerking the hilt sharply upward. Edge met spearshaft, throwing the spearman out of balance; a step with his other foot brought body and sword around and a dark round mass—a head—fell, rolled.

Thundersmith Falls pounded on, unheeding.

Men were pointing, opening and shutting their mouths in shouts that could not be heard. As Dane's blade lifted again they cowered back and moved toward one another. Without going off guard he danced back through the leaves.

The instant he judged himself out of sight he whirled and

ran like hell. His feet must have made a tremendous crashing through underbrush, but the falls took care of that. He darted to the cliff edge and hurled himself down the steep ravine. Half-running, half-sliding, he went down in a shower of small stones.

Halfway down he reached out with his free hand, and snagged a sapling. He had skinned his legs smartly in his rapid descent. He wiped his sword and sheathed it, looking up to the top of the ravine. Had he been spotted? Or were they still slinking back through the woods, expecting him, and the others, to jump them from cover at any moment?

Time. That was the important thing. Time for Aratak and Dravash to make it into the valley.

He went on down. At the bottom of the gully he shouted to Rianna, and his disk crackled a reply, the words indistinct. He jumped out on the ledge and frowned. The glassy stone was level, but slippery. He would have to keep close to the wall. . . .

"Dane—" the disk said in his throat, and Rianna's arms were around him, fast and hard, then she let him go. "You're all blood—"

"Theirs," he said. "Skinned my legs sliding down." He looked over the edge, barely able to see the dim forms of Aratak and Dravash, toiling down far below.

"We're probably going to have to delay them here," he said, looking quickly around the ledge. It was nearly four feet across at this point, and a little broader where he stood, at the opening from the ravine. Behind him it widened to six feet, giving him a clear advantage in fighting room—if he could keep them bottled up, on top of one another, in the mouth of the ravine.

Across the Great Gorge the shadows rose, climbing the cliffs like a tide, as Belsar sank lower in the sky. The massive walls below were dull maroon above; jet-black below. Dravash and Aratak were lost in the shadows now. The sun must strike the treetops soon, he was sure. Vast flocks of birds were fluttering and whirling in the cloudless sky, home to their roosts in jungle and valley.

The clamor of the falls would hide any sound his pursuers made, coming down the ravine. He looked up, but saw nothing between himself and the sky.

The three of them could easily hold this narrow ledge— though he was not sure Joda would be any use to them. The boy's eyes kept shying to the awful drop from the ledge. Actually, he thought, it would only take one to hold this ledge—

In the back of his mind he saw Dallith's eyes, open, empty, staring, dead, as he had last seen them. He saw Rianna lying dead on the floor, the spear poised. . . .

"You two start on down," he heard himself say, "I can hold them; you'd only be in the way."

"You're insane," Rianna snapped, "You sound like that —that idiot Cliff-Climber! That was how *he* got killed! What are you trying to prove?" She moved to his side, her jaw-muscles tight, and her voice in his ear was as determined as he had ever heard it.

"I'm staying, Dane. Don't try to argue."

"Now look," Dane said, reasonably, "I've had more climbing experience than either of you, and heights don't bother me. And I can make it down the cliff faster. If—"

He stopped; a tiny movement had caught his eye.

A pebble rolled out of the ravine; struck the ledge and bounced into the abyss below.

Other pebbles rolled out as he watched, and a good-sized stone or two.

"Too late now," Dane said. "Here they come! Look out!"

Stones falling, the ear so numbed now by the sound of the falls that the pebbles bounced in a surrealistic silence. Waiting, fingers squeezing the sword-hilt; Rianna's hands sliding along her spear. . . .

Master Rhomda leaped out on the ledge, spear poised at the ready.

Behind Dane's eyes Master Prithvai's face poured blood. *Master Rhomda!* And the spear already in deadly motion at him, reaching deadly steel . . .

It was all some sort of hideous mistake . . . ganjir bells jingled in his memory, and a kindly voice asking, *Hungry? Your employers shouldn't need you* . . . but his blade was already sweeping across his vision like a windshield wiper, sweeping the spearpoint to one side, and then he was stepping in, arms swinging up for the cut. . . .

The spear-butt caught his arm just above the elbow, and his bicep slammed into his cheek with the force of a punch. His cut, deflected, skipped harmlessly along the spear-shaft and he jumped back as the butt drove for his solar plexus.

I'm going to have to kill him. . . .

Rhomda snapped the spear up over his head as Dane cut

again, and stepped in, the spear-shaft pressing against Dane's blade, holding him for a moment motionless.

. . . if I can!

The tough wooden shaft stuck to Dane's blade as if glued there. Dane tried to jump free, almost lost his footing on slippery stone, but Rhomda closed the distance before Dane could cut.

In desperation Dane twisted away, hurling his shoulder against the spear-shaft, drawing the blade back and stabbing over his shoulder at the spearman's throat. Rhomda leaped away and Dane swivelled on the balls of his feet, stepping back. Rianna's spear darted suddenly past his shoulder, stabbing at the spearman, but Rhomda's weapon whipped round to flick her point aside, without offering Dane any real opening for an attack.

We're not working out in a dojo! This is serious, damn it, he'll kill Rianna and Joda too. . . . It seemed that the ghosts of Cliff-Climber and Dallith were gathered close, watching over his shoulder *. . . warning him! Look for me in the morning, you shall find me a grave man. . . .* Madness flicked through his mind. His arm smarted from Rhomda's blow. The shadows were thickening. *When the sun goes down the Hunters stop fighting . . .* but they were not Hunters! The far cliff no longer glowed.

The spear flickered again at him.

"Rianna!" he shouted, desperately, "Take Joda and get out of here!" His mind went on shouting long after he shut his mouth down.

Rhomda dodged away from Dane's return cut and again the spear darted, snakelike. Dane brushed it aside and hurled up his blade for another stroke, a killing stroke this time . . . the spear spun in Rhomda's hands. The spear-butt crashed solidly against Dane's head and he felt his knees give way.

Hard stone crashed into his body. He tried to push himself up from the sheet of glass where he lay, his sword still gripped in his right hand, but then the world went out and hurled him into an endless twilight where there was nothing but the eyes of ghosts, the eyes of Dallith, cold and dead and waiting for him to join her. . . .

Thundersmith Falls was silent too.

CHAPTER ELEVEN

It was all a big lie, like everything else. They said it didn't hurt to die, that after you were dead the pain went away and you didn't care any more. But the pain hadn't gone away. It came back worse than ever. And he couldn't see. And the man who had killed him was with him in the blind and aching darkness; Master Rhomda's voice.

"There will be none of that! Remember the words of the Blessed Ones! *Vengeance belongs to Us,* they have said . . . justice will be done! Hands off, there!"

"The Blessed Ones were not so squeamish when we were cleaning out the white devils," a second voice grumbled.

"That was different," Rhomda said in the dark, "Do you really think this is a Star Demon, you fool?"

Thundersmith Falls was still there in death, too, only more quietly, so that Dane could hear what they were saying. And he realized that he wasn't blind, his eyes were closed; but there was a reddish light seeping in under his eyelids, so the old stories about the fires of hell were true, after all. Somewhere a rasha screamed, so there were rashas in hell, too. Well, that figured. But the scent of flowers didn't fit in, somehow.

"My sister and her sons were in that village they burned with their devil-fire," the second voice snarled, "They're demons, all of 'em! Who's to say a demon can't look like a man? I say kill him now and hunt down the others as fast as we can and kill them too!"

"Saint A'assioo said that hatred is a sickness," Rhomda said, "There is much of that sickness in our lands, and much healing is needed, but killing will not heal it." His voice hardened. "I will hear no argument; I speak with the voice of the Order, carrying the commands of the Blessed Ones, and I myself am under their discipline, even as with all of you. Obey me!"

Dane's head throbbed to bursting; he blinked. Wood smoke filled his nostrils. A new discomfort forced itself through the general ache of his whole body; something hard was digging into his back. He tried to wriggle off it—

His eyes snapped open. His hands were tied together. Firelight threw vague moving shadows on the white gauze which had been spread above them to shield men's souls from the stars. Duller shadows flickered on the wall of stone at his left. Beyond his feet, well under the cloth, Master Rhomda stood, braced, hands on hips, facing a number of men whose teeth were gleaming and whose eyes were red in the firelight.

"I go to make my report," Rhomda said, calmly, "I shall return as soon as possible; guard them well." His voice hardened. "If I do not find them safe and sound—both of them—you will all answer to the Blessed Ones; I promise you that in the name of the Anka'an."

He turned and strode off calmly into the blackness of the jungle night, vanishing from Dane's sight between one blink of the firelight and the next. It kept flicking in and out, light and dark, like his wavering vision. A rasha screamed out there in the darkness; the fire crackled, making the shadow flap against the gauze overhead like black bat wings.

Rolling his head, ignoring the thunder of pain that roared through it, Dane saw Joda, roped and tied, his face smeared with blood and mud. But he must be alive. They wouldn't have bothered tying up a dead prisoner. Joda's feet were free, if he wanted to run. But rashas were hunting, out there, in that haunted darkness beyond the tent. Even if you weren't afraid of Star Demons, there were rashas, and granths, and God knows what else . . .

Dane's head felt as if it had been slit like Master Prithvai's, he could feel the split line down the middle, surely if he moved it, the left half would fall into the fire and the right half would roll out there into the jungle, for the rashas . . . *no, that was crazy* . . . Dane got the rope tying his hands into focus, saw that the rope stretched from his hands, was tied to a stake driven into the ground. It hurt like hell to move his eyes, making the dark waver and flicker and descend—or was that the uncertain light of the campfire? More urgent than pain was something else; he twisted, ignoring the shattering pain, ignoring the way in which his vision blurred and darkness came down, searching frantically with his aching eyes for a third roped and tied form, somewhere inside the canopy. *Rianna! Where was Rianna?*

But there was no sign of her. There were the men, clustered in the improvised Belsar version of a tent, under the gauze which shut out the demon-haunted stars. There was Rhomda, out there in the jungle—*and why wasn't he afraid of the stars, and their demons?* And there was Joda, tied up, dead or unconscious or asleep.

But Rianna wasn't there. Nowhere, in the flickering darkness that came and went with the small uncertain fire, was there any sign of Rianna, or of her unconscious body.

They wouldn't bother tying up the dead.

So that meant she was dead. They'd killed her.

Dallith, Cliff-Climber. Now Rianna. . . .

Savage men were laughing around their fire, the fire they had built to ward off Star Demons and hunting beast-eyes and the ghosts of their dead. And Rianna was dead out there for the rashas and the prowling scavengers of the night.

Had they killed her cleanly, at least? Or had she been left wounded, prey of the first hunting-cat? Or had those vicious savages taken pleasure in violating a wounded, dying spear-woman, delighting in the knowledge that she was conquered at last, and at their mercy? Dane's arms tensed, muscles knotting at his wrists, and the cords cut into his skin.

Rianna . . . dead under the demon-stars of Belsar, her body thrown to the prowling scavengers of the night . . . he'd teach them to laugh! He'd teach them to fear Star Demons!

At his feet he could see, now, wavering black forms flickering in and out of darkness; the men of the raiding party, coming and going across his field of vision as they spread their blankets for the night; huddling together in the flapping wings of the firelight, hiding from the stars. A single man stood guard, spear at the ready, not too far from the fire. Somewhere out in the night, a rasha screamed at the kill.

Dane's arms swelled and strained, trying to force his wrists apart. His teeth clenched with effort, and his head was splitting, his eyes flickering in and out of focus—or was it the flicker of the fire? He realized dimly that part of it, at least, was the way his eyes were behaving. He must have concussion; first the blow he had taken escaping from the city, then Rhomda's spear, knocking him out.

He'd had concussion once before, the day before a karate tournament; he'd felt like this then, sick, dizzy, aching; he'd gone in and fought anyway. He hadn't won, but he'd made a good showing. He could do it again. *Rhomda's spear had*

*killed him, but he wasn't going to let a little thing like being
dead stop him, was he?*

Blackness hovered beyond the shifting firelight, making the
motionless form of the spearman dance against the gauze.
Part of Dane's brain knew he was not rational, and he
struggled to focus eyes and mind.

His nails were cutting into his palm. The ropes bit at his
wrists with little twisted teeth. The ghosts of all those he had
failed to protect were watching him reproachfully from the
shadows, Cliff-Climber's yellow eyes mocking him, Dallith's
brown eyes like those of a wounded fawn, the cool, practical
green eyes of Rianna somewhere in the darkness, her face
dyed to an even duskiness, making all of her but her eyes a
part of the shadow. Waiting for him, out there with Dallith
and Cliff-Climber. Killed protecting that damn kid. Another
score against Joda. He would get loose, and kill a few of
these barbarians to avenge her, and then he would go into
that darkness to join her, and Dallith. . . .

Dane blinked fiercely, the vision of Rianna's cool green
eyes fading back into the darkness with his flickering sight.
*Come on, Marsh, think! Use your brain, not your muscles!
Your muscles aren't in such good shape right now!* A little,
complaining voice inside his head said, *Neither is your brain.*
But he ignored that.

He forced his arms to relax, and wriggled his elbows down
the side of his body, to wedge them firmly against his rib
cage. *Leverage, that was the trick!* His fists clenched again,
and he twisted his arms outward, the ropes tearing into the
rigid, straining muscles, ignoring the pounding hell in his
head and the way the firelight made his vision blur and
flicker, going in and out of focus with the blink of the fire
and the pounding of the blood in his temples.

Then he felt a single strand break and pop. Another. He
stared at the rope between his fists, watching it stretch and
thin out, watching strands break and unravel. His head
pounded until he felt the blood must break out and splatter
the campfire, put out its flickering light. . . .

There was a loud *crack* and his hands flew apart. The
ropes around his chest came loose with a rush. The sentry,
leaning on his spear, snapped his head up, rushing at Dane
with lifted spear; but he had to turn aside in his rush to avoid
stepping on the sleeping bodies of the other men, and that
gave Dane a moment to roll away from the poised spear.

Then the sentry was looming over him in the flickering light, spear drawn back to stab.

Still fumbling with the rope, he rolled his hips, his right foot sweeping out to knock the spear aside. Gravel dug into his right shoulder as he curled on his side, body and arms tensing like a tightened spring. Then, uncoiling, his elbow digging into the ground, hurling his hips upward, he felt the jolt of impact all the way down his suddenly straightened left leg, all the way into his head. With a new jolt of pain, he saw the guard hanging doubled and gasping over his foot.

Rianna! One for you!

He kicked the man's feet out from under him, hurling him to the ground, realizing that it was probably wasted motion. He pulled himself free from the loops of rope and rolled to his feet. The sleepers were stirring, blinking in the wavering light, falling over one another as they fumbled for weapons.

The two nearest leveled their spears at Dane, but he pivoted and swayed to the right, slapping the nearest spear aside. *His sword! Where was his sword?* The spearman was between Dane and the other, and over his shoulder Dane saw the other man's face, winking in and out of focus as the swaying darkness shook firelight around him—or was it his own eyes? Dane's arm shot over the nearer man's shoulder like a striking cobra, toward the man's eyes. His fingers sank into wetness, and he heard the man scream, saw him lurch away somewhere into the darkness, hands to his eyes.

Dane whirled, throwing another naked man he never saw clearly, into the fire, with an extra, bone-breaking twist; there was a howl of pain, and the firelight blacked out, darkness came up and bounced. *Another one he could forget about.* He grabbed a loose spear and broke it across somebody's face. He threw away the pieces and stepped across the body, toward the others that were watching them, faces in the shadows of the cliff behind, ghost-faces, Cliff-Climber, Dallith, Rianna's clear green eyes somewhere, watching him. The men were spreading out, trying to surround him, but somewhere outside that circle was Rianna, and she was dead, dead and waiting for him in that darkness . . . his fists were hammers and his legs battering rams, and the men coming at him were naked, weapons snatched up awkwardly. They were easy to disarm, to fling aside, helpless. He never knew how many of them he killed, how many lay moaning, unable to rise. A spear thrust at him, a machete hissed toward his head. He caught the hand with the machete, hurled the swordsman

across the spearshaft. He punched, with a practiced snap of
his shoulders, a savage twisting punch across the heart. He
heard bones crack. . . . The spear-butt hammered Dane's
ribs. Bone bruised on tough wood as his arm blocked another spear, thrust it aside. He jumped over the body to face
the men who had killed Rianna, to crush them and shatter
them and leave them for the scavengers of the night as they
had left her. . . . In the flare of the firelight he saw their
heads swivel, focus on something behind and to the left of
them.

"The She-Demon," someone yelled, and then they were all
gone, running in panic, stampeding. He gaped after them,
turned to look. Rianna's ghost stood there, a flickering wraith
fading in and out of sight with the flicker of the fire. She had
come for him. No wonder they had run away. No doubt at
any moment, Dallith would appear beside her, and Cliff-
Climber . . . he waited for them to appear, but there was
only the blade of her knife, flickering in the firelight. She was
cutting Joda loose.

"Don't bother," Dane heard himself say stupidly, "He's still
alive, he can't come with us . . . where is Dallith?" Rianna
seemed not to hear. Of course she couldn't hear, she wasn't
there. Or was it because he hadn't spoken out loud at all?

"Dane, get your sword! Hurry! They'll be back soon!"

That made sense. *The sword of the Samurai is the soul of
the Samurai . . . life or death, it went where he did . . .*
where was Dallith? His head hurt, and something seemed to
have gotten into his eyes.

"Your *sword*," she said urgently, and pointed. "Over there,
by the fire!"

Dane saw the sheathed blade, lying where Master Rhomda
had placed it. He staggered toward it; stumbled; went down.

"Dane, what's the matter with you? *Hurry!*"

Joda's bonds fell away, and he sat up, hugging Rianna
close.

Why did she run to Joda instead of me? Dane hauled himself up to his knees, groggily, beside the sword. There was
blood on his fingers. He dropped his forehead to the ground
in the full ceremonial bow to the sword and then lifted it and
tucked the scabbard through his sash. The touch, the ritual,
steadied him.

*The sword of the Samurai is the soul of the Samurai, even
in death . . . snap out of it, Marsh, this is no time to go
nuts!*

"Dane!" He felt her hand on his arm. Warm, living flesh! Alive, not a ghost! "Are you all right?"

"Confused. Rhomda's spear knocked me out," he heard himself saying, and the world spun as he shook his head. He pulled himself stiffly to his feet, aware of bruises in his arms, hands, everywhere. He was one mass of aching muscle.

"Come on. They'll be back. They'll be more afraid to tell Master Rhomda they ran, than they are of ghosts—or rashas," she said practically. He followed her into darkness, hearing weird cooing cries in the jungle, like those he had heard after Dravash had killed the rasha. Paws moved in the bushes; he saw faint skeletal forms like shadow hounds.

The sky widened as they moved away from the cliff, and the ground around them grew plainer. Black clumps of trees were scattered here and there, but Rianna kept well away from these, the natural hunting-ground of the rashas. Starlight glittered icily from glassy outcrops of rock, but most of the land was furred with dark vegetation, underbrush and tall grass.

His head was splitting, and the ground did not seem to stay where it belonged; he kept stumbling, and his hands were shaking. How many men had he killed? Were those cooing things jackals?

"Where are Aratak and—" he almost said Dallith, and stopped himself. "And Dravash?"

"I don't know," she said, "They must have reached the bottom safely, but do you know how big this valley *is*? They could be anywhere down here."

"Did they—" Dane realized what he had been about to ask. But that was only a nightmare, seeing her killed, violated—he amended: "How did you get away from them?"

"I didn't," she said, "I went over the edge of the ledge! I ended up in the top of a tree; and when I found out where I was, I saw them carrying you and Joda down the trail. So I hung around outside the camp in the dark, hoping I could sneak in when they were all asleep and cut you loose." He could just see her mouth quirk in the darkness. "Then you broke your ropes and started all hell breaking loose."

They lay up for the night between two tilted, jagged slabs of glass, surrounded by thick scrub. Rianna still had her pack; she dug in and got emergency rations, sharing a packet with Joda, forcing Dane to eat.

"If they have your packs," Dane said grimly, "the fat's really in the fire. And they've got mine anyway. Rhomda

must have taken it off me when I was—in shock." He realized
he had started to say, *when I was killed.*

Her fingers moved over his head exploringly. She said, and
he heard her voice trembling, "That must have been some
crack on the head you took. Fortunately your head is too
hard to break."

"Yeah," he said, letting himself go limp in her arms, "but
they sure bent it out of shape."

"Lie down." She forced him back, laid her wadded spare
skirt under his head. Joda wedged himself tight against them.
Dane lay in Rianna's arms and shivered, and finally slept.

At dawn the sky overhead turned pale; a wash of rose-pink
crept slowly down the western cliff, while the bottom of the
gorge where they lay was still in shadow. Dane watched the
light, motionless, wondering where in all this enormous valley
Aratak and Dravash had found shelter. Joda slept the limp
unconscious sleep of the very young, nestled snugly in Rianna's arms, and Dane's mouth hardened as he watched her,
still sleeping, shift her body to accommodate the boy's weight
against her side. Joda wasn't all *that* young. Finally Belsar
peered over the eastern rim of the Gorge, splintering shards
of crimson light from the glassy layer in the cliff.

Dane reached out and touched Rianna's shoulder.

"We'd better go on."

The bottom of the Gorge was rough and broken, with
great slabs of glassy rock slanting out of the rich alluvial soil
that was thickly overgrown with reedlike grasses or tall,
heavy bushes thick with sharp thorns. In the morning it was
chilly, and they huddled their thin clothes about them, until,
near noon, the sun began to sweep across the canyon floor;
then they pulled spare clothes over their heads, baking and
sweltering.

Dane felt weak and dizzy as they moved through the blazing heat. His head hurt, and he knew he should be taking it
easy, but that was just too bad. His concussion would simply
have to look after itself. He wanted his head to stay on his
shoulders, addled or not.

Eroded islands of rock jutted from the canyon floor; flat-
roofed spires, inverted cones, pyramids, flat tablelands roofed
with the glittering glass, resting on dark walls of shale rock
and slate. Rianna was fascinated by the signs of the by-gone
cataclysm, pointed out the thick layers of sedimentary rock
under the layers of fused stone. She would have enjoyed it,
Dane knew, if they had not been hunted.

As it was, three times they had to hide in the thick underbrush, watching, while parties of men went by, searching for them. Nowhere, in that long afternoon, did they see any trace indicating that Aratak or Dravash had passed.

Sunlight crossed the canyon and crawled up the eastern cliffs. Belsar vanished behind the towering walls, and they looked for a place to camp. A fire would mark their position all too clearly for any pursuers; Rianna said so.

"Yet if we camp without a fire, it is all too much like opening up a—a tavern for rashas," Joda argued. "And if they believe we are all Star Demons—" he said it defiantly, "—they will keep away from our fire!"

"And a fire might draw Aratak and Dravash to us," Dane said, thinking aloud, then shook his head, and wished again that he hadn't. God, how he wished these people had developed aspirin!

"Too risky. I don't think Master Rhomda believes in Star Demons at all. Anyhow, he said he didn't believe I was one. And he walked right out into the night, stars and all. I don't want that man on my trail again."

Yet paradoxically he was glad he had not had to kill Rhomda. . . .

Rianna pointed. "We may not need a fire," she said. "Look." Against the pale face of the cliff there was a shallow cave-mouth, high up along a steep outcropped spire.

"I doubt like hell if a rasha could get up there," Dane said, "Let's go."

The cliff was weathered enough that Dane could scramble up easily, and Joda, clawing his way nimbly up behind him, hauled Rianna up after them.

The cave roof, what they could see of it in the last dim twilight, was a solid cap of glassy stone, the floor of the fine sandstone that formed, so Rianna said, in the bottom of shallow lakes. The bottom of the cap was, surprisingly, hung with what looked like small stalactites but Rianna told them, later, that they had been formed by gobs of the glassy stuff which had flowed, still molten, into pockets and crevices of the softer surrounding stone which had long since eroded away.

Dane looked down the cliff, satisfied. A rasha might, conceivably, scramble up if he was starving or desperate—but they'd hear it coming. They ate in the cave mouth watching the valley below them. Belsar had long vanished, but above them the light lingered. The sky slowly darkened, and the great eyes of the stars flashed out above them. Down here in the gorge there was no jungle to shelter them; if Rhomda brought his men down here, he'd really have to fight against their fear of Star Demons!

A long purring snarl announced that the night's hunting was about to begin. A fragment from a poem heard in a world long lost haunted Dane's memory—*Ye hear the call; good hunting all, that keep the Jungle Law* . . . but he had been prey himself; the old automatic excitement of the hunter was no longer in the words.

A rasha screamed in the jungle. He was still prey.

Somewhere in the valley floor a red star flashed. So Rhomda had managed to get his men down there after all.

Joda, exhausted with the long day's trudge and the final climb, had curled up near the back of the cave and fallen asleep. Rianna came and sat beside Dane in the cave mouth. Thank goodness, they were alone for once. Not that it would do them much good, in the shape his head was in.

She asked, "Could that be Dravash and Aratak?"

"Why should they kindle a fire? They wouldn't attract hunting rashas. More likely, it's Master Rhomda and his witch-hunters. No way to tell from here, though."

"Why not?" She brought out her telescope, and he recalled that she had salvaged her pack. It made him worry about his own pack, in Rhomda's hands. She pointed it, twisted it to focus. "I don't know, it doesn't look like—"

Her body stiffened; she dropped the telescope, with a gasp. Dane caught it before it could roll over the edge.

"What—"

"It's one of—of *them*," she gasped, almost babbling, "one of the white things, the things Vilkish F'Thansa saw before they disappeared—one of them, a white saurian, and men dressed like the natives of this planet—Dane, what *is* it? It was *white*!"

Dane already had the telescope trained on the distant campfire. While he struggled with the focus he thought he saw something, a fuzzy patch of whiteness, a ghostly moving form—but when he got it focused, it was gone. He could see, clearly, the flames and even the black logs of the campfire, tiny irregular bursts of light that confused the lens—the small scope was only a toy, he wished for a really good pair of night glasses! And around it the tiny shapes of men in pale-colored jackets, spreading their blankets for sleep. That was all.

"Did you see it, Dane?"

He shook his head. "Nothing but natives getting ready for bed. I don't think there was anything there. That light's pretty tricky, and it's not much of a lens."

"Damn it," Rianna snapped at him—or some invective that her translator disk made into *Damn it*—"I know what I saw, Dane! It was a protosaur about Aratak's size—but, I tell you, it was white, pure white! It was standing in front of a group of men and gesturing, as if it were lecturing—"

Doubtfully, Dane raised the glass and scanned the faraway camp again, without result. One man stood guard. The others were rolled in their blankets, under a stretched canvas stretched on poles.

"It had its arms out," she insisted, "as if it were lecturing. Or something."

He snorted laughter, not amused. "It sounds like the ghost of Saint A'assioo," he said. Rianna was a skilled observer and not likely to allow her imagination to make a blur into a giant saurian. Deliberately he unfocused the glass. Certainly there was no white blur there now, nothing resembling the ghostly blob he had seen. But on the other hand, a solid saurian Aratak's size, even a white one, couldn't have vanished into thin air. And there was no jungle around the camp— they, too, had been wary of tree-haunting rashas—and nothing but low grass and bush to obscure any such figure.

"Well, if it was there, it's certainly lying pretty low," he said, "but we'll have a look tomorrow at that campsite. Let's get some sleep."

He was glad for Joda, snoring softly at the back of the cave. He wanted to be close to Rianna, reassure himself again, after the recurring nightmares, that she was warm, alive, still with him. He drew her close to him, remembering with an ironic flicker—*just like a protosimian, basic instinct in the face of danger and death*—Well, why not? And he resolved that if Joda disturbed them right now he really would kick the kid's ribs in this time!

CHAPTER TWELVE

Dane woke with Joda's hand touching him in the dark. His head hurt, but not nearly so much, and his mind was clear; he was instantly awake, hearing below him, on the cliff, the scratching of claws on rock and a constant sniff-sniff-sniffing sound. He rolled out, sword in hand, while Joda waked Rianna, and stepped to the cliff edge.

The sheer drop below them was shadowed by the huge capstone which projected well beyond the eroded sandstone of the floor, so that only a part of the mass of stars could light it, dimly, compared to the glitter of the rocks around.

In that dimness something moved. A shadow, longer than a man, that *writhed*. The thing's claws scrabbled on the rocks, blended with the harsh snuffling sound as it smelled out their handholds on the stone. Now its scent rose, a sharp nastiness; and then that impossibly supple body twisted out from the cliff. A sharp, streamlined head, tiny hungry eyes that glowed in the starlight, for a moment, before the head whipped back into the dimness, dark fur blending with rock-shadows.

"A granth," Joda said, in a whisper.

With incredible speed the thing whipped its long body up the last few feet, curling itself away from the spot where they waited, dodging Joda's awkward spear-thrust as it hooked preposterously tiny forelegs over the cliff and, with a lightning arch of its back, was on them.

Dane had once seen a weasel loose in a henhouse. In speed and ferocity this thing was their equal; but it was eight feet long! It hurled itself at Joda with a hissing snarl, only to dart its head aside at the last moment to avoid impaling itself on the boy's spear. Tiny biting teeth clicked in the air near Joda's sleeve; it drew back on its haunches, like a snake coiling to strike, and suddenly that entire length of furred cable was shooting at Dane's throat.

His blade snapped down. The thing flexed back and Dane

144

suddenly knew how a cobra feels when a mongoose dodges its stroke. Rianna's spear grated on sandstone as the thing wove from side to side, and then the lean head darted in, little rat eyes gleaming. Dane lunged for an eye; managed to rake his point along the thing's head. It recoiled with a hissing shriek, and Joda's spear sank into its shoulder. Dane leaped in, hewing with his sword. The granth jerked itself off the spearpoint, weaving to one side, and the blow that was meant to shear off its head only tore a long flap of skin and meat from its side. Dane had to jump back to keep those teeth from his ankle.

But the three of them were working together now, Joda and Rianna driving with their spears from either side while Dane kept to the center. The thing gave ground and writhed away as Joda thrust in and ran on to Rianna's spearpoint. Its head lashed at her, and Dane's blade swept down; it twisted so the sword glanced from its skull and sheared off an ear.

God! Can that thing be killed at all?

Then Joda's spear drove cleanly into its side. With a hissing shriek it tore free from both spears, and Dane, watching in incredulous horror, thought it would charge them again; instead it jerked, howled and fell into the darkness below, almost pulling Rianna with it. Dane caught her arm as she swayed on the edge, hauling her back to safety; she collapsed and lay exhausted, clutching the sandstone floor.

In the brilliant starlight below the thing jerked and writhed like a huge snake, then, with a final paroxysm, lay still.

"We killed it," Joda whispered, "we killed a granth!"

"Actually," Dane said, "*you* killed it," and Joda stared, his jaw dropping.

"But, but, you don't understand. Killing a granth . . . and there were only three of us! And none of us are even wounded. . . ."

"I'm proud of you, Joda," Rianna said, rising to her knees, hugging the boy. *How about me,* Dane wondered, with an odd tightness in his chest, then was angry at himself. Hell, she was just encouraging the kid, and he needs it. *Yes,* he reminded himself, *and he deserves it, too.* He remembered Joda saying, the night he had first stolen out to watch the stars; *I'm a coward, a very great coward . . . my father says I am only fit to end my life in a rasha's belly, and no doubt he is right . . .*

"No one could have done better, Joda. I couldn't have killed it alone."

From the brush below came a long-drawn-out cooing sound. Others answered it from far away and drew closer.

Rianna glanced at the sky. "My watch. You two get some sleep."

Dane crawled back into his blankets. The cave stank of blood and the oddly disturbing smell of the granth. It reminded him, very remotely, of skunk. Granths, he remembered, were supposed to be fairly rare. They'd have to be, he thought, or protosimians would be *extremely* rare—or extinct! No wonder Joda was stunned at the thought that he had killed one.

The thing was so *damned* fast! And it had dodged their weapons with intelligence, he would swear . . . and suddenly he remembered the words of the men in the tavern, speaking of the mysterious white beast.

Faster than a rasha. Faster than a granth . . .

And suddenly, he shivered and moved closer to Joda in the darkness.

Dawn, and the stars fading into the sky. Dane looked over the edge, and saw, below, the clean-picked bones of the granth. Something that looked like a starved fox on stilts was still worrying a bone between surprisingly powerful teeth. Its fur was grayish black. Dane's foot turned a pebble on the ledge, and the thing's head swivelled almost all the way around on its shoulders; then, with a startled *Coo!* it scampered into the bushes and vanished. Well, now he knew what made those cooing noises at night!

A thin thread of smoke marked the fire they had seen the night before. Dane and Rianna scanned the site with the telescope, looking for some sign of the improbable apparition of the night before; but they saw only men, very ordinary looking men with dark skin and gray jackets, and one in the blue tunic of the Anka'an Order. That surprised him a little, until he thought about it. He and Rianna were disguised as natives, their skins and hair darkened to pass without comment. It was the logical way to proceed. But then, why were the white saurians not darkened, as Aratak was?

And surely the disguise of an Anka'an spearman must be one of the most difficult to maintain. Surely they had their own secret signs and passwords of recognition! Could "demons from the stars" corrupt or suborn a *real* Anka'an spearman, he wondered? Or—he shuddered, recalling the

Hunters, who were shape-changers—kill one, and go around inside his body and brain?

They watched the men break camp and march off across the gorge toward the river. Carefully marking the route of the other party, Rianna and Joda descended from the cave to the thick brush below. Joda went to the clean bones of the granth and wrenched out a long, sharp tooth, prying it loose with his knife and surveying it proudly. It was bluish-white and faintly luminous.

He urged Dane and Rianna each to take one, too.

"It is proof you are a worthy hunter," he urged, "No one would ever believe I had been at the kill of a granth unless I had the tooth to show!"

Rianna smiled. "It's your granth, Joda. You take the tooth," but he said, "Every spear who is in at the kill is entitled to a tooth—" and finally, indulging him, Rianna took the tooth he wrenched loose for her, and tucked it into her pack. Dane realized that the kid was entitled to strut a little, it would be good for him, but he brusquely refused to take a tooth himself, until it suddenly occurred to him that no one might ever believe there had been such an animal, that he might, some day, come to forget the thing's size and ferocity himself. A granth was a hard animal to believe in.

Rianna looked at the cliff above them. "I wish there was some way we could leave a message for Aratak and Dravash, if they should come that way—"

"Why don't we leave them a note?" Dane asked, and Rianna stared. "You don't happen to have a scriber or voice-writer tucked into your pack, in defiance of regulations?" she asked, sarcasm heavy in her voice.

Now it was his turn to stare. "Hell! I don't even have a pack! But we could scratch a few words in sandstone," he said. "It's soft enough that the point of Joda's knife there would leave marks."

She said, "You mean your people are *that* primitive? I thought that was an art contemporary with flint-chipping!"

"It's a useful art," Dane said, "Don't your people write *at all*?"

"No," she said, "A scriber or voice-writer is much handier, and even if I had one, a portable model wouldn't imprint a symbol in the sandstone there!"

Dane snorted. "Then, I suppose, it's up to the primitive! Give me your knife. I can just about remember the ideogram for 'Sapient being.' That ought to draw their attention. I can write my name in my own script and make some kind of scratch figure for my sword."

By the time he had scratched the emblem for "Sapient being" on the rock, she got the idea and began to trace a couple of Universal ideograms on the rock with her finger for him to copy. The final message read, "Marsh, Rianna, friend safe. Off-planet white saurian sighted, investigating. Rendezvous."

"Let's hope the white critters don't read Universal," she said, "which is why I didn't put in any directions for finding us. Whether they do or not, there are probably Kirgon on this planet—and *they* do."

Then they set off through the thick bushes; tiny, blue-furred monkeys played among the purple leaves, and tiny birds, even smaller than hummingbirds, skimmed above the bushes. A huge insect, the size of a swallow, dived out of the sky, grappled with a tiny bird and fell with it into the underbrush.

At a distance they saw a herd of something like wild cows. Dane knew nothing about them; but, remembering the reputation of the Cape Buffalo, kept well away. And once he'd been treed by a Holstein bull and knew even tame cattle could be dangerous.

They had no trouble finding the abandoned campsite. The rich alluvial soil took footprints perfectly, and the trail of a dozen native sandals was so clear that even Rianna could make it out; a mound of moist earth had been tamped over the fire, and long depressions in the grass showed where the men had slept. Dane stopped Rianna and Joda outside the camp and moved in to study the prints.

He searched carefully among the muddled prints of men—then, off to one side and perfectly clear in the damp soil, purple grass crushed beneath them, a clear set of deeply-embedded saurian feet.

He hunkered down and stared. The tracks were in soft turf; they walked in, rough crescents that began and ended abruptly. They did not go anywhere. They did not *come from* anywhere.

Dane felt the hair on his neck rise and prickle. The toes showed direction clearly enough. Those two prints, side by side, clearly showed the start of the trail, unless the thing had walked backward, and he didn't think any ordinary saurian could balance doing that. Aratak couldn't. It had taken two, three, five paces forward, turned to the left . . . no, to its

own right . . . stood there, facing a mass of smaller san-
dalled feet . . . the prints there were more deeply embedded,
and somewhat smudged at the edges as if the creature had
shifted its weight more than once. Then another stride, a turn
to the right, and then. . . .

And then the tracks stopped. Right there, it had *vanished*.
Or had sprouted wings and suddenly flown away. Or had
turned on an anti-gravity belt—that wasn't any sillier than any
of the other assumptions—and stopped weighing down
enough to leave footprints.

Could it have stepped into a vehicle? No. Anything big
enough to hold a saurian Aratak's size, or larger, would have
had to leave some kind of marks—wheels, or tires, or rollers,
or drag-marks. Could it have stepped up into some kind of
hovering craft, without moving its feet, or leaving a mark
where it had stepped aboard? Even a hovercraft would have
flattened the grass underneath.

A flying carpet, maybe? Dane felt tired and his head
started to ache again.

He called Rianna over and showed the prints. She was as
puzzled as he was.

"It looks like the magic of the Blessed Ones, that they tell
about," Joda said. "But they're only a myth!"

"Looks like whatever made those prints is a myth," Dane
said grimly, "but it either vanished into air, or else it's still
standing there in its tracks, invisible, watching us."

Rianna shivered. *"Don't!"*

But Dane walked over to the prints and moved his hands
through the empty space over them. He knew it was ridiculous, but so was everything else connected with that nonexis-
tent white saurian.

*Everybody who's seen it, like those poor devils at the Unity
Base, has vanished into thin air, and never been heard of
again!*

"There must have been some form of aircraft," Rianna
said, but Dane shook his head. "Impossible. We'd have seen
it."

"Not if it was running without lights. It could have left the
camp when I dropped the telescope and been well away by
the time you got it focused again."

That made sense, but Dane, remembering the white blur he
had seen during the focusing process, was not comforted. The
Unity personnel had all vanished. Every one of them.

Taken by something that could get through a Third Level forcefield.

Suddenly a faint buzzing sound reverberated . . . Dane switched his head round impatiently, trying to find out where it was coming from. A strange, crackling, buzzing sound that seemed to be inside his head. . . .

"The communicator!" Rianna said, and fumbled among the tangle of amulets and trinkets she still wore, in a thick mass, at her throat. With a sigh of relief and a sheepish grin, Dane sorted through his own layers of junk jewelry until he found the small disk and snapped it on; heard it buzzing in his throat disk;

Rianna? Dane? Aratak. I am here, where you left your message. . . . Well is it written that in the diversity of Creation we may find endless resources which would never have occurred to us . . . for which saying I apologize to Dravash, who I suppose, has already rejoined you . . .

"Dravash? No," said Rianna, troubled, "we thought he was with you . . ." and Dane could hear her voice reverberating through the disk in his throat, too, eerie multiple layers of communication. Aratak's voice came again:

If he survives, which now I fear is unlikely, he would be troubled at the thought of using our communicators; he forbade me twice to attempt it while we were together. I fear we must maintain radio silence as he demanded. Further, he would demand we change our position at once, so you should not wait for me there. Will you rejoin me at the cave?

"Halfway," Dane said with a quick squint at the sun, "Walk straight along the line formed by your shadow and we'll meet you in an hour or two. Radio out, then. Good luck, Aratak."

"The Divine. . . ."

And the communicator went off. Dead, silent in mid-proverb, and Dane shook it, staring, but it was wholly dead, useless, as the communicators on the Unity Base had been. He had the eerie sense that some invisible hand had reached past him and turned off the switch; he tested it again but could not hear the sound he made even in his own throat disk, and finally he switched the almost-invisible button to the "off" position. Rianna was still staring at her own, stupefied. She said in a whisper "Like the ones on the Unity Base . . ." And Dane knew she was following his own thoughts.

Rianna said, "Aratak would never stop in mid-proverb; not even Dravash could make him do that."

Joda was staring at them. He said, "Whom are you talking to?" and Dane realized that without a throat disk, without that inbuilt translator, all the kid would have heard would have been Rianna, talking into a small amulet! No wonder he was confused.

Joda put an arm around Rianna and said, "You are troubled, Lady Mistress? Don't be afraid, I will protect you—I, Joda granth-slayer!"

Dane concealed a snort of irritable laughter. Killing that miserable overgrown rodent had certainly made a change in the kid! Dane wondered if he didn't like him better as a coward! And it didn't help that Rianna stood quietly in his arm, snuggled against Joda. She said, "I'm not afraid of anything right now, *zabav*, but I know I can trust you to protect me if I need it." She added, and Dane had the sudden galling thought that she was doing it dutifully, not to hurt his, Dane's, feelings:

"Between you and Dane, I wouldn't have anything at all to worry about if I ever should need protection."

"But what has happened? You were talking at that strange amulet—"

"Oh, God," Dane said, cutting off her beginning explanation of radio, "You can complete his education some other time! I want to get out of here, and at least, now, we know that Aratak is alive!"

"I rejoice to know that the Venerable survives," Joda said, "but you knew it through that amulet? Is it then like the buzzers little children make of *riknelli* shells, without the gut-string to connect their voices?"

"Something like that, yes," Rianna said, slashing a proud, startled look at Dane, and he nodded grudging approval. The kid was bright. Judging by the way he picked up even a smattering of scientific analogies and worked from them, he might even be a genius, anywhere off this godforsaken world.

But he wished Rianna would keep the kid's hands off her! Maternal solicitude, he thought sourly, went just so far . . . and if Joda was a granth-slayer he was a lot too big for sitting in her lap or being babied!

Was it even maternal?

Who knows, maybe to her the kid is handsome!

"We'd better back-track," he said, sighting along the sun-line he had suggested to Aratak, "That way. . . ."

"But if you follow the sun," Joda said contemptuously,

"you will end by walking in circles as it moves overhead! Any tracker old enough to carry a child's spear knows that!"

"We won't be doing it long enough for that," Dane snapped. "Do what I tell you!"

Rianna put her arm around Joda as they walked, talking to him in a low voice, the communicator in her hand; Dane supposed she was explaining radio to him in words of one syllable. Well, better her than me, but what is going to happen to the kid after this, when she has to drop him back into his village culture?

It was not more than half an hour before they saw a huge, dark shadow, moving slowly through the bushes. Rianna hurried toward him; Dane followed almost as quickly.

"Aratak!" she cried out, and hugged the huge, leathery body; he closed his claws, with exquisite delicacy, on her face, wrapping her in an enormous hug.

"I rejoice to see you, dear friend," he rumbled, put her down and treated Dane to the same enormous hug. "For the thought of being abandoned alone on this desolation of rock even the Divine Egg could offer little philosophy, except that sore trials come alike to good and evil men, and that was small comfort."

"We killed a granth," Joda informed him proudly, and Aratak rumbled approval. "I know not what a granth may be, but no doubt, like many other of the forms of life here, it richly deserved killing. Rarely have I seen a world with so many inimical forms of being whose uses to the Cosmic All elude my perceptions! No doubt the—the Divine Forces," he amended, with a glance at Joda, "displayed their own unfathomable purposes in creating the rasha, the granth, and the infernally created bovine creatures by whose stampede Dravash and I were separated; but that purpose is one I cannot, for all my philosophy follow."

"Perhaps, Venerable—" Joda said, with a soft respect which reminded Dane, suddenly and tellingly, that Joda, like Master Prithvai, had grown up in a culture which took the protosaurian First People wholly for granted in a way Dane or even Rianna could never do, "—the beings in question were created by the Blessed Ones in order that we Second People should never grow complacent or lazy. Or so the Wise Ones in my home village said to me and my companions when we were small."

"It may well be, small brother," said Aratak kindly, but Dane interrupted—the last thing he wanted was for Aratak to go off on a philosophical lecture, and he sounded all set for one; and Dane wanted facts. "Tell us what happened to you! We had hoped to catch up to you and Dravash at the bottom of the ravine. . . ."

"And we had intended to wait there," Aratak said, "but our space was invaded by a herd of some cowlike creatures, stampeding—I can only assume that something had frightened them, for I heard one of them bellowing. Perhaps it had been seized by the first rasha of the night, but I did not hear the cry of any rasha. In any case, when they stampeded, I was forced to climb some rocks in most un-philosophical haste; and though I believed Dravash immediately behind me, when the creature had gone I found no trace of him. I sought him and called for him—I even risked using my communicator, but it would not operate; I cannot imagine by what freak of sound or magnetism it operated for a moment when we communicated a little while ago. Then the dark descended while I still sought Dravash; and I was forced to find shelter in a cleft rock where I could see any prowling rasha. One of them scented me, but did not attack, knowing I was not edible; for which I was grateful, having no weapon; I lost my spear in the stampede and found only fragments afterward. When daylight came I began to look for landmarks where we might rendezvous, and found the cave where you had left your ingenious message. And the rest you know."

"Did you see a fire in the night?" Rianna asked. "Or—or anything?"

"I saw the fire," Aratak admitted, "and came near to approaching it, wondering if it might not be *your* fire. But as I approached, I saw many forms and knew it was either your pursuers—or something else. So I returned to my hiding place."

There was no point, Dane knew, in asking if he had seen a giant white saurian. Protosaurian eyesight was not all that much better than human; on the contrary. But Rianna knew what Dane wanted to ask, and after a moment of thought she asked, "Did you see any trace at all of—of what might have been an aircraft of some sort? A hovercraft, perhaps, running without lights?"

"No, nothing of that kind." Aratak's eye-ridges twitched, as they did whenever he was perplexed. "Why do you ask, dear friend?"

She sighed. "No reason," she said, "there probably wasn't

one." She looked, troubled, at Dane, and he heard her whisper into the throat disk, hardly more than subvocalizing, *did I really see anything?* Dane had been wondering about that himself. After all, when he thought he had seen something, he had still been suffering the after effects of concussion and shock.....

But if we *both* thought we saw it? What was it that we both didn't see? Suddenly the skin on the back of Dane's neck prickled. Everyone who *had* seen the thing, had vanished—were they too going to vanish, snatched into nowhere?

Was that what had already happened to Dravash?

CHAPTER THIRTEEN

While Aratak told his story, the sunlight had moved across the canyon floor as Belsar made a perceptible arc in the sky; Dane said, "We'd better move along," and they began to travel again. When they paused for a bite of food, Rianna said to Dane in an undertone, "Our food's running out. After this, we'll have to hunt."

"Shouldn't be hard to find something edible," Dane said. And indeed, the floor of the Great Gorge was abounding with game, none of which seemed particularly wild; either it was too difficult of access for most hunting parties, or most likely, the combinations of rashas, the occasional granth and the herds of wild cow-creatures like Cape Buffalo, kept hunters from coming here very often. "Those little rabbit things ought to be pretty good eating."

Rianna nodded. "And Joda says the small things like deer—the harlik," she used the native word, and Dane knew she meant the medium ruminants he would have called gazelle or antelope, "are a highly prized delicacy; some farmers even raise them for meat. But techniques of hunting must be highly specialized; remember that throwing a spear is a kind of ultimate taboo here, so you'd almost have to run it down, and they're a lot faster than anything *I'd* want to chase!"

"Aratak has it easy," Dane said, watching the giant saurian complacently munching on a huge, six-inch thing like a flying termite, and Rianna chuckled. "Still, I do not think you or I would care for his meal."

"No," Dane admitted, "but he can catch food the way you or I could if ham sandwiches grew on every bush."

Joda heard that, and said, "In my village the children are told a story of a wonderful underground where boiled-milk sweets grow on every tree like greenberries."

As they strolled on, Dane found himself whistling, and after a moment, amused at himself, put words to the half-forgotten tune he was whistling:

"Where the bluebird sings,
    at the lemonade springs,
By the Big Rock Candy Mountain!

At the Big Rock Candy Mountain
The cops have wooden legs,
The bulldogs all have rubber teeth
And the hens lay hard-boiled eggs,
The village pumps all run with beer,
And the trees grow bread and honey . . ."

There was a line in that somewhere about a ham-sandwich bush, too, he was sure, but he couldn't remember it.

They finished the last of their emergency rations late that evening, and camped on the shores of the inner gorge, the steep-walled bed of the Mahanga which flowed through the center of the Great Gorge. At the bottom, white water frothed with a savage roar of rapids. Rocks were like fangs in the broad water.

"How in *hell*," Dane asked, "are we going to get across that?"

"I had hoped we could rendezvous with Dravash before we crossed," Aratak said, "Once across the Mahanga, there is wider territory in which to become separated. I suppose, in the last emergency, we could attempt to communicate with Farspeaker, to make certain whether he still lives. . . ."

Dane thought, grimly, *Better you than me.* There were not many things he was afraid of, but Dravash's albino companion was one of them, and the thought of trying to re-establish that revolting telepathic contact—which, he reminded himself firmly, was just as revolting to the Farspeaker as it was to Dane—was one of the things he didn't mind admitting he was afraid of.

"I do not believe it has reached that state of emergency yet," Aratak said, looking down into the boiling rapids, "but we cannot cross here, even I could not assay those rapids in safety, and none of you little people could even attempt it." And Dane had to admit, much as he hated to, that the giant saurian was right. Nothing human could live in that boiling water.

Rianna said, "Let's walk upstream. If Dravash is still alive, he'll have to look for a place to ford the Mahanga too and if there's a really workable ford, he'll have to cross there; and he'd know we'd be looking for a ford which we protosimians, could handle. I'm sure the Captain has enough sense to think of that very elementary precaution."

So all the next day they walked upstream along the banks of the Mahanga, meeting no dangers except a stray rasha whose neck Aratak broke before Dane could get out his sword. Dane was thinking; if there's a *known* ford here, that hunting party looking for us will be looking for it, too. In fact, they might try to ambush us at the ford. . . .

But they did not, in that day's walking or the next, find a really workable ford, and at last they compromised on a narrow stretch of water which looked passable; they could waste a long time hunting for a ford, and every day the wasted meant more chance that the party headed by Rhomda would come up with them.

Or the *other* party, the one with the mysterious white saurian with it. . . .

If there was any white saurian at all, and it wasn't a hallucination or a boojum. . . .

"I think we can make it," Dane said, and Aratak nodded, then looked at Rianna and Joda. "But can *they?*"

Dane drew a long breath. "We'll have to try. We'll put them between us."

Rianna said, "Dane, I'm almost as strong as you are. If you can make it, I can make it!"

"Strong? Maybe," Dane said, looking at the rush of water, "but you haven't the weight, and neither has the kid." Then he was annoyed with himself; why was he worrying about Joda? The brat made it abundantly clear that he considered himself quite able to take care of himself in anything that might happen. *That granth's tooth certainly worked magic on him. I wish I believed in it that much. . . .*

"Are you afraid to cross the ford?" Joda asked, with a cocky lift of his dark brow, "I shall cross and protect my Lady Mistress as well!"

"Not afraid," Dane said, scowling, "trying to figure out how to get you and Rianna across without getting you drowned or smashed to pieces on the rocks."

Small loss. If anything, the damn brat got on his nerves a lot worse as a winner than he did as a loser! Joda the granth-slayer was even harder to take than Joda the great coward!

He muttered something like this to Rianna and she flared, "You would rather despise him, wouldn't you?"

"You don't need to be afraid for me," Joda said, "If you can cross the torrent down there, I can follow!"

Dane tried to make his voice reasonable. "I'm not doubting your bravery, damn it! But I could pick you up with one hand; you don't weigh much more than half what I do, and the river isn't going to give you a chance to take your spear to it! It won't ask whether you're brave or not, just whether you have the weight to stand up against it!"

"We will rope up to each other," Aratak said, taking a light, strong length of line out of the pack, and Dane nodded.

"You go first and anchor us all, and I'll come at the end, and pick up anyone who gets swept off their feet," he said, and braced himself as Aratak stepped in; Joda was instantly knocked down and battered, and Aratak stooped and picked him up. He struggled and protested, but the noise of the water drowned out the sound, and Rianna signaled to him to be quiet and let Aratak carry him. She clung to Dane as they stepped in, and Dane felt the blind insensate force of the water seize his ankles. It was ice-cold; he gasped, his arm around Rianna, and felt the current struggling to take them, as they stepped in further, going in up to their thighs.

Clinging to one another, they could feel the river trying to take them, hurl them upon the frothing fangs downstream. Dane felt one foot slip on slimy rock, struggled for footing, and then Aratak was there, his great bulk steadying them all against the battering water; Joda in his arms, while Dane and Rianna clung to him, no longer feeling the slightest false pride about it. The river was their enemy and Aratak was the only one of them with the weight to stand, like a rock in mid-stream, fighting the current. In the deepest part Dane's

feet went out from under him and only Aratak's grip on his
belt kept him from being hurled away from the others,
smashed on the rocks; Rianna was clinging for dear life to
Aratak's free forelimb; he had Joda clinging round his neck
like a small monkey. As they came up the far bank out of
the boiling, swirling water, Aratak's foot slid on a stone; he
flung Joda to safety on the far bank, the boy landing
sprawled, but safely out of the water, the breath knocked out
of him. Then they were all floundering in the water, Rianna
rolling over and clinging to a rock, Dane half stunned. The
water filled nose and eyes and mouth, as he scrabbled, felt
Aratak grab him painfully, claws grinding into his bare shoulder, haul him hard up the mud and stones. He shouted with
pain—he couldn't help it—as the claws scraped skin from his
arm and shoulder, and lay coughing and spluttering water
from his lungs while Aratak scooped Rianna off the boulder
where she clung.

Even Aratak lay exhausted on the bank for a long time,
gasping, unable to move. Rianna had an assortment of rapidly darkening bruises on her thighs, and Dane had lost a
few inches of skin from one shinbone on rough rock, as well
as the long, bleeding scratches where Aratak's claws had met
in his shoulder. Aratak, when he finally could move and
speak again, looked in consternation at the blood he had
drawn.

"My dear friend, did I unfortunately do that to you?"

"Better you than the river," Dane said, wincing as Rianna
smeared some stuff from her medical kit on the skinned shinbone, and for once Aratak could not match or better it with
a saying of the Divine Egg.

"The way our luck's been running," Rianna said wryly,
"We should have gone downstream instead of upstream and
there's probably a good wide ford and maybe even a bridge."

Dane quirked his mouth in a grin. "And Master Rhomda
with twelve spearmen waiting in the middle of it. Anyway,
we're across. I hope Dravash made it."

If, he thought, *Dravash is still alive and hasn't met up with
a granth or that white protosaurian thing!*

"The Divine Egg has wisely remarked," Aratak said, "that
any adventure which one survives is a fortunate adventure.
Do not impugn the quality of our luck, Rianna; it seems to
me we have been singularly fortunate." He reached out and
delicately caught a buzzing insect in mid-air and began to
crunch it. Joda, who had had the breath knocked out of him,

but had recovered quickly, was scaling the walls of the inner gorge, and waved, calling to Rianna.

"Here is a greenberry tree, Lady Mistress, we will not go supperless to bed."

Dane, filling his stomach with the tasteless greenberries, still thought he would prefer something more solid to eat. Tomorrow he'd have a try at catching one of the little rabbit-like things. Even if he had to hide in the long grass and make a noise like a carrot.

For four or five days, then, they tramped through the thick brush toward the black-and-red wall that shut off the sky. Dane had hoped they would leave pursuit behind on the other side of the Mahanga, but no such luck; once they had to hide in the brush, Aratak lying full length beside them, and watch Master Rhomda jog past with sixteen men at his back.

For some reason, the groves of trees were closer together this side of the river, but they were able to stay well away from them; they saw rashas several times, but the big cats were afraid to attack in the open, daunted perhaps by Aratak's great bulk; the beasts would stalk toward them, snarling through the grass, then turn away again and slink between the trees of the nearest grove. Joda stumbled into a covey of nesting birds, managed to grab one and break its neck, and they had roast not-quite-partridge that night for supper; it was delicious. They found a huge fumbling bird, like a bustard, which could not fly, and Joda, waving to Rianna to circle around ahead of it and head it back toward him—the birds were evidently incredibly stupid—speared it through the wishbone, which, Dane thought, must have been the size of a turkey's. Dane wondered how anything so enormous and edible had managed to survive when it was that stupid, but when they cooked the bird he found out; the flesh was oily and rancid, and only sharp hunger made it edible at all. Joda told him that even the rashas would not eat the creatures unless they were desperate, old and toothless and too slow to strike down anything else.

But it made a meal better than raw bug, and they could carry some of the meat in their packs for emergencies, smoked and partly dried over a campfire. They found bird's eggs, too. Joda ate them raw, but Dane and Rianna fried them on a flat stone.

Before them stone filled the sky, rising higher and higher, all black and mottled gray at the base. Looking up, they could still see the pale streak of crystal above them, the glass band, water-pale, under the sunset colored pastel of the sandstone just above it.

But there was a break in that wall, toward which they had been steering for days, and as the sky vanished from in front of them, the faintly green-tinged crack opened out into a steep gorge, down which water skipped, silver and flashing, over an irregular staircase of waterfall, while trees hung above the spray like green clouds.

Dane inspected it with the telescope and frowned at Aratak. If there was any path in the far canyon wall which the giant saurian could get up, it was probably here; but the bush and vegetation made it hard to see, from the bottom, just how rough the climb would be; and the bottom of the waterfall gorge was blocked by a great cluster of trees. With rashas in them, of course, like balls on a Christmas tree. Well, at least they would be out of the sun for a change. Dane, with his skin darkened, didn't sunburn, but the glare gave him a constant headache, and he'd be glad to get into the shade.

But, once inside, it would be raining cats on them. Not dogs, just cats.

Out here on the grassland at the bottom of the Great Gorge they'd caught glimpses of another great cat, a lion-sized animal with vaguely purplish fur, but it hadn't shown the slightest interest in them, even when they almost stumbled over it, feeding on the fresh-killed corpse of one of the big buffalo-like animals; it raised its head with an odd roaring snarl, but made no attack. Joda had a name for the cat, but said it had never been known to attack any human unprovoked. And down here its natural prey was evidently easily come by.

Here at the foot of the waterfall gorge several streams flowed, making their way leisurely across the grasslands to the Mahanga. Aratak knelt beside one of them, trying to find some real fish in its depths . . . far too many of the swimmers were small mammals, like miniature seals, or small furred whales about six inches long, and Aratak would not eat any warm-blooded creature. He was as nauseated at the sight of blood as Dane and Rianna were by the thought of chomping up flies; he had shuddered and virtually retched when they plucked and eviscerated the bird, and averted his eyes as at an obscenity when they cracked and ate the eggs—Dane imagined that he, being from an egg-laying species, had the same revulsion toward eating eggs that Dane would have had toward killing and skinning a baby gorilla.

Leave to others their Otherness. . . . At least Aratak hadn't minded when *they* ate the eggs, though Dane had a shrewd suspicion that if there had been plenty of other food available, Aratak might have protested.

Along the wide grasslands, Dane spotted a small herd, six or eight of the antelope-like harlik, quietly grazing.

"Look," Joda whispered, pointing. "One of them will feed us for several days, I will go there and hide in the underbrush, with my spear. Lady Mistress, you circle around—" he gestured with his arm, "—and drive them in this direction." She nodded and made off, but when Dane would have followed, he shook his head.

"No. Two will stampede them and they will scatter too much. Stay here with the Venerable One."

He crept off, running as noiselessly as a rasha, and Dane watched, feeling an odd disgruntlement. Joda's hunting skills had fed them all for several days. Evidently the taboo against throwing a spear, extending even to hunting, had forced the natives to develop incredible skill at tracking and running down game. He watched as the boy found a place in the long grass, flattened himself in it so skillfully that even Dane's sharp eyes could not see that there was anyone there. Rianna circled behind the herd, making no effort to hide herself; the lead beast caught her scent, throwing up a horned head, and they began to move uneasily downwind, in the direction of the grass where Joda lay. She yelled and waved her arms, and they broke into a run; Joda leaped up from the grass and his spear flashed in the sunlight. A large harlik fell, pierced to the heart at the blow; the others stampeded in a rush of flying tails, and Joda rose out of the underbrush, bent over the bawling, struggling animal, and cut its throat with a single merciful stroke. He called jubilantly to Rianna to come help carry the carcass back to their camp; she ran toward him, laughing, and as she came he flung his arms around her, hugging her hard.

Dane, watching, saw that the embrace was not the swift comradely one Rianna had given him before; the boy prolonged it, holding her, thrusting his body against hers; and Rianna, laughing, exhilarated, allowed it. Then, still clasped close to Joda, she raised her head with a peremptory call.

"Dane! Come and help us carry this here!" She added,

laughing, as he waved assent, "After all, we've done all the real work!"

Stung, angry, fighting an ignoble surge of jealous rage, Dane went toward them. *That goes a good long way beyond encouraging the kid, or building his confidence,* he thought.

Underfoot the ground was tufted with years of rough grass-growth and underbrush, lumpy and ridged; Dane stumbled for a footing, and almost at his feet, a covey of small birds stirred, the delicious small fowl-like patridges that they had roasted a night or two before. Dane grabbed at one as it fluttered, but it evaded his hand; without stopping to think, he reached down, grabbed up a stone and, taking quick aim, flung it. The bird fluttered, fell in a squawking heap at his feet. He wrung its neck, feeling that somehow, now, he had redeemed himself.

"Here," he said to Rianna, as he came up to them. "Now I've done my share too; we can roast this one for tonight and dry the harlik meat to carry with us up on the plateau. It will last better that way."

But Joda was staring at him, his mouth open in shock and disapproval. After a long moment, he said, "But I—I thought you people were *civilized! You threw a stone at it!*" There was dismay and shock in his voice, and he even broke away from Rianna, standing and looking at her in consternation, as if he had seen her, too, commit an atrocity. And Dane, too, late remembered the planet-wide taboo against a thrown spear, a hunting arrow . . . even a thrown stone!

"Dane!" Rianna said sharply, "How could you!" In their own language, so low that Joda could not hear, that Dane could hear only through the vibration of the translator disk in his throat, she said quickly, "Do you know you may have undone all I have done, for his loyalty? Don't you know that is their greatest cultural taboo?"

Dane said aloud, defensively, "We are not among the people who observe that taboo, Rianna. Joda knows we are not of his people; you told him. Surely he is reasonable enough to understand that in a universe of so many people, different people have different laws, and this is not one of ours." He spoke, looking at Joda, as near to an apology as he could make it. "I simply forgot the laws here, Joda. I am sorry if I offended you. It isn't our law, but I've tried to keep it. Is it so important, out here where none of your people except you, who understand us, will see and be offended?"

He could see that Joda was struggling with that, and told

himself, *yes, I did a damnfool thing, but the kid is bright enough to understand!*

Joda said, and there seemed to be real distress in his voice, "I thought . . . civilized behavior . . . I did not think you were the kind of man to throw his spear!" Blinking, troubled, he turned his back on them and walked away.

Dane bent to hoist the carcass of the harlik on his shoulder. Rianna turned on him in dismay and wrath, "Dane, how could you? How *could* you?"

Dane said soberly, "I forgot, Rianna. That's the truth; I saw the bird and I reacted. You talk about his cultural instincts; have you forgotten that I have them too?" His own anger surged up again. Hell, he'd apologized, he'd just about *crawled* to the kid! "I told him I was sorry; I tried to explain. But sooner or later he's got to know that everybody in this whole big universe doesn't live by his own narrow-minded little village taboos, and if he's smart enough to accept the Galactic concept he's smart enough to live with that, too!"

"Just the same, I wanted to take one step at a time! And you pull a stupid trick like that!" She was looking at him in a rage, the temper he knew so well from more than a year of living together, flaming as it seldom did. "You may have wrecked all my work!"

"Work be damned," he flung at her, turning around to face her, the harlik carcass on his shoulder shifting weight, and she tossed her head and said in disgust, "Oh, what is the use of trying to make you understand? You are not trained as a scientist; I do not suppose you can understand the very first principles, which are to do no violence—*never*—to a planet's cultural perceptions! But I cannot expect you to know anything—anything at all!" she repeated wrathfully, "about a scientist's work!"

Stung, angry, Dane retorted, "Damn it, go hungry then! I thought I was contributing something valuable!"

"If we had had nothing to eat for several days and you were actually starving," Rianna retorted with stinging emphasis, "I might have condoned it. Can you deny you were just trying to beat Joda at his own game because he can hunt, here, and you can't?"

Damn it, that's hitting below the belt! I wasn't going to carry the argument on to those grounds at all, but she started it! He flung back at her, "And for all your talk about scientific principles, do you think I didn't see the way the kid was acting—and you, too? Holding you like that, kissing you—"

"And what if he was?" she flung back at him furiously, her eyes blazing. "Do you think that because I join myself to you with pleasure that you have owner's rights in my body, or that it is not mine to do with as I will? You are mistaken in what you think you saw, Dane," she added more reasonably, "It's his age, that is all, he has spent his entire life isolated from everyone, despised as a coward, and now he is successful, he is a granth-slayer, he is accepted and even liked—and he has suddenly become aware that I, his spear-master, am a woman too. It would be unreasonable to be angry about that; he is a boy in his first awareness of manhood. It means nothing to me, Dane; why do you have to be jealous and spoil it?"

They were approaching the camp, and Aratak, hearing their quarreling voices, raised his head in mild dismay, stared at them, then, with a philosopher's shrug, turned his back and tactfully went off to catch flies. Dane had known him long enough to know that the Divine Egg probably had a proverb about the fruitlessness of mixing into the quarrels of protosimians and their mates. The thought gave him a moment's rueful pause.

But the thought of Rianna crushed in Joda's strong, exuberant young arms, her face flushed with excitement, made him angry again. He retorted, "*Now* who is rationalizing and covering the truth with easy talk about scientific principles? If you want the boy, I can't stop you—but I don't think much of your taste! A savage from a world who thinks all of us are Star Demons!"

"And who are *you*," she retorted at white heat, "to be talking about barbarians or savages?" Then, suddenly hearing herself, through her anger, she stopped and stared at him with her mouth open; but Dane did not see. He dumped the harlik carcass on the ground and bent over it—tight-lipped. He said, "We'd better get this skinned. If you want to pluck that fowl, do it; otherwise why not start building a fire so we can dry it overnight, at least?"

Out of the corner of his eye he saw her take a step toward him, irresolute; deliberately, he ignored her. Damn her, she had really gone too far this time! And as he slid his razor-keen blade along the skin and muscles of the harlik, deftly separating hide from meat, he faced again his total alienness, the knowledge that he and Rianna had nothing whatever in common, no single memory except the shared danger of the Red Moon, no single thing of common background. She was alien to him, wholly alien, and perhaps Dane himself was really what Rianna had called him, barbarian, a savage not much better than Joda. Hell—maybe not better at all!

They really had nothing in common. Did he love her, did he even *like* her? He was recalling how bitterly they had fought with one another on the Mekhar slave ship, how again her temper had flared at him. Yet under the shared dangers of the Red Moon they had come together. He remembered how he had first taken her under the Red Moon, in the sanctuary of the Sacred Prey, with the great Hunt hanging over them, the knowledge that they were only quarry to be killed heightening their closeness, the excitement of sex in the face of death . . . neither of them had been able to resist that. They hadn't tried.

But was that love? Was shared danger and sexual awareness enough to build a shared life, afterward? Dane felt, in the depths of sudden depression, that it was not. After the Hunt, when they were the only two human survivors, the memory, the strong bond of shared danger and dread, the shadow of death that had hung over them together, had created fierce companionship. But love? Love . . . what was love?

He had loved Dallith, who had died under the Red Moon . . . and with Dallith dead there was not another human creature anywhere in the worlds of the Unity with whom he had any kind of emotional tie. He was alone, alone, alone as no human being born on Earth ever had been or ever would be, and Earth itself was lost somewhere in the unfathomable reaches of the stars!

Belsar had sunk behind the western rim of the canyon long ago, leaving dim twilight; now the sunset was gone from the sky, leaving firelight and the multitude of stars just beginning to blaze down from the sky. The fire blazed up brightly. Dane finished cutting the harlik carcass into strips. Rianna, with cool politeness, accepted the meat and she and Joda started to thread them on sticks she and the boy had trimmed for the purpose, to spread them over a long firepit she had lined with stones.

"See, we'll cover it this way, with a barrier of wet leaves," she said, "and it will conceal the smoke, and dry the meat so we can carry it for many days; there is no time to air-dry it properly. No, Joda, save some of the meat for supper, don't put it all in there . . ."

Dane said, "We have the bird for supper." He noticed that she had plucked and cleaned it, and trussed it with thin green withes, over the fire.

"Throw the bird with its feathers to the virekhi," Joda said scornfully. "I will hunger before I eat of any meat killed by a dishonored weapon!"

The virekhi were the cooing scavengers of the night. Dane shrugged. "Suit yourself," he said. "I'm not bound by your taboos here; I'm sorry I offended you, but we may need the extra meat. Take the skin and bones of the harlik outside the camp for the scavengers, then."

Joda flared, "And I need take no orders from a spear-thrower!" The tone in the boy's voice made Dane realize that it was the dirtiest insult the boy knew, and Rianna said sharply, "Joda! Apologize to Dane, at once!"

For a moment, Dane thought the boy would defy her. In the blazing fire his face was drawn, clenched with wrath. Then he dropped his eyes and said, "My Lady Mistress is right. We are all traveling together, and all in a common danger, and I will try to—to—" he fumbled, caught at Aratak's phrase, "The Venerable One says we must leave to others their Otherness. I am sorry to have offended you, Dane, and more sorry to offend my Lady Mistress. But I will not eat of any meat dishonorably slain." He stooped, picked up the carcass and bones of the harlik and carried them out of the firelight. Rianna smiled at Joda, an affectionate, grateful smile, and Dane thought, his wretchedness surging up again, *she's making sure that one barbarian doesn't spoil things by quarreling with the other barbarian, while she, the detached scientist, observes them both!*

When Joda came back, after a time, while the virekhi scrabbled and cooed outside the camp, the meal was quiet, and even, on the surface, friendly. Rianna's tactful awareness that they were all traveling together and that open quarrels were dangerous, smoothed things over on the surface. But Dane still felt the cold alienation. Rianna's kindness to Joda, the way in which she had not rebuffed, but welcomed his advances, somehow made Dane think less of himself . . . he too had been one of her choices! He looked at her familiar eyes across the campfire, the only familiar thing about her now that her skin and hair had been dyed to brown darkness, but even her eyes and her smile could not reassure him.

Above their campfire the stars of Belsar blazed with eerie, haunting brilliance. Demon-haunted stars, feared by the people . . . people who also feared a thrown spear, a thrown stone! Where in that immensity of stars was Dane's own lost sun? Which of those millions of points of light encompassed a small blue world, small, and insignificant—and home? Dane chewed morosely on the sweet, crisp skin of the bird, wishing, with a physical ache in his throat, that he were in the familiar country of the Grand Canyon, not the Great Gorge of Belsar; that he could look into the sky and see the familiar distant sprinkle of stars, Big Dipper and Northern Crown and Andromeda, not this blaze of demon-haunted starlight. He had never felt so alone in his life, in spite of the familiar bulk of Aratak, hunkered close to the fire, in spite of Rianna's kind voice and false tactful smile. And yet, when he spread his blankets under the strange stars, he hungered for the reassurance of her warm body against him, something to shut out the loneliness and the glare of the stars.

Suddenly he knew why the Belsar folk spread cloths between themselves and the haunted sky, and longed for a tent above his head . . . .

Maybe Rianna would join him. She had done so often after a minor quarrel, seeking to wipe out the differences with the close awareness of their genuine similarity, after all, this strong sexual meeting that never failed them. But the night crawled on, the fire died away to a soft thread of smoke and the faint, faint smell of the covered meat in the improvised drying-pit, and she did not come.

Was she lying in Joda's arms, then, willing to confirm his newly won manhood? Dane felt wretched, angry, jealous, longing, his misery doubled. He could not sleep, and the sudden, new-found awareness of Rianna's total alienness pounded at him.

They really had nothing in common. Nothing except the memory of shared danger under the Red Moon . . . were they really bound by anything except that, and by a strong sexual tie?

Or, worse and more humiliating, was it only that Rianna was the one human being in the Unity with whom he now had any single tie, that he clung to her because she was the one familiar thing in a universe of inconceivably alien beings, and she, knowing how he depended on her, would not forsake him?

There was no one else. Now that Dallith was dead, there

was no one else . . . *it would not have been like this with Dallith,* he thought. *I loved her, and she loved me, she really loved me. It would not have come to this . . .*

Then, wryly, he knew that, too, was self-deception. He had idealized Dallith . . . and she had died before she could ever disillusion him. They had shared danger and love under the shadow of the Red Moon, and she had died, tragically, with freedom and victory already within their grasp. Every moment he had shared with Dallith had been highly colored, charged with emotion; they had never had to face any of the ordinary disillusioning circumstances of mundane living together. And so, to him, Dallith would always be his lost love, the one perfect thing in his entire life, the only memory undimmed by the tarnish of ordinary things; perfect and always glowing in his mind, with the memory of brilliant danger and love and fear, of his own youth. . . .

Rianna was real, his companion, his friend, his sword-mate . . . and she was wholly alien and she would always be alien to him. Anything else was an illusion. After a time he fell into haunted dreams of stars and thrown rocks and rashas and lonely wanderings. He woke, late. The fire had died and around it, dimly, by starlight, he made out the separate forms of his three companions, rolled in their blankets, Aratak huge and dark and with the dimmest of luminescence around his gill-slits, not wholly concealed by the darkening of his skin; Joda, looking almost as small as a child; Rianna, a separated, curiously alienated small bundle, drawn up as she always slept with her arms over her head, her face buried in them, her back turned away, alien, rejecting . . . she looked so small and alone that Dane in his own loneliness thought, *are we all, always, alone?* He wanted to get up, go to her, hold her tight in his arms, slip under the blankets with her . . . but if he did, would she rebuff him, turn him away? He stayed where he was and finally fell asleep again.

CHAPTER FOURTEEN

When he woke, it was to the luscious smell of well-cooked meat; Rianna had opened the fire-pit and was wrapping and stowing the smoked harlik meat. A small herd of the deerlike animals were grazing between their camp and the river, and Joda asked, taking a slice of the dried meat—Dane thought, tasting his own portion, that it was rather like a well-smoked, but insufficiently salted ham— "Shall we try to get another?"

"We've got all we can carry now," Dane said, trying to be gentle. Maybe the boy wasn't just gloating over his skill as a hunter, but worrying about their food supply, "Let's not kill anything needlessly, more than we can eat in a few days. There'll be game up there. . . ."

Rianna doused the fire. Aratak took a share of the dried meat in his pack, saying that he had the strength to carry it; and Rianna accepted, even though she knew Aratak would eat none of it. Dane walked away from the camp a little, studying the wood that led upward to the green canyon of the waterfall, searching, with the telescope, for an approach. There was one fairly good path, but on tracing its course it ended in a ledge he couldn't take without climbing-spikes, ropes and pitons, and even then, Joda and Rianna probably couldn't manage it at all . . . to say nothing of Aratak! Good thing he hadn't taken that path, it was the obvious one.

The harlik had moved peacefully, cropping leaves and grass, to the edges of the wood. Dane remembered how Joda had hidden in the bushes until they were almost on top of his spear. If we were going to try and get one this morning, I'd station myself *there* and have Rianna, or the kid, circle around behind under that little clump of jungly trees . . . no time now, of course.

A flock of click-owls rocketed, clicking, from the trees beyond. There was a sudden chorus of excited bird calls, monkey yells. The harlik raised their heads, sniffing the wind.

Something white glimmered in the trees.

Dane threw himself down, crouching, shouting to the others . . . but before his knee hit the ground, the thing was halfway across the open space.

Faster than a rasha. Faster than a granth. . . . a blur. A *white* blur, with six blurring legs under it. The harlik herd exploded into flight, wheeling and scattering with great leaps. But the thing was already among them, its long white neck stretching up to seize a young doe in flight.

It stood reared up, the kicking body held between those great jaws. The kicking stopped. The white neck dipped, the jaws loosened, and the harlik doe lay still between the foremost pair of legs. Red stained the snow-white muzzle.

The red stains seemed to glow. The white beast glowed against the dim green-purple background of the forest; death-white, ghost-white.

The Kirgon slave-hound!

The body was lean and graceful as a greyhound, built for speed; the six legs were slight and finely boned above large pads. But the jaws were not those of a hound, not even the legendary Hound of the Baskervilles; they were from some hunting beast of the Eocene on Dane's world, a deadly grin that went literally from ear to ear, above great rows of luminous teeth.

For an instant it stood above its prey, the eyes like tiny flecks of gold in the whiteness; then it blurred into motion again. The long, superbly muscled neck, like the neck of a stallion, or a sea lion, whipped down, and those terrible jaws fixed themselves around the body of the doe. It hoisted the body in its mouth, without the slightest sign of strain, and trotted away with the long, deerlike legs dangling limp from the jaws. The beast's own legs were moving lazily, but, Dane thought, a cheetah on Earth, running flat out, would have been swiftly outpaced.

"We've got to follow it," Rianna said.

"Follow—*that*?" But Dane knew she was right. This was the clue they had been looking for, the beast he had heard about in the tavern . . . *it came over the wall and carried off a calf. Big calf, too. Six legs. Faster than a rasha, faster than a granth* . . . that was what they had come to this world to find.

"Good God! And I wanted to get off Unity Central because it was such a nice tame world!"

"The Divine Egg," Aratak rumbled, staring into the trees

where the Kirgon slave-hound had vanished with its prey, "reminds us to restrain our desires, lest we wake up and discover them fulfilled."

Dane muttered, "Be careful what you pray for. You might get it." Even in this urgency, he was capable of being amused by the universality of proverbial language.

Aratak raised his hand to shade his eyes.

"Up there," he said, "by the waterfall," but Rianna was already focusing the glass; she stared, pursed her lips in a soundless whistle, then handed the glass to Dane.

Doesn't anything stop that beast? It was trotting up the ledge Dane had rejected, as easily as though it had been on level ground, the harlik's body still dangling limp from its immense jaws. It showed no sign of weariness. Dane watched until it vanished into a clump of trees, then lowered the spyglass.

"Where did you say that thing comes from?"

"It's from the third planet of the Kirgon system—the Kirgon themselves are from the second. There's not much known about the system—the Kirgon don't exactly encourage research—but it *is* known that the inner planets are right on the limits of heat for sentient life. A fantastically rough environment—practically unique—there's nothing like the Kirgon, so far as we know, anywhere else in the known Galaxy, in or out of the Unity—"

"Well, thank God for that," Dane said, hoisting her pack and strapping it on her back. She said "Wait; you don't know the worst thing about that beast yet."

"That the Kirgon have it trained to hunt humans?" He had already suspected that; and after seeing that ridged, triangular torturer's knife, he hoped there weren't a couple of this beast's masters hiding out there by the waterfall!

"To hunt all kinds of sentient life, yes; that's why it's called slave-hound. But the worst thing is—it's more intelligent than anything with that number of teeth has a right to be! Some scientists suspect that they are sentient. On their own world, they form fantastically coordinated hunting packs—remember, their natural prey is adapted to the incredibly rigorous environment, too."

"Wonderful," Dane said with sharp irony, "that's all we need. Not only superfast and superstrong, and able to run up steep cliffs carrying a full-grown harlik in its teeth, it has to be intelligent, too. Maybe even sentient." He trained the scope up the cliff, and was rewarded by another flash of

white between the trees, far higher than he would have believed, if he hadn't seen the thing run. He sighed and handed
back the telescope.

"Well, we were going that way anyway."

"At least," Rianna said, "at the speed that thing moves, by
the time we get up there, it will be well and truly on its way
somewhere else. I am not eager to come up with it."

"Unless it has a lair up there," Joda suggested, taking the
telescope and focusing it quickly, "Or a mate."

"I don't even want to think about that," Dane said grimly.
"Let's go."

They set off quickly across the last remaining open ground,
avoiding the forest as long as they could, until they had to
cut across it to reach the bottom of the waterfall. Aratak
went first, hacking his way through the lower limbs, while the
three followed, weapons drawn. Sure enough, a rasha jumped
off a branch just as Aratak's heavy blade hurled another cut-
off branch into its face, crouched spitting on the ground, then
ran off into the jungle.

The damned cats seemed to space themselves almost evenly
through the jungle. Probably a matter of territory size, he
thought, and wondered how they bred, and did mated pairs
share territories? Lions did, on earth; but he had never seen a
pair, or a pride of rashas—*thank God for small mercies, the
idea of a pride of rashas was nothing he could contemplate
without at least six or seven shudders*—but perhaps they were
more like tigers, solitary hunting beasts, with male territories
isolated by female territories. Or did they all get together for
one big orgy during the breeding season? He didn't even
know how to tell male and female rashas apart, and what
was more, he didn't care. They were all deadly anyhow.

He was getting bored with rashas, anyhow, he decided.
There were just too damned many of them, and it wasn't
really any challenge at all to kill them, once you learned to
keep your eyes open for them, but it would be nice, for a
change, to be able to sit down under a tree without having
one of the pesky critters drop out in your lap!

The water came gurgling over the bottom step of the falls,
not more than ten feet high; a pleasant background splashing
sound, not a roar. It spread out here into a deep calm pool,
with water flowers growing thickly all around the surface.
They stopped here for a bite of food from their packs, and
Aratak plunged gratefully into the calm water and lay there
for a few minutes, submerged. Dane didn't begrudge him his

bath; he hadn't had one since they climbed down into the
Great Gorge, and although the giant protosaur hadn't com-
plained, Dane knew that his skin must have been suffering.
And Dane wasn't in any hurry to come up with the Kirgon
slave-hound. No hurry at all. He knew they would have to report it to the Unity ship, but he supposed that they would
make contact with Farspeaker, sooner or later, and inform
them what they had found out—the known presence of Kirgon on this world. He knew, realistically, that even all four
of them together wouldn't stand much of a chance against
that animal, if it came at them. It was as much fiercer than a
granth, as a granth was fiercer than a rasha!

The smoked meat of the harlik was delicious. Dane would
have liked some bread to go with it, but he reflected that after all, you couldn't have everything, and unless he could find
that ham-sandwich tree he had been whistling about, this was
about as good as he was going to get for a while.

"Finding any fish, Aratak?" After all, he supposed the protosaurian must be getting tired of the profuse diet of big raw
insects. Unless every bug had different flavors, and he found
he didn't want to think about that.

"Not yet," Aratak said. He had come out of his swim wet
and looking relaxed, and was standing knee-deep in the shal-
lows, hunting. He scowled at one of the six-inch furred
whale-like critters, flung it splashing and spouting back into
the deepest part of the pool, then suddenly plunged deep into
the center and came up grasping a rather primitive scaly
thing. He sat down comfortably in the mud and began to de-
vour it, breaking its neck with a single merciful blow and
eating it all up, starting at the tail and saving the brain-case
for a tidbit at the end. Rianna had her sandals off and was
soaking her feet in the pool, among the water lilies. Dane
contemplated briefly going in for a swim. It was hot, and the
water was cool. Joda had taken off his kilt to splash himself
all over with the water and to rub his grimy feet with sand.
Gnawing on a final fragment of the ham-like harlik meat,
Dane yawned and watched one of the tiny whales come up to
spout. He supposed a six-inch whale wasn't any weirder than
a nine-foot weasel, which was what the granth amounted to.
But he remembered the old joke in Yellowstone Park, where
he had worked for a season when he wasn't out of college
yet. One of the great jokes among the "Savages," as the
guides called themselves, was to sit around in the hearing of
tourists, and tell stories about the jackalope in the park, and

the rare furred trout which swam in the geysers . . . he wished he could take a couple of these baby whales back to Earth.

Here at the foot of the waterfall, in this peaceful quiet glade, with Aratak fishing and Rianna lying back at peace, her feet in the water, he was beginning to recover some of his sense of adventure and delight. It was, he thought in a rare moment of introspection, always like that with adventures. When you were actually climbing the mountain, or sailing singlehanded around the world—and he had done both—most of the time, your adventure was hard, grueling effort, unremitting murderous hard work, and when you had a moment to think about it, which wasn't often, you wondered why in hell you ever got yourself *into* these things!

It was only in quiet moments like this, all too rare, that you could savor it, delight in the strangeness, enjoy it. He began to wonder if he really enjoyed the adventurous life at all, or if he enjoyed *having done* it. A singer he had once known, had said to him that he didn't enjoy concerts. Not until they were all over and the applause started. . . .

He looked idly at the baby whales, and at some small, eel-like swimmers, covered in slick fur, which reminded him vaguely of otters; they wriggled up on a mud-bank, wriggling small inquisitive whiskery faces at him, then went back to sliding peacefully down their mud-slide. Whatever cataclysm had scarred this planet, it had certainly left plenty of niches for the smaller mammalian life to move into. It was much harder to hunt down and exterminate six-inch whales than sixty-foot ones!

Around the pool, on the far side, the ground rose steadily, offering an easy slope to the top of the falls. The ground was soft, and plain to see were the large, rounded prints that must be the tracks of the Kirgon slave-hound. Close to them were the prints of native sandals.

Dane knelt and studied them with care. They looked fresh, as if someone else were trailing the great white monster. He found the place where the human tracks joined the footprints of the hound. The man must have come running out of the jungle, in the opposite direction from the way Dane and his party had come.

He followed the trail back for a distance. No hurry; they certainly didn't want to overtake that thing, and he felt sorry for any native of Belsar who did. He stopped far enough from the trees to be beyond a rasha's first spring if there should be one of them waiting there. There usually was, after all; and Dane had better things to hunt than rashas, just now. By the length of the strides, and the depth of the toe-prints, the man—the Belsar native in sandals—had been running when he left the forest. As if he were hard on the heels of something—or something were hard on *his* heels. But Dane saw no other prints. It was puzzling.

Or was the native being chased by that white protosaur, the boojum thing who could leave prints or not, just as he chose, whose prints stopped and started in the middle of nowhere? *It isn't fair*, Dane thought. He had no reason to love the natives of Belsar, but they were, in general, a peaceful and even a kindly and hospitable people. Dane supposed he was coming around to the Unity viewpoint; they had done nothing to deserve being harassed this way. It was bad enough for them to have Kirgon on their planet, hunting them. They shouldn't have to put up with monstrous white saurians too!

Of course, the very peaceful status of this planet made it a happy hunting-ground for such people as the Kirgons, or the other slave-taking race, the cat-like protofeline Mekhars who had stolen Dane from his home on Earth. . . .

Dane turned back to the pool. Aratak was fishing again—not seriously, Dane suspected, but just for an excuse to spend more time in the cool water. Rianna and Joda were sitting on a ledge, deep in conversation.

What does she see in the little creep, anyhow? But that wasn't fair. After all, she had the same reason for taking up Joda that she had had for taking up Dane; the kid was being faced with culture shock and sudden awareness of a universe bigger than he had ever suspected, and Rianna—

Loud clicking brought him around. Click-owls were soaring up from the trees, back in the jungle. He stared, stretching his vision into the woods; those click-owls made an excellent alarm system.

Somewhere back in the trees, bushes were moving, and he heard a voice, too far away to distinguish the words.

Men were coming toward them, from the wood. Several men.

He turned and ran back toward the others.

"Up," he said, "we've got company! Hurry!"

They went quickly up the slope, and across the top of the flat "step" to the next waterfall. Here it was steeper; they had to climb between large boulders. Dane went warily, hand on sword-hilt, his eyes scanning the treetops overhanging the water. If a rasha jumped them now. . . .

Maybe that would be lucky. Maybe the rasha would wait for the party behind them. . . .

Three more steps, climbing among broad slabs of glassy rock which must have cracked away and fallen from the glass band above them long ago, as the softer stone eroded beneath the glass layer.

Ahead of them the ravine narrowed, with huge fangs of crystal projecting from the curtain of water and from the sides of the ravine. This one would be a difficult climb; the tough glass was worn away less than the softer rocks. There was a narrow steep trail winding up this side of the stream, with plenty of fragments of jagged black glass jutting from the soil. . . .

Master Rhomda stepped from behind a boulder and stood in the center of the narrow trail.

There was a pleasant smile on his handsome face, but the spear was poised for instant action between his two hands, the shaft across his body.

"That's far enough," he said. "It won't do any good to run back down the ravine, either. My men are coming up behind you."

Dane tensed, and the spear moved in Rhomda's hands like a snake. Joda and Rianna moved in on either side of Dane, their spears standing out on either side, but Rhomda only smiled. The place he stood on was too narrow. The three of them could not close in on him at once; even two would be too many to come at him.

He said calmly, "You can get away from them now, Joda. Just come over here and stand behind me; I won't let them hurt you."

Joda snapped, "Go throw your spear! I stay with my Lady Mistress!"

"Is it like that?" Rhomda looked disappointed. "Of course, while she was your teacher, I would not have expected you to betray her. But I had hoped that when you found out what she was, what she *really* was, you would have left her. I cannot believe you would be willing to help destroy your own world."

"I have known what they were from the beginning," Joda said harshly, "and I know they mean no harm to our world! And what has this world ever done for *me*, that I should be loyal to it?"

"I am sorry you feel like that," Rhomda said, "I knew how bitter you were; if the—the woman had not beaten me to it, I was intending to speak myself to your father, ask him for your fosterage in the Anka'an Order. If the Blessed Ones are merciful, that may still come to pass—"

"Never!" Joda said angrily, "I am a granth-slayer and I bear a tooth; I need no favors from anyone! And I have found out that there is more in life than running all over the woods and forests sticking a spear into people who don't have the advantage of Anka'an training! I would as soon apprentice myself as fosterling to a rasha!"

Rhomda looked at him sadly and shook his head. He was preoccupied with the boy; Dane chanced a quick look over his shoulder at Aratak.

"Any sign of his men yet, Aratak?" he called, and the giant saurian twisted his great head to look down into the ravine.

"They are still far below."

Dane commanded, turning quickly between Joda and Rianna, "You two fall back and help Aratak *if* Rhomda's men come up." At least, he thought, the kid was on their side—that was *something!*

He didn't want to kill Rhomda. The Master Spearman was a good, honest man, and he was really trying to protect his people from what he saw as a very real danger.

If I could only talk with him! Just sit down and really talk and explain, as Rianna did to Joda!

The spear swung gracefully in Rhomda's hands as he saw Dane move toward him. Under the blue robe, the broad shoulders moved in little loosening gestures. Dane slid his sword free and moved cautiously up the narrow slope. The spear swayed in Rhomda's hands like a cobra about to strike.

Dane set the hilt back against his body, Japanese style. *Like a baseball player with his bat,* he thought grimly. *And the last time I came up against Rhomda, I struck out!*

Rhomda's spear drove toward his throat. He batted it away with the full force of his shoulders, and whipped the blade back up as the spear-butt swung for his head . . . as he had known it would! The heavy wood slammed into the blade, and Dane lunged forward, his point driving down for Rhomda's throat.

But Rhomda slipped away from it and suddenly the spear-shaft was pushing Dane's blade down, then, sliding like a bil-

liards cue through Rhomda's hand, the butt moving toward
Dane's solar plexus.

There was no way to block that one. Dane spun frantically
to the left, out of the way, his sword circling behind his back.
Then he had gone full circle, and his sword was whipping
over his head, down on Rhomda's. . . .

Damn! I don't want to kill him . . .

Rhomda pivoted on his right foot, swinging at the last second out from under the blade, his spear sweeping around and
up. Dane's sword shaved a long sliver from the tough wood.

Rhomda's spear dipped; the point was in Dane's left wrist.
A wash of red flooded up toward Dane's thumb. He ducked
as the spear-butt flailed at his head, swept his foot around to
hook his heel behind Rhomda's knee, all the time staring in
surprise at the bright red paint running down his left hand,
which had inexplicably lost its grip on the sword-hilt.

Rhomda fell sprawling against the rock; as he was coming
up, spear poised, Dane felt himself seized and lifted into the
air by a huge hand.

Aratak's voice rumbled through his throat disk.

"You are wounded, Dane. My turn!"

Even Master Rhomda seemed daunted by ten feet of
muscle and leathery hide: Dane saw the Master Spearman's
tongue flick nervously over his lips, and thought, of course,
the First People, on this world, don't fight, they are healers
and merchants and peaceful folk . . . he may not know how
to fight a protosaurian! But he stepped smoothly back into
the narrowest part of the trail, where Aratak must balance
precariously between the stream and a large glassy boulder
that projected from the side of the cliff. His spear was lifted
high, butt-end level with his shoulder, point high above his
head.

Blood dripped through Dane's fingers. His other hand
fumbled for pressure points. Rianna fumbled indecisively for
the straps of her pack, but he gestured her, imperatively, to
where Joda was edging against the cliff, creeping up behind a
boulder. For an instant he wondered if the kid was running
away again; then he saw what was in Joda's mind. If he
could get around behind Rhomda. . . .

Rhomda's voice was calm, respectful.

"Do not make the mistake, Noble One," he said, "of thinking that your size or the thickness of your hide will protect
you from my spear. Even among the First People there are

sometimes criminals, and the Anka'an Order has special orders to deal with them."

The pain in Dane's wrist suddenly cut through the layer of numbing shock and confusion that had walled it away from his conscious mind. The blood was flowing, not spurting; it wasn't an artery. But suddenly there was howling pain all up his arm, and he clung to it with his fingers, shaking, hearing Rhomda say, "Go back, Noble One. I have no wish to kill you, but I will if I must."

"But I, too, am one of the Demons from the stars," Aratak said, and his huge paw swiped out, grabbing at the spear. The weapon blurred from under his hand, and the sharp point darted for his eye. Aratak moved to avoid it, and then Joda, balanced atop the boulder, thrust his own spear down, darting it toward Rhomda's shoulder.

The Master Spearman ducked it easily, and the shaft of his spear swung, almost casually, catching Joda a hard blow across the ankle. Joda pitched off the boulder, and fell sprawling almost into Rhomda's arms, and while the spearman stepped back inadvertently to avoid him, Aratak grabbed the spear-butt, wrenched it. Suddenly Rhomda's feet were dangling half a meter off the ground as he clung to his spear-shaft. Aratak's other hand whipped around in an openhanded slap, and the blue-clad figure flew like a rag doll through the air, and fell in a heap against the rock, lying there motionless.

Then Dane's wrist was in Rianna's hands, and something that felt like liquid fire poured into the wound. He gasped and tried to pull his arm away, but she held it firmly. Then a gentle coolness replaced the heat, and the throbbing stopped. She slapped something over the wound. It looked like a thin sheet of transparent plastic. She tore down through her spare skirt—the long one she wore in the villages—and fixed a rough sling.

"I won't be wearing it again," she said.

Aratak lowered himself beside Rhomba, touching the huddled body. It looked from here, Dane thought, as if the spearman's neck was broken. Joda asked, "Is he dead?"

"No, but he will sleep for some time." Aratak rose to his full height. "I, too, feared I had killed him; though I tried to strike gently. He is a valiant man and should not lightly be killed." The spear was still gripped in Aratak's huge paw. He looked down the ravine.

"I cannot see his men, but they certainly are not far behind. We had better go."

And, bending down, he placed the spear carefully beside Rhomda's limp hand.

CHAPTER FIFTEEN

As they climbed hurriedly up the ravine, Dane was alert for the slightest sound behind them . . . twigs or gravel moving under feet, anything which would indicate pursuit. But by the time they heard anything, they were too far up to hear such slight sounds; all they heard was a sound of men's voices, exclaiming, and they knew the pursuers had found Rhomda. There was a chorus of shouts and mutterings.

That ought to slow them down for a while—longer than finding him dead. Anything could have killed him, even a rasha. But something that would knock him out and put his spear carefully back into his hand?

The voices grew fainter, were left behind. The series of waterfalls went on and on. Joda was limping; the climb was more difficult now, and Dane wondered how they would get up, if it grew any worse. I can't help anyone, he thought, with my wrist in this shape. The stuff Rianna put on it had taken away the worst of the pain, but it was limp and he couldn't use it at all.

Aratak, who was leading the way, suddenly stopped. Rianna pointed, and a heavy cat odor filled Dane's nostrils.

Almost invisible among the leaves, a rasha hung above the trail, perfectly motionless, waiting.

"I will go ahead and drive it off," Aratak said, "Wait here, Rianna, Joda; have your spears ready in case it eludes me and charges."

"Wait!" Dane said. He looked carefully at the walls of the ravine, and turned to look back, seeking something his eyes had passed over without fully registering.

Above the tree there was a faint irregularity in the rock

where a narrow ledge jutted from the eroded stone. Down the trail behind them a rockslide had left a gradual slope. He touched Rianna's arm and pointed.

"Think you can climb that?"

She blinked at him, puzzled. "I think so. Why?"

"The rasha won't attack Aratak. He's too big, and not edible. If we can get above him, on that ledge, he won't be able to get at us. But when Rhomda and his men come along, he'll still be there. It might buy us some time. And we need it."

She looked at him doubtfully. "I can climb it," she said, "but can you, with that wrist? And have you seen Joda's ankle? I think there may be a chip of bone knocked loose."

"I only need one hand to get up there," Dane said, "And if Joda can't make it, Aratak can carry him." As he spoke he moved up beside Aratak, and walked almost to the range of the rasha's spring—but not quite—then began to back down the slope, setting his feet as carefully as he could in the tracks he had left.

"What *are* you doing?"

"Leaving a false trail. You do it, too. Step back into your own footprints; then it will look as if we just walked on, under the tree."

"I hope you know what you're doing," Rianna said, but she obeyed.

"Aratak, pick up Joda and carry him on. We'll meet you on the other side." He handed Aratak his sword—it would only be in the way while they climbed. Rianna gave him her spear. The huge protosaurian swept up the boy like a child, walked directly under the tree. They saw the cat tense, saw his hungry eyes swivel to follow; but it did not attack, and Dane relaxed.

When he came opposite the pile of rock he jumped away from the trail, landed clumsily, hurting his wrist. Rianna joined him a moment later, and they looked at the trail they had left, critically. If they didn't look *too* closely . . . anyway, they wouldn't see where he and Rianna had left the trail. He clambered carefully up on the rocks. The cliff was rough here, and sloped; there were footholds and handholds, and at any other time he could have scrambled up it like a monkey, but climbing one-handed, it took all his long mountaineering experience to crawl up the cliff until he could get one knee over the ledge and haul himself over. Rianna followed.

Then came a long nightmare of inching along the slippery, narrow ledge. Below them the rasha, aware that it had been cheated, snarled and rose on its branch, face upturned, its tail lashing back and forth as it watched them pass by well out of its reach.

The ledge was *very* narrow, at times narrowing to a mere bulge of the rock. Rianna went slowly, her face set and grim, clinging to the rock, but Dane knew that if her skin had not been dyed, she would have been white with dread. Dane had to try to use his injured wrist to cling to the cliff; his fingers would not work right, and he was reduced to hugging the wall and leaning, inching along with his toes digging hard against the rock wall. Just when he thought he would lose his balance and fall into the claws of the waiting rasha, they were past the tree and the ledge widened. Ahead of them the ledge ran out to join the top of the next waterfall, where Joda stood waiting. Aratak climbed clumsily up to join him.

They climbed on.

When, at long last, they reached the top, there was no sign of pursuit—which was just as well. Aratak, in particular, needed rest badly. Dane's wrist was giving him hell—whatever painkiller Rianna had used on it had worn off a good long time ago—and Joda could hardly walk. They flung themselves down, gasping, without strength enough even to get food from their packs.

Joda, younger and more resilient, recovered first. He got out the dried harlik meat from Rianna's pack, and Dane was startled, and even touched, when Joda cut slices for Rianna, and even for Dane himself, before settling down to satisfy his own hunger. Aratak hauled, from his own pack, the second fish he had caught by the pool—was it only that morning? It seemed ages ago. It smelled distinctly over-ripe, but Aratak bit into it with relish.

The jungle here seemed thicker, if that were possible, than that on the far side of the Great Gorge. The river flowed glittering between tree-shrouded banks, the open air above it like a wall of gold. Gazing from the shadow of the trees across the band of sunlight, Dane could see bright-plumed birds and jeweled insects flitting above the leaves on the far side. There was a whole other world up there, he realized, up there in the forest canopy, a world of wind, sunlight and bright colors.

Down here, away from the bright cleft of the river, this was a dark and shadowed world. A world of stacked, mildewed leaves and crumbling, powdery logs covered with fungi, and with the slender stalks of some alien plant, growing on the dead logs like some impossible combination of asparagus and mistletoe. Vines like spiderwebs wove between vine-shrouded trees, some already dead in their thick coating of vines, others with leaves interweaving with the vine-leaves.

Under purple masses of leaves that hung far out over the water, Dane could dimly see the trail of the Kirgon slave-hound in the moist turf. It had followed the line of least resistance along the river bank, and here and there, crashing through the tangled vines, it had left a clear trail for Dane and his companions to follow.

After they had rested, and eaten, they rose to follow its trail. Dane turned his back on the Great Gorge almost with reluctance. Never, he supposed, would he see anything like it again.

The river gurgled at their left; to the right, twigs crackled and leaves rattled as the denizens of the shadow world went about their own cruel business. Monkeys chattered in the thick roof of leaves, and small rabbit-like things scurried in the underbrush. A flock of tiny birds darted chirping through the clearing ahead of them, like leaves or snow driven by the wind. Snow . . . had it ever snowed on this world? Wiping sweat from his dripping face, Dane found it impossible to believe.

Huge flowers nodded on the vines that wreathed the trunks of the trees, filling the air with a perfume that warred with the scent of moldy leaves.

When night came they had no choice but to build a fire. The huge stars were sealed away by the forest roof, but constellations of eyes gleamed around them, while the voices of the jungle mourned and clamored on every side.

The next day Joda's ankle was better, but Dane still had no feeling in the fingers of his left hand, and began to worry for fear he had severed a tendon. The trail of the Kirgon beast was growing old. Just how much territory, Dane wondered, had that creature covered at that incredible speed? It had drawn far ahead of them by now. That suited him well enough. He hoped he never set eyes on the thing again.

And, although neither he nor Aratak spoke of it, he realized that by leaving the Great Gorge behind, they had, in effect, virtually abandoned all chance of rendezvous with Dravash. Probably the Captain was dead; rationally, Dane realized it was all but impossible for the Sh'fejj to have sur-

vived alone, at the mercy of rasha, granth, the other
unknown dangers of this world, with Rhomda and his men
on their trail.

At last the tracks turned aside from the river, and followed
a game trail, a mold-floored tunnel through the trees. The
gloom of the jungle deepened as they left the sunlit waters
behind. A rasha snarled from a low branch; fled as Aratak
broke a stick over its head. The air was stuffy, hotter than
ever, thick with the odors of leaf mold and too-sweet flowers.

Leaves rustled in the path ahead, and from behind a rotted
log that lay across the path, a tiny head, almost like the head
of a weasel, popped up and regarded them with tiny hard
eyes. A thin neck covered with fur rose higher, and higher
still, and Dane froze, feeling a wave of lunacy. It looked like
a huge fur boa rising behind the log. Surely it was a puppet,
someone was pulling it on a string!

No, he thought, stifling a hysterical impulse to laugh, it *is* a
fur boa . . . a fur boa constrictor! The tiny head was swaying four feet above the log by now. On its belly he could
make out dull plates of greenish-black horn . . . or was it
hardened hair? The furry snake watched them, then the head
slowly descended, but not before Dane had seen a double row
of small pinkish buttons on its belly. It slithered calmly away
across the log. Well, now he had *really* seen everything. A
mammalian snake!

Well, he supposed it was no stranger than the six-inch
whales. For that matter, in many parts of the Unity, a sapient
tool-using ape was about as unlikely a creature as the Sh'fejj,
for instance, could imagine.

Through the gloomy shadows they saw, at last, light before
them. A clearing, the end of this interminable tunnel! They
hurried forward, feeling that even a small clearing, even a
brief exposure to air and sunlight, was now as necessary as
rest or food. A faint clean-smelling breeze brushed away the
smell of dead vegetation and oversweet flowers that it
seemed, to Dane, he had been breathing ever since he could
remember.

Then they were blinking in burning sunlight, their aching
eyes at first unable to make out more than blurred shapes.

At the center of the clearing was a silver flare of light.

The growth here was all new and short. Tiny seedlings
thrust up through fast-growing scrub. Here and there, around
the roots of the larger plants, soil showed; black soil, and
gray.

Ashes. There had been a fire here, and as their eyes adjusted to the light, they saw the cause.

The silver glare, dazzling them under the blue-white rays of Belsar, was a twisted shape of metal.

Once, Dane thought, it had been mostly wings. But now it was crumpled like a candy-bar wrapper, and partly melted. Green vines were already beginning to climb up its side. But near the top, dull white things lay against the metal. They walked toward it, and Rianna drew a breath of horror.

A human skull stared down at them, through caves and eye-holes of bone. Some of the bones were blackened and burnt.

"A Kirgon airship," Rianna breathed. "A landing-craft. . . ."

The ground was scarred where the plane had come burning out of the sky, leaving behind it only a long treeless patch. The swift-growing jungle was already inching in, with vines and creepers, but the scar would be there for many years.

How long had it been there? Dane was no judge; it was not a familiar jungle and he didn't know that much about rates of growth. He would have guessed, from the way the creepers had moved in, that it had been more than one growing season, a Belsarian year or more. But he had no way of knowing. Looking at the bones, thinking of the Kirgon knife, he wondered: have we found the remnants of the vanished Unity personnel? On the ship that brought us here, the Prrzetz captain said the Kirgon were white, and Vilkish F'Thansa referred to a white shape. . . .

No. These bones are human—protosimian, anyway. The Unity Base personnel were Sh'fejj, Dravash said—all of them. So it wasn't a Kirgon slave raid on the Unity Base. Suddenly, Dane shuddered. Had Unity personnel and Kirgon raiders both been destroyed by a third force more frightful than either?

The slave-hound tracks went on past the plane, over the fast-growing creepers that covered ashes and plowed earth, straight down the center of the long strip torn out of the jungle by the burning aircraft. They followed.

The Kirgon craft had flown less than a mile from its base.

Here, too, the jungle had been burned away, and was only now crawling back, slowly, to reclaim its own. Piles of melted slag still held the shape of some kind of huge weapons that made Rianna grimace and shudder, and Aratak bare his teeth with a scowl. Joda only looked stunned. Human bones lay half-hidden in the new growth. Brilliant blue flowers blinked through the eyeholes of a bare skull.

Vines were tearing apart the burnt walls of what had been some kind of prefabricated housing. A circular wall of green enclosed an area littered with what Rianna said were slave-collars. Two skeletons lay by the gate, the bones nosed but not scattered by scavengers, and tattered strips of cloth still lay about them.

Star Demons, and stories of men being carried off in the bellies of their metal carts. . . .

Dane looked about him constantly, searching for any flash of white, the tips of his good hand caressing the hilt of his sword, while icy nettles wriggled along his nerves. At any moment he expected the slave-hound to dash out upon them; so wrapped up was he in this guarded search, following the traces, which here became confused and jumbled, that only slowly did he realize there was something strange about the forest beyond the burned-out area. Was it only the shimmer of the heat?

His skin prickled. Someone was watching him. Years of wilderness living had taught him to heed this instinct; he gripped his hand on his sword, muttering "Look out—" to Aratak. Rianna grasped her spear, circling behind him. He knew, beyond a doubt, that any moment now, that snow-white elegant creature would whiplash into sight, and the great jaws would tear them all apart. . . .

A huge black form reared up from behind the wall and Dane jumped back, his blade flashing in the sun.

"Easy there," a voice rumbled through Dane's throat disk. "It is I. I was sure the tracks would lead you here."

Dravash strode out from behind the wall. The brief leather kilt he wore hung in battered strips, and he was leaning on an immense knobby walking-stick; but he still had his pack.

"You're wounded!" Rianna said, seeing how heavily he leaned on the stick to walk, the long plastic patch covering a portion of his scaly hide.

He shrugged that aside. "The rocks by the waterfall are not kind to protosaurian integument, and I fear I shall never be as good at climbing as any protosimian. Perhaps my pre-human ancestors may have excelled at crawling over rocks and boulders, but I am no more fit for it now than you and Dane are fit to swing through the trees like your lower simian relatives. But that is not important now. And I beg you, comrade," as Aratak turned to him, baring his teeth in a friendly greeting, "spare me any proverbs of the Divine Egg, or the Blessed A'assioo, or any other saintly philosopher, about the reunion of comrades; I rejoice to see you, and I hope to make it known to you at leisure just how relieved I am to know you had not been seized, or hunted down and killed. At the moment, we have really urgent business at hand. I think there may be a survivor from the Unity Base hiding near here. As soon as we find out what's behind that forcefield—"

"Forcefield?" Dane said, startled, and Rianna said in disgust, "What a fool I am; I should have known! That shimmer I thought was heat from the jungle. . ."

Dravash nodded, and Dane realized that what he had taken for unbroken jungle, shimmering in the heat, was the faint, but perceptible visual distortion of the field . . . perceptible, once you knew what to look for, and what you were seeing.

Rianna fumbled with the key at her neck, but Dravash shook his head.

"Save yourself the trouble, *Felishtara*," he said, "The keys we were given are good for a forcefield up to seventh level . . . since our Unity Base was only second level, it never occurred to anyone that we would need stronger ones. This—" he waved one clawed forelimb at the wavering film of jungle, "is probably a level ten or twelve, perhaps more. We can't break into it. Forget it. But there is one trick we can try," he added, "I couldn't do it with only my own. But now you are here—lend me your key, Aratak. Rianna, tell me when I am approaching distortion."

With a puzzled look, Aratak complied. Dravash took a key in either hand, and moved toward the shimmering jungle. As he moved toward it, it rippled slightly, and Dane saw the Sh'fejj's straight walk divert slightly to the left.

Rianna called, "There it is; you just started to go sidewise. . . ."

"So." Dravash began cautiously, a key in either hand, moving them toward one another, twisting the controls on one of them as he moved it toward the other.

Suddenly sparks shot between the two keys and the wall of jungle dissolved into whorls of color. Dravash, forcing the shivering keys closer together, peered between them.

Dane could see between the keys, past the ripples of green and silver and purple, a strange, high shape . . . domed, round, glassy-metallic, flickering. Dravash struggled to hold the keys together, but finally, his hands jerking in spasms, was forced to drop them. He stooped and picked them up, being careful to keep them at a safe distance from one another until he had adjusted some essential control on each; then handed one back to Aratak.

"I thought so," he said, grimly. "Did you see, colleagues? There's a Kirgon starship in there!"

CHAPTER SIXTEEN

Dravash led the way across the clearing and away from the forcefield. "There could be a horde of Kirgon in there—" he said, "though, from the wreckage I saw, I don't think so. Did you find it?" he asked, and when Aratak nodded, said, "The whole Kirgon base seems to have been wiped out, slave-quarters, everything. Any force that could destroy all those Kirgon—" he shook his huge black head, the eyebrow-ridges twitching.

"It's certainly nothing from *this* planet," Rianna said, and Dravash nodded. "Which means—we'd better get away ourselves. As soon as we make camp, I will call to Farspeaker and ask him to send down a landingcraft for us. We know, now, that the Kirgon have been here—and another race, powerful enough to destroy *them*."

"The white protosaur I saw," Dane said, and Dravash flicked his head round with that single movement which reminded Dane that after all, this giant sapient being was reptilian in origin.

"You saw it? I too caught a glimpse of it," he said, "It was the night we became separated."

Aratak said, "I am curious about that, dear friend. Why did you not rejoin us?"

"After that incredible stampede by those—those cowlike disasters-upon-four-legs-each," Dravash began, and Dane found himself wondering what word in Dravash's own tongue was rendered that way by the throat disk, "I discovered that my attempts to elude them had carried me farther into the floor of the Great Gorge than I realized; and before I could find my way back to where we had been separated, darkness was upon me. I was grateful—not for the first time in my lengthy existence—that I was not of protosimian stock; the rashas were all about me in the night, but fortunately I am not of a people they consider suitable for prey. I concealed myself in a tree, and sought to compose myself, wishing I could draw upon some of your philosophy, Aratak; I have seldom spent so cold or so wretched a night. The next morning, I debated attempting to rejoin you, but I did not even know if any of you had survived. Therefore I struck straight across the Great Gorge, knowing that we must meet at that series of waterfalls—the map had convinced me that if Aratak still survived, and I knew he had done so because on the second—or was it the third—morning, I heard your communicators functioning for a moment. I considered speaking to you, but they ceased to function again before I could do so. And in any case—" He hesitated, looking searchingly at them. "—it might have given away our position to any followers equipped with Unity technology, or better. At that time, not knowing the Kirgon base had been destroyed, I expected at any moment to be ambushed by Kirgon."

"There's one left," Dane said. "A slave-hound. It's evidently what those people in the tavern had seen."

Dravash dismissed that. "Without its masters, it is capable of survival for a long time, on a planet abounding with wild game," he said, "but probably incapable of serious planning on its own. The beast is intelligent, but I, for one, have never put much credibility in the theory of their sapience. Why, for instance, would a sapient creature, who could live well upon the herds of small beasts in the Great Gorge, return again and again to the site of its dead masters? Habit and patterning, certainly, but of an animal kind, not creative sapience intelligently applied to survival. Or the creature may have been fitted by its masters with a key to the forcefield, as collar or ear-tag, and thus found the shielded site of the starship a convenient and safe place to return for sleep."

Rianna surmised, "Perhaps it, too, has caught a glimpse of the white protosaurians—"

"Yes," Dane said, "Tell us about that, Dravash."

"There is, really, nothing to tell. It was larger than Aratak, and white, and I saw it for only a few moments, so I assume it had some form of antigravity device allowing it to make swift progress without regard to the kind of terrain under foot—which I, unfortunately, do not. However, I did not see it again."

He went on telling his story as Rianna led them along the trail, wary of prowling rashas, but otherwise listening carefully. Dane thought how greatly his own attitude had changed; at first the rashas had seemed the most fearful menace on this world; now they were only a nuisance to be knocked out of the way and driven off, not even killed unless necessary. Of course they were stupid and easily frightened, and after seeing the granth, and then the slave-hound, a rasha seemed no more frightening than a housecat.

After the night which he had spent in the tree, and seen the white protosaurian, Dravash had struck out directly across the Great Gorge, using all the survival skills he had learned in youth, as captain of explorer ships on wild worlds. He had gone warily to avoid the great buffalo-like beasts, had lived well off insects and the remains of his emergency rations, not stopping to fish, because the sight of the great white protosaurian had reminded him uncomfortably of Vilkish F'Thansa's story. And again at the foot of the cliffs, while he was looking for a way up, he had seen something large and white at a distance; he had not known whether it was the slave-hound, or the mysterious white protosaur.

He had found a narrow trail to the top of the cliffs, and had met an Anka'an spearman coming down.

"He had not been expecting me," Dravash said, "and for a moment was not sure I was not one of his own First People. That gave me a moment to evade his spear and to seize him from behind where he could not get at me. I am a peaceful man, and I do not like to kill, but I broke the spear over his head, and banged that head against the rock a time or two. I do not think I killed him, but I am also sure he was in no shape to follow me. That is the only wound I have which is not from the rocks and sharp glass of this monstrous place; the accursed spear caught me in the shoulder." From these few words Dane caught a tantalizing picture of a battle he would have liked to have seen. On second thought, he had had enough of battles for a time.

Dravash had discovered, soon after that, that he had walked into a furious manhunt; and had had no resource but to conceal himself in the underbrush while it raged around him. And from things the Anka'an spearmen, their leaders, and the villagers who followed them said within his hearing, he surmised that the quarry of the hunt was neither the slave-hound—some of the villagers had grumbled because they were not giving their time and energy to hunting that monster which had killed so many of their cattle—nor the four who had escaped from Rahnilor.

"Otherwise," he said, "I'd have gone back out of the Gorge the other way, and headed back for the Unity Base to try to get a ship down for us. We've done our work here; we know there are Kirgon, and we know about the white protosaurs, and once the Council of Protectors hears this story, they can monitor all approaches to Belsar, and stop whoever it is. Although I do not like to think that the protosaurian kind could spawn such a fierce race of pirates. But when I heard that, I realized there was probably a survivor of the Unity Base hiding out somewhere around here."

Rianna asked, "How do you know it was a survivor of the Unity Base?"

"Because," Dravash said, "I saw an arrow—a fairly crude one. No native would have used it; and after I found the wreck of the Kirgon base, I knew that any race which could have done *that* would have had no scruples about hunting with a weapon more effective than bow and arrow. The Unity people on the Base knew about the taboo here, but when a last survivor was starving, he might not be so careful to observe such a prohibition."

Dane wasn't so sure; the same might possibly apply to some criminal of the native population, exiled from a village. "But if it is a survivor from the Unity Base," he asked, "and he has been able to hide out from the whole Anka'an Order, how do you think that *we* are going to be able to find him?"

"Our throat disks," Dravash said. "If we can get within normal range, his disk will pick up the vibrations of ours, and he will know we mean him no harm."

"That's a lot bigger *if* than I like," Dane began but at that moment there was a sudden hiss in the air, and an arrow drove quivering into the ground by Dane's foot.

His heart lurched; his sword sparkled sunlight as he pulled it free. His disk in his throat vibrated suddenly to speech— strange speech.

"Come on, you filthy subhumans! You'll not get me this time, either!"

There was a second hiss in the air and Dane suddenly rolled his good wrist upward in a swift movement, a foil-guard. The arrow skittered on his raised blade and flew off at an angle.

"Wait!" Rianna shouted. "We're from the Unity! We're friends!" She peered toward the thick brush of the jungle, and a human figure prowled toward them. Dane thought, in confusion, *human, I thought the Unity personnel were Sh'fejj . . .*

The human kept itself in the densest part of the shadows, but Dane could see the bow, still half-drawn.

"I have no friends in the Unity," the voice sneered, "So you've finally gotten around to this dung-ball, have you?" The bow moved up in his hands. "Was it you who did—this?" A comprehensive gesture took in the desolation of the Kirgon base around them.

"No," said Dravash, "we had nothing to do with it; we found it only a little while ago. Come out, why don't you, and talk?"

"One of you overgrown rock-creepers? Sh'fejj, by the Great Fire," the sneering voice said from the shadows, "Where's your ship?"

"In orbit," said Dravash. "Now come out where we can see you, and talk."

Rianna whispered, "A Kirgon."

The man in the shadows hesitated, and then, lowering the bow once more, moved toward them out of the shadows. The pallidness of his form was, Dane decided, a close-fitting silvery suit that made Dane think of early flying gear; his hair, too, was silvery, and his skin pale in the shadows, with a faint grayish hue that made Dane think for some reason of photographic film.

He stepped into the full sunlight—and suddenly his face and hands glowed pearl-white, beautiful as a haloed angel. Prismatic shimmers rippled along the highlights of his cheekbones, and his eyes were mirrors from which the sun flared a blaze of light. His hair had become invisible, a reflector casting off sunbeam brilliance.

He was wearing some kind of close-fitting coverall of grayish leather, trimmed with fur; Dane wondered how he endured the heat. Round his waist was a black belt studded with metal, supporting the sheaths of two blades, and an empty holster which must once have held a pistol-like weapon. The bow was new, made obviously from native materials.

"So you didn't know the Unity had a Base on this planet?"

Dravash said, and Dane, following his thought processes, knew the unspoken part of that was, *so you didn't find it, if you people had found it, it would look like this.* Dravash, with a gesture, indicated the wreckage around them.

"How did this happen?"

The flashing eyes were like silver mirrors and unreadable, but Dane saw the lips move, and fancied a sneer as the Kirgon asked, "Why do you want to know?"

"My superiors, in orbit, have ordered me to investigate," Dravash said calmly, "Belsar is a peaceful world, and under the protection of the Unity."

"If I tell you what happened, will you take me off this—this desolation of rock and jungle, and send me home?"

"I can promise to take you off this planet," Dravash said. "I have no authority to promise anything more; your ultimate disposition will rest with the Council of Protectors."

Again Dane saw the lips move, but was baffled by the metallic blankness of the eyes. A smile? The hint of a sneer?

"Transport off this hellishly cold world should be sufficient," the Kirgon said, and Dane, almost roasting in the direct blaze of the Belsar sun, stared. "After that, I suppose, it will be a matter for the—diplomats."

He's got something up his sleeve, Dane thought. *He gave in too fast. I hope Dravash doesn't think he's surrendered to us!*

Joda, who had been staring, with an expression of horror, at the Kirgon, ever since the alien had come out of the shadows, touched Rianna's arm and Dane heard him whisper.

"Why is the Noble One standing here and parleying with this—this spear-thrower?" Loathing and revulsion filled his voice. The boy, of course, had not been able to follow their conversation through the translator disk the others wore. "This—this is truly a Star Demon! Look at his skin—his eyes—his hair—"

Rianna kept her voice level as she answered, in a flat, nononsense tone, and Dane remembered that the Kirgon, too, wore a translator and could hear what she said. "His people come from a very hot world circling a blue-white star. With skins like yours or mine, they would be burnt to a crisp instantly. So his people evolved a different kind of skin, that's all; he changes color because his skin adapts to the light, darkening in the shadows to absorb heat, and in the sun, reflecting all light. No more than that."

"He is evil," Joda said with conviction, "He would have

killed us all while he hid in the shadows! Why is Dravash holding parley with him?"

"He has information that we need," Rianna returned calmly. The Kirgon had by now noticed that Joda had no translator disk, and was watching him through his blind-seeming eyes.

"A native boy? I see you people are not beyond picking up a souvenir which will fetch you a good price later on!"

"He is not a slave," Rianna said quietly.

"Oh, a female?" The Kirgon's eyes glinted around to Ri-anna. "Is he *your* toy, then?"

"Never mind that." Dravash's voice was deep with calm authority. Dane was reminded again of the old Norwegian skipper with whom he had sailed, years ago. He seldom got angry—but when he raised his voice, even if it was only to say "Let go the ropes," it could be heard over a six-knot gale. "Tell your story; who destroyed your Base?"

For the first time the sneer dropped from the Kirgon's voice and he seemed to hesitate. Finally he said, "I don't know. I have never seen anything like them before. I can't tell you where they came from, or anything about them, except that they are—are lizards, like you—only bigger. And pale—pale like something you would find under a rock." Dane tensed as the Kirgon went on, "I didn't see much of them. That's probably why I'm still alive."

His voice held real horror.

"We were just getting the slaves pacified, and sorting them out, deciding which would make good off-world merchandise, which we should keep for labor here. We had to bomb a village or two, and my friend and I were out rounding up refugees when the alarm came. I rushed back—but the place was—" he raised his hand with a blinding glimmer of light, "like this. The guns blew up—not just the big ones at the gate, but hand weapons too. I managed to throw mine away before it exploded—that is why I am still alive.

"The white lizards were—were everywhere," he went on, stammering, "I think they must have had some sort of—of disintegrator ray, because one or two men disappeared while I looked at them. No corpses, nothing else. The Captain and one or two others made it back to the ship. I saw the force-field go up, and I ran; I believed the Captain would take the ship up and bomb our attackers.

"But the ship never took off. It's still in there. It never moved. A few of us hid out in the hills, while the natives hunted us. For a long time the place was swarming, either with the lizards, or with the natives in the blue robes. Then everything quieted, so we sneaked back into the ship, by night. But it was deserted. No bodies. Nothing. Everything was—was just gone."

Like the Unity Base, Dane thought.

"Then, suddenly, one of the men yelled—I turned, and saw—one of *them!* I don't know where it came from, or how it got through the forcefield. But suddenly it was there, and—and our man wasn't. We ran—all of us. Eleven of us went into the ship. I think I was the only one who came out. My friend and I are the only ones left. I have come back three times since—gone into the ship to set a distress signal. I've left the signal on each time, and when I come back it has been turned off. Once I got the Unit to operate—I was actually getting a signal out—then it stopped, just cut off in the middle of a sound. I got away fast. I've kept away since then. My friend and I are alone now."

"Your friend?" Dravash asked, "Where is he?"

The Kirgon turned his mirror-eyes until they flashed in the sun, and pointed.

"Over there. In the jungle on that hill."

The sun was low enough that its beams shone directly into their eyes as they turned, and Dane shaded his eyes with his hand.

"Oh, is that dim candle of a star too bright for you?" the Kirgon asked, and Dane heard the lift of mockery in his voice again. "How could I have guessed that it could bother any sapient being? You cannot believe how sorry I am!"

And now, Dane thought grimly, *he knows another of our weaknesses. But if he calls Belsar dim, what in hell is his home sun like?*

"Do you intend to leave your friend here?" Dravash demanded sharply. "Have him come out into the open where I can see him! I don't particularly trust you, and I certainly won't trust anyone I can't see, with a weapon I don't know about!"

"Oh, very well." The Kirgon's hair flamed and shot sun-haloes as he whirled and called, "Windspeeder! My beauty! Come to me!"

And a chill coursed down Dane's spine as he realized what the Kirgon's friend must be.

Birds flew up screaming in terror from the jungle trees.

Outstripping them, blurred like wind-driven snow, the slave-hound came.

Before they could panic it was among them, frisking around its master like a puppy; but a puppy, Dane thought, the size of a stallion! The Kirgon laughed aloud and took the great jaws between his hands, rubbing playfully.

"Yes, my beautiful one, my treasure, yes!" The huge head swivelled to look at the others, and the Kirgon's bright glowing face streamed prism colors as he laughed. "Yes, Windspeeder, my treasure, these are mine, so you must be careful not to hurt them. They are—useful to us—for the moment." The blank glowing eyes moved toward them, to be sure they got the point. He laughed again and stroked the whiplash body with his hands.

Why, he loves that thing! And the thing loves him! Dane thought in amazement.

"This is my friend," the Kirgon said, "my only friend. He does whatever I want. Shall I have him kiss you, Sh'fejj?"

A white blur; and the creature stood in front of Dravash, staring directly into his face, the great jaws almost—but not quite—closed. "Or you, swordsman?"

And Dane was looking into a red cavern, where white spikes were set in rows like chairs in a theatre.

"Or your female, or the slave—pardon me, the native—" Rianna managed to stand her ground as the thing faced her, but Joda tottered back and tried to raise his spear. The slave-hound had to raise its head—but only a little—to sniff at Aratak; then it was back at its master's side. The Kirgon's hands toyed with the white ruff around its neck.

"He thinks as I think. His mind is mine. He kills when I want to kill and spares whom I wish to spare. He and I are one, in a way none of you deadskins can ever understand. He tells me things. He has told me now, for instance, that there is a pack of the blue-robed natives following you, and another following me. Do you not think it is time we left this place?"

They stared at him, without answering.

"Come," he said arrogantly, and pointed west, and a little north, "There are some excellent hiding places there; I have had a long time to learn the best of them. Or will that take you too far from your rendezvous point? If you prefer another direction—"

"This will do," Dravash said, "Let us go."

The Kirgon patted the dazzling white neck and the slave-hound darted off into the jungle in quite another direction, while the Kirgon took the northwesterly path he had indicated.

"What of your friend?" Aratak asked.

The Kirgon's mother-of-pearl lips writhed to show perfectly ordinary teeth. Somehow Dane had believed they would be fangs.

"Windspeeder will make it certain we are not followed," he said.

Ahead of them a game trail opened in the jungle wall. The bright figure leading them plunged into its shade. Instantly the glow of his skin was extinguished; a grayish tint washed over the smooth mother-of-pearl hue. The Kirgon seemed to hesitate, blinking.

Dane thought: *if Belsar is such a dim star to him, if he can look straight into it without blinking . . . then this must be pretty dark to him.*

So he knows one of our weaknesses . . . but we know one of his. I'd make a guess that he's as near to blind, in here, as makes no difference, and he's able to lead us without stumbling because he knows the way.

Of course, he's got that Thing to help him. Windspeeder, or whatever he calls that monster.

They followed into the darkness of the forest. Dane could find his way fairly well, after his eyes adjusted to the dim light filtering down through the trees, but the Kirgon was only a dim, blurred grayish figure. At any other time Dane would have been fascinated, trying to figure out how the curious metabolism of the alien reacted to light, so that in the sun he glowed like reflecting glass and in the darkness, the brilliance of his skin was all put out.

Strange adaptation, you'd think he would glow in the dark, or something. Like Aratak . . . of course, it's not dark enough here for Aratak to start glowing, even around his gills.

Aratak was bringing up the rear, on the alert for prowling rashas. Dravash was at the front of their party, immediately after the Kirgon.

The Kirgon. Dane realized they still thought of him as the Kirgon. *Strange,* he thought. *He must have a name, and whatever the Kirgon equivalent might be of a rank and serial number. He must have lost companions and perhaps friends and family; if not he has a family somewhere. He's a moderately ordinary member, I suppose, though of a very strange*

*race. He can't even be an outstanding member of it—he's the
one who ran away and hid, instead of fighting. Yet he didn't
tell us his name and we didn't ask. He didn't ask our names,
either.*

We know the slave-hound's name, but not his.

*He called Dravash "Sh'fejj." He probably addresses all
members of lesser races as "slave" anyhow. No—what he
called us was "subhuman deadskins."*

But why didn't we ask his name? Not even Dravash asked.

Dane wondered; was it perhaps an attempt to keep the
Kirgon from becoming a person, an individual in their
minds? Did he want to think of him as simply the alien—the
enemy?

Behind them a man shrieked, a horrible scream of agony
and terror. Other voices were shouting in the distance.

The Kirgon turned and his teeth flashed pale in his darkened face.

"They will not follow quickly," he said.

Dane thought of Master Rhomda, and all he had heard,
little snippets, in this culture, about the Anka'an Spearmen.
He remembered the Spearman's courteous unwillingness to
kill Aratak, a courtesy they had returned by leaving him his
spear. Suddenly Dane felt sick. What was he doing here, running with this—this slave-catcher, this pirate, this invader,
who smiled while that ghastly monster of his tore apart a
group of good, decent men who thought they were trying to
protect their homes from demons? And, having seen the
slave-hound, who could blame them? It wasn't fair, he was on
the wrong side, he'd take Rhomda's side any time, if he was
given a choice. . . .

He hadn't been. He had *no* choice.

CHAPTER SEVENTEEN

Light glowed through the leaves ahead of them, the end of the leaf-floored tunnel, lighted by Belsar's declining beams. They hurried on. Behind them, but at a considerable distance from the previous screams and shouts, came shouts, a terrible hoarse dying yell. The Kirgon laughed.

"Windspeeder," he said, "he has struck the other group; he will go from one to the other, keeping them both busy—and off our trail. He will kill a man each time he strikes!"

His eyes looked different; in the dimness there now seemed to be a moving pupil, not that disturbing blankness. Evidently his eyes, too, adjusted with the light.

Like built-in sunglasses, Dane thought. The Kirgon stepped into the light, and his skin flamed again, his hair throwing a sunflare of reflecting sparks.

Lucifer, the flaming angel, the light-bearer. . . . I'm getting as superstitious as Joda, Dane thought angrily. But the thought persisted, *Lucifer, Son of the Morning, how thou art fallen. . . .*

They came to the edge of a small side canyon. Below them wind and water had worn the coarse sandstone into twisted shapes that made Dane think, with a homesick pang, of Arizona. They looked down a series of broad ledges to the bottom of the canyon, where a small river was trying to saw through the layer of glass.

"What's that?" Aratak pointed to where something jutted out of the wall of the canyon. It looked like a huge bubble of the crystal glass-rock, broken at one side.

"A house," the Kirgon said, and his skin rippled into prismatic colors with the movement of his face in what Dane thought must have been a grin. "Yes, a house; one of my favorite hiding places. A fossilized house. Come and see!"

He led the way down. Dane was glad that there was a path, that he could walk, not scramble down the rock; his injured arm was giving him absolute hell. He wondered if Rianna had any more of that painkiller stuff in her pack.

The bulge of glass was not quite regular, more square than round, and ridges led away from the corners. Like melted walls!

There was a great crack in one side, that ran across the roof. The entrance was filled with shards of glass and other rubble that must have fallen only recently.

"Go in, look around. Welcome to my temporary home," the Kirgon gestured, a mocking invitation. "Look around. I am not sure it would be worth looting—the statue might be worth something, though everything else is pretty well fastened down."

Rianna made for the crack in the door, picking her way carefully between fist-sized lumps of glass. Dane held her back. He wasn't sure he trusted the Kirgon, and that invitation to enter had held enough mockery that he wondered if the alien had an accomplice waiting for an ambush inside. But the crack was barely wide enough for Rianna to squeeze through; reason told him that no sane being would bottle himself up in there. He moved away, let her put her face to the crack.

"Oh, look!" she cried out, and her voice was rapt, almost reverent. "By the Void-spirit! Aratak, Anadrigo was right! Here we have the proof!"

She slipped between the glass walls. Aratak wedged himself forward, but there was no way his massive bulk would fit through the crack; nor could Dravash do more than put his big head inside, and one forelimb. The two protosaurs withdrew to let Dane slide through after Rianna—and even for him it was a tight fit.

The interior was mostly dark, but a bright streak of sunlight lay across a gemmed floor. Rianna was kneeling on the floor, ecstatically staring down at the mosaic beneath her; sealed here for countless millennia, while sand had settled into stone above it, and then slowly worn away again, sealed here until, in some fairly recent landslide, the stone had cracked . . . to reveal this ancient dwelling.

There, drawn in tiny mosaic stones in the floor, saurian huntsmen rode on things like tailless dinosaurs, like a cross between a small diplodocus and a horse, and shot with bows at a monster that might have been Tyrannosaurus Rex himself. The saurian "horses" were made of bright red stones; their riders, with protosaurian muzzles, were of inlaid jet; the

menacing beast that towered above them was sapphire and
amethyst, with pure white stones set in as teeth; even the pictured beast was as tall as Dane. A green stone jungle surrounded riders and quarry; a tiny pterodactyl of polished
golden gems soared in a pale-green sky. And all this sealed
away under their feet by a layer of the transparent glassy
stone that had dripped in over it, sealing it away for millennia.

"Delm Velok was wrong," Rianna said, excitedly. "This is
proof of Anadrigo's theory, proof that would convince Delm
Velok himself! There was no Sh'fejj starship to colonize this
world; look, before whatever monstrous cataclysm built up
this layer of molten glass, there was already a whole sapient
saurian civilization here, independently evolved! Aratak—
Dravash," she cried out, "Do you know what a treasure this
is? And after the cataclysm—perhaps this world collided with
an asteroid, or a truly gigantic meteor shower in space, perhaps it was a polar shift with enormous volcanic activity—after that cataclysm, a few of them must have survived, driven
back to barbarism, and a new mammalian civilization, protosimian, evolved all around them!" She paused and looked
doubtful.

"But it must have been *millions of years*, Dane! And the
sandstone layer *above* this—that was formed in an ancient
desert. The first several thousand years, anyhow!"

Dane stared at the mosaic, sealed under its layer of glass.
His eyes, as they adjusted to the dim light, saw that the interior of the shell-house was neatly laid stone, rough grayish
natural stone. The outside had been melted into glass.

"But what kind of cataclysm—" he stopped. He *knew* what
kind of cataclysm would be required to do that. There was
only one force in the Universe that could have done it.

"It must have been—well, a swarm of giant meteors, perhaps a collision course with an exploded moon—that asteroid
belt out there—" but Dane interrupted her.

"No," he said, "this was no natural disaster, Rianna. They
must have done it to themselves."

She raised her head, staring at him. In the flicker of sunlight inside, Dane could see the sun picking out the coppery
roots of her dyed hair. For Rianna, whose people had been at
peace for countless millennia, it was logical to assume a
natural disaster for such destruction as this. But Dane had
grown up under the specter of atomic holocaust; had awak-

ened hearing planes going by in the night, and knowing, with a horrible certainty, that this would be *it.* . . .

"Atomic war," Dane said. He rose and walked to the shadowed corner where a saurian statue, a meter tall, sculptured from some unknown translucent violet rock, posed with calm detachment on a pedestal, thinly glazed with its coating of atomic glass. He could see it all now.

"Maybe that's their reason for the taboo against thrown weapons; some memory survived of where that leads. They taught it to the simians when they began to evolve. Maybe the fear of the stars comes from confused memories and legends of rockets falling out of the sky, bombs, blitzes. . . .

"I'll bet if you excavated under here, you'd find the traces of fallout shelters, big caverns underneath—" he stopped. Pieces of an enormous jigsaw puzzle began to fall into place in his mind. The statue, the blunt muzzle like the statue of Saint A'assioo in the marketplace of Rahnilor. Caverns underground, and a memory of white cave fish, all the useless color in their skins bleached away by aeons of darkness. *For us the Saints come to suffer in the sun.* . . .

"*Though the blessed land is quiet and cool,*" he finished aloud, "Good lord, it's been staring me in the face all along! Rianna what do you remember of those tapes of native religion?"

She sat back on her knees, looking up at him, her hand tracing tenderly along the gemmed line of the great lizard-like quarry with the jewelled white teeth, under glass. "There was not a great deal of it," she said, "and what there was, was vague and confusing. The good forces were all underground, and the evil forces came from the night sky. And all the Saints and Gods were protosaurian except for a couple of mammalian fertility goddesses presiding over purely protosimian functions."

"And the color of purity?" Dane prompted, and she stopped, staring at him.

"White, of course. And the blessed Saints. . . ."

Joda stood hesitating in the entrance, then wriggled through, stepping on the mosaic, then crowding back away from it, his eyes widening with wonder at the sight of the statue in the corner.

Dane phrased his words carefully in the boy's own dialect of the Kahram tongue.

"Joda," he said, "Since we left Rahnilor, we've talked quite freely in front of you, but I know that sometimes we've slipped into our own language and used words strange to you. Think. Have you ever heard us talking about white—" and carefully, Dane used the word, the Kahram phrase that the people of Rahnilor used to differentiate the protosaurian peoples, "First People?"

"Only that morning at the strange campfire," Joda said, "and I thought you were jesting with my Lady Mistress, for you made a reference to the ghost of Saint A'assioo, and spoke of a myth, a thing with no tracks. . . ."

"You see?" Dane said to Rianna, "and what color are the Blessed Saints, Joda?"

Joda stared at the statue in the corner. He said, in a whisper, "They are white. White, but like the First People. . . ."

"And why do the Saints always die, in the stories?" Dane asked.

"By the Mothers," Dravash exploded, his huge black head wedged into the door, "Farspeaker must know of this!"

Rianna repeated Dane's question, urgently.

"*Zabav*, why do the Saints die when they come to suffer in the sun?"

"Why—they just die," he said, "they cannot endure the cruel sun after the blessed cool and dark of the Realms of Purity. . . . some of them seem to have died from the heat, and others were struck with horrible disease and wasted away. . . ."

"Dane!" Rianna caught at him in excitement, and he nodded.

"Some of the protosaurs survived," he said, gesturing at the floor beneath them under the long-sealed atomic glass. "Survived underground in their fallout shelters. After the radiation died down, some of them must have come out, and evolved—evolved into the First People of today. But some of them stayed in the caverns, used their science to keep alive, developed their technology and improved it . . . they've had millions of years to improve it, down there in the dark!"

"But—white, Dane?"

"Genetic drift," said Dane, "Albinism, growing dominant through centuries—hell, millennia! After a while their descendants *couldn't* come out—not without those long robes and hoods. Didn't work very well—Belsar throws out an awful lot of ultra-violet, and probably the robes kept them alive just long enough to accomplish their missions, like Saint A'assioo disarming the barbarian hordes and preaching to them at Rahnilor, or Saint Ioayaho's disarming the archers of

Ashrakhu—and then they would die, probably of fulminating skin cancers. . . ."

"But those stories are all myths!" Joda cried out, "They can't be true! Or, if they are true—" clearly, the boy was frightened. Rianna went over to him, put her arm around his waist and began talking to him soothingly.

Dane got up, climbed carefully over the rubble and out of the ancient house. His arm was aching frantically, a nasty, throbbing ache that went on and on. He moved his fingers; there was no strength in them. He hoped none of the nerves were damaged. Probably it was no more than a nicked tendon, but God, it hurt! Aratak had gone down by the stream and was kneeling there, his forelimbs in the water, fishing, or simply enjoying the coolness. Dravash seemed to be in a trance, probably reporting to Farspeaker. The Kirgon, too, was standing immobile, his hair flashing in the sunlight, meditating, or perhaps communing with that vicious hound of his, revelling at a safe distance in the slaughter. . . .

Down the canyon he could see a huge opening flooded with light; and beyond that, the dim green-and-purple floor of the Gorge. Belsar was sinking slowly; there was not more than an hour or two of sunlight left. He wondered if the Kirgon had any night vision at all.

They would all have to camp here tonight, he supposed, then begin the long slow journey back to the Unity Base. That wasn't a pleasant thought, with the Anka'an order hunting them all the way. He didn't like the idea of having that damned slave-hound guarding them, either. The Belsarians, even the Aanka'an Order, didn't deserve anything like *that* let loose on them!

Maybe the shuttle landing craft would come down and pick them up in the Gorge. There was plenty of landing room, and if it came in at night, no one to see it. He felt very tired, and the ache in his wrist was maddening. The thought of being back inside a Unity ship, with hot baths and medical attention and cooked civilized food, was tempting. He'd had just about enough of this adventure, and he was glad to know it was nearly over, mission accomplished. The rest would have to be finished up by the politicians. They would deal with the Kirgons. He walked back up and found a ledge that was comfortable to sit on, watching the others like toys below him. He heard Joda's voice, and Rianna's, though he was too far away to hear what they were saying. Joda's voice still had a hysterical note. *Poor kid, he's been through a lot.* Poor Ri-

anna, too; she'd really be in seventh heaven, with an archaeological find like this, and she hasn't got time, or the proper
exploring equipment, to check it out properly. But, at least,
she could report it and have the pleasure of knowing that it
was her work which had proved Anadrigo's theory—or had it
disproved it? Dane never could keep it straight. Any how,
she'd get a footnote in archaeological studies, and from what
Dane knew of that kind of scholarship, that would be quite
enough for her. Meanwhile—

Dravash suddenly shook himself and came out of trance,
glaring around him, his body tensed as if to fight. He strode
toward the Kirgon, who stood unmoving, his body glittering
in the sun.

"Kirgon!" he roared.

The gleaming figure jumped back, startled. Dravash lowered his voice, speaking in a level, compelling growl.

"Farspeaker informs me that you are planning to seize our
shuttle when it comes down!"

The Kirgon shrank back; Dravash was, Dane decided, im-
pressive enough that he would be frightened too. Still, on instinct to rally to their leader, Dane got to his feet and began
to move down from the ledge.

The Kirgon blustered, "I don't know what you are talking
about!"

"It is not possible to pretend innocence with me," Dravash
said, with level menace, "The Farspeaker heard you talking
of this with—your *friend*."

"That's impossible!" raged the Kirgon, "You subhumans
cannot—"

A stone struck the slopes near Dane and rolled. He came
quickly around, looking up the sandstone slope behind him.

A man in a torn blue robe was coming down the cliff,
steadying himself with his spear. He was sweating and breathing hard, his skin marked by thorns, but his dark eyes were
steady, with indomitable purpose.

Master Rhomda!

Behind Dane, lower down, the Kirgon and the Sh'fejj still
argued; Dane could hear their voices rumbling in his throat
disk, but Dane was not listening. He looked up the sandstone
cliff, expecting at any moment to see the Kirgon hound hard
on Master Rhomda's trail. He could tell that Rhomda had
run fast and far. He was alone; what could he do if that
white terror came down the slope on Rhomda's track? Dane's
blade came out of his sheath as if of its own accord. If it

came to that, he would stand with Rhomda against the slave-hound, no matter what that flaming fallen angel down there had to say about it; he would not stand there and watch it take an exhausted, wounded man!

Rhomda stopped and the spear moved like a live thing in his hand.

"So, Dane," he said, and his voice was infinitely sad, "I was right—and I would rather have been wrong. Even now, I would not believe that you had joined forces with that bright demon down there. I had hoped it was some kind of dreadful mistake—that when I delivered you to the Blessed Realm, the Blessed Ones would be able to grant mercy. But there is no chance of that now."

What is he talking about? Blessed Ones, the Blessed Realm? Is he jabbering superstition? Or—Dane's mind made an enormous leap, *was I right, all along, then, about the saints and all the rest of it?*

"Rhomda, there is no need for us to fight. If you will just listen to me for a little—" Dane began, searching for words, "you don't understand. It's a terrible, tragic mistake. Won't you come and talk to me first—or better, talk to Aratak or Dravash?"

Slowly, the Master Spearman shook his head. "It is too late for that. Because of my own weakness, you have escaped me twice. Not this time. The evil from the stars will end, for this generation at least, and our world will have peace."

He raised his spear. Dane backed away, watching the point of the spear moving in small, deadly circles. The brawling voices from below had stopped. Rhomda's eyes were slitted against the sun, and Dane circled to the right, without thinking, so that the spearman's eyes avoided the direct light.

I don't want to take him at a disadvantage.

Dane brought his left hand up, trying to close the stiff, strengthless fingers around the hilt. A feeling of helplessness washed over him. In the two-handed Japanese style, the left hand provided all the strength, while the right was used only for control—and his left hand was all but useless!

"You are wounded, Dane," Rhomda said, sorrowfully, "and you could never stand against me, even at your best. If I thought there was still the faintest chance of mercy for you, I would urge you to surrender to me now. But I am afraid that the best I can do for you, now, is to kill you as quickly and mercifully as I can."

The spear point punched suddenly for Dane's throat. He

knocked it aside somehow and stumbled back, in desperation bringing the blade up in a saber guard, pulling the useless left hand back to rest on his hip. The blade's balance was not too different from that of a cavalry saber.

But Rhomda is right. I've never been a match for him, he's beaten me twice, now ...

"The Anka'an Order will be true to its trust," Rhomda said, "the world will not be destroyed a second time!"

He knows!

The spear stabbed in and Dane's blade flickered, left, then right, knocking the point aside and leaping up to catch the butt-stroke he knew would follow. His blade quivered as the tough wood crashed into it, then lashed at Rhomda's scalp. The spearman leaped back, sweeping the sword away with the metal point of his spear. His dark face looked surprised.

Dane brought his knee up as the spear-shaft swung at his groin, and as the wood rapped painfully against his calf, his wrist and forearm looped the blade around and sent it hissing toward Rhomda's temple.

The spearman ducked and stumbled back, dragging the spear butt on the sandstone—the first awkward movement Dane had ever seen him make. Dane brought down his foot, realized that he had fallen automatically into a karate stance instead of the standard saber stance, and swiveled his right foot to point at Rhomda. But what was the matter with the Master Spearman?

And then he knew.

Rhomda had grown accustomed to Dane's style—the two-handed Japanese style. But he had never encountered the saber style before. The timing, the logic-pattern of guards and cuts, all were different—Dane knew Rhomda's style. But Rhomda no longer knew his.

Rhomda was staring at him incredulously; but he brought his spear up again, ready if need be to carry on an old and legendary war, on behalf of a world that had ended before his own simian ancestors had evolved from the tree-shrew and lemur. *The waste of it,* Dane thought wildly, *the tragic waste!* He could see the strain in Rhomda's eyes, could hear the others closing in behind him, and he saw Rhomda set his mind on death; death with honor.

I don't want to kill him, damn it!

Desperate, the spearman leaped in, trying to kill, his spear a blur of motion. Dane knocked the point aside again, and as the butt swept for his temple, guarded it *up,* pushing the shaft

above his head; then whipped his blade down, low, lower
than he would have been allowed to cut in a match, drawing
the edge sharply across the tendon behind Rhomda's
knee. . . .

He jumped back as Rhomda lashed out with the butt end
of the spear, and fell sprawling on top of it. Rhomda rolled
over, tried to get up, and fell again. Dane, sheathing his
sword, felt a cold horror at what he had done. Hamstrung,
the tendons in his leg gone, the spearman would never walk
again.

He backed up a little and discovered Rianna and Aratak
behind him, their weapons at the ready. Joda was looking
from Dane to Rhomda in cold horror. Dravash stood a little
apart, his eye-ridges twitching with some unreadable emotion.
And the Kirgon was walking very slowly toward them. . . .

This was the real enemy. Dravash had found that out, in
conference with the Farspeaker, just before Rhomda had
come. Dane was glad. He preferred the Kirgon as an enemy;
the thought of having him, even temporarily, as an ally, re-
volted him.

He turned his attention back to Rhomda. The Master
Spearman had rolled over, disregarding the spreading pool of
red beneath his leg, and using the spear to lever himself into
a sitting position. His arms were shaking with pain and effort.
Dane walked toward him; Rhomda's face, contorted in agony, glared up at him and he tried to twist the spear-point
and level it at Dane, but nearly fell over. Dane ducked past
the point and knelt at Rhomda's side.

"Rianna," he shouted, "bring your pack, get out the medical supplies! Let's get that bleeding stopped. . . ." His voice
was shaking. So were his hands. Rhomda tried to swing the
spear toward him; Dane caught it between his hands and
wrenched it away, hurting his own injured left hand in the
process. He flung it out of reach, then put his arms around
Rhomda's shoulders and held him.

"I'm sorry," he said. "Stupid thing to say, but it's true. I
didn't want to fight you. I didn't want to kill you—even to
hurt you. I'm not your enemy, Rhomda."

Pain, panic, rage, all those struggled briefly in Rhomda's
dark face. Then he drew a deep breath, held it, fought to
control his gasping breaths, and Dane saw calm and stoic
resignation settling over his face. He made no protest as Rianna knelt beside him and began cleansing the wound and

stanching the blood. Aratak stood by, holding Rhomda's spear carefully.

The Kirgon came up behind them, flaming in the brilliance of the last sunlight.

"Leave him," his voice snarled through the disk in Dane's throat. "My friend will take care of him."

"No!" Dane snapped his head up and he spoke, deliberately, in Kahram, "I will take him to a place of safety myself."

The sunlight glared in his eyes as he spoke. The Kirgon had deliberately placed himself where they would have to stare directly into the sun to see him, and he flamed and glowed as if he were made of molten metal.

"I have had the blue-robed deadskins on my trail far too long. I don't allow myself to be harried by slaves! Leave him!" the Kirgon ordered.

Dane felt Rhomda's body slump limp in his arms. Exhaustion, shock, horror had finally drained the Master Spearman's iron reserves. *It would have been kinder to kill him, perhaps. To give him the same swift merciful death he offered to me.*

"You aren't giving us any orders at all here, Kirgon," Dravash snarled. "We are finished with you! What we do is no concern of yours!" He jerked his head along the trail. "Go where you please; we won't interfere. But you betrayed our bargain—and we will leave you to the natives, and if they leave you alive long enough, to the Council of Protectors when they come to investigate. Go!"

Dane lowered the crippled spearman to the ground, standing up slowly, his hand on his sword. The Kirgon threw back his head and laughed, a ringing sound, flaring out like the scintillating flames of his hair.

"*You* threaten *me*, Sh'fejj? You subhuman fools! You really believe I would lower myself to make a bargain with such as you? You have been my prisoners all along, and too stupid to notice! Stupid slave!" He made a menacing movement toward Dravash. "Get that shuttleship down here, if you want to live! It will be *you* who are left at the mercy of the natives—if you are quick, and provoke me no further!"

Dravash's voice was deep, calm, reasonable.

"What good would a shuttleship be to you? It cannot even leave this system."

"No," the Kirgon said, "but it will be equipped with communication equipment, and once off this infernal planet, I can send a tightbeam signal home, and my friend and I can wait in orbit and be warm while we wait for a ship, with no deadskins hunting us. A warship will be sent to pick me up, and we can snap up a quick shipload of slaves, and knock a hole in this planet to remember us by—besides, our ship is down there for transport. Now tell your superiors to send a shuttleship down, before I lose patience—there is room to land down in the Gorge there. Quickly!"

Slowly, Dravash gestured in refusal.

"No. No shuttleship will come down on this planet while you are within any distance of us. Farspeaker has you, and your friend, marked now. It is no use."

"Then," said the Kirgon softly, "you will have the pleasure of watching my friend eat your companions, one after another. He has worked hard for us today, and has not been given any real reward. I think I will let him begin with that one . . ."

He pointed to Rianna, where she still knelt beside the unconscious spearman; and even as he spoke, the birds hurtled up from the jungle and a white blur poured over the sandstone and loomed suddenly above Rianna, the huge jaws open.

"Do not do anything rash!" warned the Kirgon. "You have until he has finished playing with the native, to repent your decision and bring the ship down!"

Rianna had dropped her spear to tend Master Rhomda's wounds, but it lay beside her. She reached out for it and the slave-hound's great paw came down on her wrist, the huge jaws gaping within inches of her.

"No!" Joda shouted.

And threw his spear.

It was not a good cast—the boy had never thrown even a rock before—but by sheer luck it came down point-first and scratched across one golden eye. With a howl like a rusty door-hinge the thing reared back in a frantic blur, and stood shaking blood from its torn eye over the ground fifty feet away. Rianna scrambled to her feet, snatching up her spear; Dane was instantly at her side, his sword drawn. Joda was running toward the Kirgon, his machete gleaming as he ran directly into the sunlight.

"Windspeeder!" roared the Kirgon, "kill them! Kill them all!"

And suddenly the white shape was looming over them again, its eye still dripping blood, and the gaping cavern of its mouth filled Dane's vision. There was no time to do anything but stick his sword out, thrusting up into that red and dripping roof. . . .

The terrible jaws snapped shut just below the guard of Dane's sword, and the hilt was nearly jerked from his hand. He tightened his grip and tried to bring the stiff fingers of his other hand around the hilt to hang on, felt himself jerked from his feet while blood poured down over his arm. He held on, frantically.

Held on, while earth and sky moved in a confused blur; then with a sudden burst of sense stopped trying to use his useless left hand, and instead brought his forearm down on the back of the blade; as his feet touched earth, wrenched sharply at the blade.

He staggered back and fell, just as Aratak and Dravash hurled themselves on the wounded beast from opposite sides. It staggered under their combined attack; Rianna thrust in with her spear, which sank almost to the wood in the white shoulder; but the beast hardly seemed to notice. The head whipped around, and the great jaws, with their rows of teeth, clamped into Aratak's shoulder.

Aratak howled with pain and rage, an infuriated, sky-filling bellow; Dravash raised his machete, but before it could fall the beast had released Aratak and turned to seize Aratak's leg. Aratak staggered, blood streaming down his whole upper body. As Dane reeled to his feet, he noted a movement of blue in the corner of his visual field, and saw Master Rhomda, rolling toward Joda's fallen spear.

Rianna had pulled her spear out again, and drawn it back for a second thrust, when Dravash's toppling body crashed on top of her, knocking her off her feet. Dane, still dizzy from the shaking, ran toward them.

God! Did nothing stop that thing? From the front it looked like a pinto pony now, its dazzling white fur splotched and dyed with great patches of blood. No pony had ever moved that quickly. Its head whipped back to Aratak, whose knife had been driven to the hilt into the beast's flank; he hung on grimly, though his leathery hide was streaming blood from the shoulder where the hound's teeth had torn a great ragged wound. The huge head writhed around at what Dane would have sworn was an impossible angle, to clamp great teeth in Aratak's forelimb. The giant protosaur hung on, howling with rage and pain.

Can that thing be killed at all? Dane wondered, and ran

toward it, his blade raised for a cut at the magnificently muscled neck. *There must be an artery in there somewhere!*

But as his sword came down the whiteness blurred and something struck Dane with the force of a battering ram.

He staggered back, and the great jaws snapped shut an inch from his face. He fell back, and caught himself with his injured arm; for a second the pain almost made him black out. Aratak still held on grimly, driving the machete again and again into the hound's flank, his shoulder and arm streaming blood, as the creature crawled toward Dane, dragging the lizard-man's great weight with it. Dravash had rolled over to let Rianna crawl out from under him; and between Dane and the beast Master Rhomda rolled, Joda's spear clutched to his side. Dane raised his sword again, feeling his good arm drag, and knew it was his last effort as he staggered up to meet the great beast, still glowing with the last rays of Belsar. *Burning bright . . . in the forest of the night . . . Blake should have seen this thing,* Dane thought wildly, feeling the weight of his sword drag hard on his hand, and wondered in a frantic moment if the sword would drop from his wrist and roll away. With the great jaws opening to close over him, Dane thought in a last mad moment, *Did He smile his work to see, Did He who made the lamb, make thee . . . ?*

A spear in Rhomda's hands stabbed up from the ground. The slave-hound reared, and for the second time Dane heard its shrill voice squeaking. Aratak lost his grip and staggered aside, leaving his knife in the beast. Dane jumped in, his sword slashing down, cleaving deep into the white neck. The beast hurled itself backward and crashed over, all six legs kicking in the air, Joda's spear jutting from its chest. It rolled to one side and lay still.

Out of the sun's glare a voice, distorted with rage and anguished grief, screamed: "Windspeeder!"

Rhomda rolled up on his elbow, smiled crookedly at Dane and collapsed again, his face in the dust.

Dane looked wildly round. Aratak was still on his feet, his bitten arm and side streaming dark blood; Dravash sat up, clutching at his chewed and mangled leg. Joda—where was Joda? Then he heard Joda scream. Dane whirled and saw Joda staggering back, weaponless, clutching at his arm, while blood dripped from his fingertips, splattering on the rock. And beyond him, out of the blinding sunset, the Kirgon came, glowing like Satan walking white-hot out of Hell. In his hand one of the long, shovel-like torturer's blades was dripping with the boy's blood.

Rianna caught Joda and shoved him behind them, while Dane squinted into the light.

"Die, slave," the Kirgon snarled, "You have killed Windspeeder, but you will not live to boast of it! Can you see me, slave? I am here, in the light!"

Dane remembered working out against people who always tried to maneuver you so that the sun was in your eyes—and was, suddenly, immensely grateful to them; their dependence on that cheap trick had taught him how to overcome it—and would save him now.

The Kirgon moved in the glare, blazing like a steel mirror of the sun; Dane heard his weapon hissing, then steel clashed as he knocked it aside and whirled his blade out in a cut. He felt the edge jar through flesh and grate on bone in his unseen enemy.

The glowing figure swayed and fell.

Dane blinked and looked away. Behind him his shadow stretched and wavered, long and black, toward the others.

Joda was clutching at his arm and moaning, while tears streamed down his face. Aratak was kneeling beside the fallen Dravash; Rianna was pulling her medical supplies from her kit. Beyond them, like a blood-stained snow bank, beside the motionless body of Master Rhomda, lay the Kirgon's "friend."

His *only* friend. Yes. Dane thought with savage irony, *They were lovely and pleasant in their lives, and in death they were not divided.*

His first good look at Joda's wounded arm turned Dane's stomach, even though, seeing the blade that made it, he should have expected it. A chunk of flesh the size of his fist had been gouged out of the boy's upper arm, scooped away from the bone. Even the terrible bites on Aratak's shoulder and forearm—and the arm was broken—and Dravash's thigh, seemed insignificant by contrast.

Master Rhomda stirred, and Dane felt a surge of relief. He moved to prop the Master Spearman up against a rock; Rhomda looked at Joda, who sat before Rianna, teeth clenched in his lip, while she patched the massive wound.

"You saved my life, lad," he said with a wan smile, "but you dishonored your spear."

Joda stared fiercely at him, tears of pain drying on his cheek. He said, obviously quoting, "The honor of the *zabav* is the honor of his—of his Lady Mistress," he amended, "and I have learned a larger law than yours. I shall never again think it dishonor to save a friend's life against a dishonorable enemy."

Dravash rummaged in his own pack for medical supplies for his own wounds, and Aratak's. While they bandaged and patched their massive wounds, Belsar dropped low in the sky, painting the brilliant heavens above them with unbelievable colors. Rhomda said, "I suppose it is my duty to inform you that you are all my prisoners. And you, at least, Thra'vasha, will find it difficult to run away. Not impossible, perhaps, but difficult."

"Surely, Master Spearman," rumbled Aratak, "your duty cannot require you to make any further efforts in this direction. Your efforts have already been superhuman. Furthermore—" he looked down sympathetically at the helpless man, "you are seriously injured, and whatever your attention to duty, none can blame you if you—um—find it impossible to prevent us from escaping. Regrettably, I fear the truth is that you are *our* prisoner, although we would prefer not to regard you as such, but as a friend whose zeal has unfortunately been misplaced."

Rhomda shook his head and sighed. He said, "Alas, I have only the word of a Healer from Rahnilor that you are anything but the travelers from Raife which you pretended to be. And these two bodies make a powerful argument for the claim that I have fulfilled my trust and the hunt for demons from the stars should be ended." He shook his head. "But no. I fear it is not that simple. I heard both of you talking to that—that creature, in a language that was not of Raife, or any other tongue known to our world; and the conclusion is inescapable, that you folk, as well, are Star Demons—"

"What makes you think that only demons can come from the stars?" Joda demanded fiercely. Rianna had finished bandaging his wound; he was pale, his arm in an improvised sling, but he was chewing on a strip of dried harlik meat, as he sliced another for Dane and for Rianna, then cut a large one for Master Rhomda and held it out to him. "Yes, *they* were demons, or worse, from the stars. But there are evil criminals even in Rahnilor, and in my own village, and evil First People as well! Perhaps there may be a demon or two in your precious Blessed Realm, and the sky may harbor a Saint or two!"

Rhomda took the strip of dried meat from the boy, and

spoke gently. "These are not matters for a boy. Leave them to your elders, my dear child."

"I am not a child," Joda retorted angrily. "I am Joda Granth-slayer, and I bear the tooth of a granth, and I am wise enough to know that my Lady Mistress is good, and her consort, and the Venerable One from the stars! And for all that you wear the blue robe I have been taught to obey, you know nothing of these people, while I have traveled with them for more than a moon! It is you who are ignorant in these matters and should leave speech to those who know what they are talking about!" He swallowed hard, then said, "I do not want to be rude to you, Master Spearman, you have been kind to me since I was a cowardly child being beaten by my father, but I know these people and you do not, and it was you who first told me that only a fool talks about things he does not know and has not seen."

"The Divine Egg has said wisely," Aratak rumbled in the language of Kahram, "that on certain matters the unhatched may speak with the wisdom their elders have forgotten. Master Spearman, we mean you no harm, nor anyone from your world. I regret it more than I can say, that Dane was forced to injure you. I could wish there were no ill will between us."

"Ill will?" Rhomda asked, surprised, "If there were ill will between us, I would not fear to be derelict in my duty. Until the word came from those I am sworn to honor—" he made a curious, near-ritual gesture, "I liked you all well, and recognized in the Swordsman, one of my own kind."

Dane thought, holding dried meat with his good hand while he tried to tear off a strip with his teeth, *That goes double for me, buddy.* He could not remember having met anyone, for a long time, whom he had liked as much as Rhomda. The Anka'an Spearman's words had relieved him considerably.

"Should you not, then," Aratak asked Rhomda, squatting massively at his side, "have left the chase to others, and searched for enemies against whom you have some personal animus?"

Rhomda shrugged. "Why should we dislike our enemies? Personal likes and dislikes are poor grounds for choosing sides in important matters. Frequently the reason for our likes and dislikes are trivial things, dress or appearance, patterns of speech, a fancied resemblance to someone else we have reason to dislike or to love. Often we must work together with those we dislike, in alliance—and as with our al-

lies, so with our foes. It is the *goals* of our enemy we must
oppose, not the person himself. For we can never know another person as he is, but only as he appears to us; and since
we must see him dimly through the jungle of our own habits
and prejudices, how can we form any judgment whatever of
his moral worth?"

"But if a being has enough in common with you that you
find him personally admirable," Aratak argued, "how can his
goals differ from yours sufficiently to form cause for a death-
struggle? Must not the goals of similar persons be themselves
congruent, if not identical?"

Dane stared in amazement and a certain amount of amuse-
ment at this spectacle—the Anka'an Spearman and the great
protosaur, calmly arguing philosophical points.

"I can admire the rasha, Venerable, yet have no desire to
be his dinner," Rhomda said with an air of finality. "No, sir,
you must allow others their Otherness, as Saint A'assioo said
so wisely; how else could humans and First People ever reach
agreement even on small matters? How, indeed, could males
and females ever live together in harmony? You cannot judge
another person by yourself. A person whom you like, indeed,
one whom you love, may have goals and needs very different
from your own; just as one you have reason to dislike greatly
may be striving in his own way to further your own cause.
Were you not, in fact, willing to join forces with *that*—" he
pointed at the dead body of the Kirgon, from which all the
light had faded, "at least for a little while, in a common
goal?" With his knife, he began cutting the harlik meat into
strips he could manage more easily, held one out to Dane.
"Here, my friend, with your injured wrist you will have difficulty in cutting these. My hands, at least, are uninjured."

As Dane took the slivered meat from him, Dravash asked
quietly, "What are we going to do with him? We can't leave
him for the rashas, and in this state, he can't even climb out
of this canyon!"

"We'll just have to carry him," Dane said, "There must be
a village somewhere that we can leave him. I'm responsible
for his being crippled; and he's a brave and decent man. I'm
not going to leave him here!"

Dravash frowned, slowly shook his head. "The sentiment
does you credit, Dane, but as you may have noticed, many of
us are wounded; and our mission here is truly accomplished
now. I have told the Farspeaker that he should send a land-

ing craft down into the Gorge, as soon as it is fully dark; and before dawn we will be safely off this world."

"Then we'll have to take him with us," Dane said. "We can't leave him for the rashas—or for *those*," he added; as the great stars of Belsar began to wink in the sky over them, dark skeletal forms were beginning to coo and slink from the jungle, nosing around the fallen body of the Kirgon slave-hound.

"Dane, don't be a fool," Dravash said in exasperation, "We can't take him with us; I tell you, a landing craft is going to take us off, probably before the night is half over!"

"Then it will just have to land somewhere again," Dane said, "and land him near Rahnilor." Suddenly he wondered about Joda. Dravash shook his massive head. He said, "I don't know if I can convince the Captain that it is either necessary or possible."

"Then, damn it, leave me here too," Dane flared. "He killed the slave-hound and saved us all from worse wounds, even if he didn't save our lives! I tell you, I will not leave him here, crippled, for the first rasha to kill!"

"Dane is right," Rianna said, her teeth set. "If we have to, Dane and I will stay here on Belsar until the Council of Protectors can arrange to have us taken off." She looked down at the canyon and said, with a small, quirky grin, "It will give me time to be an archaeologist for a change, instead of a spearwoman."

"I will stay too," Joda said, in a small fierce voice, moving to Rianna's side, "While the Venerables rejoin their sky-wagon, I will build a fire here and remain with Master Rhomda. I am a granth-slayer; I fear no rasha in the jungle."

Dravash shook his massive head again, and Dane knew the Sh'fejj was musing upon the incomprehensible ways of proto-simians. Finally he said, "I cannot stand against all of you. Let it be as you will, then. Perhaps, under cover of night, the landing craft can make another brief landing, and leave the spearman near to an inhabited place."

"The Divine Egg wisely tells us," Aratak began, and Dravash exploded:

"The Divine Egg has told us all the accumulated wisdom of all ages and of a hundred Galaxies, Aratak, and if I may be allowed to quote his wisdom once for myself, he once said that there is a time for philosophy and a time to attend to mundane matters! I respectfully remind you that in the voice of your own wisdom, this is a time to attend to mundane matters! Let's get moving!"

"Wisdom is wisdom, even on the lips of the unwise," Aratak retorted equably, and stooped to pick up Master Rhomda in the crook of his good arm. He offered Dravash his shoulder to lean on, and the Sh'fejj, after a step or two, stumbling with the support of Rhomda's spear, accepted. Dane and Rianna went behind, and in the darkness he felt her fingers reach out, close over his. He squeezed them in return.

His comrade, his sword-mate, the sharer of his life . . . and of all the things that were important to him, as well. After a moment he beckoned to Joda to come and walk between them. The boy was hurt; it was unfair to keep him away from the comfort of Rianna's presence. And watching Joda, a small, valiant figure in the dusk, his bandaged arm white against his dark skin, Dane felt a surge of warmth and pride. Stunned and incredulous, he knew he was thinking, *That's our kid. . . .*

Above them the great stars of Belsar leaped down from the sky. And suddenly, out of the darkness before them, a white blur appeared. Dane's hand flew to his sword-hilt, and he heard the hiss of breath between Rianna's teeth. *The white saurian!*

It was taller than Aratak, gleaming moon-white under the stars. It stood before them, blocking their path.

Rhomda breathed, from the curve of Aratak's arm, "Blessed One!"

And inside Dane's head, not through his throat disk, Dane heard words form, and knew they came from the great white figure looming before them in the starlight.

Stop! Who are you, and what are you doing on our world? It is time that I heard it from your own lips; what is your purpose here?

CHAPTER EIGHTEEN

Around them the jungle night was silent. Even as the words were forming in his head, Dane could hear the pounding of his own heart, the countless voices of the night, even the small sound of leaves rattled by the wind that was drying the sweat from his body, Joda clutched Rianna's arm with a frantic grip that must have hurt.

"They are *real*, my Lady Mistress! It is one of the Saints of the Blessed Realm, and they are *real*, not tales to frighten babes! They are *real*!"

Through the boy's babbling, Aratak's voice was a mild rumble.

"The Divine Egg tells us that the fool sees the shell of the egg; but the wise man sees the hatchling who will emerge in time. Since you speak of 'our' world, my distant kinsman, one may assume that you regard yourselves as the possessors of this small, but not altogether insignificant world. If this be true, let me give you a warning. From whatever world you may come, this world is neither yours nor mine. It belongs to those who dwell here, and who have lived here since the beginnings of time. I suppose that the Council of Protectors is not unknown to you. Mark me, no further depredations will be allowed against this innocent world. There is a Unity ship above us in orbit; all that befalls us is known, and the Council is prepared to take the strongest actions against any offenders. On the other hand, if it is true, as I am beginning to surmise, that you speak of this world as 'ours' by right of being the descendants of the ancient inhabitants, then I greet you in the name of Universal Sapience, and acknowledge your right to question us. We are searching for our colleagues, who vanished without trace from the Unity Base north of Rahnilor—"

"Blessed One!" Rhomda interrupted, sitting up in the crook of Aratak's arm. "I beg of you to hear me! Remember the

Judgment of the Mind! I beg of you, take no further action until these can be heard—"

Aratak continued, as if there had been no interruption, "where they were making harmless measurements of the weather, the climate and the radiation of the sun. I now require them at your hands."

The Judgment shall be honored. Once again, Dane felt the words form in his own language, deep in the speech centers of his brain, and knew them for the words of the reptilian ghost before them. *The Judgment of the Mind of the Race, aliens, was that we should destroy no more of you without searching within your minds and hearts for your motives. But seek no more for your vanished colleagues; they have been destroyed. You have required an accounting of them; know, then, that we too have questioned the justice of this action, and those who counseled it shall be held to account by the Mind. Be calm; your own hearts and minds shall judge you, and until that is done, you have nothing to fear.*

Starlight gleamed on another white shape to Dane's left; it had not been there before. Out of the corner of his eye he could just see a third . . . but before he could focus on them, the world reeled under his feet, and the starlight was gone.

He swayed in darkness. He was blind! Under his feet was stone; cold and smooth. The air was still, damp—immense space seemed to rise, unseen, around him. He heard Joda cry out in alarm, Rianna's reassuring murmur. Fighting panic, he felt in the darkness for his companions, but could not reach them.

Slowly, he realized it was not all dark. Faint, colored lights, far dimmer than the thickly clustered stars of the Belsar night, glowed dimly here and there. He heard water dripping, somewhere, not far away, in the immensities around him. Hollow dripping. Like an echo in a cave.

"Fear nothing." It was Rhomda's voice, speaking with calm assurance. "By the Power of the Blessed Ones, you have been admitted to the Blessed Realm."

. . . . *the Blessed Land is quiet and cool* . . . He clutched in sudden panic at his sword-hilt; found, instead, that he was squeezing Rianna's wrist.

"Dane, where are we?" she whispered. He tried to moisten his dry lips to form some kind of reassuring answer. But before he managed it, Dravash's voice boomed in the dark.

"Relax, everybody," the commander said, "They've got matter-transmission, or teleportation, or something of that sort. Remember, they've had a few million years down here, to fool around with such things. I'd say they've brought us down to those caves you were talking about, Dane."

"Their Blessed Realm. Of course." Rianna was trying to sound cheerful; to Dane she didn't quite manage to sound convincing.

He muttered, "I think, if I were setting up a heaven, I'd want one with a little more light in it."

We had not realized, the voice sounded again, *that it would seem inconveniently dark to you. That is simple enough to remedy.* The faint patches of irregular light began to brighten; around Dane the forms of his companions slowly took form in the dimness.

To their right a sheer wall of stone appeared, arching into unguessable spaces above them, beyond and around them, except for dim pale shapes, moving in the twilight. Dane shivered; a land of spooks!

Aratak's voice sounded cheerful. "However strange these people may be, it would appear that courtesy is numbered among their virtues; and as the Divine Egg has justly told us, concern for the well-being of others is the first virtue of civilized thought. At least we are not now among barbarians indifferent to the welfare of another race; and at least it is an improvement over the philosophy of the Kirgon. And as the Divine Egg has further said, any improvement, however small, in one's condition, should be regarded—"

"The Divine Egg—" Dravash began impatiently, then swallowed in the darkness around them, audibly, and said with unaccustomed meekness, "has wisdom for all occasions. May we hear it at some further time, Aratak?"

Before the echo of his voice could die, words were forming again in their minds. *That distant companion with whom you have been communicating must also be brought here, that he too may face the Mind of the Race.*

The darkness trembled. Suddenly another white shape materialized immediately before them. But this one was less than half the size of the others . . . with a cry of terror, it collapsed to the ground, to lie there, quivering.

Dravash cried out, in consternation:

"Farspeaker! Consecrated One!"

A second white form, towering above them all, appeared above the fallen telepath, holding in his hands a metal framework; Farspeaker's walker.

Peace, little one. We regret the oversight . . . you have

need of this. You, at least, are in no danger. The huge white saurian bent, tenderly helped the small whimpering form to his feet and into his walker. In the great head, vast eyes glowed rose-pink in the dim twilight. *And now one more from your ship, and all is in order. . . .*

And the Prrzetz Captain was suddenly standing beside Far-speaker. He dropped instinctively into a fighting crouch; a hand dropped to his belt, seeking a weapon that was not there.

"Steady, Captain," Dravash said. "There's no danger yet—not that kind, anyway. Take it easy. . . ." That was how it came through Dane's translator, anyhow—"we're all right, so far."

The protofeline whirled, his eyes seeking them in the darkness.

"Dravash! *Where's my ship—what—?*"

"We're in a cave somewhere under the surface, I think," Dravash began in his usual ponderous manner, but Far-speaker interrupted, his voice sharp with hysteria.

"We are about two hundred meters below the surface, not far north of the Ocean Crater. These monsters teleported you here from the ship!"

"Teleported? But that's impossible—" the Captain stared wildly around, watching the ghostly figures moving in the dimness, at the giant saurian who stood close to them. "Who are these people?"

"Monsters!" Farspeaker cried. He sounded frenzied, and clumped his walker toward the others, away from the tower-ing white creature who had helped him into it. "Monsters, I say! Telepaths, the most powerful in the Galaxy—so power-ful they were able to hide themselves completely from me un-til they had captured Dravash—able to reach into the ship to get us—no living thing can be trusted with that kind of power! They destroyed the Unity Base, they could destroy our ship, they make a mockery of the Council of Protectors—destroy anyone who tries to meddle with that phony little Utopia they're maintaining up there—they've got us trapped! We'll vanish without trace, ship and all, like the last expedi-tion—"

Peace! The great calm voice throbbed in their brains. *Trust to the justice of the Mind of the Race. If your hearts bear no evil will, you may put aside your fears. Now come; some of you are injured, and all of you need care.*

The towering saurian stepped toward them, and for the first time the great jaws moved.

"Follow me, please," he said in hesitant Kahram—not as if he were unfamiliar with the language, but as though the business of moving his mouth to produce audible words were strange to him.

The twilight moved with them.

Dane fell asleep, he thought, while they tended his arm; not surprising, he thought, considering all the marching and fighting he had done that day. He awoke to see Aratak's gill-slits glowing in the darkness, and found his left arm had been fitted into a tube filled with liquid. Moving his fingers brought no pain, only pleasant warm tinglings.

It heals, the voice said in his brain. *The injured nerve has been stimulated, and is being nourished to grow again.*

Dane wondered if they were reading his mind again, all the time.

Of course. This thing you think of as privacy, it is not known to us, we regret your discomfort, no harm or disrespect is intended, strange small one.

He had to think that over. No privacy, even in thought? Were they a group mind, a hive-mind like the Hunters? No, not necessarily; they must have individuality, for earlier they had said, *we too have questioned the justice of this action, and those who counseled it shall be held to account by the Mind* . . .

Dane could see Joda lying beside him on a stone slab; as he looked, the boy yawned and sat up. The cave where they lay was small enough that they could see all four walls, glowing dimly from those faint patches.

"It *was* true then," the boy exclaimed, "There *is* a Blessed Realm, and we are in it!" He jumped to his feet, ran to one of the glowing spots on the wall. Dane reflected that to the white saurians, living in eternal darkness, this was probably a brilliantly lit room, perhaps painfully bright. Their eyes, supposing that they still had functional eyes, were probably hypersensitive to the faintest light-sources.

Joda moved his hand toward the glow; away again.

"It's not hot!" he breathed.

"Still, you'd better not touch it," Dane said, "No telling what kind of—" he paused; there were no words for *radiation*, or *exposure* in the boy's language. "It might hurt your skin to touch it, even if you didn't feel it right away."

"But this—surely—" Joda hesitated. "This is the Blessed Realm, after all . . . surely nothing *here* could hurt us!"

"Most likely not," Dravash said. "But remember, they might not know what would hurt us. They've been down here a long time. They might be, shall we say, a little out of touch with the needs of your people, Joda."

Dane's skin prickled. Indeed they had been down here a long time. Sixty or seventy million years, if humanity had evolved in the interval from the lowest of rodent-like mammals . . . what kind of technology could you evolve in *that* kind of time?

Aratak sat up, his gill-slits glowing in the dark. He said, "If these people are indeed of the race which sent the Blessed Saints to mankind on this world to teach and inspire, the race of Saint A'assioo, then I think—"

"You never *think*," Farspeaker snarled. "Your thoughts are only feeble and sentimental emotings disguised as philosophy! You hope for justice or compassion from *these*? Can't you understand that in their eyes you are no more than one of the lower animals, and all your wretched philosophy is no more to them than the thoughts of the rasha as he awaits his next meal? With their power, they could conquer the galaxy, and now that they know how primitive we are, no doubt they will promptly proceed to do so! These people have evolved so far that no doubt they will make the whole universe into a series of planets like this one, with themselves ruling as gods over all the lesser races—"

"Nonsense," Rianna said soundly, "The galaxy has plenty of telepathic races and races which are functional espers, and most of them are worthy and ethical members of the Unity."

"But none as powerful as these," Farspeaker warned, ominously. "They are beyond any we know, beyond the powers which our forefathers believed held only by their gods! So far as we are concerned, they might as well be gods, and that being so, they could squash the Unity as you crush a bug for your dinner!"

"Even if all this were true," Aratak said in his gentle rumble, "It need not be as you fear, Farspeaker. You speak as if all races were like the Kirgon or the Mekhari, that because a creature is possessed of power he must necessarily use it only to prey upon those who have it not. If this were true, my friend, there would be no Council of Protectors, and neither you nor I would be here."

"You doddering fool!" Farspeaker cried out, his voice

again with that frenzied, hysterical pitch, and he levered himself, with trembling forelimbs, into his walker, clumping toward Aratak with a heavy, hollow, metallic sound. "You really believe the Council of Protectors are a noble race of selfless beings? You think that if there were anything on this god-forgotten world worth having, that they wouldn't already have turned it over to the Unity, to enrich the Council members? Don't you know that three or four *major* medical breakthroughs were already reported here from observations, and have already gone out to enrich the Unity? The motto of the Council of Protectors, that oh-so-noble group you believe in, runs as follows: *each world has its own unique contribution to make to the culture of the Unity* . . . and to the purses of the Members of the Council, I might add. But they never say *that*, I notice."

"Yet the ideal is served," the Prrzetz Captain said quietly, "Even by you, Farspeaker, sneer as you may."

Joda was standing confused by the light-patch as they quarrelled, turning back and forth as their angry voices moved back and forth, evidently not understanding a word. *Just as well*, Dane thought.

"Consecrated One," Dravash said, "with respect, is it wise to speculate and argue in this manner before the trial we face? All of us will need our courage—"

"Courage!" Farspeaker jeered. "What good will that do, before beings of such power? We are helpless, and we may as well admit it to ourselves! Or is your arrogance so great that you still believe we can speak to these people and they will actually listen?"

"Consecrated One, I intended no disrespect or arrogance, I only wished to say—"

Suddenly Dane exploded.

"Damn it, Dravash, if anyone else in this room started to yammer like that, you'd shut him up before he could finish his first sentence! I don't know just why you Sh'fejj make a fetish out of this pampered, bad-tempered, bleached-out mind-reader, but I'm sick of listening to him, and it's time he shut up, before I shut him up!"

He had expected shocked silence; instead Dravash burst unexpectedly into thunderous laughter. Dane stared, turned to stare at Rianna, who had started to giggle too and was trying to smother it. He opened his mouth to ask what was so funny, but before he could speak, Joda cried out, in dismay.

"My Lady Mistress! What have they done to you? You are

white—white as a saint—white as the spirit of the dead—oh, what have these people done to you!"

And Dane, staring shocked at his own hand, suddenly realized what had seemed inexplicably out of key, what had struck him as strange about Aratak.

"Rianna! Aratak! Our skins—the dye is gone! We're back to our original color!"

Aratak looked down at his huge paw; laid it against Dravash's. Dim as the light was, it was perceptibly grayish against the jet black of Dravash's Sh'fejj hide.

"Interesting," he remarked. Rianna reached out and patted Joda's hand. "Don't let it trouble you, *zabav*," she said gently, and then the voice boomed in all their brains, disembodied, passionless, the giant saurian they had dealt with before:

It is so. The artificial pigmentation which protected your skins from the sun of this world has been removed; you have no more need of it.

Joda said valiantly, "You are still my Lady Mistress, whatever the color of your skin. But—but," he faltered, "you seem strange to me now—"

Now that you are all awake, the voice resonated in their brains, eat and refresh yourselves. *The Mind of the Race awaits you.*

Huge lizard-ghosts appeared in the chamber, vessels of food in their hands. Dane found himself eating flat cakes of the native grain, covered in thick sweet syrup, and other foods not quite so identifiable, but all tasty. Even Joda seemed to lose a little of his awe as he ate. But the drink with which the meal was washed down was neither water nor the thin Belsarian wine, but an odd-flavored sweet fluid that looked faintly bluish in the light, and seemed to wake him up and sharpen his senses; not like a drug, but rather like the half-forgotten effect of a good cup of strong black coffee, in his former life on Earth. . . .

Rhomda was no longer with them. Dane supposed that was natural enough. But he hoped the Anka'an spearman had not died of his injuries. Although, if he was going to be crippled for life, perhaps that would be better. . . .

When they had finished, a single ghostly figure remained with them. Dane briefly entertained the thought of rushing the lone lizard-man, but dismissed it at once. Even if more guards did not appear—and obviously, if their thoughts were being continuously read, that would be the first thing that would happen—escape would only leave them lost in the endless labyrinth of caverns. Anyhow, his sword hand was immobilized in the tube of healing fluid. Although the sword itself was still at his side. Why had they not taken it from him? Because they knew it would be useless against their powers? And a faint wisp of thought, slightly apologetic, reached his mind from somewhere: *Your kind has need of weapons, small brother; we would not deprive you of any-thing which contributes to your sense of security . . . not while you still have need of them. . . .*

Come, said a clearer voice in his mind, *The Mind of the Race awaits you.*

Their single ghostly guard, or escort, moved to guide them, and as they gathered and began to move along the long hall-way, Joda at Rianna's side, Dravash protectively close to Far-speaker, Dane remembered the brief telepathic contact he had had, before, with Farspeaker, aboard the ship. This was wholly different; there was no hint of the bitter alienation, the overlap of conflicting viewpoints. Above all, there was none of the bitter hatred and contempt.

It occurred to Dane that Farspeaker's twisted view of the Universe might be one of the worst dangers facing them. Suppose those spooks judged them all by Farspeaker's twisted and hating heart and mind?

The twilight moved with them as they walked through seemingly endless tunnels, the light brightening overhead and immediately ahead of them, dimming behind. Out of the darkness curious machines—at least, Dane *supposed* they were machines—emerged at intervals; great disks of crystal, webworks of glassy rods through which lights and colors moved. Once a light before them resolved itself into a lattice-work through which purple fire pulsed and crawled.

The dark corridors stretched on and on. Dane sensed that they had walked more than a mile. Ghostly in the dimness, they saw the white cave-saurians moving about their own af-fairs, taking not the slightest notice of the group of prison-ers—or were they prisoners?

Farspeaker clumped along in his walker. Dane heard him muttering under his breath, and felt sorry for the poor crippled wreck. He didn't mind the long walk in the cave himself—it felt good to stretch a little—but if these people read minds, couldn't they see that Farspeaker just wasn't up to this kind of long hike? Dravash was trying, unobtrusively, to give him some help, which, judging by the grumbling, was being sullenly rebuffed. *Farspeaker can't really be as bad as all that, or Dravash wouldn't be so attached to him, so ready to make excuses for that filthy temper of his. A real fetish.* And that reminded him of Dravash's sudden explosive laughter, Rianna's smothered giggles. He touched her hand in the dark and asked, "By the way, what was so funny about what I said back there, just before Joda discovered we were back to our natural color and got us off the subject? When I was telling Farspeaker to shut his trap before I shut it for him?"

Rianna giggled again. "You called him a fetish. A fetish! In the oldest civilization in the Galaxy? And protosaurian at that!" She snickered again. Dane shook his head, finally concluding that his translator had made a one-way joke, and somehow come out with the perfect and exact phrasing to puncture some bubble of Sh'fejj psychology; his translator had somehow "made a funny" which was meaningful in the Sh'fejj linguistic context, and for some odd reason in Rianna's too, and it could not be translated back.

And Farspeaker *had* shut up. Except for his muttered, painful protests, and considering the creature's physical condition, Dane wasn't surprised at that. Suddenly, the muttering changed to a howl, almost a scream, of panic and fury. The clumping of the walker was silent, and looking around, Dane saw the walker gliding along smoothly about half a meter above the ground, while the little telepath held on, shrieking, for dear life.

Fear not, Little Brother, said the silent voice. *You will not be allowed to fall. We regret that we did not perceive your difficulty of motion.* And after a minute, when Farspeaker realized that he was indeed being transported smoothly, without danger, the shriek of terror subsided.

Black tunnel mouths branched away on every side. Now an archway opened out before them. A thick scent, heavily reptilian—Dane had smelled it, before, in the protosaurian city of Rahnilor, but less concentrated and better ventilated up there—drifted from the archway; the echoes of the footsteps took on a different quality. Farspeaker made a small, terrified, whimpering sound. Dane set his chin, but could not help thinking, *Double that for me, Buddy.*

Their guide waved them on.

Enter, and abide by the judgment of the Mind of the Race.

There was an impression of vast cavernous space. The patch of twilight in which they walked was surrounded by darkness—darkness filled with shapes, reptilian, saurian, maggot-pale. Instinctive, bone-deep, gene-deep, terror moved in Dane. He struggled to control it, fishing in his mind for memories of vanished Earth. A painted scene, ancient Egyptian; the dead stood waiting in the Hall of Judgment, waiting to be judged by ancient gods with the heads of beasts; Osiris, Thoth, Anubis. There stood the great scales, where all the sins of the human heart were to be weighed against the lightest feather from the wings of Truth; and those who failed that test were cast to the waiting jaws of the crocodile. . . .

Was the Eater of the Dead waiting, somewhere, in the vastness of the great Hall?

Somewhere out there, among the row upon row of pale, worm-pale shapes, with great reptilian jaws . . . hundreds of them, thousands of them . . . they were in a monstrous amphitheater, the size of which was frankly unguessable; Dane sensed that they could have set the Cathedral of Notre Dame down inside it. Was the whole underground race waiting there to judge them? Or, more frightening still, was this only a selected jury? They crossed spaces cleared for them, moving in twilight that still followed them, and dimly, climbed stairs, waited. Saurians blinked dawn-pink eyes.

Aratak muttered, "Look. To them, this is *bright* light."

From all around them came a tense slithering and stirring. The overwhelming reptilian odor set Dane's nerves on edge; he gripped at his sword-hilt, forced himself to relax. That was no good here.

Rhomda walked into the circle of dim light.

Dane smiled at him, spontaneously. Thank God, the spearman was alive! Then he stiffened, in automatic rejection.

No! You don't walk with the tendons cut through in both legs! Even if I was mistaken, and the tendons only nicked a little, it would take months . . . years. . . .

He wriggled the fingers of his hand inside the tube of fluid. No pain. For the first time in days, no pain. Nerve regeneration? *That was impossible. . . .*

Well, Rhomda was walking. That was a fact. Rhomda smiled at them encouragingly, and Dane, even in the midst of everything that was happening, felt a surge of joy, for Rhomda and for himself. He wouldn't be crippled . . . his hand would be all right!

Let the Mind of the Race assemble for Judgment!

A loud hiss of breath, and a brief stirring sound, came from the darkness around them, and stopped. For a moment it seemed nothing was happening; then Dane felt a strange inward sensation. As if he stood at the very edge of a great orchestra and the conductor raised his baton. As though out in that darkness, a thousand willing, practiced hands were building some mighty edifice, raising enormous stone blocks effortlessly into position.

His ears expected music, his eyes some incredible piece of architecture; and despite the silence, the darkness, he knew that *something* was being shaped around them. The symphony was being played; he was deaf, but he could feel the harmonies in every cell of his body. No, not a symphony; a complex choral work, in which each individual voice had its own part, in which he, too, *almost* had a voice. . . .

His ears heard only silence. His eyes saw only darkness. Yet around them he could *feel* his companions; Aratak's calm and wonder; Joda, torn between a child's fear and a sudden, amazed, adult acceptance; Rhomda, concerned and yet peaceful. And Rianna, warming him like a strong flame.

Built into these familiar harmonies were other notes; Farspeaker, troubled, still hostile; Dravash and the Prrzetz Captain, whose name, he reflected, he had never known; curiously alike, these two, despite the sharp contrast of protofeline electricity with saurian depth. Steersmen, these two, accustomed to authority, to decisions which could mean the life of hundreds. Something in Dane, abashed, translated this in an old way, *The buck stops here.* He could feel that in both Captains, the female cat, the male lizard. Dane felt suddenly small; *I can do that, but only for myself. It hurts me too much to be wrong. They can even accept, and live with, the knowledge that sooner or later they are going to make wrong decisions which may cost lives . . . am I ever going to be that big? What do they say, never judge the other guy till you walk a few miles in his shoes?*

The unheard music swelled; then from the cresting wave of power, voices and words formed, no single voice. Was it the voice of the Mind of the Race?

These two of our own are also on trial; they are your accusers and their accusations are their defense. The light seemed to brighten, suddenly, around two of the giant saurians who stood sharing the open space cleared for the aliens from outside.

Creatures from the stars destroyed our world long ago. Somehow Dane knew that the words in his head came from the one of the giant saurians who stood to the left, not from the other, or from any of the massed white reptilians in the caverned darkness, *When the first ship from the stars came, we were frightened; some of us said, wait, ages have passed and it may be that these mean us no evil. Wait, and see. We waited. But that first ship was followed by another; it settled among the villages and rained fiery death upon all the people of the surface. The action we took was necessary.*

And suddenly Dane understood. It had never occurred to these people, any more to the folk of Rahnilor, to doubt a common origin for all the "Star Demons." And so the Unity Base had been destroyed—because the Kirgon ship had tried to enslave the harmless villagers. They could not, or would not, distinguish between the two groups; they had not inquired into their minds, but merely, seeing what the Kirgon had done, struck to destroy all invaders . . . and left the survivors to their surface arm, the Anka'an Order of Spearmen.

The second saurian on the platform turned to them.

When we had destroyed all of the invaders, we set again the ancient watch upon the skies, and we saw that the creatures had once again occupied their original Base. These, too, we cut off and destroyed.

So much, Dane thought, for the expedition led by the unlucky Vilkish F'Thansa.

Yet when it was proposed that we destroy their ship, we were divided, and no one would act; we saw the ship turn and vanish from our skies. And now, see, they have come again. Are we to sit and await again the destruction from the skies?

And a part of the unheard chorus, it seemed to Dane, cried out in a vast shout for revenge:

We too could travel among the stars! Let us avenge the ancient sorrow! Let us make our world and our people forever safe!

But even as that cry surged up, the Mind of the Race, divided against itself, merged into strophe and antistrophe:

What manner of justice is this? They know nothing of the ancient crime, their people had not evolved from small running things when it was done, we know by looking at them that they are no kin to the Ancient Destroyers.

Dane blinked; light made him cover his eyes. He felt as if he had wakened from some strange and confusing dream. He looked into the great cavern, saw rows and rows of the pallid cave-creatures, most of them shielding their hands with their eyes. The white light vanished. Curiously solid and substantial, hanging in the spaces of the cavern all around them, a planet glowed, Belsar—Belsar as he had seen it from space! But a Belsar unpitted by ancient craters; a Belsar unscarred, covered with wide blue seas and continents, over which moved thin layers of cloud.

Remember, my children! cried the Mind of the Race, *Behold our world as it was!* It was a threnody, a mourning cry of sorrow and memory.

Rich greenery and vast swamps; huge shapes, not unlike the vanished dinosaurs of his own world . . . yet these had built glittering cities, streets and highways . . . here they had risen from the beasts . . . pictures played in the light, not projected flat on the wall like a movie, but somehow projected to full dimension, showing the ancient saurians, sailing in wooden ships, planting and harvesting, shaping iron and wood; at first, a simple agricultural people, then a technological society . . . there was less war, Dane thought as the "film" unrolled, than a comparable history of Earth would have shown; but there were clashes of isolated groups, hints of dreadful weapons tested and put aside. At the height of an industrial culture, they had built these tunnels, fearing that some hand would unleash on them the disaster of their weapons. . . .

But wisdom prevailed; our world united in peace, and we thought all the dangers past. And then, when we least expected it, the disaster struck. . . .

Again a planet hung in space, and Dane remembered the star the natives had called World-Destroyer. A sun near to Belsar, perhaps just too near. . .

We will never know why they attacked us. But Dane shuddered, now, his mind unable to take the sight of the only interplanetary war he would ever see—he hoped. The glare of terrible light on the screen, the familiar mushroom clouds. Death and destruction . . . and the tunnels, built, and abandoned when their world grew peaceful, suddenly crowded with the dark-skinned saurians. A world blasted; Belsar, scarred by craters, a dead world, seeming as lifeless as Earth's moon. Silent. Useless even to the attackers . . . a planet, seen through a telescope; huge bursts of light, splitting, exploding. . . .

Rianna whispered, "The asteroid belt!"

Our world was gone. We destroyed their Base; but the price of our folly was too high. Never again will our descendants live under the open sky . . .

Time. Millennia. Weather, erosion, earthquakes, hurricanes, small plants sprouting unseen, to cover a world not quite as dead as they feared, while the tunnels swarmed with the saurian civilization underground.

Generation after generation, millennium after millennium, we labored underground, discovered new energies, created new arts and sciences . . . at last a time came when we looked out on the world we had left, thinking to find only ruin and desolation. And behold, our empty world again held life. . . .

A desert; small tough bushes grew, tiny mouselike shrews scampered across the sand. Something like a hawk darted from the sky, and the mouse-thing took shelter in the bushes, the swift escaping, the slow perishing. . . .

Ages passed . . .

A ripple of the light; grass covered a broad prairie, nomad creatures roamed, creatures who stood upright, fighting away the fierce cat-things with stones and spears. And again the caverns, crowded with dark-skinned saurians. . . .

Leaders arose, preaching that life on the surface could be ours again, that we could go forth and wrest this world from the ape-things who had won it. Yet we would not do to them as the creatures from the star World-Destroyer had done to us. We, too, resolved to make a new beginning. And we would make certain that those of our sons who went forth to live beside the protosimians, never allowed them to climb to such dangerous heights. . . .

And so, as man evolved, next to them were the cities of the dark-skinned protosaurians, the First People, side by side . . . and then the ice came, and some of the reptilian people had returned to the caves, rather than resorting again to the dangerous technology which had once before come near to destroying their world. . . .

And during some of those recurrent ages, our people had lost the ability to survive on the surface. Those of us who had returned to live beneath the sun had adapted to its changed radiations. But we could not. And now the change had come. The simians under the brilliant sun of Belsar were dark-skinned; the dark-skinned saurians worked and built cities beside them; but those who had remained in the caves were pale, and no longer able to tolerate the radiations of their own sun. The time when they could have left their self-chosen exile was past. It was forever too late for them.

Yet we watched our children, in secret, making certain

they would never destroy themselves as we had done, never reach a dangerous technology . . . and that no invaders would ever come upon them from outside. . . .

But now the time has come when we rejoin, if not the people of the surface, at least the people of the outer world, beyond our stars, the vast antiphonal Mind of the Race soared into awareness again. *There are people of good will there, dedicated to protecting the helpless . . . to using technologies, not abusing them . . .*

No, a cry came from one of those who shared the platform with Dane and Rianna, *We have built a perfect world on the surface there, a world without danger or injustice or evil. . . .*

Joda's voice, very small in the huge cave, spoke up and said, "But it isn't so perfect. What about the rashas?"

Do you not understand, Little Brother? They keep you from outbreeding your food supply and dying of hunger, yet your people find pleasure in breeding. And pleasure even in fighting the rashas.

Joda said, "I think some of us would like to choose whether or not we wanted to kill off the rashas, and then we could find other things to do with our lives. Fighting rashas is fine, for people who like it, but people like me shouldn't have to die because we're no good at fighting, either. I'd like to learn something about—about the sciences my Lady Mistress talks about. Maybe if people from the stars can learn not to destroy other planets, my people could learn not to destroy ourselves with wars, too. But the way you keep us, we don't have any chances. The best thing you can think of to do with people like me is to put them under the protection of the Anka'an Order, and that's just more fighting. My Lady Mistress taught me how to fight, and how to kill. I could go back to my village and be Joda Granth-slayer and spend the rest of my life as a respected man, not a coward. But there's nothing else I can do. Why can't we decide for ourselves how we want our world? Are we all that stupid? You are—" Suddenly he choked, and Dane realized what the boy was doing, defying every cultural precept of his life. "You are the Blessed Saints, and this is the Blessed Realm, but to me, you look like a lot of scared old men hiding in a cave from something that happened billions and billions of years ago, and you won't even let us try to do better. You say because you failed, you won't even let us try. Is that being *Saints*?"

He fell silent. From somewhere a small trickle of agreement began. It swelled into a mighty concord.

The boy is right. His people should be free, and masters of their own destiny.

But if they destroy themselves . . . ?

The Prrzetz Captain said quietly, "Are you gods? Nobody can be right all the time."

The Mind of the Race swelled again into a mighty harmony.

We have seen. We have judged. These people shall be returned to their own place . . . and the people of the surface shall follow their own destiny. But it must be their destiny, not ours. We cannot at once bring all our sciences to them. They must discover, and rediscover, their own. They are not ready for ours.

And suddenly the cavern was dark again, except for the dim figure of the one saurian who had destroyed the Unity Base and counselled destroying the ship. It shone in the darkness like a star; and suddenly light bloomed around them and they were on the surface of the world, two giant saurians looming around them.

One of them said, squeezing his eyes painfully against the light, and Dane recognized, from something in his tone, that he was the one who had destroyed the Unity Base.

"I am Vasa'ariyo. This is my punishment; I shall go to suffer in the sun, exiled forever from the Blessed Realm, and perhaps I can bring healing to the lands wasted by the Kirgon."

Rhomda, standing with his spear, knelt in reverence.

"Saint Vasa'ariyo, I will go with you and guide you."

"Some punishment," Rianna said, "becoming a saint." But only Dane "heard" it through his throat disk. He said, in the same murmured language, "Don't you know that he's just sentenced himself to die of skin cancer, probably slowly and agonizingly? Believe me, it's punishment enough."

Farspeaker was leaning heavily on Dravash and the other saurian. "Where is my walker?" he demanded querulously.

"You do not need it, Little Brother," said the giant white saurian, "Take a step, I beg you."

Farspeaker lurched forward, his whole attitude showing fear and dread . . . but he did not fall. He moved again, and again, and Dane, in amazement, saw that the crippled telepath was moving with cautious care . . . but moving freely, without pain. A look of delight and amazement came over his face.

The other saurian said, "You are still in need of healing,

Little Brother. We beg you to remain with us, as the Ambassador from the Unity." He turned to them and said, "It is time for you people to rejoin your ship. Speak with it, I beg; your communicators have been restored to action."

The Prrzetz captain pulled out his—no, Dane thought with sudden detachment, *her*—communicator from the belt loop where it hung. She spoke into it, urgently, and a crackle of excited speech came from it, which Dane's translator rendered as a jumble of What-the-hell-happened-to-you-Captain, and What-shall-we-do-about-it?

"Nothing," said Dravash, "The Captain and I, and all of us, are all right, and waiting for you."

"We'll send a shuttle right away—"

The giant white saurian said, "There is no need for that, we can restore you instantly to your ship—" and stopped. Then he said, "No. Allow your ship's shuttle to land. There is no need for you to suffer further disorientation."

Rhomda clasped Dane's hand briefly.

"I wish you were coming with us," Dane said, but he knew, as he spoke, that it was only his way of saying he would miss Rhomda. Rhomda was entirely suited to his own world. He was in a position of strength and responsibility.

"I am committed to be servant and helper to the Blessed Saint," said Rhomda, indicating Vasa'ariyo, who was blinking painfully in the light, "So long as he lives, I shall never leave him."

"Nor I," Aratak said suddenly. "The wisdom of the Divine Egg has shown me that all wisdom is one. I, too, will remain and sample the wisdom of a race older than mine. Bid me farewell, my dearest children."

Rianna flung her arms around the huge lizard-man. Dane felt his throat tighten. Aratak had been at his side since he awakened in a cage on the Makhar ship, and this parting was anguish. He tried to smile, but the words would not come. Aratak was a philosopher, not a fighter. And he, too, would be an ambassador to this world, perhaps a truer ambassador than the still-warped Farspeaker, bringing the wisdom of the Egg to join with that of the Blessed Saints. He said at last, his voice sticking to his throat, "Leave others their Otherness. I'd like to stay here, too. But—" he looked at Rianna, and Aratak's huge paw descended, gentle, on his shoulder.

"Your fate lies elsewhere, my friend. Farewell. Think sometimes of me." He went to the side of the great white saurian . . . *Saint Vasa'ariyo. Have all the Saints been criminals condemned by their kind?*

Rhomda said quietly to Joda, "You go with your Lady Mistress? I shall bear word to your kin that you are safe and well, and gone to the lands beyond Raife; the truth would only hurt and frighten them beyond bearing." He laid both hands on Joda's shoulders, and said, "You have chosen wisely, my son. You have dishonored your spear; there is no place for you here."

Joda said quietly, "I think there never was a place for me here, Master Rhomda. I was lucky; I found my place. Some day, though, will you try to help some other boy who is not as lucky as I and cannot find his place?"

"I swear it." Rhomda touched the hilt of his spear. "Farewell, Joda Granth-slayer."

Joda shook his head. From around his neck, where the amulets were clustered, he took the granth's tooth and said, "I don't need it any more. Keep it to remember me by, Master Rhomda."

Rhomda silently put it around his own neck, lifting his spear in tribute and farewell. And then, above them in the sky, the shuttle ship from the Unity was descending slowly to the ground, and Aratak and Rhomda were leading the saint away, down the hill, from the painful glare. They disappeared into the darkness of the jungle.

Dane sat in the observation lounge, watching Belsar recede in the screen. Rianna was already making notes into her voice-scriber, watched by a fascinated Joda.

Utopia, he thought. *For me, after Dullsville, it was a marvelous world. But one man's Utopia is another man's hell. Dullsville was hell for me.*

"I suppose," he said to Rianna, "that you'll spend the next couple of years making notes and anthropological observations on what we were doing here?" But he really didn't need to ask.

"I'm afraid so," she said apologetically. "And I've got to find a place for Joda to be educated, somewhere where he won't suffer too much from cultural shock. Central City is too big, too mechanical . . . perhaps the University Preserve on Spica Seven . . . oh, Dane, do you really mind so much? I'm afraid it's going to be *years* before we get that anthropological observation-trip we wanted. . . ."

He shrugged. "For a while," he said, "Dullsville's going to

be fine. A chance to rest up. And when I get tired of it, this time . . . ."

He leaned over and kissed her, knowing he no longer resented it, that her needs and wishes were alien from his own. He loved her; he would always love her, always come back to her. But he was no longer wholly dependent on her. It was a big galaxy out there. And somewhere, like Joda, he could find a place in it. He leaned over, hugging her exuberantly close in his arms, and she returned his kiss with a passion that wiped out all the resentments of the days on Belsar.

Dravash, watching Belsar in the observation screen turned to look at them, and shook his head with a sigh.

"You protosimians!" he said, scowling; then, suddenly, laughed.

"The Divine Egg has rightly told us," he said, while Rianna and Dane gaped at him, "That it is well to leave others their Otherness. The Unity is large enough to embrace all kinds of differences. I shall go and make a final contact with Farspeaker, and assure myself that all is well with him."

He left the lounge, and Dane, smiling affectionately after the big Sh'fejj, thought: *what was it Aratak always said? I rejoice in the diversity of Creation.*

It's a big galaxy, out there, he thought, looking joyously out at the wilderness of encircling stars. And somewhere in it, there's a place for everybody. Somewhere.

He gripped his Samurai sword, and drew a deep breath. For now, he had Rianna, and Joda growing up, and a place to find. And out there . . . *well, who knows?*

Rejoice in the diversity of Creation! Which, of course, was just another way of saying, *Leave others their Otherness.*

But then, as the Divine Egg said, all wisdom was one.

And in a world where Dravash could quote from the Divine Egg—well, anything could happen, and probably would.

DAW

MARION ZIMMER BRADLEY
NON-DARKOVER NOVELS

- [ ] **HUNTERS OF THE RED MOON**   UE1968—$3.99
- [ ] **THE SURVIVORS**   UE1861—$3.99
- [ ] **WARRIOR WOMAN**   UE2253—$3.50

NON-DARKOVER ANTHOLOGIES

- [ ] **SWORD AND SORCERESS I**   UE2359—$4.50
- [ ] **SWORD AND SORCERESS II**   UE2360—$3.95
- [ ] **SWORD AND SORCERESS III**   UE2302—$4.50
- [ ] **SWORD AND SORCERESS IV**   UE2412—$4.50
- [ ] **SWORD AND SORCERESS V**   UE2288—$3.50
- [ ] **SWORD AND SORCERESS VI**   UE2423—$3.95
- [ ] **SWORD AND SORCERESS VII**   UE2457—$4.50
- [ ] **SWORD AND SORCERESS VIII**   UE2486—$4.50
- [ ] **SWORD AND SORCERESS IX**   UE2509—$4.50

COLLECTIONS

- [ ] **LYTHANDE** (with Vonda N. McIntyre)   UE2291—$3.95
- [ ] **THE BEST OF MARION ZIMMER BRADLEY** edited
  by Martin H. Greenberg   UE2268—$3.95

Buy them at your local bookstore or use this convenient coupon for ordering.

PENGUIN USA   P.O. Box 999, Bergenfield, New Jersey 07621

Please send me the DAW BOOKS I have checked above, for which I am enclosing
$_____ (please add $2.00 per order to cover postage and handling. Send check
or money order (no cash or C.O.D.'s) or charge by Mastercard or Visa (with a
$15.00 minimum.) Prices and numbers are subject to change without notice.

Card #_____ Exp. Date _____
Signature_____
Name_____
Address_____
City _____ State _____ Zip _____

For faster service when ordering by credit card call **1-800-253-6476**

Please allow a minimum of 4 to 6 weeks for delivery.